I0600030

DECODING THE HEART

THE CYBER HUNTRESS CHRONICLES

BOOK 1

A.M. MARYLAND

MARYLAND
MEDIA PUBLISHING

Decoding the Heart: The Cyber Huntress Chronicles, Book 1

© 2025 A.M. Maryland

This is a work of fiction. While the story is set in recognizable locations, all characters, events, and depictions are purely fictional. They are not intended to represent any real people, situations, or institutions.

Second Edition: January 2026

Published by: Maryland Media Publishing

ISBN: 979-8-9921225-0-3

For permission requests or inquiries, contact:

author@cyberhuntresschronicles.com

Losing family has a way of reminding you that life is finite. You will be missed, Mary Ethel 🤍

CONTENT NOTICE

Note: Located at the back of the book. Consume at your own discretion.

CHAPTER 0

LOS ANGELES, *California – Pulse*
  July 27, 01:58 PDT

VIBRATIONS from the floor match the speed of my heartbeat as the bass thumps. Strobe lights flash and chaotic shadows shift across the crowded club. The DJ cues Juvenile's "Back That Azz Up," and everyone explodes. I saunter to the center of the dance floor, the beat coursing through my veins.

My body moves instinctively, hips gyrating, dipping low, rising with a precision that commands attention. The crowd forms a circle around me, each calculated twerk drawing hollers and whoops from my onlookers, their eyes glued to my direction. The heat wraps around me, slicking my skin with sweat, but I don't care. This is my moment. My stage.

I catch sight of two men. Their eyes lock onto mine, slowly closing the gap with each seductive sway. Ignoring the intense warmth inside the venue, there's an anticipation that summer always brings. The season holds a special place in my heart, despite my given name being Winter. But now, all that matters is the magnetic pull of those two men edging closer, drawn into my orbit. I don't wait for them to make a move. With a sly smile, I beckon them over, and it's magic the way they rush toward me. One presses himself behind me, his body warm and firm, while the other faces me, hands on my hips.

The song eventually changes, the energy waning, but the man in front remains, his hands squeezing my hips lightly. A slight tipsiness clouds my thoughts from the four long islands I had earlier, but I focus on the man with me in his arms—tall, a head above me, and muscular. His waist grinds into mine with a rhythm that makes me want to lose control. Under the neon lights, his ebony skin glistens, while his midnight-blue shirt hugs his frame perfectly. His short hair shines as we dance, and I imagine all the ways I could let him ruin me.

"Do you want to take this somewhere else?" His voice is almost a whisper and gruff, with an accent I can't quite place.

I nod enthusiastically, and he chuckles. I beat him to what we're both thinking and grab his hands, pulling him through the crowd toward the elevator.

The door dings open, and before I can react, he shoves me inside, pinning me against the wall. He smiles, and I hit the button to disable the elevator. The only sounds are the muffled music and our heavy breathing.

He brings his lips down to mine, but there's nothing gentle about it. Our tongues dart around each other's mouths, and the taste of whiskey is surprising as he doesn't fit the mold of a typical drinker. I press closer, hands roaming his hard muscles and broad shoulders. Although a nice addition, this isn't for exploration; it's for urgency. He lifts me, my soft moan echoing as my ass hits the railing. He grins and kisses me again, his grip steady around my thighs. My short black skirt rides up, and I silently thank myself for skipping the tights I assumed would add character. His hand trails up my thighs as he finds my most sensitive spot. He latches onto my neck, and I reach for his pants, fumbling with the buttons until they drop. He pulls away with a laugh. "Eager, are we?"

I laugh too, but there's no humor in mine. "You have no idea."

His fingers shift my lacy panties aside, a couple dipping within, teasing but brief. As he enters me, the sensation is overwhelming. My screams fill the elevator, and I don't care if anyone hears them. I'm damn near losing my mind, and his grunts aren't helping.

Catching our breath, he steps back, fixing his fly. "That was something," he says, and I hum in agreement. I'm not interested in exchanging pleasantries about how good it was. Hopping off the railing, I pull down my skirt, hit the open button, and strut out of the elevator.

"We're wrapping up. Last call."

"Jack on the rocks, please." The bartender slides the drink over, and I tap the glass on the counter. With a smile, I murmur, "To blue shirt," before taking a deep, satisfying swig. Another night well spent. There's something intoxicating about knowing I can have any guy I want.

As I savor my whiskey, someone bumps into me. Brushing it off would do me well, but the conversation unfolding on my left is hard to ignore. "I told you to stop talking to my girl."

"Damn. I said I'm sorry. I really didn't know. I'm leaving."

"Oh, so you think you can just go?"

Another brush. *Let it go, Washington.* I think to myself, yet I still decide to turn and find two men in a scuffle: one significantly larger, clearly the boyfriend, going to town on the smaller guy, beating the life out of him.

Let them be. This doesn't concern me. But then another shove sends my drink splashing onto my ivory silk top.

"That'll do it." I intercept the large man's next punch, twisting his arm behind his back and angling it just right, eliciting a yelp from him.

In a sweet whisper in his ear, I say, "You've had your fun. You're done. Ignore this, and I'll snap your arm in two." To further prove my point, I bend his body forward, increasing the pressure on his wrist until he cries out again.

"Now go." I release him with a push toward the exit. He leads his girlfriend out, and I follow after. It's time to go home.

About three miles away from my place, the night air feels refreshing. L.A., I'm told, isn't the type of city where a twenty-six-year-old woman should walk alone late at night. But I welcome anyone brave enough to come and try me.

The streets are almost empty, a person here and another a few yards away. Sirens sound in the distance, but I don't head toward them. A different me would've rushed to the flashing lights to see what was up, but that would defeat the purpose of my move. I promised myself not to engage in anything remotely close to my old life.

I am no longer a vigilante.

CHAPTER 1

DOWNTOWN LOS ANGELES – *Home*
  July 27, 07:03 PDT

THE GRATING sound of a blender slices through my sleep, pulling me from my dreams. I reach for my phone, the screen blindingly bright as it springs to life. Squinting, I read the time and stifle a groan, realizing I barely slept three hours.

Dragging myself out of bed, my mouth dry, I hobble into the kitchen. Jessica glances up from her concoction, her expression broadcasting her disapproval of my disheveled appearance. Clad in hundred-dollar yoga pants and a matching sports bra, she embodies the results of her strict kale-and-antioxidant regimen.

"Good morning," I mumble, heading to the sink for a much-needed glass of water.

The blender roars back to life, and I suppress a wince, the sound amplifying my not-quite-hungover state. I gulp down the water and go to the coffee maker, popping in a pod and watching it come to life.

Living with Jessica has its perks, mostly when she's off at her Malibu mansion. The apartment is usually mine, and I relish the solitude. The blender finally stops, and Jessica pours her green sludge into a glass. I peer into the fridge, hoping for a miracle but finding only a few eggs and condiments.

"Nothing promising," I mutter, turning back to the coffee maker just as it finishes its cycle. I take a sip of the hot coffee and immediately regret it.

"You came home really late last night. I'm surprised you're awake," Jessica says.

I hold back a snarky reply and take a pan out of the cupboard. Her protein shake didn't exactly give me a choice.

"Any plans for the day?" she asks.

"I plan to sightsee, do the tourist thing," I reply, cracking eggs into the pan.

Her laughter rings out, light and infectious. "Aren't you a month late for that?"

I roll my eyes with a smile as I whisk the eggs. "Look, all that partying and sleeping around kept me very busy. Now I'm finally ready to see what else L.A. has to offer."

"So, what are you looking to do? Maybe I can give some suggestions."

"Well, food is an absolute must. Any cute boutiques you can think of in my not-so-rich price range, of course. Oh and any great sights to see?"

Jessica nods thoughtfully, and then her eyes light up. "You absolutely have to try this little Italian spot in West Hollywood. Their pasta and sauce are made fresh every day. The food is incredible. It tastes like heaven!"

I must look unconvinced because she quickly pulls out her phone, taps a few times, and flips the screen around for me to see. "See, they have tons of high ratings."

After some scrolling, she continues, "And for boutiques, there's a few stores on Melrose with some amazing finds. And for views? Griffith Observatory is a classic, but if you want something quieter, there's a hidden spot near the Malibu cliffs. It's absolutely breathtaking."

A smile spreads across my face, warmed by her enthusiasm. "Thanks, Jessica. That sounds perfect."

She gives a mock salute. "No worries. Your resident L.A. native is at your service." Before leaving, she offers, "Oh, before I forget, if you're free tomorrow, my dad has a show if you want to come. I promise it'll be fun."

"Sure," I say, never one to turn down a free concert. "Is it an album tour?"

"It's a mix of his greatest hits and some new stuff he's been working on. Trust me, you'll love it."

"Bet. I'm in."

"Great! Have fun today. And if I think of any more suggestions, I'll text you," Jessica waves as she leaves, her positive energy lingering in the room.

I sit down for a quiet breakfast while the sun filters through my bedroom window. It casts rays over the mess of my remaining unpacked boxes. My room feels temporary, as if I haven't quite accepted it as mine yet. As I reach for a towel, a photo tucked into the corner of my dresser mirror captures my attention. The only one I decided to put up.

My senior prom photo. The girl in the picture—smiling, naïve, in love—feels like someone I barely know anymore. She's a stranger now, standing next to Jayden, both of us lost in the present, arms wrapped around each other. My fingers trace the detailed border, lingering over his face.

That version of me is long gone. And so is he.

"What are you so dressed up for?" My mother's voice cuts

through the excitement, sneering as she stumbles into the bathroom, a bottle dangling from her hand.

"It's prom night, Mom. Remember? Jayden's on his way."

She cackles. "I'd rethink your hair situation. It looks horrible."

I lock eyes with myself in the mirror, on the verge of tears. "I think I'll wait outside by the gate."

A limousine pulls in front of the apartment less than ten minutes after I arrive. Jayden, my boyfriend or maybe just my best friend—it's unclear sometimes—is taking me to my senior prom. He lives in another state, and I miss him every day.

Jayden steps out of the limo, and my heart rate picks up. He's wearing a dark green velvet tuxedo, matching my emerald gown. His strong jawline is framed by a perfectly tied bow tie. His magnificent posture pushes his chest out, highlighting the contrast between the tux and his collared shirt. He extends an arm to me and as his hand finds mine, a familiar warmth spreads through my veins, anchoring me to the present.

"You look beautiful," he says, admiring me. He leans in closer and gives me the most passionate kiss we've ever shared. A kiss that took over a year to get. We both pull away, out of breath. His lips hover over mine, and he whispers, "We should head on. Otherwise, we're going to be late."

The driver opens the door, and Jayden enters. I try to elegantly get into the limo without making a fool of myself in these heels. The luxurious back seat in the black limousine exudes a sense of excitement. We lean back on the polished leather where a romantic ambiance envelopes the space. The scent of fresh flowers wafts through the air as our bodies instinctively gravitate toward each other, magnetized by an invisible force. I want to be as close as possible to my Jay. He puts his arm around me and pulls me into his chest. His torso molds to my body, and I can feel us breathing in unison. I missed his touch for so long.

The limousine glides through the city streets, its motion a gentle lullaby. I don't want to break the silence, but I know I won't be able to enjoy the night if I don't ask the burning question that always lingers on my mind when we aren't together.

"Are we good, Jayden? I know the last time we saw each other, I wasn't the best version of myself, and then we kind of broke up, but we've been talking almost every night on the phone for a while now. I'm trying to do better every — "

I can feel myself rambling and spiraling, and I can sense Jayden knows this too. He cuts me off by kissing me almost more lovingly than he did in front of my apartment, but this time, there's something more meaningful about it. He cups my face with his hands that smell of cacao butter and looks me in the eyes.

"There is no other county, zip code, or coordinate in this world I'd rather be in than with you, right here and right now. I see you, and I'm proud of what you've overcome. Winter, I love you."

Until he used both his thumbs to wipe the tears from my eyes, I didn't realize that I was full-on bawling. He quickly turns to shuffle in his bag, and before he can reveal what he has, I pounce on him. I take his lips with mine and completely catch him off guard. Despite this, he doesn't hesitate to return the same energy. He picks me up and settles me on his lap as we continue making out.

If it wasn't for the abrupt breaking and the horns blaring outside, I'm not sure we would've stopped. Over the intercom, the driver informs us, "There's an accident. I need to make a detour. Our ETA is five minutes out."

Jayden clears his throat and shows me what he was grabbing before I distracted us. He reveals a beautiful cream corsage. He places it around my wrist and kisses my forehead.

I open my clutch and pull out a pocket mirror and a makeup wipe. My reflection shows smudged mascara, so I decide to take everything off rather than look like a panda for the rest of the night. As the limo comes to a smooth stop, the driver exits the vehicle. Jayden, sitting beside me, catches my eye with a sparkle of his own.

"You look even more amazing without makeup," he says, a teasing smirk playing on his lips. *"I should make you cry more often."*

The limo door opens, and we step out, the grandeur of the governor's mansion of Ohio rising before us. The venue is filled with a flood of formal gowns and sharp suits, laughter and music. Waiters weave through the crowd, offering glasses of sparkling cider. I squeeze Jayden's hand, trying to contain myself, and he responds by gently rubbing the back of mine.

A corner of the mansion has been transformed into a photo booth, adorned with green and black balloons, the event's colors. A line of couples stretches the length of the room.

"Come on." I drag Jayden to the booth. We pose together, his arm wrapped around my waist, the flash capturing our smiles. The photographer hands us a print, and I tuck it safely into my clutch.

We head to the punch bowl, half-hoping for a little extra kick, but then I notice Colonel Walters, the JROTC instructor, stationed by the table. He doesn't miss a thing.

The Colonel and I make eye contact, and he marches over. He smiles and asks, *"Sergeant Washington, who have you brought here tonight? I don't recognize this young man."*

"This is Jayden." I point to Jayden, who stretches a hand out to Walters, and to Jayden, I say, *"This is Colonel Walters."*

They shake hands, and that's all the contact I allow, an attempt to stop whatever questioning Colonel Walters might have for him. It doesn't seem to go unnoticed by the two of them, but neither mentions it.

"Shall we dance?" Jayden smiles and bows.

His hand resting on my back, he leads the way to the dance floor. He wraps his arms around my waist, and I wrap mine around his neck. We sway to the music, and I can't help the grin that settles on my lips. But somehow, my brain, which seems to never have an off switch, is thinking about everything besides the man I have in front of me.

Jayden, astute as ever, asks, "Winter, I can literally see the gears turning in your head. What's on your mind?"

I blurt out the first thing on my to-do list: "SAT scores; have you submitted them yet?"

He chuckles, spins me around, and responds. "Yes, Winter. I submitted them two weeks ago. Remember? Our admittances are a done deal. All that's left is figuring out our housing. Now would you relax and enjoy the dance?"

I rest my head on his chest, feeling the steady beat of his heart. He's right. I need to enjoy tonight, the moment. We have the rest of our lives to figure out the little details.

"You know," I say, looking up at him with a smile, "I still can't believe you joined the soccer team just because it was the closest thing to football at NYU."

He laughs, the sound soothing to my nerves. "Hey, a guy's gotta stay active, right? Plus, it's actually kind of fun."

The night goes by with Jayden and I never straying far from each other. We stand side by side, get snacks together, and he even walks me to the bathroom. It feels like we're making up for all the times we were apart, savoring every minute we have together. As I watch him, his easy smile and the way he seems to understand me so effortlessly, I think back to how foolish I was to ever consider another guy the same way I thought of Jayden. He's always been the one who made everything feel right.

I lean against him, watching the last few couples dance. "Tonight," I murmur, "didn't go as badly as I thought it would."

"Told you. Sometimes you just have to let go and enjoy the ride." He kisses the top of my head, his arm around my shoulders.

"Hey, Winter. A group of us were going to Anthony's place afterward. He's throwing a little thing. You want to come?" Andrea from government class offers.

"No, thanks." I squeeze Jayden's hand. "We already have plans."

The second the hotel door closes behind us, we're all over each other. It feels like a continuation of the kisses we shared in the limo, but we don't have anywhere else to be here. Now, it's just us and our desires in the driver's seat. Jayden pulls me flush against him, and that's all it takes to drive me crazy. Our clothes come off in a heated frenzy, hitting the floor one after the other. He follows as I lay back on the bed, pausing as he straddles me.

"Look, I don't want to pressure you into anything, Winter. This would be the first time that we... ya know, since—"

I kiss him to stop him from stumbling any further, and ruining the mood more than he already has. My hands cradle his face, locking eyes with him. "I love you, and I trust you, Jayden." I push away the wandering thoughts, choosing him, choosing us.

CHAPTER 2

WEST HOLLYWOOD – *Shoppes at Melrose*
   July 27, 11:32 PDT

WITH JESSICA'S help and some online research, I've mapped out my day. It's packed with places to explore, spots for great photos, and maybe even opportunities to meet some hot guys.

The sidewalk overflows with people, each absorbed in their own worlds. Stepping into one of Jessica's recommended stores, I plan to shop a bit before lunch. I know my bank account will take a hit from the clientele exiting the store. Still, I pick out a mustard yellow two-piece set and head to the changing room.

"I love this style. Can you bring me similar items?" I instruct the attendant. I'm ready to swap my signature all-black wardrobe for more colorful outfits. So far, I've only managed denim-blue and white. Without the need to keep a low profile anymore, I'm ready to make some noise. A new wardrobe for a new city and a new me. "L.A. will be good to me," I mumble under my breath, hoping it'll stick.

The bottoms fit perfectly, showing off my lean frame. The cropped shirt is a bit loose but still looks good. I fluff my curly hair, courtesy of my mixed genes.

"Great choice! I love the way those pants look on you." The attendant knocks on the door with more outfits.

I try on a few. "That top is perfect!" she assures me. I nod, knowing I won't buy more than three sets. After one last glance in the mirror, I change back into my clothes and gather my things.

Lunch is at the raved-about restaurant. I twirl my fork in sun-dried tomato pasta, savoring each bite. The flavors burst in my mouth, and I intend to tell Jessica all about my taste buds coming alive. I'll exaggerate the experience, but the idea will be communicated. The restaurant's décor deserves its own review—a massive chandelier creates a radiant shine, manicured plants add a touch of nature, and the wooden floors and furniture create an inviting atmosphere.

From my table, I can see the Hollywood sign in the distance. The iconic letters call to me; I decide to hike up there without much thought.

No one warns you how challenging the hike to the Hollywood sign is, especially while clutching three shopping bags in the L.A. heat. By the time I reach the top, I'm slightly out of breath, a humbling reminder for me to get my ass in the gym soon. I might be boycotting vigilantism, but I'm not giving up staying in shape.

The view from the sign is breathtaking. L.A. sprawls out below, the smog producing a hazy halo across the city. Behind me, the dark outline of the hills cuts into the sky, while the distant mountains stand like jagged, silent sentinels. I snap a photo, capturing the moment. Despite the path's popularity,

I'm alone up here—thanks to the unusually scorching day. I take a deep breath, the warm air filling my lungs.

Classes start next month, but I moved early as a birthday treat. Between my dysfunctional childhood, losing Jayden, and my former life as a vigilante, I never had the chance to slow down. Grad school will be a piece of cake compared to everything else. A full ride to USC was too perfect to pass up and a step in the right direction. I needed life to cut me some slack, and maybe this degree can be that.

I take deep, calming breaths, focusing on happy thoughts—though most of them involve Jayden, despite the heartache he brings, and by no fault of his. The last time I attempted a fresh start in a new city to earn another diploma, I wasn't alone.

After a long inhale, I open my eyes and count to ten before starting my descent.

I head straight for my room and dump the bags by the corner of my bed when I get back home. I'm ready to fall into the sheets and forget the day. But something catches my eye. A piece of clothing pokes out of one of my unpacked boxes. I don't need to pick it up to know what it is. My dad's old pilot jacket. The one he wore every time he flew, his lucky charm. I thought I'd buried it with all the other memories I was trying to leave behind, but here it is, staring back at me.

The sight of the worn leather always pulls me back to that day—when everything began to fall apart.

My mother is in a hurry, and thirteen-year-old me can't understand the urgency. She's sober, or at least she appears to be. It isn't just the hurry I can sense. She's angry too, but then again, when isn't she? But I've never seen her like this.

She shoves items into boxes, and I notice just then how many there are. I look around our little house and then back at my mother, who keeps muttering to herself as she puts more and more of our stuff into the boxes. She doesn't know I'm in the room with her; she would've put me to work immediately if she did. Suddenly, I'm grateful for her ability to ignore me at the oddest times.

A headshot of my father is in her sights now. She snatches the frame hanging on the wall. Normally, she'll stop and stare at the picture for a while as if she has questions to ask the man in the photograph. I guess you run out of questions after asking them for two years.

"Don't just stand there looking at me," my mother snaps when she finally notices me, "Help me out." She places the photograph into one of the boxes and moves around to grab more off the wall.

"Mom, what are you doing?" I'm aware of the panic in my voice. I know what it looks like, but I hope to God it's something else. There's nothing I need more than it being anything else.

"We're moving. I got a job in another state," my mother plainly states without even looking at me. She seems obsessed with packing our lives and memories into the cardboard she has scattered everywhere.

I don't want to argue with her. It never ends well. But I'm not about to be hurled to whatever state she thinks is the new thing to change her life. I haven't been able to recognize her since Dad died.

"Why do we have to move?"

"Because I got another job and we have to be closer to where I work, wouldn't you think?"

I hate when she does that, when she makes the worries I have seem unreasonable and insignificant. My whole life is here. My father's scent is still in this house. I can still hear his voice if I focus hard enough. Is it that hard for her to be around things that remind her of him?

She grabs Dad's favorite jacket, the one he wore as a pilot in the Air Force. I watch her look at it for nothing more than a second before she flings it to the side. I know enough about moving to know whatever doesn't make it into the box isn't coming with us.

I rush after the jacket, tears blurring my vision. "What are you doing?"

"Now, don't be difficult, Winter. We need to get packed up and get going."

"I don't want to go," I raise my voice at her, but she barely registers what I say. Whatever I'm going through doesn't matter to her, it never did.

"Well, it really isn't up to you, is it?"

I let out a piercing scream because I know there's nothing else I can say that'll get through to her, and I don't have any words left. My mother spins around quickly, holding a fire in her eyes. Her braids, peeking out from beneath her bonnet, fall just to her shoulders. Her red lipstick is slightly smeared as she purses her lips and takes a deep breath.

"Listen, I can't afford to pay the mortgage anymore. With your father gone..." She draws another breath as if to steady herself before going on, "I can't pay it off. And now, we have to go where I have a job. I can provide for us there."

I shake my head quickly; it's more than my father's memory keeping me here. I have a life here. My family is here, my friends too. Jayden.

Jayden and I have something going on if the kiss we shared was anything to go by. I've waited nearly my whole existence for him to notice me this way, and now, he's finally doing it. There's no way I'm going to let her just rip me away from him.

"We can ask for help from—" I step back in fear. My mother smacks one of the lamps, sending it flying across the room, shattering into pieces once it hits the ground. I blink rapidly, wondering why she did that.

"I don't need anybody's help! I am your mother, Winter. It's just me and you now. It's about time you get used to it. If I say we're moving, then we're moving. Even if it's to some remote village in the middle of God knows where."

There's a tightness to her voice I recognize from when she's trying to convince people she's okay. I attempt to stop my lips from trembling, but between the both of us, my mother breaks first.

Tears fall down her cheeks, and she swipes them away. Her brown eyes cut me a look as if she blames me for them. I want to protest more, but I know better. I want to tell her to let me move in with Aunt Gina and be less of a burden to her.

"I know you think it'd be better if I left you with your aunt, but Winter, what type of mother would that make me? I can take care of you; I just can't do it here. I have an opportunity somewhere else and know it will benefit us greatly. I can't lose you too. I already lost your father."

At the last part, her voice cracks, and I feel my resolve start to dissipate. I don't say anything. I pick up my dad's jacket and shove it into one of the bins, payment for agreeing to her desire.

As the moving truck pulls out of the neighborhood, I shoot Jayden a quick text to let him know we're leaving for good. Our small town disappears behind us, and I hate there wasn't any time for a proper goodbye. Or at least that's what I tell myself because I know I couldn't face him either way.

A splintering crash breaks through the quiet. It's the unmistakable sound of fragile porcelain hitting the tiled floor with a violent finality.

"Fuck!" Jessica's voice, muffled but clear, leaks through the door as she stumbles toward her room. I believe the vase in the hallway took a tumble. She's cursing under her breath, no doubt glaring at the shards left in her wake. I close my eyes, biting back the desire to jump in and handle it. But that's not who I am. Not anymore. Not here.

I settle into the mattress, exhaling. The comforter spreads around me as I make another mental reminder to finish unpacking the final boxes.

CHAPTER 3

PASADENA – *Tulip Dome Stadium*
  July 28, 19:04 PDT

ALL THE MOVIES I've seen about celebrities did nothing
to prepare me for the chaos that's Jessica's life. Or more accu-
rately, her father's life, given that we're nothing but
spectators.

"What do you think?" Jessica asks.

What do I think? My mind alternates between thoughts of
wow and *what the fuck?* "This is crazy," I say in response, and
she nods.

"Right? The concert is going to be the craziest part. A lot
of people haven't shown up yet, but when they do, you'll
know you haven't even seen half of it."

I'm in the green room holding a glass of something
bubbly. I'm told it's champagne, though I'm skeptical. Jessica
is adamant I've just never had the proper expensive ones. I
don't argue—after all, her father is the one being fawned

over. Makeup artists surround him, while his manager switches between calling and texting. It was his idea for us to swap our basic clothes into something more glamorous.

"Something to bring out your eyes," he'd said before diving back into another call, leaving us to the stylists who had a field day with us.

I ended up in a black bra with a sheer net top over it and black leather shorts. My curly brown hair is now silky straight. Jessica wears a pink corset top, a short black skirt, and thigh-high boots that accentuate her skin tone and long legs. Her blonde hair falls in soft waves around her shoulders.

Backup dancers stretch in the corner, possessing the most flawless bodies I've ever seen. They flash us smiles as we watch them warm up. Jessica's father, now free of the makeup artists, laughs with his swarming entourage.

"Anything you'd like to eat?" the manager asks with a smile.

"No, thank you, Fabian." Jessica replies.

He nods and stands with us, watching her father joke with his friends. "He's really busy these days," Fabian remarks. "It's fabulous that you were able to come, and you brought a friend. I've never met this one before."

"She's my roommate." Jessica says.

Fabian chuckles. "Is she?"

"She can hear you," I say, raising my glass only to find it empty. Before I can react, someone refills it.

"Thanks," I mumble, then introduce myself. "I'm Winter."

"Well, it's nice to officially meet you, Winter. I'm happy both of you could come today. It's been forever since you've made it to an event," Fabian says before hurrying off to take another call.

"Allen, man!" a familiar voice calls out. We turn to see the famous movie spy Jackson Wilde approaching. My heart flutters, but I keep my cool, only allowing myself a small smile. *Jackson Wilde, in the flesh.*

Allen's face lights up as he greets Wilde. "Jack, you made it!" he says, extending a hand. He's not alone—his influencer daughters follow him.

Jessica watches her father interact with Wilde and the girls, a wistful look in her eyes. Fabian's attentiveness is starting to make sense. Aside from a quick kiss on the cheek, her father and her have barely spoken since we arrived. She feels my gaze and turns to smile at me, but it doesn't reach her eyes.

The Wilde sisters, in their immaculate designer outfits, stroll over, their eyes sweeping the room with practiced scrutiny.

"Jessica!" the elder sister exclaims, air-kissing her on both cheeks. "It's been ages! How are you?"

Jessica returns the air kisses effortlessly. "I'm good, Serena. Just here to support my dad."

The younger sister gives Jessica a once-over, her expression reeks of mild disinterest. "Nice outfit," she comments, her tone flat.

"Thanks, Lily."

Their attention shifts to me, standing slightly behind Jessica. "And you are?" Serena asks with polite curiosity.

"Winter," I say, offering a small smile. "Jessica's roommate."

Lily's eyes narrow slightly, and she smirks. "Never thought I'd see Jessica Glory mixing with the common folk," she says, her tone dripping with condescension.

I open my mouth to respond, but Jessica steps in

smoothly. "I wouldn't call Winter common. She redid my whole Wi-Fi setup in like ten minutes. She's a genius!"

Serena nods, her attention already drifting elsewhere. "That's nice. Tech support is such a hassle to deal with," she replies airily.

Lily gives me a half-smile. "So, Winter, how are you finding L.A.? Must be quite the adjustment from… wherever you came from."

"New York," I reply, keeping my tone light. "A bit of a change, but I've been loving it, until now."

"Small world. Lily and I just came from the Hamptons," Serena says absently, already engrossed in her phone as it buzzes with a new notification. "Well, enjoy the show, ladies." With that, the Wilde sisters drift away, their interest in us waning as quickly as it had sparked.

Jessica lets out a small sigh, her shoulders relaxing. "I'm so sorry about that. They're a lot. Lily can be such a bitch sometimes." Her eyes meet mine with an apologetic look.

I raise an eyebrow. "You don't say?"

She laughs softly, draping an arm around my shoulder. "Come on, the show is going to start soon. How excited are you?"

"I can't believe I'm here, about to see the great Allen Glory on stage." The thrill is evident in my voice despite how much I try to disguise it. The attention is addictive. I could get used to star treatment.

"This is our VIP section," Jessica leads me to a luxurious box suite. We share the booth with Fabian, who comes and goes, too busy to sit still for long.

The crowd's excitement is palpable as the opener takes the stage. He's a new act that Allen's record company just signed. Yet, the audience sings along to every word. I nod along too. I don't hate it.

To my right, Jessica seems lost in thought. Although I think I can piece together what's going on, I still ask, "Are you alright? You seem kind of bummed out."

"I'm fine. Dad's going to kill it." After a pause, she adds, "He's just really busy is all. You know how it is for people like him. Their jobs take them away all the time. He's doing what he loves, and that's all that matters. At least I can see him now. He's touring less, and he's more local."

"You know, it's okay to want more from your parents."

Jessica gazes out at the crowd, watching them scream and bounce on their feet. "I can't complain. It's not a good look. Most people would kill to be where I'm standing. Besides, that's why I invited you. I knew he'd be too occupied by everyone else to notice me."

She's right. There's still a silver spoon, no matter how cold it might be.

A drone buzzes past our box, reminding me of her father's intentions to make a tour movie. There's a lot of hype around it, with news outlets speculating on everything, including an old feud that needs answers.

The door to our box springs open, and Fabian enters, carrying a tray of the most exquisite deli sandwiches I've ever seen and several bottles of imported water. He places them on a chair and looks at us.

"You've had too much wine. How about a change of beverage? And maybe some food?" It sounds like a suggestion, but it's clear it isn't.

"I don't suppose we can have some tequila after this," Jessica says, grabbing a sandwich half. I follow her lead.

"At the concert? Hell no. But maybe something can be said for the after-party." Fabian turns and leaves the box, closing the door behind him.

Intrigued, I ask, "An after-party?"

"Yeah, it's usually for the guests, a thank you for co—"

"LADIES AND GENTLEMEN, GIVE IT UP FOR THE AMAZING ALLEN GLORY," the announcer booms.

The lights dim, and the crowd goes wild. I'm grateful for the earplugs dulling the noise. Jessica and I scream along as her father rises from the stage floor, lights focusing on him. He dives straight into his first song, wasting no time. If you weren't a fan before, you are now.

$$-\!\!\!\!\bigwedge\!\!\!\!-$$

ON TO THE AFTER-PARTY. Jessica grabs my hand and pulls me into the black car that picked us up from the apartment in the morning. "This isn't just an excuse for people to party. It's for people to make connections, exchange contacts, and, more importantly," she says and leans in, "hook up with just about anybody. Because who's going to talk about it?"

Her words linger in my mind, especially the last part. While hooking up wasn't exactly on my agenda, I've definitely noticed a few people who've piqued my interest.

"This is going to be a night you'll be talking about for a long time," she assures me, and I don't doubt her for a second.

The party is one of the wildest scenes I've ever witnessed. Celebrities are everywhere, mingling so casually it almost feels surreal. I spot two singers, rumored by the media to be broken-up, unable to keep their hands off each other.

"It's one of my father's many houses," Jessica explains. I scan the room, but her father is nowhere in sight.

"Where is the amazing and great Allen Glory?" I joke.

Jessica shakes her head with a smile. "This isn't the Alister party. It's for the B-listers. The real deal is at a different location. That's where the business happens. This one's just for fun. You could come with me, but it's usually a snooze-fest." I take in the scene around me. "They all hope to score an invite one day," she adds.

The singer who opened for Allen approaches us with a grin, wrapping an arm around Jessica and pulling her close. "I haven't seen you in forever," he shouts into her neck.

She gently shoves him away. "This is my friend, Winter. She's new to L.A.," she introduces, gesturing to me. "And this is Felix, but he goes by Kid Lix. He's my father's newest object of interest."

"Kid Lix?" I repeat, looking him up and down.

"The one and only," he replies, taking my hand and planting a light kiss on my wrist.

Felix waves the bartender over and orders a round of drinks. "So, Winter," he says, handing me my glass, "How are you finding L.A.?"

I take a sip, savoring the familiar taste. "It's been great so far. I'm loving the change."

Jessica, perched on a nearby stool, chimes in. "Winter's been exploring the city. I gave her a whole list of places to hit."

Felix nods. "L.A. has its charms. Have you been to the Santa Monica Pier yet?"

I roll my eyes playfully. "Come on, Lix. That's the best you can suggest? That's such a tourist's answer."

He chuckles, raising his hands in mock surrender. "You've caught me. I must confess I'm not from here."

"Oh really? Where's home for you, then?"

"Born and raised in Miami. But I've been all over. L.A. is just the latest stop on my grand tour."

Jessica interjects. "Felix here likes to pretend it's actually *his* world tour."

He puts a hand over his heart, feigning offense. "You wound me, Jessica."

"Hey Kid! You want in on this?" A yell comes from a high-stakes poker table in the corner.

"Deal me in." Felix downs his drink and gets up. "Well, welcome to L.A., Winter. Good seeing you again, Jessica."

We watch him head toward the table. "So, you and Lix, huh?"

A hint of something reminiscent lies in her eyes as Jessica smiles faintly. "Almost. He left to go on tour before anything happened. Then I met my current boyfriend."

"You're the girl, right?" A petite woman approaches, poking Jessica's shoulder and whispering passionately in her ear.

Jessica's smile tightens. "It seems... that there's like a clog in one of the bathrooms. I need to call maintenance." She glances around briefly before she excuses herself. "I'll be back, Winter." With a quick nod, she heads off, tugging the woman along, leaving me alone at the bar.

"Another one." I hold up my glass to the bartender and take in the environment again. My eyes roam over the mansion's foyer and entertainment space; I'm in awe. The wealth in this house—nay this room alone—is unreal. I estimate the combined spending power to be the GDP of half of South America.

"Here's your martini. Would you like anything else?" He palms a small baggie with an assortment of pills in it.

"No thanks, I'm good with the drink." Vices are easy to indulge in, especially under the guise of spontaneity. I'm not looking for such regrets tonight.

The thought is quickly taken away from me when an arm

wraps around my waist, pulling me close. I look up to see Felix gazing down at me with a playful expression. Before I know it, his tongue is in my mouth. I don't fight it—why would I?

He leads us up the stairs. Though I had one of the backup dancers in mind, I'm not upset with who the universe has sent my way.

CHAPTER 4

HOME – *Bedroom*
  August 19, 10:13 PDT

GIVEN the number of times I've moved, you'd think I'd be immune to the jittery nerves of being the new student. But as I stand in front of the mirror on my first day of grad school, my stomach churns with anxiety. I scrutinize my reflection, questioning if I look good enough. Jessica isn't here to give her opinion, so I'm left to rely on my own judgment. The mirror, once a trusted friend, now feels like a deceitful stranger.

Taking a deep breath, I scold myself for acting like a child. I'm not that awkward teenager anymore, the one who was constantly shoved into class after class and forced to introduce herself to indifferent faces. I'm a master's student now, an adult. I can handle this. With one final look, I grab my backpack and phone and head out the door. The morning sky is gloomy as I walk toward the bus stop, trying to shake off the lingering nerves.

As I step onto the school grounds, a familiar apprehensiveness tightens in my stomach. I can almost hear my mother's voice, insisting it wasn't as big a deal as I was making it out to be. After the first move, I stupidly thought it would be the last. My mother promised she had everything figured out, but with every address change, she only managed to disappoint me more. It always struck me as ironic that the number of leases increased after Dad died, even though he was our only connection to the military lifestyle. "Military brats," they called us, but without him, we were just aimlessly moving from place to place.

This time, a choice I made all on my own, I stand before another unfamiliar school.

It's the fifth one in three years. You'd think I'd be used to it by now, but nothing ever feels right to my mother. We always move. We haven't managed to spend more than a year in a particular location. She always finds a reason to pack up and leave, like the problem was the city and not her.

Her voice drags in my ears, loud and impatient. "Behave yourself, Winter." We walk to the entrance together, her words a constant drone. "The last thing I need is for you to cause problems here," she says, her tone condescending. I grit my teeth and nod, not trusting myself to speak. She speaks as if I'm the reason we can't settle down and her inability to keep a job isn't the real issue.

I don't need her to drop me off. I've navigated enough new schools to know the drill. After a while, they're all the same. I have a plan: keep a low profile, stay invisible, and get through the day without drawing too much attention. Making friends is pointless when I'm destined to leave them behind. Staying in touch never actually works. I spend more time thinking about Jayden than I do talking to him. In this case, I have no one to blame but myself due to all the calls I've been dodging recently. I just need some time to get my head straight, but I'm not sure if I can dig myself out of this hole anymore. I want to be back in our little town again. I'd give anything to be the same girl that left in the first moving truck.

"Now, you be good," my mother abruptly says, turning on her heel and walking away before I can respond. I watch her leave; there's something different about her. I noticed it a while back, but I've chalked it up to Dad dying, and our moves. But now, it's starting to get obvious.

I shake my head and enter the school. Whatever's going on with her, I hope she figures it out soon. I don't have time to worry about her; I have my own problems to deal with. I adjust the straps on my backpack, feeling the weight of it all pressing down on me. Another new school. Another new start. Another lie.

With my head fixed on the floor, I walk down the hallway. My plan to stay unnoticed is quickly thwarted as I hear snickers and someone call out.

"Hey, you!" a girl's voice cuts through the noise. "Why yo momma look so crazy? I know a crackhead when I see one."

On any other day, I might have let it slide, but it's the second semester of tenth grade, and the cold is ending as spring is taking its place. I can hear the birds singing, and the flowers are beginning to bloom. So much to be excited about, but it's been a rough couple of months, more so than usual, and the picture-perfect day isn't enough to stop me from snapping.

I drop my bag and charge at her, my vision narrowing in on her face.

A crowd forms around us as I punch her with all the pent-up anger inside me. Hitting her does nothing to ease my restlessness; it's as if the more I punch her, the heavier my life seems, and that makes me detest her more, makes me hit her more.

Hands grab me roughly, pulling me away, but I fight against them, desperate to get back to her. It angers me further to see someone helping her as if she hadn't just been running her mouth. I hated her for it.

I'm hurled into the principal's office by whom I would later realize is the P.E. teacher, Coach Braton, who glares at me in disappointment.

"I never would have admitted you if I had known this was how you would behave." Principal Thompson says, his voice sharp. "Lindsey, get me her mother on the phone now."

I slump in the chair, knowing I'm in for it.

"Why did you do that?" Coach Braton asks.

What is one to say? 'She was talking shit about my momma, who honestly deserved it?' Frankly, no one in the room would have wanted the real answer. Instead, I chose to just shut up and wait for my mother to handle it.

The door swings open, and she walks in. "Is everything alright? You mentioned a fight?"

"Yes, the first thing your daughter did was beat another student," Thompson states flatly.

"Well, I assure you that won't happen again. Isn't that right, Winter?"

All eyes are on me. I cross my arms and mumble, "Yes, it won't happen again. I promise."

Principal Thompson rubs his temples and exhales loudly. "Fine. I'm suspending you for three days. I'm letting you off easy since you are new. But next time you are getting expelled. Am I clear?"

"Yes, Principal Thompson."

Up until now, I've been the daughter every parent dreams of— never causing trouble, always doing well in school. My mother knows this, yet she doesn't defend me. It's like she doesn't care anymore. Coach Braton was the only one who gave a damn and bothered to ask me why I jumped her.

We leave the principal's office in silence. My mother's disinterest and the smell of alcohol hanging around her speak louder than any scolding could. I don't know why I'm surprised she went drinking as soon as she dropped me off. If only she put half the effort *into parenting as she does into finding her next drink, maybe things would be different.*

UNIVERSITY PARK – *USC Campus*
August 29, 10:23 PDT

BY THE SECOND week of classes, I've found my groove. Navigating the campus has become second nature to me, and I recognize enough faces to receive and dispense a few friendly waves. Today, I head to the library, determined to master a concept that tripped me up in my Applied Cryptography class.

Stepping into the archive, I'm immediately struck by its grandeur. The high ceilings are adorned with intricate wood-work, each pattern drawing the eye upward. Large, circular bulb covers hang from wires, orchestrating a warm and inviting hue. Despite being early in the semester, the place is already bustling with students.

A table in the middle contains one of the few empty spots available. As I approach, the two seated students glance up, offering me a brief, acknowledging nod. I return the gesture and settle into my seat, pulling out my laptop and notes.

The soft murmur of conversations and the rustle of pages create a soothing background as I immerse myself in my work. My problem set requires me to prove a symmetric encryption scheme is secure. To do this, I need to show that the scheme is indistinguishable under chosen plaintext attacks (IND-CPA secure). In other words, given an attacker with reasonable resources, they can't pull any underlying information about the scheme from an encrypted message of their choice, no matter how many guesses they make.

BAM! A stack of books falls onto the table next to me, forcing me out of my focus. The sharp sound rings through the library, and before I know it, I'm not here anymore.

Mr. Carter remains at the front of the classroom yapping about trade networks and diplomacy, and I stare at the board, pretending to care. I've made sure to behave myself since the suspension, but I can't get myself to focus today. I haven't slept much—these nightmares won't let me. Every night I relive the worst day of my life. I use everything I have in me to try and give a single fuck about the fall of the Ottoman Empire, but to no avail. Mr. Carter's voice starts to fade, becoming lighter and lighter until it disappears altogether.

And then there's only silence.

A loud smack jolts me awake. My head snaps up, and I see Mr. Carter hovering over me, his hands resting on a textbook serving as my unwelcome alarm clock. I ungracefully wipe away some slobber collecting on the side of my mouth.

"Miss Washington, I hate to bore you, but I am teaching a class right now."

"Sorry, I—"

"Doesn't matter. See me after the bell. You've disrupted the class enough."

Ooooooooooo's echo across the classroom while the other half of the class laughs at me as I sink further into my chair.

The bell rings, and I reluctantly approach his desk. Mr. Carter's stern expression softens as he looks me in the eyes. "Is everything alright at home, Winter? Are you sleeping well?"

I don't want to make this a thing if I don't have to, so I lie and say, "Yes, everything's fine. It won't happen again, Mr. Carter. I promise."

He pauses, inspecting me, and I feel like I might break under the weight of his gaze. "Since you're usually a good student, I'm going to let it slide this time, Miss Washington. But if I catch you dozing off in my class again, you will get detention."

I nod and release the breath I didn't realize I was holding. He waves his hand to dismiss me, and I scurry out of the room, heading to my locker to grab my textbook for the next class.

Turning a corner, I'm immediately shoved against the lockers, the impact knocking the wind out of me. As I regain my balance, I look up to see a guy in a letterman jacket towering over me.

"So you're the girl who beat up my girlfriend," he says. Based on the football on the front of his jacket, it's safe to assume he's some jock.

"Well, maybe she shouldn't fuck around with people she doesn't know," I say, sounding braver than I feel.

He shoves me back onto the lockers, clutching my shirt. "Since I'm a gentleman. I won't hurt you." He steps aside to reveal three large girls in track and field uniforms. "I'll let them have that honor."

As the first fist connects with my nose, I can only think about how I should've followed my own advice. I don't even have time to register the hits or their origins. A coordinated jab to my ribs brings me to my knees. But that doesn't slow them down. I'm completely on the ground as they continue to kick every inch of my body. I just stay there lifeless, waiting for them to finish.

Shouting in the distance signals the end of my beating. "That's for Amber," the biggest girl says, delivering a final kick to my stomach and a mucus-filled spit blob to my face as she runs away.

So that was her name, huh?

I don't know how long I lay there before faculty arrives to help me up. Leaning against the lockers, blood dripping from my nose and an unbearable pain radiating through my chest, I look up to see Mr. Carter. His eyes are full of pity and confusion. "Why didn't you fight back?"

"What would have been the point?" I mutter, surprising both of us.

I break out of his grip and bend over to grab my bag, igniting a fire across my torso, which makes me stagger a bit. Mr. Carter steadies me again. I pull away for a final time and shuffle toward the exit. By now, Principal Thompson is approaching, cursing under his breath when he hears I was involved in yet another altercation. I ignore him as I reach the front door. If I'm going to get in trouble for fighting, I would've liked to get at least a single lick in.

He yells, "Winter Washington! Get back here right now, or I'm contacting your mother!"

I turn around and scream, "Get in line!" The phones are cut off, and I haven't seen her in two days.

Every step to the bus stop hurts more than the last. I have no particular destination in mind, but I know I need to forget about today. I've never smoked weed before, but now seems as good a time as any. Luckily, I know just the place to find some.

I blink rapidly, shaking my head as the school library comes back into focus, and I realize I'm clutching the edge of the table, my knuckles white. The girl across from me looks up, bewilderment present on her face. I force a smile, hoping to reassure her.

"Just a bit dizzy," I mumble, giving a weak laugh.

She nods once, clearly unconvinced, but turns her attention back to her book and slips her earbud back in. I don't wait around for her to spare me another look. I gather my things quickly and slip out of the library.

I don't have any more lectures for the day, so I decide to take the long way home, strolling through the main part of campus. The sheer number of students and the bright colors of club booths help pull me out of my head.

"Winter!" A familiar voice calls out. I turn to see Jessica waving enthusiastically from a nearby booth.

I flash her a smile and make my way over. She's dressed in a pink mini-skirt and a white shirt, tucked in neatly. Her white knee-high boots are pristine, and her blonde hair cascades in perfect waves. As I approach, she pulls me into a hug, catching me off guard.

"Hey, girl!" she says brightly. "Meet my sorority sisters."

I smile at the group of impeccably dressed girls.

"We're promoting the first football game of the season." Jessica motions to her booth.

I nod, trying to keep up. "I hadn't heard about it."

She laughs and rolls her eyes. "You've got to get off that laptop of yours, Winter. So, we're having a pre-game kickback at one of the frats next Friday. It's still up in the air which one, but you should definitely come. I'll let you know as soon as it's decided."

"Sounds perfect. I could use a night out."

Jessica smiles and envelopes me in another hug. "Great! I'll see you at home."

A party is exactly what I need. Maybe blowing off some steam could be good for me.

CHAPTER 5

USC CAMPUS – *Beta Alpha Psi House*
  September 06, 21:44 PDT

THE CAR DROPS me off at the base of a hill, and I can hear the music thumping from a distance. It's a miracle no one's called the cops. The walk up is an obstacle course of drunken chaos—kids passed out on the sidewalk, others vomiting, and couples making out. Some are still dancing to the music blaring from the house.

The frat house is impressive. It's a white four-story building with numerous windows, likely dorm rooms. Flags wave from the roof, one of them the school's. The center of the lawn holds a beer fountain where two students are currently chugging the stream.

I take a deep breath and step forward. This is my first college party since moving here, and I intend to make it a memorable one. I'm on a mission tonight: find someone remotely interesting and have a good time. My skirt is short, barely covering my butt, and my top is so cropped it's practically a bra. I shove aside unwelcome thoughts, focusing instead on finding a drink.

A drunken student is bent over, and he's halfway through puking his guts out. I understand wanting to escape something, but at some point, it can't be enjoyable anymore. I ignore him and search the crowd for potential targets.

As I reach the door, heat and noise assault me. A guy stumbles out, clutching a bottle of Tito's. He looks decent but way too drunk. Dragging a girl along by the hand, he laughs uncontrollably. She looks thrilled, but something about them makes me uneasy. I step aside to let them pass, watching as he pulls her toward his group of friends. The scene feels off, but I don't have time to dwell on it as a piercing scream cuts through the air.

I spin around and spot the source through the patio glass. Some frat boy presses a girl against a tree, his hands and mouth all over her. Her eyes plead as she twists and turns to get away. His friends circle them like hyenas, laughing and cheering.

Not caring who I bump into, I push through the crowd. A knot forms in my stomach, but I force myself to take a calming breath. *This isn't about me right now.*

Once outside and within arm's reach, I grab the guy by his hair, yanking him off her with so much force he falls back into the tree, hitting it with a thud. The girl sags against the bark, her breaths ragged as she wraps her arms around herself.

"Whoa, who the hell are you?" He slurs. I can smell the vodka on his breath even from a foot away. There's an arrogance in the way he squares his shoulders, like he thinks he's untouchable.

"Let's make this simple," I say with an edge sharp enough to break through the drunken fog clouding his brain. "She said no. You're going to walk away."

He hesitates, and for a moment, I see the cogs turning in his head, trying to figure out whether to laugh it off or take a swing at me. His friends talk amongst themselves, hyping him up. "Who's this chick?" and "Don't let her talk to you like that, man."

The girl takes a shaky breath, trying to slip away, but another guy catches her by the wrist. She winces, and that's all I need to see. I step between them, locking eyes with him. "Let her go," I say, firm but steady. "Now."

He lets out a dry laugh. "What's your deal, huh? She's fine—"

"Does she look fine to you?" I cut him off, glancing back at the girl. Her face is streaked with tears, and her mascara is a black river as she trembles. I pull her free. My voice softens as I meet her eyes. "Go. Now."

She darts around me and bolts down the hill, disappearing into the crowd. I breathe a sigh of relief, but it's short-lived. The first guy steps closer. "You think you can just butt in like that?" he spits. "Do you not know who I am?"

"Not really. And I don't care to learn," I say, planting my feet. I didn't come here looking for drama, but it has a way of always finding me. I just wanted to make sure that the girl was safe. But I can tell he's not going to let this go.

He lunges forward, aiming to grab me, but he's drunk and slow—an easy read. I sidestep, slipping out of his reach before he even realizes I've moved. Before he can react, I deliver a quick, precise combo: a jab to his solar plexus followed by an elbow to his side, not enough to do real damage, just enough to knock the wind out of him and send him floundering backward.

"What the hell?" he gasps, clutching his ribs, his face twisted in shock. "You're a fucking psycho!"

I step back, casual, keeping my hands low and relaxed.

"Stop touching women without their consent. Consider this a friendly reminder. I don't like to repeat myself."

For a moment, he just stands there, his mouth open, processing what just happened. His friends exchange glances, looking more amused than concerned. Then his face hardens, anger flashing across it like a switch being flipped. He charges at me again. Before he can lay a hand on me, I sweep a leg behind his knee, and bring my arm around his neck in a flash. It all happens so quickly that by the time his back hits the ground, I'm already on top of him, my knee pressed against his chest, one hand pinning his arm while the other hovers near his throat, daring him to move. I know at least seven ways to break his hand, but I don't. It won't make the night any more enjoyable.

"Third try is always the charm," I say while the stunned frat boy blinks up at me. The hype he was receiving from his buddies is now mere silence. They shift uncomfortably, their drunken courage wavering. "But in all seriousness, try me again and see where it gets you next time. Stay down." I push off him and stand, glancing at the group of guys as they stare, slack-jawed. "Any of you feeling a bit emboldened?"

"We good. We don't want no trouble," one of them mutters, taking a few steps back, looking everywhere but at me.

"Smart choice. Maybe the GPA requirement for this frat is actually paying off," I say, as they slink away, throwing back a final look over their shoulders. The guy on the ground scrambles to his feet, massaging his side, glaring at me like he wants to say something, but he just huffs and retreats with his friends. I let them rejoin the party, leaving them to lick their wounds and bruised egos.

Inside, I navigate through the throng of drunk dancers, searching for Jessica. The party doesn't seem to have minded the whole scene from the backyard. Are people used to hearing terrified screams, I wonder. Suddenly, I hear her voice. "Winter!" she cries out, stumbling into me. She's clearly gone, and it's not just from alcohol. Her face is flushed, and white specks dust her nose.

I don't need to be told what it is. I wipe it off for her, the action causing her to giggle. "You made it!"

"Yup," I reply, forcing a smile. "You look like you're having fun."

"I am," Jessica yells.

She leans into me conspiratorially, and I do the same. "Do you want me to get you something?" She proceeds to point to her nose, and I shake my head. The night has been a downer since I got here, but booger sugar and I don't need to be reacquainted.

"Your loss. Have fun," Jessica announces and waltzes away, hands in the air and her hips swinging from side to side. *That should be me,* I think to myself. This beat is the type I get down with. I can go to the middle of the room, put on a performance for everybody and find a temporary escape with some random guy in a dingy frat house bathroom. But I can't, and it's all the fault of those boys from earlier. They managed to get in my head.

It's almost Christmas, and the weather is perfect for a Chicago winter. My phone buzzes with texts from my teammates, wondering where I am. Determined to make the best of tonight, I remind myself it's supposed to be a celebration. And I won't be here for much longer.

I need to forget the latest fight with my mother. We've been arguing a lot lately, mostly because I've finally found the courage to call her out on her bullshit. She doesn't like it one bit.

"Winter's here!" Rachel announces the second I arrive and hands me a drink. We head straight for the dance floor. The music

pulses through my body, and for a moment, I feel liberated. I can forget the tension at home and the hollow phone conversations with Jayden that leave me longing for more. I try to push away the bitterness I feel every time I remember that my mother refused to let me stay with Aunt Gina. She wanted to prove she could take care of her family, she said. And yet, the further we get from everyone we know, the less she seems to care about being a good mother. Sure, she makes sure I go to school, but only when she's sober enough.

I can't say exactly what makes me desperate for a release, but when I find it in the cheap alcohol in the disposable red cup I hold in my hand, I cling to it as if my life depends on it.

Pushing through the crowd, I shake off the memory. Jessica now sits in the lap of a guy, making out with him on the couch. His blond hair is unmistakable—Jessica's boyfriend, famous for his wild parties. She'd gleamed with pride when she told me about him. It's such a quintessential college thing to be proud of, and while it's shallow, it makes her happy, so who am I to judge?

I reach the kitchen, where a bowl of punch sits unattended. I know it's spiked, but the real danger is not knowing how much alcohol has been dumped in it. I stare at the bowl, debating whether to risk it. My head spins, and my breathing grows shallow. It's ridiculous that I'm even feeling this way. I've been to countless parties and clubs, yet tonight's different.

Deciding against the punch, I open the fridge and pull out a beer, opting for something I can control. Leaning against the kitchen counter, I nurse the drink, wishing I could enjoy it.

A ping-pong ball bounces off the table nearby and rolls toward my feet. I glance over, and a guy half-shouts, "Hey! Can you toss that back?"

Reaching down, the cool ball between my fingers, I eye the table, not really thinking, just reacting. With a flick of my wrist, the ball arcs smoothly through the air and lands dead center in one of the cups. It splashes softly, a perfect shot.

"Yo!" The guy's eyes go wide, clearly impressed. "That was clean! You wanna join? My partner's too sloshed to even see straight, let alone shoot."

The guy next to him sways a little, giggling at nothing in particular. A shrug escapes me. *Fuck it.*

Surveying the last few cups scattered in a tight triangle at the other end, I step up to the table. "No pressure, but there's just three cups left."

A half-smile creeps across my lips. Without a second thought, I take the shot. The ball sinks into the middle cup, barely disturbing the beer inside. The crowd around the table explodes with shouts and groans—celebration from my side, disappointment from the other.

My new partner slaps me on the back. "A couple more like that, and it's game!"

Two cups now, standing together like soldiers waiting to be taken down. I zone in, blocking out the noise and chucking the ball. It drops into the penultimate cup. They cheer louder, but it feels almost distant.

I step up for the final shot, bringing my hand back, ready to send the ball into the remaining cup. Just as I'm about to release, fingers wrap tightly around my wrist, stopping me cold.

Expecting some random drunk, I turn to find Jessica's boyfriend. She stands behind him, arms crossed, her eyes fixed on me. The look on her face says it all—this isn't going to end well.

"Let's take it outside," Jessica suggests. He releases me and strides out, radiating irritation. She takes my hand in hers. Her grip is loose, a stark contrast to her boyfriend's. I feel myself relaxing, just a bit. "Come on."

"Wrap it up for us," I say as I throw the ping-pong ball to my partner.

Outside, her boyfriend stands in a corner with a group of guys, laughing and talking. Some of them have girls draped over their arms. I study their faces, making sure none of them are there against their will.

"Chris has been getting complaints," Jessica says, her voice tense.

"About me?" I ask, turning my attention back to her.

She nods. "About you. And honestly, you do seem a little off. Are you okay?"

I wave away her concern. "I'm fine. I guess he was coming to ask me to leave."

"I'm really sorry. I know I invited you, but this party is a big deal to him. His entire reputation is built around it."

I nod my head in understanding. At that moment, I can see our age gap truly showing. To a twenty-year-old music major from Malibu, a party that goes bust means the end of the world. I wish I had the luxury of thinking that way. But I've lived too many lives before this.

"I'll leave," I say.

"I'm truly sorry," she repeats, looking genuinely upset.

I force a smile. "I've been partying nonstop since I got to L.A. Maybe it's a sign I need to slow down."

Jessica's eyes flicker with relief as I pull out my phone and order a rideshare.

"I'll stay with you until your car gets here," she offers. I want to tell her it's unnecessary, but I decide against it. If she needs this to assuage her guilt, she can have it.

My phone vibrates in my pocket. I don't bother to check it; I already know who it is. Ignoring my mother's calls has become a habit, one I'm not ready to break. I don't have the patience for a conversation with her right now. There's nothing I want to say.

When my ride arrives, I get in and wave goodbye to Jessica. As the car pulls onto the road, I finally check my phone. It's my mother, as expected. I don't call her back. I'm not sure when or if I ever will.

CHAPTER 6

THE STORE'S air conditioning brushes against my skin as I step inside. This upscale establishment is filled with racks of designer clothes, each piece more extravagant than the last. Jessica jumps from one display to another, her eyes sparkling with excitement.

"Try this on!" she calls out, holding up a black dress with delicate lace detailing. I glance at the price tag and choke on my own saliva.

"I can't afford this," I protest.

Jessica laughs, her voice light and dismissive. "Don't worry about it. It's on me. Consider it an apology for the party. I don't know what came over me."

"No, I can't let you do that. It—"

She shoves the dress into my hand. "I'm not taking no for an answer." She points behind her. "Fitting rooms are over there." I hesitate, but I do what I'm told.

"Jessica, this is excessive," I say, emerging from the dressing room for the sixth time. This whole shopping spree is a bit much. She's sorry about how she left things at the party, but it's fine. I get it. That's your man, and you stood behind him.

"Nonsense. You look great." She holds up another dress, this one red and equally short. "Try this one next."

I groan but obey, slipping into the dress and giving her a twirl. "It's perfect!" she exclaims. "I think if we pair it with—"

"Hey, do you know that guy?" I cut her off, nodding toward a man standing near the entrance. He's dressed in a dark suit, with an earpiece discreetly tucked into his ear. He has the look of security—tall, broad-shouldered—but something about him doesn't sit right with me.

Jessica's eyes flick toward the man, and I notice a fleeting look of unease pass over her face. "Oh, him? He's just my security. My dad can be so overprotective sometimes."

I've seen my fair share of bodyguards, and this guy doesn't exactly fit the mold. His eyes are watchful, but his stance is too predatory. I let it slide for now, not wanting to ruin the day with my paranoia.

After what feels like an eternity of Jessica pulling outfit after outfit off of hangers, we finally leave the store. I'm laden with shopping bags.

"Oh wait, can we stop in here real quick?" Jessica gestures at a high-end watch store. I follow her inside, and her eyes light up as she zeroes in on the gold section.

"What do you think about this one?" Jessica points toward a diamond-encrusted watch with a matching band. "Chris and I's one-year anniversary is coming up, and I don't know what to get him." I look at the healthy five-digit price tag and feel my throat tighten. "Again, I'm so sorry about the party. I didn't know the whole story at the time, and neither did Chris. I promise he's a really nice guy."

An attendant approaches us, his attention fixated on me. "Anything catching your eye?"

"Yes, could I see this one out of the case?" Jessica asks, pointing to the watch.

"Of course. I'll be right back with the key." He leaves us briefly.

Jessica nudges my arm. "He's cute! And he's totally into you. Get his number."

I roll my eyes. "Oh, I don't know. I think he's just trying to make a sale."

"Yeah, sure. But I don't think any sale requires that much eye contact," she teases.

The attendant returns with the key and unlocks the case. "This is an excellent choice. This classic style has made a comeback in recent years." He hands the watch to Jessica, and she hovers the timepiece over her wrist.

"I love it. I think I'll get it," she declares.

"Wonderful. Right this way." He guides us to the register, his hand lightly touching my back as he directs us. He types information into the computer. "And what are the names of the two beautiful ladies I have before me?"

Jessica pushes me forward. "This is Winter, and I'm Jessica."

"A pleasure to meet you both," he says, locking eyes with me again. "And I just need a card to complete the transaction." He turns back to Jessica.

She hands him a black card, and as he resumes typing, she starts making lewd gestures, her hands mimicking explicit movements and winking at me.

He looks up, interrupting her antics. "And we're all set.

Here's your card." He steps around the counter, shaking her hand.

"I hope you both have a wonderful day. Thank you for stopping in." He shakes my hand, subtly passing me a folded piece of paper. Once outside, I unfold the note: *Velvet @ 9?*

"See? I told you he liked you," Jessica exclaims, peeking at the invitation. "So, are you going?"

"Maybe, it is Sangria Saturday at The Velvet Lounge tonight." I say, mulling it over. "But who knows? The day is still young."

Jessica laughs and pulls me along. "Well, we don't want to be late for our mani-pedis."

She settles into a plush chair in the salon, immediately striking up a cheerful conversation with her nail technician. I watch her, noticing the tension beneath her relaxed façade. I don't understand her sometimes. She can be so down-to-earth and then, with the flip of a coin, become a full-blown nepo-baby.

Without even realizing it, the words slip out of my mouth, "Why me?"

Jessica arches a brow. I clarify, "Why did you choose to have a roommate? You don't exactly need the rent money, so why me?"

"I'm not sure." Jessica wears a thoughtful expression. "You just seemed so carefree. Moving cross country at a moment's notice. Looked like you could use the help."

I raise my eyebrow now. "Carefree? That's not how I'd describe myself."

She smiles. "Maybe not. But you're definitely... different. You don't get caught up in the drama or the pressure of being perfect. The fame or the stardom. You're just... you. Unapologetically." She trails off, "I wish I could be like that."

I take a deep breath, trying to find the right words. "Look, being carefree doesn't mean you don't have problems or stress. It's about picking your battles. You have to find your strength in who you are, not in what others expect you to be."

"Yeah, but how?"

"Find something you love and hold on to it. But don't let it control you. Perfection's a joke. We're human, we screw up. All we can do is our best," I say, though I haven't fully embraced this advice.

Jessica nods slowly. "Thanks. Hey, how did you get so wise anyways?"

"I guess you could say I had to learn the hard way."

As we leave the salon to get massages, I can't shake the feeling that we're being watched. And it doesn't feel protective; something's off.

"I'm glad we could finally do this. The semester really picked up for me," Jessica says, admiring her new nails. We turn a corner. "Oh, I've been meaning to ask, what are you going to be for Halloween? Chris and I are doing match—"

I grab Jessica's arm and pull her into a nearby alley. She looks at me in surprise, but my attention is on the alleyway entrance. The man in the suit appears seconds later, his face a mask of calm professionalism.

Stepping forward, I place myself between Jessica and the man. "Who are you?" I demand.

The man doesn't respond, his eyes on Jessica.

"Winter, it's fine," Jessica says, her voice trembling slightly. "Let's just go."

But I'm not backing down. "Why are you following us?"

The man finally speaks, his voice even. "I'm here for Miss Glory's protection."

My eyes narrow. "Protection from what?"

Before he can answer, Jessica pulls me back. "Winter, please, you're scaring me. He's just some guy with my dad's agency. Now, come on."

Reluctantly, I follow her out of the alley. But something about this isn't right. I don't think this is over.

CHAPTER 7

THE CLOCK on the wall steadily ticks as I walk inside the door. His space is much like he is—organized chaos. Stacks of papers and books hang over the edges of his desk, but there's a method to it. His keen eyes always find exactly what he's looking for. He doesn't look up immediately, attending to the glowing screen in front of him.

"Ms. Washington," he says, finally breaking his gaze from the monitor. "I haven't seen you at my office hours before. Do you need help with the project?"

I pull out my laptop, flipping it open with a calm focus. I've spent a non-negligible amount of time on this, and I know the code inside out. It's already solid, but I could use an extra eye from someone else. I'm curious to see what Donovan will think. He's a world-renowned network security consultant after all. His opinion could help me weed out a few rabbit holes. "I made a few adjustments, and I wanted to see what you thought."

He scrolls through the script I've written, his brows knitting together. His fingers tap lightly against the desk, scanning my work with a meticulousness that makes me a little uneasy. Hovering over the touchpad, he occasionally stops to study certain lines of code. I wait for him to speak, to critique, but instead, there's a long silence.

"What are you trying to do here?" he finally asks, glancing up at me from behind his black-rimmed glasses. His gaze is filled with curiosity.

I clear my throat, sitting up straighter in my chair. "I... wanted to challenge myself. Make it more robust. I know it didn't need to be this complex, but I figured—why not?"

He motions for me to continue, so I do.

"I automated the routing rules," I explain, tapping the screen to bring up the relevant section of the code. "Instead of manually configuring each, I created a system that analyzes network traffic in real-time. It gathers data from IP packets, and based on certain parameters in the headers, it adjusts the routing automatically. It's a heuristic approach."

His eyes narrow slightly as he leans closer to the screen, focus sharpening. "Heuristics, you say?"

I shrug. "I figured manual configurations are too slow and inefficient. Let the system learn and adapt as it goes. No need to hard-code every possibility when the data itself can inform the routing. The program detects anomalies, flags potential issues, and optimizes the firewall without needing human input."

Donovan leans back now, folding his arms as his gaze shifts from the screen to me. "You've managed to automate something most only know how to handle manually. That's... impressive."

"You sound surprised, Professor."

A hint of a smile flickers across his face. "Not surprised, just intrigued. I wasn't expecting something like this. Not even from my doctoral cohort. Most students would've just stuck to the basics." He nods, still studying the code. "Have you tested it against realistic scenarios?"

I nod, pulling up the results of the trial runs. "I did a few tests last night. I have it adjust the routes in about five milliseconds, with only a slight latency spike during the reconfiguration. I'm almost done optimizing that part."

Donovan studies the data, his fingers tapping against his desk again. After a moment, his eyes are back on me. "You've built a foundation that could evolve into something much larger. With the right fine-tuning, this could revolutionize how systems handle network traffic. It's scalable, adaptable— it's smart."

I smile, feeling a sense of satisfaction at his words. "That's the plan."

He glances at the clock, then back at me. "We're about out of time, but keep refining it. Tweak those parameters and see how far you can push it. I want to see how this evolves."

"Will do," I say, standing up and packing my laptop.

"Winter," Donovan speaks again, and I pause at the door. "If you need extra lab access, let me know. I'd like to see where you can take this before the semester ends."

"That won't be necessary. Give me a couple of days to tinker with it and it should be ready to go. I'll keep you posted, Professor."

HOME – *Living Room*
 November 07, 14:57 PST

A CRUMPLED piece of paper flies toward my head when the apartment door opens. I manage to dodge it in the nick of time and it hits the wall in the hallway behind me, bouncing off with a light thud.

"Sorry!" Jessica calls out from across the room. She sits on the couch, her guitar in her lap, fingers poised over the strings, but her expression is anything but relaxed. She's staring at the notebook in front of her like it just insulted her family. Another balled-up piece of paper lands near her feet.

I drop my bag by the door and remove the litter from the building's hallway. "Any reason why I almost got my head taken off?"

Jessica groans. "I've been at this for forever, and it's just not coming together."

The faint melody she'd been strumming still hangs in the air when I step further into the living room. It's soft, tinged with melancholy, and carries a hint of something... unresolved. It doesn't fit Jessica's usual preppy, rich sorority girl vibe. "What are you working on?"

She taps her pen against the notebook, looking more like she wants to snap it in half. "It's a new song for my mental health music class. The lyrics—they're a mess. I can't get it to feel right."

I nod, moving to the kitchen to grab a water bottle. "What's it about?"

"It's about... a girl who's in way over her head. She's trying to do the right thing, but everything is just spiraling. She's trapped between who she is, what she wants, and who she's supposed to be."

I pause, leaning against the counter, the cap of the bottle halfway twisted off. That hits close to home. "Solid theme. I think a lot of people can relate to it, myself included."

Jessica jumps off the couch and begins stretching. "I agree. So why am I having such a hard time with this?"

I walk back into the living room and sit on the armrest of the sofa. "In my experience with writing code, it always helps to have another set of eyes on it. Mind if I take a look?" I nod toward her notebook.

She hesitates for a second, then hands it over. Her neat handwriting fills the page, crossed out in places, scribbled over in others. "You're stuck on the lyrics?" I ask, flipping through a few more pages.

Running a hand through her hair, Jessica exhales slowly. "Yeah. I think I got the melody down, but the words... they feel off."

I hand the notebook back to her, thinking for a moment. "Maybe you're overthinking it. What is the girl actually going through? Try to put yourself in her shoes."

She tilts her head, her fingers absentmindedly strumming the guitar again. "She's overwhelmed. Everything around her feels too big, too risky. But she keeps pushing forward because... well, she has to. No one else is going to do it."

The impact of her words sinks in. I'm not sure if she's talking about a song anymore. But I don't want to pry. It's not my business.

Jessica hums a few notes, her voice rough from hours of work, but still beautiful. The sound wraps around the room.

"The melody is nice," I say, nodding along with the rhythm. "But it feels like it's missing something. Maybe you could try to make it more simple to balance out the intensity of the lyrics?"

Jessica stares at me with an analytical expression. "You sing?"

I shrug, suddenly feeling self-conscious. "I've been told I can carry a tune. Why?"

"Hum something," she says, shifting the guitar to her side, giving me her full attention. "I want to hear it through someone else besides me."

I blink at her, then glance down at the guitar like it's going to save me. But Jessica's waiting, her expression expectant, never pushy. I clear my throat, feeling awkward, and vocalize a few soft notes, matching the key she'd been playing earlier.

Jessica's eyes light up and she reaches for the guitar again, fingers moving faster now, working out the new rhythm. "Keep going."

I stall for a bit, but then let myself fall into the song, adding a few more notes as I hum along. The room seems to shift, the frustration from earlier lifting from Jessica as she writes down a few more lines, the lyrics starting to come together.

"Try this." Jessica hands me the notebook, her fingers hovering on the edges nervously as I pry it from her grip. The words jump out at me, raw and real.

Verse:
In too deep, lost my way,
Every step feels like yesterday,
Running fast, but I'm stuck in place,
Fighting battles I'm not sure I can face.

And the weight keeps pulling me down,
Lost in the noise, swimming against the crowd,
But I won't back down, I won't let go,
Even if I'm on my own.

Chorus:
I'm just a girl, in over my head,

Trying to make sense of all the things I did and
   said,
The world's too loud, everything to fear,
But I'm still standing, I'm still here.

I look up from the page, surprised by the depth of it. The words are unfiltered, like they're coming from a place much deeper than just a school project. "This is... pretty deep," I say softly.

"Let me hear it," she says, leaning forward.

She starts to play, and I sing along and get lost in the music. Someone in over their head, trying to push through, even when it feels like the world's their opposition; it's a story I know all too well.

When we finish, she looks at me, waiting for feedback. I chew on the inside of my cheek before speaking. "What if... you softened the bridge a little? Like, before it gets to the final chorus, give the listener a moment to breathe? And then we can hit them hard with the first line of it."

Jessica raises an eyebrow, intrigued. "Show me what you mean."

I hesitate for a moment, but I take the guitar from her, awkwardly holding it as I strum a few chords. I'm not a pro, but I've picked up enough over the years. I start singing, adjusting the pacing of the lyrics:

But I won't back down, I won't let go...
Even if I'm on my own...
I'm just a girl, in over my head...

She listens carefully, then grins. "Yeah, that's it! That's exactly it."

I return the guitar to her, feeling flushed from putting myself out there. It's been years since I've sung for anyone else. "You've got something here," I say, my voice lighter. "It's good. It really makes you stop and think."

She starts strumming the revised melody, nodding her head as she works through the changes. "I've been stuck on this for days. I was caught up in trying to say something, but I just didn't know how to get it across."

The leather creaks as I lean back on the couch, replaying the lyrics in my head. "There's nothing wrong with the song," I murmur, breaking the silence between us. "Maybe it's not the lyrics you're stuck on."

Jessica looks at me for a beat, like she's weighing whether or not to say something. But she says nothing, just sighs, her fingers falling back into a gentle pace. "Maybe."

The light strumming fills the space, a quiet conversation all its own. Jessica looks… vulnerable. There's a weight on her shoulders I don't think many people notice, but I do. Because I've felt that same pressure. She's not only the wealthy, stubborn roommate I've gotten used to. She's more than that. And tonight, I get a glimpse.

Withdrawn, she picks at the strings, lost in her own thoughts, and I find myself doing the same. My mind drifts back to long drives with my mother while we were constantly on the road. The old sedan flying down the highway with our voices carrying over the sound of the engine. I remember her singing voice being so full of soul, filling every seat of the car. She used to sing in small clubs before she met my dad. Sometimes, when the road stretched out endlessly in front of us, she'd start belting out tunes, and I'd join in just to fight the boredom.

Jessica's voice pulls me back into the present. "Where did you learn to sing like that?" she asks, a teasing lilt in her tone, though her eyes have genuine interest. "How dare you hide those vocals from me all this time!"

I shake my head. "It's not that serious. My mother was a singer back in the day. We used to sing together on road trips while we were moving. I guess some of it stuck."

"You sure that's all it is? Because it sounds like you've got more in you than just some road trip karaoke." She gives me a playful nudge with her knee.

I shrug, my smile fading a bit. "I don't really sing much anymore." I haven't been in a sing-along mood for quite some time. The truth sits there for a while, and I don't offer anything more. Silence fills the room, overshadowed by the distant drone of the refrigerator in the kitchen.

"Does that have anything to do with why you moved out here? From New York?" she asks softly, probing deeper into my past. I flick my eyes to the guitar, and how her fingers float over the instrument like she's waiting for my answer to shape the next chord.

A familiar urge to deflect resurfaces, to shut down the conversation before it gets too personal. A need to keep my true self hidden. This time is no different; old habits kick in, and my guard snaps back into place.

"What about you?" I say, flipping the question back at her. "Does your song have anything to do with your 'bodyguard' from a few weeks ago?" I arch an eyebrow and cross my arms awaiting her response.

Jessica's fingers stop on the strings, the music halting. Her eyes meet mine, but she doesn't answer right away. Instead, she exhales, a sound between a laugh and a sigh, and gives me a knowing look.

"Touché," she says, her lips quirking into a small, tight-lipped smile. "How about we just... drop it."

I nod. If anyone understands keeping things close to the chest, it's me.

CHAPTER 8

HUNTINGTON PARK – *La Clínica*
November 27, 15:12 PST

IT'S the day before Thanksgiving, and I'm spending it in the far end of a waiting room, waiting for a nurse to call my name. I'm not sick, but regular check-ups are a priority. Considering how active this quarter has been for me, I figured it was time to stop in.

Jessica isn't going home for the holiday, something about wanting to spend time with her boyfriend. "I see my parents more than I see him," she said when we shared our plans. "My parents won't mind."

My plan for the holiday is simple. I'm going to stay indoors, pretending not to know it's Thanksgiving while everyone else is with their families, sharing what they're grateful for.

A baby next to me lets out a piercing scream, and I purse my lips to keep from saying anything. How do mothers do it?

If I had something like that screaming my ears off, I'm certain I wouldn't be able to take it.

The mother hurriedly shoves her nipple in the baby's mouth to quiet her, and the baby babbles happily before settling down. I think about what she would have done if the baby refused. My thoughts then drift to whether there's ever been a baby its mother couldn't soothe. It's a strange notion, but it's better than reading the infographics on the wall for the hundredth time.

My mind wanders to my mother, or rather the lack of a relationship with her. Does she remember all the things she put me through? Sometimes, I wish she had at least one more child. I would've had someone to talk to, someone who understood everything without me saying a word. But then again, that would mean another person sharing this scarred life, and I wouldn't wish that upon anyone.

I do a pass over the waiting room trying to take my mind off the overwhelming antiseptic smell. I had hoped to see a familiar face, but there's no one. In the few months I've been in Los Angeles, Jessica and a handful of classmates are the only people I've really connected with. In front of me, two girls lean into each other, giggling. Sisters or friends, I wonder.

"Winter Washington?"

"Yes." I grab my things and follow the nurse. Time to cross this off my to-do list.

The doctor is a middle-aged woman with brown hair in a ponytail and no makeup except lip gloss. Her smile is the prettiest thing I've seen today. Her name is Isa Rajit.

I answer her questions as best as I can. No sense in lying to the woman.

"Are you on birth control?"

"Yes. An IUD."

"When was the last time you had sex?"

"Yesterday."

"With protection?"

"Yes."

"When was the last time you had unprotected sex?"

"A week ago."

"Do you have a partner?"

I shake my head. "No, I don't."

She nods and enters the information into my file. "Multiple partners, then?"

"Is that what you call it when you hook up a lot?"

She gives me a thoughtful look. "Yes, it is. Do these partners," she gestures, indicating every guy I've been with, "ejaculate in you?"

"There have been occasions," I say with a smile as memories flash by.

Noting something in my file, she nods again. "How often do you get these tests done?"

"I try to get them done as often as every two months, but I've been so busy, so the last one was maybe four months ago. I haven't exactly gotten one since I first moved here."

"With your activity level, you should try to get these tests done every forty-five days to catch any issues early. And you should practice safer sex."

I wonder if she's struggling not to judge me. But, I can't imagine I'm the only promiscuous woman in L.A.

"Well, that'll be all," Dr. Rajit says. "The results will be ready in ten days. The clinic will contact you. The nurse will take you for the tests now."

As if on cue, the door opens, and a nurse with a friendly smile gestures for me to follow her. This is where the doctor should reassure me and tell me I'm in safe hands, but Dr. Rajit says nothing of the sort.

The nurse tests me for everything in the book. I decide Dr. Rajit is reason enough to visit the clinic regularly. She doesn't ask many questions and is straightforward. Others would try to psychoanalyze my sex life, but I don't need to pay someone $165 an hour for them to tell me I'm fucked up. I know.

I walk home to take in the fall air, and just relax. The weather is nice and people around me are so caught up in their activities that I'm forced to watch them.

A couple is arguing, but it doesn't seem serious. He pulls her close and kisses her forehead. I look away when she blushes, feeling like I've intruded on something intimate. An older woman passes by and tells them they're a lovely pair. I suddenly wish I were old, able to look into others' relationships and drop kind comments without feeling my heart twist at the thought of Jayden.

Droplets land in my eye. I extend my hand and raise my head to gaze at the suddenly cloudy sky. *It's drizzling?* I can't help but release a smug smile. Somehow, I think I managed to bring rain to Southern California.

CHAPTER 9

HOME – *Bedroom*
November 28, 07:21 PST

I STAY in bed longer than necessary until hunger finally drives me to the kitchen. Thanksgiving breakfast is pancakes and a cup of joe. After eating, I get some fresh air and head to the patio. Leaning against the balcony, I inhale the frigid fall scent, my coffee in hand. Everything looks peaceful, and it brings a rare genuine smile to my face. Maybe this city could actually be my permanent home.

When I look down, I see a pair of feet and recognize the shoes as Jessica's. I hurry back into the apartment, setting my mug on the table before rushing out into the hall. How drunk was she last night that she couldn't make it inside? I know Jessica can handle her liquor. Did she fight with her boyfriend? The last thing I have energy for is comforting a hungover person with a broken heart.

I push the door open and hurry over to her. "Jess, you shouldn't be lying out here like this."

She lies a few steps from the door, looking like she's been placed there rather than stumbling there herself. A shiver runs through my body as I take in her appearance. Her hair is disheveled, dirt clings to it, her knees are scraped and bloodied, and her hands are blue. A faint puncture wound on her arm jumps out at me. I will myself not to think the worst. My heart hammers loudly, and when I reach for her wrist, my fears are confirmed.

Jessica now too? I rush back into the apartment and grab my phone. The logical thing to do here is call this in.

"911."

"My roommate's not moving. She passed out in front of our building. Please send help. I think we need an ambulance." My throat feels dry as I speak.

"Ma'am, what's your address?"

"722 West Olympic Boulevard."

"Help's on the way."

The sound of the dispatcher confirming that the paramedics are en route hardly registers. My legs move before my brain can catch up, taking me to the balcony, looking down at her body. From up here, Jessica looks too still. My pulse pounds in my ears as I grip the railing, my eyes glued to her, even though I want to look away. It reminds me of my dad, the first dead body I ever saw. I remember his limp form being wheeled away, the wheel squeaks echoing alongside my mother's screams.

I try to snap out of it, to go to Jessica and attempt to revive her, but I can't bring myself to do it. It would be a wasted effort anyway. I hear sirens in the distance, and for the first time, I don't feel the urge to be near them. But I know I have to face them. The paramedics will have questions when they arrive.

Forcing myself to move, I sprint down the stairs two at a

time. The cold air slaps me in the face as I burst through the door and walk toward her.

I stop a few feet away from Jessica. My legs threaten to buckle beneath me, but I stand still. I won't touch her again. I can't. *This is now an active crime scene.*

A distant cry, growing louder, closer. I hear the screech of brakes, and in moments, the ambulance pulls up. The paramedics climb out and rush over. One of them kneels beside her, checking for a pulse I already know doesn't exist. His partner pulls out equipment, going through the motions they've probably done a hundred times before, but I see it in their eyes when they meet mine. They know too.

The one still standing looks at me, his face unreadable. "Miss, we'll take it from here," he says softly, and I step back, trying to make myself smaller, less noticeable.

Soon after, blue and red lights flash against the walls of the building. A police cruiser pulls up. Two officers step out, but my eyes lock on the younger one first. He's tall, barely early twenties, with the kind of face that hasn't yet been worn down by the weight of the job. His badge catches the light as he approaches me, his eyes taking in the scene with careful attention to detail.

He stops before me, standing stiff. "Officer Parks," he introduces himself, his voice all business. He motions at his superior. "We need to take your statement."

I nod, feeling numb.

His eyes flicker to the scene behind me. He clears his throat. "Would you be more comfortable discussing this down at the station? We can get you away from here while we secure the area."

"Yeah," I mutter, my voice barely audible. "Sure." He gestures toward the cruiser. I follow in silence, my shoes scraping against the concrete.

As long as I cooperate, everything will be fine. I can't let them dig too deep. Not into me. Not into my past. The focus needs to stay on Jessica.

The door to the cruiser closes with a soft thud. As Officer Parks drives, I stare out the window, watching the city blur by. Jessica's face lingers in my mind, but it's not the Jessica I saw yesterday morning. It's the one with a white sheet over her corpse.

I sit in the sterile, fluorescent-lit room at the police station. Parks sits across from me, a notepad in hand, waiting for my statement.

"I really don't know," I begin, my voice trembling slightly. "Jessica said she was going to spend Thanksgiving with her boyfriend, Chris, the president of Beta Alpha Psi. When I woke up this morning, I made breakfast and took my coffee to the balcony. That's when I saw her."

Parks looks up, his pen hovering over the paper. "You saw her from the balcony?"

Swallowing the lump in my throat, I nod. "At first, I thought she was black-out drunk. But... she wasn't. I called the ambulance, and the next thing you know, I'm sitting here."

He scribbles down notes, asking me to repeat the story multiple times. I even write it down, my hand shaking as I scrawl the words on the paper.

"Don't leave town anytime soon," he says, sliding me a business card. "This is the detective assigned to the case. If you remember anything else, contact him immediately."

I take the card. "I just want to make sure you find whoever did this," I say. "Jessica didn't deserve this."

"We'll do everything we can," Parks replies, but his words feel hollow, a standard line meant to comfort.

"What about Jessica's parents?" I ask, my thoughts

drifting to the people who must be devastated the most right now.

"They're already on their way. You can wait if you want," he tells me. "But you're free to go." I don't think I can sit around and comfort a couple who just lost their daughter. So, I decided to leave.

On the way home, I sit in the backseat, unsure of what I'm supposed to do now. Am I going to trust the cops with this investigation? The sanest choice is to let the police do their jobs. Jessica isn't just some kid who had the unfortunate luck of being killed; she's the daughter of someone who has a voice and influence in the world.

I exhale. It's no longer *Jessica is…*

My hands are shaking by the time the car arrives in front of my building. This was such a crazy way for Turkey Day to go. Her parents will never see this as anything other than the day they lost their daughter. Besides their millions, they can't possibly have anything to be grateful for.

The door latches shut, the sound fading as the car pulls away, leaving me stuck. The apartment building looms before me, just as still. I pray my eyes are playing tricks on me, but they're not. It's not the now-empty sidewalk, where men in uniforms crowded earlier, that throws me for a loop. My mother stands out front, and I almost laugh at how ridiculous today has been despite it barely being noon.

"Gina told me where you stay."

Expressionless, I say, "You should go back to wherever you came from."

"Listen, Winter, I know I wasn't ever mother of the year, but I'm willing to make amends. I want to right my wrongs and—"

"Jesus Christ," I spit out with all the venom I can muster,

"I don't care about the reformation you're going through. Go through it and leave me out of it."

A part of me itches to tell her that I just lost my friend, but I don't. She doesn't deserve to know that much about me. I turn my attention back to her.

"You shouldn't have come," I say, noting how skinny she looks. Clearly, she put a lot of effort into her appearance—her hair and nails are perfectly done.

"Winter, I—"

"No, Mom! What did you think would happen when you decided to show up in Los Angeles?" I yell, anger threatening to take over me. I let out a strenuous breath. "You know what? Don't answer that." I turn away. I don't want to look at her for too long. Memories I wished to forget are already resurfacing. She may be willing to make amends, but I'm not.

"Stop calling me," I say sternly. Without waiting for her reply, I enter the lobby and slam the door behind me, hoping she got the message and will leave me the hell alone.

CHAPTER 10

WITH A BANG, *the door opens, distracting me from my work at the computer. I whip my head around to see my mother and Luke, her new boyfriend, staring at me. My mother looks irritated, while his face is smug.*

Luke stands in front of her, chest puffed out, while my mother hovers behind him, heaving. I don't need anyone to tell me I'm in trouble, though for what, I haven't a clue.

He's the latest in a long line of boyfriends, each one worse than the last. I never saw them as father figures, just obstacles to navigate through different stages of my life. Luke is no different—complaining, taking, never adding anything positive to what's left of this family.

I can tell he's zeroed in on something worth taking today, and I have a bad feeling about what that might be. My hands feel sweaty on the mouse, and it takes everything not to squeeze it too hard to gain some control.

Asking what's wrong is something I wouldn't dare to do. Knowing both of them, there's always an issue in how I do things. The air around us is thick, and I'm aware that any simple act on my part will break it. It still doesn't stop me from facing my screen again as the only option was to keep having a staring contest. I don't have time for their drama. I'm in the middle of crafting a SQL query to inject into a database that contains all the students' grades at my school. A kid paid me 150 bucks to update his final score.

I realize too late that turning was the wrong move when a scoff escapes one of them. "What did I tell you about her and that computer?" Luke starts, his voice dripping with disdain. "I told you she's in front of that damn thing all the time. It's spoiling her brain."

He's literally never mentioned this before.

"Look at the state of the house," he continues, gesturing wildly. "Nothing gets done. She doesn't even go to work. Doesn't pull her weight around here. Just sits there, staring at that damn screen while we do everything. She hasn't paid a bill in forever."

I roll my eyes. I shouldn't have to contribute. I'm still a high school junior. I must've missed the memo that said I needed to bring home the bacon too.

A high-pitched sound escapes me as Luke shoves me away from the computer, chair and all. I hit the floor harshly but scramble to my feet, certain of what's coming next. My mother is already reaching for the monitor, yanking at it, but the cords are tangled.

I rush to grab the tower, but Luke gets to me first. I don't expect it, so I have no way of shielding myself from the hand that lands across my face. The impact of the slap stuns me to the floor. As I hit the ground, I hear the crash.

Everything goes silent. I don't move or say anything. I keep my eyes fixed on the ground while my mother's voice hovers above me. I hear laughter, but all I focus on is the cracked motherboard and broken hard drive before me.

My vision blurs with tears that I refuse to let fall. All of it I hold inside of me because I don't want to show them weakness. I don't want them to know they can break me. I crawl toward the remains of what used to be my PC, it's for the hope that it might be worth saving, something I can still hang on to.

The keyboard lands in front of me, and I flinch. It's been snapped in two, and some of the keys are missing. The sob forces itself out of me before I can reel it in. I feel wronged, and the argument rests on the tip of my tongue, but I know better.

I can't believe my mother would let this man, this stranger, hit me like that.

Besides, what do they know about what I've been doing in the house if they're high half of the time? All the time, even. I'm the reason the lights are still on in this bitch. I worked the entirety of last summer to pay the bills and to build this PC. I picked up coding in my spare time. I saw how programmers were making headlines everywhere. They were transforming industries, and I wanted in on that. To be a part of something I was certain would take me out of this hellhole.

I think of all the friends that I have online, and all the forums where I'm able to have a community. People I've never met, people I feel like I've known for years. The tears flow freely now, my body shaking with each sob. I don't hear them anymore; they're gone. The door slams, and I cry harder.

Dad needs to come back so I can tell him everything and he can kick Luke's ass. But tonight confirms what I already knew—I can't count on anyone, not even my own mother.

Facing the wreckage that's been left for me to deal with seems daunting. Instead, I lay on my back and trace the patterns created from the leaks the slumlord won't repair on the ceiling. I wish I could tell the future from such markings. I imagine it must be good because I can't see it getting much worse than this.

Pushing my body to cooperate with me, I finally get to my feet. I pick up the remnants of my computer and place the non-salvageable parts in the waste-bin.

CHAPTER 11

I DON'T TRUST the police. They always manage to mess things up. But I'm determined to make sure Jessica's case gets the attention it deserves. Not that they need me for motivation—her parents must be all over it. Still, I want to know how far they've come in the investigation. What are their leads? Was there foul play? How close are they to finding the bastard who did this? Bastards, if the bastard had an accomplice.

The station is busy when I step in. A man is having a loud argument with a detective, drawing the attention of everyone in the waiting room. It's a spectacle; some people are laughing, others egging on the detective to fight back.

"I'm telling you," the man yells louder, "I didn't do anything. I don't even know what's going on."

"Maybe if you let me get a word in, you'd know all about

it," the detective retorts. I ignore the scene; it's not why I'm here.

"I'm here to see Detective Gillian," I tell the receptionist.

She doesn't even glance at me. Her eyes are glued to the chaos in front of her. Laughing along as if I'm not standing right there.

Her hair is packed in a bun, and she has warm brown eyes. There's a name tag that sits on the upper right part of her chest that reads *Garcia*. She doesn't have the excitement of a newbie, or the professionalism of an old-timer. Must've been someone who screwed up on duty and is serving her way through retribution.

I turn my attention to the wall behind her. There's an image of the president, and he seems younger and healthier in the picture than he currently is. The LAPD logo covers almost every surface, and lines of walkie-talkies decorate the tables around us.

When I return my attention to the receptionist, she's wearing a frown and I offer her a fake smile. It must not be nice getting ignored.

"Detective Gillian, please," I say in my most sugary voice.

"Is he expecting you?"

He's not, but she doesn't need to know that. "Tell him I'm here for Jessica Glory's case. I was her roommate."

She picks up the phone and calls, presumably to Gillian's office. My plan is simple: find out what I need to know to see if they have this under control, then leave. She speaks briefly into the phone, listens, and then hangs up. Before she can say anything, a loud bang distracts her, and this time, I look too.

The man from earlier is now being restrained by two offi-cers. Spit flies from his mouth as he yells, and the detective yells back.

"I wonder who'd win if they're both allowed to have a go

at each other?" Garcia mutters. I raise a brow, and she turns her head to the side and points down a hallway, "Fourth door on your left."

I offer her a smile but don't say thank you.

The fourth door on the left has a plaque: J. Gillian, California Investigator of the Year Award. Given the victim's high profile, it's no surprise they put one of their best on the case.

I knock twice on the door and push it open. Gillian looks up from a file. I see him trying to reach a conclusion about me based on how I'm dressed. I'm wearing cargo pants with an oversized hoodie.

He stands up, and his shoulders tell the tale of days spent in a gym. His handshake is firm, and there are calluses on his palm. I offer a polite smile, strands of my hair sticking to my lip gloss. He points to one of the visitor's chairs and I take a seat.

"Officer Garcia tells me you were Jessica Glory's roommate."

I nod. "I came by to know if you've found anything that will tell us who did this to her."

He keeps his eyes on me for a while and leans forward on his desk. "I'm told you're the one who found her."

"Yes." It's not something he doesn't know, seeing how I was brought here for questioning on the day I found her cold body at the front of the steps.

"Is there something new you remember that might help the case?"

"Besides the detailed report I gave on the day, a week ago?"

"Ms. Washington, is it? The LAPD is doing everything we can to determine the cause of death."

"She was murdered," I say and fix him with a stare. "She was killed."

Gillian sighs and rubs his forehead. "We don't know that she was murdered."

I stay quiet, waiting for him to come to his senses, or laugh and say he's pulling my leg. What does he mean by he doesn't know that she's been murdered? Did she kill herself at our front door?

When I don't say anything, he says, "Look, I know how you feel."

"If you don't think she was killed, what do you think happened to her?"

"Listen, I assure you we are doing everything in our power to bring the case to fulfillment."

Fulfillment? This isn't a drop-shipping warehouse, and Jessica wasn't a damn order. Jessica was a generous girl who was fiercely loyal, full of love even when she wasn't getting any herself. She wasn't perfect, but she didn't need to be.

My vision blurs, and I look up to the ceiling to push away the wetness gathering in my eyes. "Is there anything you can tell me?"

"It's not a murder investigation yet, like I said. We just don't have enough evidence to make it one. Our medical examiner's results are inconclusive. We have reason to believe that the injuries could have been self-inflicted. The best option now is to send it up to another lab before it's decided as a murder case."

"How long is that going to take?"

"Here," he says, handing me a pen and paper, "Give me your number, and I'll try to keep you posted. It's good to see someone caring about the case that isn't paparazzi, but kiddo, you have a life to live. Don't let your roommate's death consume you."

My head is computing close to a thousand thoughts per second once I leave the station. The meeting didn't go as I expected. I went there hoping to make the detective slip the name of someone they think might have done it, and what did I get? They think she did it to herself.

A loud crash makes me stop in my tracks. When I turn around, I see a ghastly collision. A white sedan has collided with a black SUV.

I'm planted in my spot as the occupant of the SUV, a man, hops out of the vehicle. People have gathered, and amongst the crowd, phones are recording.

Let the professionals do what they do best, Washington. I watch the SUV driver approach the white car. He's attempting to free the woman from the driver's seat.

I should help, but I don't move. The sirens are getting closer now, wailing through me like a promise I can't keep. *Leave it alone, Washington. Help is already on its way.*

He manages to free her, and they hobble toward the sidewalk. I think it's over, but something in her body language catches my eye. She's shaking him off, refusing his help. Her legs are weak, stumbling, but it's the desperation in her eyes that makes me pause. I glance past them, to the smashed frame of the car.

There's still a little boy inside. My chest tightens, and for a second, my feet start to wiggle, revving up to do something. But I stay in place. A flash of heat rises up my neck. What the hell is wrong with me?

Every instinct screams at me to act. The kid's just sitting there, too shocked to cry. It'd be so easy to rush in and get him out. To do what I thought I was good at—stepping in when no one else could, or wouldn't. But the last time I put that mask on, someone didn't walk away. The last time I tried to save everyone, I failed. And people died.

That pain is still louder and heavier than the weeping of the mother before me. I didn't come to L.A. to keep playing some version of a protector. I gave it up for a reason. Thought I could escape the wreckage of my own choices, have a clean slate, let the first responders handle the messes. I wanted to leave it all behind. This was my chance to stop controlling a world that can't be understood. To walk away before I did any more damage. Intentionally or not.

The paramedics will be here any second. They'll know how to extract the kid safely. I'd probably just make things worse if I got involved. Yet, my eyes shift back to the scene. Fuel drips from the black car onto the white one.

It's going to blow.

I let out an exasperated sigh. "Who am I kidding?" I ignore the voices in my head as I pull my hoodie up and take off down the street. Toward the wreck.

The side where his mother was pulled from already has flames in front of it. Going in through there isn't an option. I grab the door handle on the other side and pull it. It's locked. The boy inside is no more than ten. He's not looking at me. His eyes are on his mother, who's being held away from him. He snuggles an action figure against his chest, his back turned to the door. I bang on the window to get his attention.

It works, he looks at me. His cheeks are stained with tears, his lips trembling. I point to the lock and wave my hand down, hoping he would get the hint. Luckily for me, he gets the message and unlocks the door. I smile at him, desperate to offer a calm that neither of us feels.

Something is preventing the door from opening, and as I tug from outside, the boy tries to push from inside. It's a joint effort that yields no result. I motion for him to scoot back and drive my elbow into the glass with everything I've got. The window finally gives in, and I pull him out immediately. He clings to me, and I move to make a break for it. His mother, a few yards away, looks hopeful that I'm able to get her child to her in one piece.

A loud boom. I wrap my body around the kid and turn him away from the explosion. A fiery force pushes me forward. Everyone screams and drops down to the ground.

The world tilts on its axis as the adrenaline drains from my veins, my vision swimming for a second. The boy's small frame slips from my grip, his mother swooping in with shaking hands, pulling him against her chest. She's sobbing, clutching him so closely I wonder if he can even breathe. Each of her cries stabs the quiet space between us. Now safe in his mother's arms, her tears soak the boy's hair as she rocks him back and forth. Relief washes over her face, but her grip stays firm as if she's afraid that letting go might mean losing him again.

My body aches, and I try to breathe easy as bruises bloom beneath my skin. A face is above mine, talking rapidly. I can't make out what's being said. I shut my eyes tightly and try to focus on one thing, anything. The ringing in my ears makes it nearly impossible. I want to sit up, but even the thought exhausts me. Still, I know I can't pass out or be here when the cops arrive. Although I've dealt with worse, being out of action for so long makes it feel like I've been hit by a truck. The last thing I need is someone deciding I'm hurt enough to be sent to the hospital. I mentally assess myself for any serious injuries.

"I'm fine," I grunt out and push a hand away, fixing some woman with a glare.

"How could I ever thank you?" The kid's mother is in front of me, her son still in her arms. "God bless you. You are my hero."

"I'm no hero." I say, getting to my feet. Pain shoots

through my back, and I try not to make the discomfort show on my face.

"Let me take you to the hospital," another voice says. It's the man who owns the SUV. "This is all my fault."

Talk about an XY who owns up to his faults. He has shoulders broad enough to suggest he'd probably be good in bed, and I quickly scold myself for letting my thoughts drift there, especially now.

"I'm fine," I repeat, trying to sound convincing. "Don't worry about it."

I turn to leave, but a small hand tugs at me. I glance down, and the kid clings to my sleeve. It takes considerable effort to crouch to his eye level, and pain shoots through my knee as I do.

"What's your name, little man?" I ask and dust off some of the soot from his jacket collar.

"Ryan." He smiles. "And yes, you are."

I give a puzzled look. "What am I exactly?"

"A hero. You saved me." He jumps off the ground with his hands in the air. "Only a hero would do that!"

"Is that so?" The sirens get louder, and I give a sad smile. "Look, Ryan, I've got to go, but you be good and stay out of trouble. Okay?" He nods his head vigorously.

I get back to my feet, ignoring the breeze I feel on my backside and the looks I'm certain to be getting. As I head home, I realize I can't keep ignoring who I am, who I've always been. I am the Cyber Huntress, a vigilante through and through. It's time to stop pretending otherwise. If I want to find Jessica's killer and make them pay, I'll have to do it myself.

For that, I'm going to need another suit.

CHAPTER 12

BELLFLOWER – *Beary Hungry Diner*
   December 07, 05:52 PST

THE FIRST RAYS of the sun are just beginning to peek over the horizon when I approach the entrance. A jingle greets me from the bells above the door as I step inside the sparsely occupied establishment. A young couple with a backpack sits in the far corner, but I don't stare at them for long. If they're running away, I don't want them to think someone is onto them. The only other occupant is a man with a long blond beard, wearing a leather jacket. A Harley motor-cycle is parked outside, and I don't doubt for a second it's his.

A waitress heads toward me as soon as I take a seat. I'm not here for the food—just to meet an old contact, hoping I won't be stood up. Thorne—whose real name I never both-ered to ask—has always been punctual, so I pray today isn't the first time. He's reliable in the way a snake might be. Cunning, quick, and only predictable when he's getting something out of the deal. I didn't trust him. Not fully at least. But he's my only hope of getting back into the game officially. He pays well, and crime-fighting gear isn't exactly cheap. My scholarships barely cover my living expenses.

I glance at the menu as the waitress stands in front of me, pen and pad in hand. She offers me a bright smile, clearly a morning person. There's no other reason a person has to be branding such happiness this early. "Have you decided, or do you need more time?"

"I'll have coffee and whatever the dish of the day is."

She looks behind her, and I follow her gaze. It's written in chalk: a classic burger with a fried egg and fries. I nod. "I'll have that and the coffee, please."

I face the door to see when Thorne enters. We first met in New Jersey about four years ago. He agreed to be on a heist I led. If you could reach him, it meant he'd been expecting you. It's safe to say when I contacted him on a dark web chat, his quick reply was a surprise. He picked the place for us to meet, and I knew better than to request somewhere else.

His reputation is a tangled web of truth and fable. Some say he was one of the best thieves in the world until his partner died on a mission, and he blamed himself. Since then, he has committed to a solitary life so no one else could get hurt. Or the story that he was ex-military, and he's been on an anti-establishment streak ever since he went AWOL. Others say he never had a partner, but during a job, he got a little girl accidentally killed, and his life has never remained the same since. The common thread in all the stories was a life-defining bank robbery. It was a success, but it cost him dearly, and he didn't have it in him to do big jobs again.

My breakfast arrives. "Enjoy," the waitress says before walking away.

Another jingle from the door, and someone steps in wearing a gray sports tracksuit and a Dodgers baseball cap.

When he looks my way, I straighten my spine instinctively. Not out of fear but in preparation. The kind of readiness that comes when you know you're stepping into the ring with someone who's always got a few tricks up his sleeve. Thorne walks over with that same easy swagger, a confidence that says he's always in control. As he drops onto the bench across from me, he doesn't say a word at first—just looks me over, taking his time.

"For some reason," he says, "I thought you'd look different. Maybe dyed your hair or gotten an insane number of piercings or tattoos."

The waitress arrives before I can respond. "Coffee. Black," Thorne says without looking at her.

"You don't see me in forever, and that's the first thing out of your mouth?"

"Would you prefer a party?"

I scoff at his response and take a sip of my coffee. He looks as good as the last time I saw him. His jaw is as sharp as ever. I could definitely use it to cut the burger before me into two. His gray eyes twinkle with mild excitement.

Of course, there's the mark that runs from his chin to right eye. But I never ask. I've been through it once; I'm not asking for a reenactment. Seems like a sore subject.

His coffee arrives, and he takes a sip. "So, what's up, Snow? Our last interaction in New York gave me the impression I'd never be meeting with you again."

Yeah, I thought so too.

I take shallow breaths as I focus on the tangled mess of wires. "Red to blue, green to yellow, brown to orange," I mutter to myself. Sweat trickles down my temple despite the cool fall evening. 1:30. 1:29.

"Everyone, please calmly leave the area. Bryant Park is officially closed until stated otherwise," NYPD cops shout into a megaphone.

Red, it has to be red. "K.A.R.M.A. are you seeing this?" I capture a photo with my phone. "Which wire holds the denotation logic?"

"Red has the highest probability, ma'am."

I reach for the wire cutters, steadying my hand, but my mind is racing. Time seems to slow as I analyze the circuitry, my brain running through every permutation, every potential disaster. "Please be right," I cut the red wire.

The timer surges forward. 0:30. 0:29.

"Shit!" I frantically scan the bomb again. Focus, Washington, focus.

Thorne snaps his fingers, bringing me back to the present. I recall his last question. "You know how it is. I had to clear my head, and I needed some sun."

"Where did you just go, Snow?" He waits for a response, but I've become comfortable with silence. He laughs and shakes his head. I amuse him. "Since you only call me when you need spending money…" He pauses, leaning in with a cynical smile, and says, "I have good news for you."

"What is it?"

"I have a job. It's not a standard one, so I need to know you're really back in this."

"Of course, I am. What's the job?"

He leans over to take a few fries off my plate. "Your eagerness reassures me." Thorne smiles as he looks at me, and I know that smile. "I simply need you to place a USB receiver in a server room. The job pays twenty grand."

"Just to plant a USB? For twenty K?"

"Correcto. Aren't you excited? It's so much money for such a small task."

I sigh, already afraid of the answer. "What company?"

"You'll love this," he says and leans forward again. "Blue Life."

"Blue Life for only twenty? Hell no."

"It'll boost your resume. Clients will be all over you when they know you've infiltrated one of the biggest tech companies."

"I don't need a boost. I'm one of the best hackers in the world."

"For now. I say this with a lot of concern; you'll really need to. These new guys, they're not messing around. I'm giving you something to stand out from your competition. A year is a long time to be out of this world."

I lean back and cross my arms. "You might as well take it to them then."

"Alright. Name your price."

"Fifty."

"To plant a drive?"

"You want to do it yourself?"

"Absolutely not. My client needs me alive and outside of police custody to see things through if you succeed with this mission. I'm a very sought-after man myself."

"I'm sure you are."

"You know what, let's make it thirty-five." I squint. He chuckles dryly. "Fine, fifty." Thorne pulls a mini-USB drive from his jacket. "Plug it in somewhere out of sight."

I take the USB. "You have nothing to worry about. I always finish the job, don't I?"

He nods. "Can't dispute that."

"It'll be done by the end of the week." Thorne stands up from the booth, and I ask, "Do I even want to know why you need this done?"

"No," he utters, tipping his hat and placing a hundred-dollar bill on the table. He leaves the diner, disappearing back to wherever he came from.

CHAPTER 13

HOME – *Bedroom*
December 07, 11:09 PST

GIVEN that I basically speak binary, it's hard to ignore one of the top three companies involved in data analysis in the country and maybe even the world. Blue Life's customers range from banks to health care providers. They're on the payroll of the most influential organizations across the globe.

I try not to wonder what Thorne might need from their servers. The next thing I know, I won't rest until I find out exactly what he and his client want from monitoring them. Still, fifty thousand is fifty thousand. That would be a good start toward an even better setup than the one I had in New York. If I wasn't so determined about not being a vigilante, I might still have some of my old equipment. But selling it off was a way to prove a point and to show I was done and dusted with that part of my life. *So much for that.*

And of course I did keep one thing. Something I put too much time and energy in to give away. I'm currently rifling through the back of my closet looking for the box I shoved her in. I finally manage to free my petabyte solid state hard drive.

"There you are, old friend," I whisper, heading for the lobby.

My lair is in the building's basement. The property manager thinks it's just a study and research space, so he quickly agreed when I asked for it. It's supposed to be storage. Now I've turned it into something much more.

I plug the drive into my desktop. "Welcome back, K.A.R.M.A."

K.A.R.M.A. is the artificial intelligence I developed. She was neither cheap nor easy to build. Putting her together proved to be one of the hardest jobs in the world. She can do *almost* everything I can. But there's always going to be a problem that a machine can't solve. Once I set her up completely, she'll have eyes and ears in the hideout and apartment through a highly advanced security system.

"It's good to be back, ma'am. Performing system diagnostics and updates." K.A.R.M.A.'s mechanical voice responds.

"Do that in the background. I need your full attention right now. I need you to tell me everything you can find on Blue Life."

HOME – *Lair*
December 11, 20:04 PST

INFILTRATING a company is no easy task. There are about a billion things you need to do if you intend to slip in and out undetected.

First, what's the layout of the building, and what's the

purpose of each room? How do you find that out? Simple. A blueprint.

Most people don't know that blueprints are fairly easy to come by. They're often printed in famous architectural magazines. But the one I found of Blue Life isn't as detailed as I'd like, which left me with the second option of getting it from the county office.

And of course I can't just walk in and get it; that's equivalent to announcing my existence to the world. There'll be a record, and if something like a heist happens, I'll be at the top of the list for people to question about what I did with the copy I requested.

Another option, the easiest of them all, was to steal it. For an organization that holds the plans for every building in L.A., they don't seem to take their jobs seriously. But the negligence is appreciated.

The next bit was confirming that Blue Life didn't mess around and change the floor plan as seen in the submitted diagrams. In order to do that, I had to confirm it with my own eyes. Getting access to Blue Life isn't as hard as you'd think, especially if you're a janitor. And a janitor's ID is the easiest to fake because who's going to ensure that the person who scrubs their toilets is the same one who did it yesterday?

Nobody, that's who.

It took me four days to sweep through every floor and confirm what I needed to know. It's funny how much you can get away with if people think you're the help.

The data room is the most secure part of the building, and for good reasons. It sits on an entirely underground floor, and there are cameras nearly everywhere. It can only be accessed by a select few employees, mainly security and IT personnel.

An idea is to be one of the few people that are able to gain access, but I'm just a lowly janitor who isn't even getting paid for her services. And you can't just start a new job and get access to the mainframe on the first day, which leaves me with no choice other than to become a desk employee myself.

On my second-to-last cleaning run, I took pictures of an ID card left out carelessly. It seems the difference between a regular Blue Life employee and an employee with access to the server room is a custom red dot printed in the corner of the badge. Since I've taken the liberty of hacking into their local systems, I know for a fact that instead of scanning the chip like the other employees, the server room scans that dot.

I can't recreate the signature of a valid dot in the seven-day timeline I've set, which means I'll have to find a way to bypass the security of the server room altogether. Operation Blue Life is going to be as ordinary as I can make it. I won't be going in there guns blazing like I'm robbing a bank. I'll walk in and walk out like it's a normal weekday morning, and I'm just another employee participating in the endless cycle we call the American dream.

FINANCIAL DISTRICT – *Blue Life HQ*
   December 12, 08:42 PST

DRESSED IN BLACK SLACKS, a white button-up shirt, and an argyle print vest over it, I reach the base of the steps. I'm the new hire, and I've made sure the information regarding my onboarding has been sent and authorized by the company. It's fake, but none of the guards need to know that.

To sell my disguise and put it as far away from my current appearance as it can be, I've decided to give myself a limp. My eyes, with the help of contacts, are dark green. Like an evergreen forest, at least that's what was written on the lens case.

I'm wearing a wig, short and bobbed. Something you'll never catch me wearing on a normal day. I wear thick glasses to give the impression that I'm as blind as a bat.

Time to earn my keep.

I enter the lobby. "You must be Evelyn." A stout man approaches me. "I'm Lucas, your manager. I'll walk you to your desk and have you settle in. Sophia will drop by soon and give you a quick tour of the campus and answer any questions you might have."

"Sounds perfect; lead the way." I follow my manager through the rows of cubicles to the edge of the building where the windows let in a large amount of sunlight.

He stops at a square with *Evelyn Brooks* labeling its side. "This is you. I'll set up some time for us to connect tomorrow. I've got a lot of offsite meetings today." He points towards an office a few feet away. "That's me when I'm here. Sophia will give you everything you need to get started on your first project. I don't imagine you'll get far today, so we can do an overview of it when I get back." He turns to leave but stops and knocks on my desk. "And it's great to have you on the team, Evelyn." Lucas leaves for the elevator.

I look around my workstation. There's a stapler, some post-its, a notebook and pen, a large curved monitor, and a new laptop in the box. Beside the box are some adapters and a Blue Life coffee mug.

I'm impressed. Blue Life's HR department is surprisingly competent and quick. In less than a week's time, they managed to onboard me. Maybe I should actually consider them for full-time employment post-graduation.

"Hi, Evelyn. I'm Sophia." I turn around and find my buddy for the day. She's wearing a long cardigan and slacks.

"Hi Sophia. Nice to meet you." I extend my hand with a bright smile. "Looking forward to jumping straight in."

She gives a light laugh. "Relax Evelyn. Lucas isn't here anymore. You can let your guard down. There's no need to rush into any work. Let me give you a tour of our facilities." She walks away, and I follow after.

We exit the main building and land in a courtyard. "All of these food trucks are free for employees. They rotate weekly, so if you see something you like, try it before it's gone." She runs to a coffee kiosk. "Oh, this booth has the most amazing strawberry mocha. I definitely recommend it."

She points at two other buildings, and if you include the building we left from, the courtyard sits in the middle within a triangular shape. "Those buildings are mostly for clients when we host conferences and technology summits."

I follow her back into the building. "Every floor has a break room, but ours has two." She whispers the next part: "Our department is the highest paid because of the sectors we analyze." She points out the break rooms on opposite sides of the floor. "Of course, all snacks are free to grab."

"Ladies' room is right down the hall. It's essentially a private bath. Women in STEM, am I right?" We do a sweep of the floor and end up back at my desk. "So that's Blue Life. If you have any questions, don't hesitate to ask. I know what it's like to be new. Oh yeah, there should be an email in your inbox with the project specifications. Let me know if anything is unclear; I will admit some of our documentation could use some fine-tuning."

"Thanks for everything, Sophia. I'll set up my laptop and take a glance at everything."

"I'm one desk away, so just holler." Sure enough, she heads to a cubicle a few feet away, right next to me.

Regardless of what anyone tells you, data analysis is the

most daunting thing to do in the universe. That is if statistics is not your strong suit, which I identify with. I don't know if I'm losing my mind or if I'm overreacting, but I stare at the data I was provided for so long, the hours stopped moving at some point. When time finally progressed, I had a better idea of what I was looking at. Unfortunately, it takes forever for the last person to leave the floor. Data analysts can be a bit overambitious.

"You should go home," Sophia says as she leaves. "The job is still going to be here tomorrow." I offer a smile and a weak thanks. I wait a while, get to my feet, and head to the bathroom, aware of the cameras in the four corners of the room.

The bathroom has a blind spot just in front of it, but I don't linger there. I head inside, into one of the stalls. Naturally, there are no cameras in here, but there's an air vent. I set the toilet seat down and jump on the lid to pull myself into the vent.

My smartwatch has the blueprint, but I added a twist. There's a white dot indicating where I am at all times, and a green one indicating where I'm supposed to be. Between those is a blue pointer to show which direction I'm supposed to go.

It's paramount that I move carefully because I don't even know if these vents can hold my weight for long. The elevator that will take me downstairs is already heading up. I need to be there as soon as it arrives; then K.A.R.M.A. will replay a thirty-second clip of the same scene. An empty hallway.

Cobwebs cling to my skin, and I shove them to the side with my hand. Every breath I take is too loud for my ears, and each exhale puffs up dust before me. A sneeze tries to force its way out, but I stop all movement and push it back. It takes longer than I'd like because of all the particles that keep making their way into my sinuses.

When the sneeze finally passes, I move faster, dragging myself through the vent and ignoring the dirt clinging to my outfit. My white shirt is sure to be brown the second I'm done. I make it to the exit and hover for a bit to scope out the scenery. There's no one.

"K.A.R.M.A., now." I whisper, opening the vent as quickly as possible.

I leap down and jab the elevator button, my impatience growing as the doors refuse to open fast enough. My vision switches between the timer and then the camera.

5. 4. 3.

The door slides open, and I fling myself into it as the countdown comes to an end. The air rushes in and out of my lungs. The elevator *CAN NOT* be taking this long to open and close. I beat my chest. *This is a miscalculation.*

The elevator plays another clip. But the difference between the last clip and this one is a seamless loop. I double-check the layout on my watch. The server room is actually a series of rooms that have been merged together to give the illusion of a single space. And it's located at the end of the hall. The only problem is that the server room directly faces security.

My head pokes out of the elevator before the rest of my body follows. Another thirty-second video is already playing, and I see my destination right in front of me. I speed walk there, my heart beating as fast as it can. Before I can get to it, the door to the security room springs open, and I throw myself into the room closest to me.

"Yo man, I can't see you on any screen."

My eyes go wide, and I shake my head. Who do they have on duty today, and why the hell is said person paying so much attention to the screen? Don't they usually play games or watch porn?

"Are you sure?"

"Wait, I see you now."

"Are we getting hacked?"

There's silence as the men, I don't know how many, take in the information. I wonder if now would be the best time to have K.A.R.M.A. disable the video when they break into a laugh.

"Nah, I think the camera is angled wrong. Maybe something is blocking it."

Okay, not the brightest crayons in the pack, but it's not a loss on my part. I can't go back out in the hall, leaving me with no option besides going up the vent again. I use my watch to navigate my way to the server room. The vent goes over security, and I hold my breath as I scooch by. I raise one leg as slowly as I can, and drop it with the same care. It takes me eternity to get past, but soon, I begin to feel the cooler air flow and see all the wires running across the room. I don't need the watch to tell me I've reached my destination.

I open the vent cover, but my hands don't grasp it firmly enough. It opens with a bang. I close it back quickly and move out of view.

The door flies open.

"Who's there?" a guard says from the door. I hold my breath and squeeze my eyes shut. If I'm caught now, I'll be spending the rest of my life in prison on several counts of breaking and entering as well as impersonation.

Footsteps move further into the room, and my heart hammers even louder. My back aches with the way I've positioned myself. I'm too scared to move. A single creak will encourage them to look up here.

The door shuts again. "Did you see anything weird?"

"Nothing out of place."

I allow the tension to ease out of my shoulders as much as the situation allows. I try to ignore the tightness in my stomach that makes me want to run to the toilet. I unlatch the air vent again, and this time, I'm much more careful about it. I hang onto the sides and lower myself to the ground, landing as elegantly and silently as possible.

There are thirty rows of server racks back-to-back. I close the vent and head toward one of the CPUs. I allow myself to imagine going through all of this and still forgetting the USB. Luckily for me, the drive sits in my pocket, and I locate the server rack at the edge of the room, plugging it into the slot. I place it in a port facing away from view, using a few wires to cover it.

Mission accomplished. *Escape? Pending.*

I hurry back to the air vent and leap a little to open it. I land on my tippy-toes before hopping back up and pulling myself into the HVAC system again.

Faster, but as quietly as I can, I make my way to the elevator. I hang back and wait for it to come down, and when it does, another guard steps out. After he leaves, I hop out of the vent, shut it, and slip inside.

The doors slide closed. "We didn't see you come down."

The guard who just came down happens to be the one who has the brains in the bunch. "Go do a sweep! Clear the office building."

I get back to the bathroom without a hitch, but I know they're alerting everyone to be on the lookout. I open one of the water systems and pull out a sealed plastic bag with the same outfit. I get dressed quickly, inserting the old clothes into the bag. I return the bag back to the toilet tank with a dissolvent solution to get rid of any evidence.

Now out of the bathroom, I head to my seat. I'm mid-stretch when the guards come running. My face is blank when I look back at them. I go the extra mile of raising my brows.

"Why are you still here?"

"First day on the job. You know what they say. First one in, last one out," I reply.

"Did you see anyone come down this way?"

"No. Why did something happen?" I ask with concern.

They shake their heads. "Don't worry about it." I exhale slowly as they walk away.

"Are you sure you heard something?" the third guard asks, but now, the men don't seem too sure of themselves. A smile threatens to break through, but I hold it back. To further sell my cluelessness, I shrug my shoulders and turn my attention to the computer, adding the final touches to my resignation letter. It's scheduled to land in Lucas's inbox at 08:00 tomorrow.

"See you tomorrow." I project to the guards at the door while walking out of the building. One waves goodbye, and I wonder what it'll be like if I cancel the email and turn up tomorrow like a good little employee. But alas, I have a final project on Malware Analysis to complete, so I'm afraid this is my first and last day as a data analyst at Blue Life.

HOME – *Lair*
December 12, 19:51 PST

"IT'S DONE."

"I knew you wouldn't let me down. Let me just confirm the connection... and we are online." Thorne announces. I hear the soft clatter of a keyboard in the background. "Everything looks good. Transferring funds now. Pleasure doing business with you as usual. Oh, and welcome back."

My burner phone clicks out.

I check my account balance; my fifty thousand sits there shining at me, congratulating me on a job well done. Now that I have the funds, it's time to splurge on some high-tech equipment and catch Jessica's killer.

CHAPTER 14

LA CLÍNICA – *Dr. Rajit's Office*
   December 13, 11:12 PST

WHEN LIFE CHOOSES to kick you in the ass, it does so with all its might. I finally got around to checking my voice-mail and now I'm sitting, reading the results of my tests. It must be someone else's. But Dr. Rajit's serious expression tells me otherwise. Her eyes bore into me as I review the words again.

"It says I'm pregnant," I say, my voice foreign to my own ears.

"Yes, congratulations."

This is the third time she's congratulated me today, and I wonder what part of the news is festive. Though being free from STDs seems like something one should commemorate.

"And we're sure this result is mine?"

Her nod is firm. "Yes, of course." The laugh I want to let out is lodged in my throat, and the tears that I don't want to fall are lurking in the corner of my eyes.

"This can't be mine. I can't be pregnant! I have an IUD!" The paper trembles in my hand. This isn't real. I can't be a mother.

Rajit interjects calmly, "Technically, IUDs are not one-hundred percent effective against pregnancy. No form of birth control is. You always run the risk of pregnancy with every sexual interaction you have."

"I know how the birds and the bees work, Doc. I don't need an abstinence lecture."

One month pregnant, the results say. The thought of getting rid of it fills my mind for a moment, and I force it out in a panic. I'm shaking now; I can't remember the last time I shook this much.

"Maybe we can call someone to come and get you; parent, the child's father?"

I laugh, a sharp, bitter sound. "Sure, let's call the child's father, whomever the hell that is." Calling my mother is out of the question.

Of course, I don't know who the father of the child is. I made sure to tell her about the copious amount of sex I have, and how some of it is unprotected. My eyes drift back to the report, and I bite my bottom lip. The timing couldn't be worse. I literally just decided to become a vigilante again.

"I'm fine," I say finally and let out a deep breath.

The doctor leans back in her chair, her face placid and professional. "You do not seem fine."

I am not fine. I'm woefully unprepared to be a parent, and I'm freaking the fuck out. But Dr. Rajit was just doing her job, and I'm sure she's heard enough of me and my outbursts for one day. I force a smile. "I'll figure it out."

She nods, standing as I do. "There are plenty of resources available. Are you sure you'll be fine?" she asks, her concern genuine.

I nod, trying to believe it myself. "Yes."

"Since you have an IUD, it is recommended that you return within two months to remove it and avoid any potential complications. Although there have been plenty of healthy babies born with it. The choice is ultimately up to you."

"I just need a moment to think about it."

"If you need help with anything, I'm willing to provide assistance as far as I can."

I smile at her kindness but say nothing as I leave her office. My hands ball up the results, cramming it into my pocket as I head to the restroom. Splashing cold water on my face, I stare at my reflection. Two options; get rid of it or keep it. Neither seems ideal, and I don't want to think about it, not right now. I release my grip around the sink's edge, my knuckles aching from how tightly I'd held on.

Later — I'll deal with this later. Now, I need to find a dress for tonight.

USC CAMPUS – *University Club*
December 13, 19:13 PST

"DR. DONOVAN AND MY GUEST." My Network Security professor informs the receptionist, threading his arm through mine. We're given numbers for coat check and ushered inside.

USC's 77th Annual Winter Donor's Gala is all anyone at school has talked about for months. It's an evening where rich aristocrats and overly educated professionals can come together over hors d'oeuvres. Experiencing this event before graduating seemed essential, so I accepted Donovan's invitation. I'm not blind; I know how he looks at me, but invitations like this are rare.

The hall is full of professors I recognize from the university directory. Fairy lights shaped like snowflakes twinkle, shifting colors from white to cream, then blue, then a darker blue. The décor triggers a wave of nostalgia, eerily similar to my eleventh-grade winter formal. The pianist plays the same haunting tune from that night, the night everything with Jayden unraveled.

I'm wearing a light-blue gown. Jayden is my date, but it isn't as exciting as I thought it would be. It's an event I was looking forward to because I haven't seen him in so long. Both of us can sense there's an issue, and yet neither one of us is brave enough to speak up.

Jayden and I barely talk anymore. Our everyday phone calls slowly became weekly and sometimes biweekly events. Whenever he tries to reach out to me, I always find an excuse to avoid him.

It's almost been a year since the party, and I'm still lost, unable to find my way back to normal. I don't have anyone to talk to about it; the best thing is finding a way to forget about it completely. It's easier said than done because anytime I close my eyes, an invisible weight clings to my skin, an echo of an unwanted past touch.

My appearance no longer mattered to me. I was slowly becoming my mother, and I hated myself for it. But if there's anything I can thank her for, it's making sure I knew how to get drugs. After an afternoon in a crackhouse, you could say I made some connections in the business.

And the thing with drug dealers is they don't care too much about the person they sell to. What they are after is the money in your pocket. As long as you pay them, they'd supply you even if you were a newborn.

"I know you're running from something," my dealer said as he exchanged the cash in my hand for the newest drug on the street. It

started off small at first, a few blunts here and there. I soon gradu-ated to coke, and after a while, I was being introduced to some sort of new drug every week. Each one stronger than the last. I had something to forget, and chasing a high was the most effective way to do it.

"We need to talk," Jayden says, grasping my hand. This entire night has been a struggle for me because I don't use around Jayden. I don't want him to see that part of me.

"Is everything alright?" I ask after we come out in front of the school. I hear the song playing from the speakers, and I know all the couples are dancing together. Something we could be doing if he didn't lead me out of the school gym to have a conversation.

"I'd like to ask you the same thing."

I pull my hand away, crossing my arms defensively. "What do you mean?"

"What do I mean? Winter, we've hardly talked for a whole hour this month. You keep avoiding me, and then there's all of this," he says, waving his hands over my person.

I'm stunned by his audacity. What's that supposed to mean, and who's he to judge how I look?

"I have no idea what you're talking about. And what do you mean by this?" I wave my hand over his body the same way he did to me.

"Winter, you've lost so much weight. You keep shaking, and whenever I try to touch you, you flinch."

"That's all in your head. I'm fine, and I told you, I've just been busy with stuff. I'm working out more these days. That's why I'm losing so much weight and I'm on this new diet." The lies fall off my lips so easily that it concerns me.

"I don't think you're working out at all," Jayden says, and it sounds like the accusation he intended it to be. And as if to further prove his point, he stretches his arm out to touch me, and I instinc-tively recoil; it takes me a moment to realize my mistake.

"What's going on, Winter? I can't help you if you don't talk to me!"

"I don't need your help. If you have some hero complex and are looking for where to unleash it, how about you find someone who actually needs it? Stop poking your nose in my business."

It's when he opens his mouth, closes it, and then repeats the action two more times that I realize I said the last part out loud. I watch his face fall, but the last thing I'm going to do is apologize for my words. I don't know how to tell him what happened to me. All I can do is simulate the hurt I felt.

"If that's how you feel, then fine." Jayden turns to walk away. Instead of going back into the gym, he walks down the street, away from the dance and away from me.

I stand there and watch him leave, wondering why my legs won't move or why my mouth won't scream for him. My heart feels heavy, and I hate myself for thinking about how I need a fix to deal with the fact that I just lost the love of my life.

Blinking back to the present, my professor looks at me with a smile on his face. I'm sure he was saying something, but I was so far away I didn't hear a damn thing.

"I'm sorry, I didn't catch that. I was really admiring the décor; it looks lovely," I say, looking around to prove a point.

"I think so too," he replies, but instead of looking around, his eyes stay on me. "You're really pretty, and I love the dress choice." I'm in a burgundy gown with a V-shaped dip and a thigh-high slit for the night. I thought it contrasted my caramel skin tone well.

"Thank you. You don't look so bad yourself, Professor."

He laughs. "Please, call me Will tonight. I was asking if you'd like to dance."

I nod, taking note that most of the room is already swaying to the beat. Even though he's my professor, and rumor is bound to spread, I'm still his date, and I owe him a dance.

Donovan leads me to the dance floor, and I brace myself for the usual awkward shuffle that often accompanies these situations. But the moment he takes the first step, I'm caught off guard by his fluidity, the easy way he glides across the floor. We move into a slow waltz, and it becomes clear he's no stranger to this kind of dance. His movements are precise, almost elegant, guiding me effortlessly through the turns and steps. He lacks the concentrated expression of a man focused on not stepping on my toes. Instead, I find him looking down at me with a relaxed smile. It's disarming, really—this unexpected side of him.

"So, about your network automation side project—again, impressive work. You've got something there," he says, his voice low and close enough that only I can hear. He guides me through a gentle turn, his steps surprisingly sure for a man I'd pegged as the typical computer nerd, the kind who spends more time debugging code than engaging in anything remotely social. But here he is, proving first impressions aren't always accurate.

"Thanks." The soft lighting catches the edges of his expression, turning his usual reserved demeanor into something warmer. "I do what I can."

He shakes his head with a knowing smile. "You're selling yourself short, Winter. I've never seen anything like your work before. You are one of my best students by far. I've been thinking, with some minor refactoring, this could be groundbreaking. Ever considered going any further? Maybe a PhD? I could connect you with some people here or at UCLA, or even Stanford and Berkeley—folks who would kill for work like yours."

He pulls me back into the dance, and I have to focus to

keep from mis-stepping, bamboozled by the suggestion. Academia. A PhD. I know I can't be a vigilante for my entire life. It doesn't exactly come with health care or vision. A younger me would've considered that kind of future. But now, I'm not so sure. "Maybe," I say, keeping my tone light, even as a dozen thoughts tangle in my head. "I'm not sure if that's the direction I'm heading in right now. I'm looking for a different kind of challenge."

His eyebrow quirks subtly, a smirk playing at the corner of his lips as he dips me low, then pulls me upright again. "Different how? Because from what I can see, you're already tackling some of the most challenging problems out there. With ease."

I allow myself a small, private smile, but quickly tuck it away. "Not all challenges can be solved in a lab."

For a moment, Donovan watches me. There's something in his gaze—a sense that he knows I'm not just talking about code. But he doesn't ask any follow-up questions. "Fair enough. But just know, if you ever decide you want to explore the academic side more seriously, the connections I have are not the type to let good talent slip by."

There's a change in the tempo causing the music to shift, and he adjusts without missing a beat, leading me through the transition perfectly. "Thanks, William. I'll keep that in mind. And you know, you're surprisingly good at this," I finally say, a little breathless, more from the unexpected rhythm we've fallen into than from the dance itself.

His chuckle lingers in my ears as we turn, his hand tightening slightly around mine. "There's more to life than just algorithms and firewalls," he teases, the warmth in his tone lessening the edge of his words. "Though, I'm guessing you've already started to figure that out."

I return his smile, the tension in my shoulders easing. "It's still a work in progress for me," I admit. "I guess I didn't expect you to be this graceful."

"People often assume I'm a basement dweller," he says, spinning me effortlessly. "But we all have our hidden talents, don't we?" His words make me curious about other surprises he might have tucked away.

Before I can ask anything more, the music halts abruptly, and a few people ascend the stage, microphones in hand, ready to present awards. I take the opportunity to slip away. "If you'll excuse me, I need to hit the powder room." A yawn creeps up as I head for the exit of the ballroom, rubbing my tired eyes.

Jessica's case occupies my thoughts. Chris's story about not seeing her that night doesn't add up. According to police records, he was at a party. Beta Alpha Psi hosted a Friends-giving, and he was there waiting for Jessica to show up, and she never did. He called her a couple of times, and the one time she picked up, she said she was going to be a little late. The police seem to believe this story, but I don't think the cops know exactly who they're dealing with. That man is the president of Beta Alpha Psi, only the biggest frat house on campus. Not to mention, he's from a long line of Beta Alpha Psi legacies. His family has their own plaque on the law building for all their donations. Who would dare to cross him?

"We would like to welcome doctoral candidate Harris to the stage to discuss how this recent joint partnership with UCLA will bring about massive change to our Biomedical department and change oncology research—"

A stack of papers falls to the floor when I bump into some-one. I dive after it, muttering an apology after apology. The person is doing the same thing, and we both reach for the papers at the same time, causing our heads to collide. I straighten up immediately, ignoring the throbbing in my skull.

"I'm so sorry. I wasn't looking where—"

My eyes go wide, and my mouth feels numb. Right in front of me is one of the few people in the world who knows about some of the demons I'm running away from. He looks way different, but those almond-shaped jade eyes haven't changed a bit.

"Winter?"

Not a word escapes my mouth. I just walk away from him as quickly as possible and exit the gala. My heart is hammering so loud that it's the only thing I can hear. My throat feels like it's closing in on itself. Using the side of the building for support, I just breathe for a while.

I could use a drink.

"Rough day?" I nod at the bartender as he places the strong drink I asked for before me. I stumbled into a cocktail bar close enough to campus. I go to pick up my glass, but stop midway.

Oh wait, I'm pregnant. It pulls a laugh out of me, and I can't believe what my life has been like these last few weeks. It doesn't take long for everything to fall apart. First, my roommate gets murdered, and my mother, whom I haven't seen since God knows when shows up wanting to worm her way back into my life, the same day my roommate died, of course. Then I find out I'm pregnant and, as if the universe has not seen me having enough, I run into the one person I never thought I'd see again.

When it rains, it pours, huh?

"Are you alright?" the bartender asks.

I try to stop laughing, aware of how unhinged I must look. He'll have a story to tell tonight, even if my life is in shambles. "I'm sorry, I just had a bad moment and forgot that I'm pregnant."

"Oh," he says, glancing at the drink. I hand him money, insisting he take it despite his protests. I wasted his time and made a scene. If there's ever a sign that I'm not going to be a good mother, it's staring me in the face looking like a Hennessy Manhattan.

I attempt to stand gracefully but end up looking like someone pretending to have their shit together. I'd like to think I had it all together before I ran into Xavier. But that'd just be a lie.

Fucking Xavier.

CHAPTER 15

I LOCATE THE NEAREST GYM. If I can't drink it down, I'm going to hit it out. I answer all the questions asked of me by the receptionist, and follow her instructions to the room where the punching bag hangs.

Kicking my heels off, I shift as much strength as I can to my fist and punch with all my might. I'm gifted with a loud smack, and the bag sways a bit. Another punch and then another. I keep going, the past rising to the surface.

Both the boys' and girls' basketball teams qualified for the state championship, so we decided to have a party to celebrate. It's sophomore year, and everyone knows it's the time when you need to solidify what clique you're a part of. I'm the new girl who plays basketball really well. A bit of a legend at school, but I keep to myself and a few friends.

All my so-called friends have ditched me and are currently occupied with trying to lose their virginities by sixteen. So there's no one to save me from the one person I've been avoiding since I arrived at the party.

"Hey stranger. Congratulations on another win."

I like Xavier. He's cool, but I'm not looking for anything. I have Jayden. Even though we're long-distance, it's working out pretty well. I guess as well as any teenage romance can go with thousands of miles between you. When our schedules align, we talk to each other all about our day. We fall asleep to each other's breathing. He's the only person I can rely on. He's my best friend.

Xavier is someone I've known for about a year now, and we've hung out a couple of times. I guess it's nice to have someone who's physically there. It didn't feel like I was doing anything wrong. Until that night after practice, when Xavier kissed me, I didn't pull away—not quickly enough, anyway. His lips were warm, his hold gentle but firm. It felt nice to be kissed again, to be held. I pressed closer, and though his hands stayed respectful, part of me wouldn't have minded if they hadn't. That's when I realized I needed to create some distance between us. And yet, here we are again, alone in the backyard of a party.

"Look, I'm sorry if I crossed a line with you that night. Rachel mentioned that you already have a boyfriend. I didn't know. That kiss was a mistake. It didn't mean anything and it won't happen again."

He's right; it was a mistake. But I'm not sure if either of us can truthfully say that it didn't matter or it wouldn't happen again.

"Relax, Xavier, I'm not mad. It happened, and now it's over. Let's have some fun." I open the cooler and toss him a beer. I'm moving away in a week during Christmas break, so there's no point in ruining the night over a dumb kiss. This is supposed to be my one last party for the road.

The crowd eventually migrates to the backyard, and somehow, Xavier and I end up roped into a game of Truth or Dare. My turn is up again.

"Winter, truth or dare?" my teammate asks.

"Truth."

"Stop being a lil bitch, Winter! You've chosen Truth this entire game."

"Fine. Dare."

"I dare you to kiss Xavier."

"Alexis, I'm not kissing Xavier. Give me another dare."

"That's not how the game works, Winter. Live a little. Kiss him."

All the people playing the game start chanting, "Kiss! Kiss! Kiss!"

I glance at Xavier. His eyes have both amusement and challenge in them.

"Come on, Winter!" Alexis goads, her grin widening.

I roll my eyes but inch closer to Xavier. The chanting crescendos. "Fine, but just to shut you all up." I say before leaning in. I give Xavier a quick peck on the lips.

"Winter be serious. If you're going to kiss him, kiss him right! That wasn't a real kiss."

Normally, I find Alexis being an instigator entertaining, but now that I'm the subject, it's starting to piss me off. I turn to face Xavier as the chanting ensues again. He's wearing his lovable smile.

"You know you don't have to. We can stop playing," he says.

"You're probably right, but I think we have to give the masses what they want."

"Well, by all means, kiss away then."

We already shared two, so what was one more?

I tug on Xavier's collar, bring his lips back to mine, and nothing about this kiss is fleeting. It's passionate, heavy, sweet, and somehow everything in between. It isn't until the chants turn into cheers that I realize I'm making out with Xavier in front of half the school.

Alexis shouts, "Now that's what I'm talking about!"

I pull away from him abruptly, and our eyes meet as we catch our breath. Xavier repeats my name as I stand up and exit the circle. I don't look back. I just keep walking until I cross through a bedroom and head into a bathroom. I need to snap out of it. Placing my hands under the running faucet, I rub some sense into my face. I try to convince myself that the kiss didn't matter, doesn't matter.

It can just be a seasonal fling. *No. I can't two-time Jayden with him, out of the question. It's ridiculous that I'm even considering it. I step out of the bathroom and someone is in the room with me.*

"Oh, my bad," I say.

I don't completely recognize the face, but parts of it are familiar. He says nothing, just allows his eyes to roam my body, which not only makes me self-conscious, it makes me uncomfortable. He's bigger than me, a clear indication that he's an athlete. He also doesn't look to be in high school; he has to be at least twenty.

"Hey, aren't you that new girl who won state as a freshman?"

"Yep, that's me." My eyes travel to the door, but before I get to it, he beats me there. The smirk on his face is so sinister it turns my stomach as he shuts the door.

I start to say, "Listen, I don't want any troub—" but he shoves me onto the bed and mounts me immediately.

"If you cooperate," he whispers in my ear, "It'll be over before you know it."

Between the loud music and the hand he raises to my lips, I know no one is going to hear my screams.

"Shhh, just stay still. I don't want to have to hurt you."

I try to fight, anything to get him off me, but it's a losing battle. My underwear is ripped off, and he shoves his fat fingers inside me. The tears are falling now.

"You're so wet. You must really enjoy this. Does being forced turn you on?"

Please stop, *I want to say, but the words don't escape my lips.*

He takes his fingers out, and I make the mistake of thinking it's over, but then his dick is being shoved in me. And all the fight I had left is gone.

"You know, you deserve this," he says. "My brother tells me that you've been acting brand new since the summer. Sometimes, you just gotta put a bitch in they place."

Desperately, I try to block out his groans filling my ears, forcing myself to think of anything else, something that'll make me forget this is happening. Eventually, the weight on me disappears, but I still can't breathe. Someone is shouting, and someone else is asking if I'm alright. The words don't come.

A final deadly right hook to the punching bag sends it flying off its chain, and sand begins to pour out of it. I stand there, breathless, my heart pounding in my chest.

"Goddammit," I pant, hands on my knees, "I'm probably going to have to pay for that."

CHAPTER 16

HOME – *Jessica's Room*
   December 17, 14:42 PST

I STAND IN THE DOORWAY, the scent of jasmine sending a shiver down my spine. My eyes roam over the meticulously organized room. Each framed sorority picture, concert ticket, and poster weaving together the story of Jessica's carefully curated life.

Stepping inside, I move silently across the plush carpet, feeling like an intruder in a life I barely knew. The closet door creaks open, revealing a rainbow of designer dresses and neatly stacked shoe boxes. I run my hand across the fabric, letting it slip through my fingers, trying to grasp the essence of Jessica's existence.

Under the bed, there's nothing but dust bunnies and a forgotten pair of heels. Moving to the dresser, I find a picture of her and her father at a red-carpet event. I open each drawer with a sense of urgency. The top drawer holds a delicate assortment of underwear and an old sorority pin. The second drawer is a chaotic mix of makeup and hair products. In the bottom drawer, my fingers brush against something hard wrapped in silk. Unwrapping it, I discover a small, ornate box. Inside, a vibrator lies nestled among various types of condoms.

Fair enough.

"Calendar alert. Network Security Final in ten minutes," K.A.R.M.A. interrupts.

Shit. I throw the toy on the bed and hurry to the door.

USC CAMPUS – *Computation Hall*
December 17, 18:00 PST

"PENCILS DOWN! Pass your exams to the front," Donovan announces. "I hope everyone has an amazing winter break."

As I hand my answer sheet to the person in front of me, I grab my bag, ready to leave. Donovan's voice rises above the muffled shuffle of papers.

"Miss Washington, could you hang back for a minute?"

My stomach sinks, of course. Late to the final, disappearing from the gala—this was bound to come back around. I take a deep breath and walk over to his desk as he finishes stacking the exams, keeping his usual efficient demeanor.

When he looks up, his expression is calm, but there's a hint of concern in his eyes. "You've been pretty elusive lately," he begins. "You left the gala in a hurry and were late to the exam today. Is everything alright?"

I shift on my feet, debating how much to say. "Yeah... personal stuff, you know? It's been a lot lately," I reply, trying to brush it off without sounding dismissive. My phone buzzes in my pocket, but I ignore it, willing my mother to stop calling.

"For what it's worth," he says, leaning back in his chair, "I'm relieved to hear it wasn't something I did. But you know I have to address the fact that you were late to the final."

"Right," I say slowly, bracing myself for what's next. I knew this was coming, but I still feel my chest tighten.

"I have to dock your score by fifteen percent," he continues, almost apologetically. "It's department policy. I can't make an exception."

"Fifteen percent! Really, Donovan? You can't cut me some slack this once? I've been a top student."

His face softens, but he stands firm. "Winter, I can't bend the rules, not even for you. I'd love to, but it's not fair to the other students."

I bite back a slick comment, crossing my arms. This isn't his fault. I know that. But it doesn't make it easier to hear.

"I get it," I finally say, trying not to sound too bitter. "Just... frustrating."

He nods, his expression understanding. "I know. But even with the deduction, you're still in a strong position. I'm confident that with an eighty-five percent mark on your final, you'll be in the A range. You've done solid work all semester."

"Yeah, whatever you say," I mutter, though I know he's just trying to help.

"Lighten up," he says with a smile, "I have no doubt you earned a one hundred percent before the adjustment. You'll be fine."

I nod, trying to let his reassurance sink in, even though I'm still pissed at myself for letting this other life and case interfere with the one thing I wanted to accomplish when I moved to L.A.—getting my master's degree.

My phone buzzes again, louder this time, and I finally glance down, seeing my mother's newest number on the screen.

Donovan notices and says, "I won't keep you any longer. Seems like someone's eager to get in touch with you. But if you ever need a recommendation or anything down the line, don't hesitate to ask."

I force a smile. "Thanks, Donovan."

"Take care, Winter," he calls out to me as I walk out of the lecture hall.

I sigh and hold my phone to my ear once I step outside. "Hi Winter. It's your mother again. I would really love to reconnect. Call me back when you get this."

Clicking on her contact icon, I block her. It's too late for amends now. Where was she when I was a child who needed a mother? The damage is already done.

Shaking her off, I focus on the task at hand. Tonight is the last frat party of the semester for Beta Alpha Psi, and it's my last chance before my prime suspect leaves for break. I want to be the one to point the cops his way, but if I do it without any evidence, I'm just making noise. Which is why I decided to be more proactive tonight. According to his course schedule, Chris should be on his way to take his last final for the semester. I need to place this bug on him undetected.

I spot him as soon as he exits Hoffman Hall; I pull my hoodie up and run into him, placing the bug on his shoe. All the while, I'm continuing to rush toward the hall, spewing some apology about my tardiness for my exam in a questionable accent. After a quick lap around the building, I head back home.

Now it's time to wait and listen.

When I enter my hideout, there's a large red present with a bow placed on top of my desk. My heart rate increases as I quickly survey the room to check if I'm alone. Who the hell came in here? I examine the box and see a note attached.

> *My client was extremely impressed with the swift-ness of your work and felt you deserved a bonus. I couldn't agree more. I figured you would get the most use out of all this stuff.*
>
> *P.S. Invest in better locks*
>
> *XOXO,*
> *T*

Of course, it's from Thorne.

The first item in the box has my logo on it. I palm the material. The designer of this costume made my first one. I originally sent off the details of my dad's pilot's uniform to be incorporated in it. He kept the same style but made it lighter and flexible. There are weapons: a long staff, some nun-chucks, a few daggers, and more importantly, two pistols. The last remaining items include a high-tech set of binoculars, a grappling hook, and schematics for various evil-scientist-type inventions. ·

I set the box aside and absent-mindedly listen to Chris' conversations. He and a frat brother are doing a beer run for the party they're throwing in a few hours. After a mind-numbing debate over the taste of Coronas versus Modelos, I'm ready to pluck out each eyebrow follicle one by one. Thankfully, a chime breaks my focus; there's a notification on ProfessionalsLink. A new message; it's from Xavier.

    Hey, Winter. Are you free for
    coffee sometime soon? -X

For far too long, I stare at the text, my mind racing with conflicting thoughts. Do I want to catch up with him? Sure, it'd be nice to know what he's been up to after all these years. But the thought of sharing what I've been doing makes my stomach churn. Where would I even start? I sigh, rubbing my temples. Despite my reservations, the choice feels inevitable, and with a deep breath, I type out a reply:

> Hey Xavier, I'd love to catch
> up. How about we meet at the
> start of the next semester? -W

I hit send before I can overthink it, the message disappearing into the ether.

Jessica's name snaps me back to reality. I rewind the recording, scanning for anything I might have missed. I hone in on the following interaction.

Frat Bro 1: *Hey man, you look like shit.*

Chris: *Damn man, good to see you too.*

Frat Bro 1: *I'm just messing with you. But listen, I just found out I passed my OChem final and I don't have to take it again in spring. I'm trying to get fucked up tonight! Can you use your connect to get me some molly?*

Chris: *... Sorry dude, no can do. I don't have it anymore.*

Frat Bro 1: *Oh stop being so stingy. I only need a couple of tabs for me and the homies. I know your girl is the hook up.*

Frat Bro 2: *Dude shut up already. Haven't you heard that Jessica's dead? He can't get you any more.*

Frat Bro 1: *Oh shit. I'm sorry, C. I had no idea.*

Chris: *Just leave me alone guys.*

Duh! Jessica was a drug dealer. How could I have missed this? I suppose it does explain her behavior at the frat party. Come to think of it, a few other situations too.

Okay, so Jessica dealt drugs, but who did she deal for?

CHAPTER 17

MY MENTOR always stressed the importance of understanding the lay of the land. I don't know enough about L.A. when it comes down to it. And if I intend to be a productive vigilante in this city, I need to learn everything I can about my new home. And by everything, I mean every detail —from city council members and corporate bigwigs to top criminals, police response patterns, and where the Wilde sisters last had brunch during their most recent visit to the West Coast.

I decided to spend the entirety of Christmas break speeding up the process of becoming an L.A. native. From dusk to dawn, I've been keeping watch on the city for the past few weeks, covering as much ground as I can on foot. Tonight, I'm focusing on police operations. In New York, response times varied drastically depending on the area and the nature of the crime. I need to know how long it takes

LAPD to arrive at the scene after a report is made and their movement patterns.

Standing atop a building in a high-crime area, I watch the city below. Over the past weeks, I've noticed peaks of criminal activity here. I'm geared up: a black padded cropped leather jacket with an illuminated red *CH* resembling a power button across my chest, tailored black cargo pants held up by my utility belt, and custom combat boots.

The cold night air nips at my face as I tune into my police radio, listening to the chatter. It's a lot to monitor—cops, emergency lines, and the fire department. Buildings in L.A. seem to catch fire frequently, more so than in New York. Maybe it's the dry weather, but the fire department's response time is notably faster than the cops.

There's a call for assistance on the radio. "We have a pursuit heading southbound on Harbor Freeway, possible 23152. Requesting additional units, Code 3."

I roll my eyes and look in the direction of the sirens. With the aid of my binoculars, I see the car chase. The driver is in an Audi and acting wasted, swaying his car and body from one side to another. I doubt he's even aware that the cops are following closely behind him. All they need to do is overtake him, and that'll be the end of it.

Scanning the streets, I'm surprised by the emptiness. You'd think a city like this would be bustling. I lift the binoculars to the sky, finding the Ursa Minor constellation almost instinctively. The North Star remains in my focus.

"211 in progress at Hollywood Presbyterian Medical. Four suspects reported." *Robbery. That's more like it.*

"K.A.R.M.A. what's my ETA to Hollywood Presbyterian on foot?"

"Three and a half minutes if you run."

I take off, the city blurring as I sprint toward the hospital.

Four men burst through the emergency room doors, arms loaded with stolen medical supplies and drugs.

The first man, tall and burly, charges at me. I sidestep, letting his momentum carry him past. I hook his ankle as he stumbles, sending him crashing to the ground.

The second man, covered in tattoos and wielding a knife, lunges at me. His slashes are wild, but I remain calm, deflecting the assailant's attacks with precision. I seize his wrist, twist sharply, and disarm him with a swift kick. The knife clatters to the pavement. I punch him in the gut, and he doubles over, gasping.

The third man, carrying a bag of drugs, hesitates. His eyes dart around, looking for an escape. I fix my sights on him, my stance steady. He bolts, but I'm faster. I tackle him to the ground.

"Ma'am, I have an update on Jessica's case. Shall I continue?" K.A.R.M.A.'s voice chimes in.

"Not now, K.A.R.M.A. I'm a bit busy." The criminal struggles, but I bend his arm behind his back, pinning him down.

The fourth man swings a crowbar at me. I duck, feeling the rush of air as it whizzes past. I roll off the pinned criminal, and counter with a quick jab to his ribs, followed by a knee to his stomach. He drops the weapon, collapsing in pain.

Sirens are close, the lights are bright. *Time to go.*

I linger in the shadows as the cops park in the alley and hurry to the men I subdued. The one on the right pulls out his radio. "Somehow we're all clear at Presbyterian Medical."

HOME – *Lair*
January 03, 01:22 PST

"K.A.R.M.A." I unzip my jacket and unload my gear. "What was so important that you needed to interrupt me in the middle of a fight?"

"As instructed, after using the doorbell cameras nearby, I was able to track down security footage of the vehicle that dropped Jessica's body off in front of the building."

Your typical large, nondescript white van appears on the screen, approaching our apartment. Two sets of arms fling her lifeless body onto the sidewalk. I zoom in on the pixelated shot, focusing on the license plates.

"K.A.R.M.A., I see plates. Who does that van belong to?"

"According to the California DMV, the plates are registered to Madilyn Wright, a thirty-six-year-old mother of three from San Fernando Valley. She's married to Henry Wright, a neurosurgeon. Neither have prior records."

I slam my fist on my desk. *Dammit. Those plates were obviously swapped out.*

"Would you like to follow Mrs. Wright?"

"No, that won't be necessary. Madilyn won't help me solve this case. Instead, show me what we have."

"Certainly. Jessica Glory: age twenty, daughter of pop star Allen Glory and Oscar-winning actress Charlotte Glory. She was a junior at USC, majoring in music, part-time dealer. Found dead Thursday, November 24th, at 08:09. Van footage timestamps her being dumped at 06:33. Drivers unknown. LAPD's initial toxicology report states she died from a drug overdose. Substance unknown. Body still being processed at labs in Sacramento."

The cold, factual summary hits harder than those hospital robbers ever could. We've combed through this dozens of times, and it still doesn't sit right. Each time I hear it, I catch myself wishing that something new will jump out, something I've missed, a hidden key to this whole mess. But every time, it just feels more like a closed box, a case sewn shut by too many loose threads.

"Go over her last day again, K.A.R.M.A.," I say, my fingers tapping on the arm of my chair. "I know we've already walked this path, but I need to make sure I'm not missing anything."

"Jessica's last day, November 23rd," she begins, and I close my eyes, trying to picture it all over again. "She withdrew cash from an ATM on Western at 19:37. Surveillance footage shows signs of agitation, glancing over her shoulder, appearing anxious. Her phone then pings to a location near Long Beach, an area consisting primarily of abandoned warehouses."

"Right," I mutter, images of that deserted corner flashing in my mind. That alleyway's burned into my brain. I've dug into it—no security cams, no witnesses. Just a black hole where her trail disappears.

"She stays there for approximately an hour. No calls, no texts, no contact until her phone goes dark around 03:27," K.A.R.M.A. continues. "After that, her next appearance is the footage showing her body being dumped, roughly three hours later, at 06:33."

I let out a slow breath, my fingers tightening around the chair's edge. "K.A.R.M.A., when is her body expected to be done with the medical examiners?"

"No timeline available, ma'am. There seems to be a backlog."

Of course there is. "Alright, let's switch gears." Grabbing a pen and pad, I sketch a tattoo that stood out on one of the hospital robbers: a skull with two revolvers inside the letter O. "K.A.R.M.A., reverse image search this sketch." I hold the paper up to the camera in the corner of the hideout.

"That appears to be the logo for the Omega Outlaws gang.

They're one of the largest and most violent gangs in L.A., with the highest murder rate per capita. They also have significant presences in Atlanta and Detroit, involved in murder, drug distribution, and stolen goods amongst other nefarious acts."

"Drugs and murder, you say?" I sit straight. "K.A.R.M.A., add these Outlaws to my watchlist."

CHAPTER 18

HOME – *Jessica's Room*
   January 05, 09:14 PST

A SENSE of unfinished business gnaws at me. My last visit was cut short by a final. But now that I know Jessica wasn't just some regular college student, I step inside, determined to leave no stone unturned.

The desk is cluttered with textbooks and notes. Pulling out the drawers, I sift through pens, notebooks, and stray papers. I dig deeper, feeling along the bottom and finding a few unmarked bottles of pills. An elegant ottoman sits at the foot of the bed. Lifting its lid, I unearth folded blankets and pillows.

I inch back to the closet, pushing aside the neatly hung dresses and sneaker boxes. I prod around each wooden panel. One feels hollow. Prying it open reveals a small compartment of cash and a few baggies of pills.

So this is where she kept her stash.

My gaze falls on the bed, the last untouched part of the

room. I lift the mattress, running my fingers along the seams, I notice an irregularity. A section of the padding has been carefully sewn back together. Using a small knife, I cut the stitches. There, tucked away in the foam, is a USB drive.

This seems promising.

CENTRAL LOS ANGELES – *Sunset Brew Co.*
January 05, 11:02 PST

THE COFFEE SHOP Xavier suggested is one I know well. I arrived way earlier than our set time because the hours spent cooped up in the basement of my building are starting to suffocate me.

Plugging Jessica's drive into my laptop, I watch as the screen flickers to life, revealing a series of encrypted files. Upon first glance, they appear to have a level of encryption that's unusual for your run-of-the-mill Valley girl. The longer I'm investigating Jessica's life, the more I'm starting to realize she wasn't just a pretty face.

You can tell a lot about a person by their effort to protect their secrets. Ironically, the act of hiding something so securely only draws more attention to it. I prefer hiding things in plain sight. My eyes are glued to my terminal screen, absorbed in breaking the encryption, when a shadow falls over me.

I glance up to see Xavier standing there, smiling softly. Unlike the day we bumped into each other, his face looks rested, his eyes have no bags underneath them. His ebony curls are more voluminous than they've ever been before.

"I didn't think you were going to accept my invitation," Xavier says as he settles himself into the chair in front of me. I try not to think of him as the boy from all those years ago. I try to focus on the man in front of me.

"Well," I start to say but I can't think of anything to follow up with, so I leave it at that.

"What would you like to have?" he asks. I look down and realize I don't have a drink yet. I remember telling the barista I was waiting for someone, but it feels like a distant memory.

"Iced coffee is fine," I reply. He nods and heads to the counter. I watch him walk away, telling myself to stay calm. It would be easy to do except I feel a certain way about how he's looking at me. It looks like he remembers something and is only looking at me through that lens.

This is Xavier, I remind myself. When have I ever known him to be judgmental? But then again, it's unfair to compare present-day him with the classmate I made out with at some stupid party over a decade ago.

He returns with two iced coffees, followed by a waitress carrying two plates of pastries. The sight of the sweets makes me want to hug him; I've been having sugar cravings lately, and it's driving me crazy.

The coffee and a slice of cake are placed in front of me. I smile at the waitress in gratitude, and she smiles back, returning to the counter.

"I was so surprised when I saw you," Xavier begins. "I almost didn't believe my eyes."

I take a sip of my drink, avoiding his gaze. "I think I was a bit too excited. Ended up running off," I say with a nervous laugh.

Xavier nods his head but says nothing. It's his turn to take a sip of his coffee. I try to remember what mine tastes like, but nothing comes to mind, so I take another sip.

"How have you been?"

I nod in acknowledgment of the question. "I've been alright. How have you been?"

"Same, I guess."

This interaction is pitiful, and so are his eyes. I'm trying not to focus on them, but they're right there staring back at me. I don't know how he managed to make his gaze both piercing and gentle. *It's all in your head.*

"What brings you to Los Angeles?" he asks, offering a safer topic.

"I'm getting my master's in Cybersecurity at USC."

"Oh," he says, positively surprised.

"How's Rachel?"

"She's good. She's still in Chicago with the family."

It feels like I've been here forever; this conversation feels so stilted. I want to look at the time, but I don't want him to think he's boring me. I wonder if the reason for his discomfort is because I'm antsy, and that's somehow putting him on edge.

No, it's the way he looks at me—with pity. No matter how hard I try to see it as something else, it's impossible. I could stay and endure the conversation, but I have no reason to anymore. It was nice to see him. However, this meetup wasn't exactly what I had in mind.

"I have to go," I announce, cutting him off mid-sentence.

"Is everything alright?" he asks, and I nod.

"I just remembered that I have this thing. I promised a friend I'd help her out because she's not in town at the moment. I totally forgot about it, and I think the deadline is today. So, I have to go and attend to that right now," I lie, avoiding his eyes as I pack my things.

Yet, I feel this urge to tell him about my life, about being the Cyber Huntress. All the people I've stopped. I want him to know about Jessica and the investigation, but I don't say a word.

He wouldn't understand.

"Can we do this again?"

"Sure," I reply, standing up and already moving toward the door. I pull out some money, more than enough to cover my share, and place it on the table. "Just let me know when."

I don't wait for his response. I head for the door, mortified by my performance.

CHAPTER 19

HOME – *Bedroom*
   January 21, 10:43 PST

JOLTING AWAKE, my heart pounds as the front doorknob jiggles violently. Grabbing a knife from my bedside table, I creep toward the entrance of my bedroom. The knob twists persistently, but the door holds fast. I'm thankful I took Thorne's advice and changed the locks for the lair and the apartment.

Peering through the peephole, I see a familiar blonde woman. *Oh shit, it's Charlotte Glory.* I tuck the knife into the hem of my sweatpants and quickly unlock the door.

"Oh, hi. You must be Winter," she says.

I take in the woman before me: her face is perfectly made up, her blonde hair layered with strawberry highlights, and she's wearing a coat that definitely costs more than half my wardrobe.

"Yes, and you must be Jessica's mother?"

"I'm sorry. Yes, I'm Charlotte Glory," she replies,

extending a hand adorned with a massive diamond ring. I shake it and motion for her to come in. As she steps over the threshold into the condo she and her husband own, she raises a hand, signaling a man in a suit and earpiece to stay put. Security, I guess. "I must have an old key to the apartment. I couldn't seem to get it open."

"Yeah, sorry about that. I just had the locks changed, given what happened. I wanted to be more cautious."

"I completely understand. I've felt quite on edge myself as of late. I was hoping to just slip in and gather up her things while you were in class."

She's right. I should be on campus right now, but I needed a quick nap before patrolling all night. "Of course. I can step out for a bit if you'd like. Give you some time."

"No, it's alright. Stay, do whatever you were doing before I came. I'll just be in her room."

I leave her to it. I think I can squeeze in thirty more minutes before getting up and returning to work. As I shut the door to my bedroom, I can't help but hear the sobs emanating from the one across the hall. My emotional intelligence might not match my IQ, and still I know it's wrong to ignore that woman's cries.

At the foot of the bed, Charlotte is weeping, clutching a necklace Jessica often wore. I crouch down next to her and simply pull her into a hug. I've lost enough people in my life to know that actions are better than condolences. Sometimes you just need to know someone cares.

After a while of us sitting in silence, I softly suggest, "Why don't we get some lunch, Charlotte?"

She nods, and I help her to her feet. Food has never failed to cheer me up, and maybe it will help her too. I figure I can console a grieving mother and maybe make some headway in the case. Having a conversation with the mother of the victim could be beneficial. I'll get to learn about Jessica from an angle I can't get stalking the streets of L.A.

She wipes her eyes. "Call me Charlie."

I grab my keys and lead her to the front door. Her guard is still standing in the same exact spot. I mean, he hasn't even moved an inch.

"Maxwell, can you get the car ready? We are going to Fig." Charlie forgets to mention that the car is a limousine. When we get in, I see there's another guard in the back seat in addition to Maxwell closing the door behind us. "So, Winter. Tell me about yourself. Jessica mentioned that you were from New York."

Ah, the dreaded interview question. "Sort of. I went to college out there for my undergrad at NYU."

"What did you study?"

"Computer Science. Computers are kind of my thing."

"Oh wow. You must be some kind of genius. I was never a science person. In fact, I went to college in New York too. But I went to Juilliard for theater. I met Allen there. I wanted Jessica to go there for music. But she wanted to stay local." She wears a somber look on her face for a while as she stares out the bulletproof window of the limo. She continues, "I have this thing where I have to ask every person who has lived in New York the top pizza spot."

"Is this even a debate? It's Maricio's on Lennox and 9th," I say matter-of-factly.

She perks up at that. "And what about Gianni's on Market and 2nd?"

"Gianni's? I thought you wanted the top one. They're top five at best."

Placing her thousand-dollar sunglasses on, she lets her lips curl into a smile. "You know what, Winter, I like you."

The limo door opens, and as we step out, people materialize from nowhere, cameras flashing, snapping as many photos as they can. They might as well have taken a video at the rate at which their fingers press their shutters because why do you need thirty photos in a second?

Charlie's guards surround us, but that doesn't stop the vultures from bombarding us with questions until we get inside the restaurant.

"Charlotte! Charlotte! Over here! Can you tell us who you are with now?"

"Charlotte! How are you holding up since Jessica's death?"

"When are we getting a sequel to *Harbor*?"

It's not until we're sitting down at our table that I can see Charlie for who she truly is. To the paparazzi and the media, this is all some fabulous scandal they can cover. The dead kid of a Hollywood mogul will surely get their likes and engagement clicks at the expense of a mother grieving the loss of her daughter. I don't care how many millions she has, she's still a person who should have the luxury to mourn in peace.

"I'm sorry, Charlie. You deserve better than that. You're more than a tabloid."

"You get used to it." She dabs her eyes with her napkin. "Anyway, let's eat."

To steer the conversation, I ask, "Can you tell me what Jessica was like as a kid? I know I was a troublemaker. I feel like Jessica must've had her moments."

Charlie lets out a genuine laugh, her eyes lighting up. "Oh, you have no idea. Jessica went through a 'prank phase' that nearly drove us all insane."

I lean in, intrigued. "Really? What kind of pranks are we talking about?"

"Oh, they were elaborate," She says, shaking her head fondly. "Once, she rigged the entire house with motion sensors connected to speakers that played animal sounds. We had lions roaring in the living room and elephants trumpeting in the kitchen. It took us a week to figure out how to turn it all off."

I laugh, trying to picture a young Jessica orchestrating such chaos. "Sounds like she had quite the imagination."

"That she did. And the resources to make it happen. Having access to her father's expense account certainly didn't hurt."

"Must've been nice, growing up with all that," I muse.

Charlie nods. "Yes, we have been quite fortunate. But Jessica was always resourceful, always looking for ways to challenge herself. She was so fiercely independent. She didn't like being told what to do, even as a little girl."

"She really was something," I admit. I didn't know her long, but she was someone I could've seen myself being friends with for a long time.

"She was," Charlie agrees, a bittersweet mix of pride and sorrow as she reflects on Jessica's spirited nature. "She had such a big heart. She cared deeply about people, even if she didn't always show it in the traditional ways."

We sit in a comfortable silence for a moment, nibbling on our food, the noise of the restaurant fading into the background as we both get lost in our thoughts. Finally, Charlie sighs and offers a small smile. "Well, thank you for hanging out with me this afternoon, Winter. It was nice to officially meet. The apartment is yours for however long you want it. Allen and I will take care of everything."

As we stand to leave, I smile, grateful for her generosity. "Thank you, Charlie. It means a lot. It really was no problem."

The limo pulls up in front of the apartment. "Thank you again, Winter. It means more to me than you know."

"How about I pack up Jessica's room for you and somebody can come and grab the boxes?" Charlie nods silently as her bodyguard closes the door.

Instead of heading for the lobby, I veer off toward the cluster of shrubs lining the side of my building. The second I reach the foliage, a sour taste rises in my throat.

I wipe my mouth with the back of my hand, closing my eyes as I try to steady my breathing, praying for the gagging sensation to subside. "I knew I shouldn't have tried the sushi."

CHAPTER 20

PURSING MY LIPS, I try to zone in on the lesson, but my concentration is shot. Every time I attempt to focus, giggles erupt from beside me. Unable to resist, I glance over and, as always, it's a couple. Today, I loathe romance more than any other day of the year.

Valentine's Day. Another year of me being a bitter bitch. My phone buzzes, pulling me from my thoughts. It's a text from Aunt Gina.

```
I hope you find the strength
you need to get through today,
and if it gets too hard, I hope
you know you can rely on me.
I'm here for you.
```

If only it were that easy.

Jayden and I share an apartment in the West Village, and

waking up next to the person you've promised forever to feels like a small slice of paradise. Sure, we have our fair share of disagreements, like any couple living together, but we always find a way to reconcile.

For Valentine's Day, we decided to go to a fair. I haven't been to a carnival since my eighth birthday with my dad, so it means the world to me that we're going. Our schedules rarely sync up because of Jayden's freshman soccer practices, so this feels special.

"I'm not scared of anything," Jayden says, a playful glint in his eyes. "So, try whatever you feel like trying."

I nod, grinning. "Of course, I'll do my best to enjoy myself with someone as capable as you by my side."

He laughs. I'm the braver one between us, but Jayden liked to call bull on that because it threatened his ego. He's the one who pledged to protect me and not the other way around.

This morning, we had the best sex we've had in a while. I woke up to his kisses, clothes quickly discarded. We confessed our love, and I told him how much he means to me. He doesn't understand the extent of it, but I told him he saved me. The act was slow and tender, and when Jayden buried his face in my shoulder, I felt the wetness of his tears and said nothing. I was just glad he was comfortable enough to be this vulnerable with me.

Afterward, we shower together. Jayden lifts me by the waist, my legs wrapping around him. Shower sex has always been my favorite —filled with passion, some flexibility, and unrestrained moans. Once, we were so loud that our neighbor banged on the wall, begging for sleep. It's one of our funniest stories.

Our first stop is a cozy diner that's gone all out for Valentine's Day. Red paper butterflies flutter from the ceiling, pink and red balloons are tied to every available surface, and the waitresses move around with heart-shaped pins on their aprons and red scarves around their necks. The place feels like it's bursting with love, and I can't help but smile as we slide into a booth by the window.

"What do you think?" Jayden asks, raising an eyebrow as he takes in the decorations.

"It's... a lot," I say, laughing as I glance around. "But I kind of love it."

He grins, reaching across the table to take my hand. "Good. I wanted today to be special."

A waitress with a bright smile and a heart-shaped charm on her necklace comes over to take our order. "What can I get for you two lovebirds?" she asks, her eyes sparkling with the Valentine's spirit.

"Pancakes," I say, looking at Jayden. "With extra syrup."

"And a large milkshake with two straws," he adds, gently squeezing my hand.

"Coming right up!" the waitress chirps before hurrying to the kitchen.

When our food arrives, the stack of flapjacks is towering, dripping with syrup and a dollop of whipped cream on top. The milkshake, complete with two straws, sits between us, a shared treat that feels like something out of an old-school romance movie.

Jayden picks up his fork and spears a hot cake, holding it out to me. "First bite?"

I lean forward and take the bite, closing my eyes as the sweetness hits my tongue. "Perfect," I say, savoring the taste.

He smiles, taking his own bite before nodding toward the milkshake. "Think we can finish this whole thing?"

"Challenge accepted."

We both lean in, sipping from the milkshake at the same time. Our faces are so close, I can see the flecks of color in his eyes. It's one of those moments where everything is right in the world, like the diner, with all its cheesy decorations, is a bubble where nothing bad can touch us.

Jayden, out of nowhere, starts laughing uncontrollably. "What's so funny?"

"Remember when we went to Niagara Falls a few months ago

and your poncho came completely off and hit a few people in the head?"

I smile, the memory instantly coming to mind. "How could I forget? It was so embarrassing. I wasn't even that close to it."

"It was an unusually windy day. Besides, if the wind wasn't going to do it, I was," he adds, with a smirk.

We both dissolve into laughter, the kind that makes your stomach hurt in the best way. The other diners might think we're crazy, but in this moment, we're the only two people in the world.

After breakfast, Jayden and I make our way to the county fair; the air is filled with the smell of popcorn and rides whirring to life. It's already packed with energy, where families and friends mill about. I can't help but feel a rush of nostalgia.

"Where to first?" Jayden asks, scanning the fairgrounds with childlike excitement.

I point toward the bumper cars with a mischievous grin. "Let's see if you can handle yourself on the road."

Jayden raises an eyebrow, a competitive glint in his eye. "Oh, it's on, Washington."

We weave through the crowd, the sounds of laughter and carnival games all around us. The line for the bumper cars isn't too long, and as we wait our turn, I can't resist leaning into Jayden, nudging him playfully. "You know I'm not going to take it easy on you, right?"

He chuckles, wrapping an arm around my shoulders. "Wouldn't want it any other way."

When it's our turn, we climb into our respective cars. I watch Jayden adjust his seatbelt, his fingers drumming on the steering wheel like he's gearing up for a race. The second the bell rings, signaling the start of the round, I slam my foot on the pedal and swerve to block his path.

"Not so fast!" I call out as I cut him off at every turn.

Jayden frowns as he tries to outmaneuver me. I keep him boxed *in, only giving him a momentary break before blocking him again. Eventually, I let him slip past, giving him a moment of victory.*

"You're ruthless!" Jayden says as he speeds away, finally free. I just laugh, the wind whipping through my hair as I chase after him.

After the bumper cars, we stroll through the fair, passing booths offering everything from giant teddy bears to goldfish in plastic bags. The aroma of fried food is too tempting to resist, so we decide to indulge. We grab a basket of deep-fried YinYangs and a massive funnel cake dusted with powdered sugar, sharing bites as we wander.

"Okay, I think I've hit my sugar limit," I groan, rubbing my stomach as we finish the last of the golden-brown encrusted cookies.

Jayden wipes powdered sugar from the corner of my mouth. "You said that after the first YinYang."

I roll my eyes, but a smile tugs at my lips. "Alright, you got me. I can't resist fried diabetes. What should we do next?"

"How about the spinning teacups?"

"Only if you promise not to make it spin like crazy," I warn, eyeing him suspiciously.

He winks. "No promises."

We head over to the teacups, and I immediately regret the decision as Jayden grabs the wheel and starts spinning it with all his might. The world becomes a blur of colors and lights, and I cling to the edge of the teacup, shrieking as the sugar rush and dizziness take over.

"You're evil!" I gasp between fits of laughter.

"Payback's a bitch, isn't it?" Jayden yells as he keeps spinning. By the time the ride finally slows down, I'm almost ready to hurl.

As we stagger off the ride, I grab Jayden's arm for balance. "Okay," I say, trying to steady myself, "My turn to choose. How about laser tag?"

We dodge kids with cotton candy who also hold oversized stuffed animals until we reach the entrance of the laser tag arena. The neon lights and pulsing music set the stage for what's about to go down. It's us against two other couples, and the last one standing takes the win.

Jayden struggles with his vest, fumbling with the straps as I adjust my own. I bite back a laugh and give him a quick peck on the cheek. "Just stay alive, okay? I'll handle the rest."

I pull him back over and fix his vest for him as he says, "Yes, ma'am."

As the buzzer sounds, we scatter. My strategy is clear: take out the guys first. They're the bigger threat, and their girlfriends look like they'd rather be anywhere else. I hug the edge of the arena, moving stealthily through the shadows. The first couple comes into view, and I lock eyes with the boy. Before he can react, I fire. His vest lights up, and he looks down in disbelief.

"What are you looking at me for?" he yells at his girlfriend. "Destroy her!"

Before I can finish the job, Jayden swoops in from the side and tags the girlfriend, who squeaks in surprise. I shoot my partner a look of admiration, and he smiles back at me, clearly pleased with himself.

I push deeper into the arena, and I find myself in a mirror maze. The walls are a bewildering array of reflections, making it hard to tell what's real and what's just a trick of the light. I slow down, mentally mapping each turn. A laser beam cuts through the air, but it hits one of my reflections instead of me. I keep moving, silent and focused, until I catch sight of the remaining guy. He's scanning the mirrors, trying to spot me, but he's too slow. I take the shot, and his vest lights up. Got him on the first try.

His girlfriend appears out of nowhere, crying as she rushes to his side. "I don't want to play anymore," she whimpers, clinging to him. I let the tears flow until my gun recharges and kill her off too. There's no mercy once you put on the vest.

I step out of the maze, and the arena's main screen flashes with our names. We're the last couple standing. "Up top!" I raise my hand for a high-five, and Jayden slaps it enthusiastically.

"Is there any reason why you're stupid good at this?"

I shrug. "Walters used to run combat simulations with us."

"Of course he did," Jayden shakes his head with a smile. "Well, I've worked up an appetite watching you do all the work. Let's go grab dinner."

"You're joking," I say as he pulls me by the arm. Jayden made reservations for this fancy French restaurant he asked me about some weeks back. I didn't know much, but everyone I knew who went had only praises to sing. It's reservation only. And you have to call weeks in advance. Sometimes, even months.

"You said you wanted to come," he says, and I still can't believe he'd go to this length for me. I feel the tears well up in my eyes. This entire day has been nothing short of perfect.

He gives his name to the hostess, who immediately gets us settled. Jayden says nothing. He just watches me take in the entire room. The lights and the decor are all breathtaking; it takes everything for my jaw not to drop.

Jayden lifts his glass. "Here's to surviving our first Valentine's Day in New York."

"And to many more," I say as I clink my glass with his.

"Are you absolutely sure you still want to see that horror movie tonight?"

"One hundred percent." I watch his face fall. "Hey, don't pout. I promise I'll kiss you whenever you get scared." The idea of making out with him for the better duration of the movie seems more interesting than watching some rom-com.

Within the nearly empty theater, I drag Jayden to the seat that people are least likely to pay attention to. "Aren't you scared the movie will be too scary for you to handle?"

I kiss his lips. "No, but I'm hoping you catch a little fright."

"Oh, I'm terrified," Jayden says as he pulls me back into the kiss and deepens it. The film has barely begun, and I'm already on my way to having a swollen lip. I can't say what the flick is about, or at what point it becomes scary because we spend the entire time making out. He settles me on his lap and kisses me more, his hand moving as far up my dress as he can go. Whatever sound tries to escape my lips, he swallows as he pushes one finger into me and then another. The drive home is a race because I can't wait to have him take my dress off, and he can't wait to do it.

"I love you," Jayden says suddenly, offering a small smile.

"I love you too," I reply, leaning over to kiss his cheek. "I'll never get to the bottom of the list of things I love about you."

"I love your hazel eyes," Jayden starts, and I grin widely because this is something I could do.

"I love your full brows," I say, leaning over to run a finger over them.

"I love the way you fit into my arms when I hold you; it makes me feel like I can take you everywhere." He pauses for a while and says, "I love you," again. I look over at him and know this is the man I will spend the rest of my life with.

Jayden pulls the car into the parking space in front of our building; he's a beast at parallel parking. I make sure to pat his back in compliment, and he laughs out loud.

He steps out of the car and hurries to my side to open the door. While Jayden makes his way around the hood of the car, I hear a loud screech and the gunfire that follow after. Glass shatters all over me while I place my hands over my head and duck down until the shots stop ringing. I'm frozen in a panic until I realize Jayden is already out of the car. I push the door open, and there he is, on the ground, the blood pooling out of him. His white shirt now red.

I let out a piercing scream and rush over to him. I hold him in my arms while he gurgles and chokes up blood, gasping for air. Amidst all this, he's trying to say something, and the only intelligible word I hear from the sentence is "… you."

"You, what?" I ask, but no matter how much I shout for him to wake up, he doesn't budge. His eyes are open and staring at nothing. I'm vaguely aware of the crowd hurrying over to us, the ones calling the cops.

"Jayden," I call, shaking him in hopes this is all some elaborate joke and he'll snap out of it. Nothing of the sort happens. He doesn't respond. When the ambulance arrives, my voice has nothing left to give. I don't need anyone to tell me my Jay is officially gone.

"Miss," someone says, laying a hand on my shoulder. "We need to secure the area." People tug at me, trying to pull me away, but I refuse to move, clinging to Jayden, my everything.

COLUMBUS, *Ohio – Colonel Walters's House*
   ***8 years ago** – May 08, 04:12 EDT*

IT'S BEEN months since Jayden's death, and the case has hit a dead end. People keep insisting he must have kept bad friends and wronged them. It was all nonsense. They didn't know him like I did.

Walters is the man I'm looking for. After mourning and realizing it isn't getting me anywhere; I turn up at his front porch in the middle of the night. His surprise is evident when he opens the door, but I don't waste time on pleasantries.

"I want to become a vigilante."

He observes the surroundings, ensuring I'm alone. I must look like a madwoman, a former student showing up unannounced, dead of night, asking him to make her into something he didn't think anyone knew he was.

"I know how this looks, and I might seem incapable now, but if you train me, I promise I won't disappoint. I lost him,

Colonel. I lost Jayden. I can't keep living like this. I don't want to feel helpless anymore."

Walters remains silent throughout my plea, his expression unreadable. Just as I start to lose hope, he steps aside and opens the door wider.

I wipe my tears and step into what will be the rest of my life.

ST JAMES PARK – *8-Eleven*
February 14, 18:48 PST

"ANY SCRATCHERS OR TICKETS?" the rugged cashier asks.

"Huh? Oh, sorry, no thanks."

"Just these items?" he continues as I nod, placing my snacks and candy bars on the counter. I required something sweet, so I stopped to grab a few things before heading back to the school library to study encryption. The hope is that the sugar will keep me calm as I try to decipher the flash drive's complexity, which is beyond what I initially thought.

A news broadcast on the store's television catches my attention: *Vigilante Spotting*. My heart races. I thought I was being careful. Until now, speculation about a vigilante had been fueled by the cops' increased success in catching criminals and the steady stream of petty offenders turning up at the station.

However, it isn't just the spotting that catches my eye; it's the mention of two vigilantes. My eyes widen as I stare at the screen. Two grainy photos are displayed side by side. How can there be two vigilantes? Surely, our paths would have crossed by now, but I haven't encountered anyone on my nightly outings.

"I thought one nutjob running around the city was enough. What are the odds of having two vigilantes?" the cashier mutters, shaking his head.

I play along, forcing a laugh. "I know, right? What dumbass goes around town dressed up as a power button to fight crime?"

"The weirdos in this city never cease to amaze me. Anyway, your total is $23.86."

CHAPTER 21

WESTLAKE – *HalfFoods*
  February 26, 15:53 PST

AS THE AUTOMATIC double doors *whoosh* open, I can't help but scoff at the *TIME* magazines displayed at the front registers titled "Who Was Jessica Glory?" After living with her and investigating her, I don't even know that answer. I highly doubt those editors do either. I needed to clear my head, and I've been putting off grocery shopping for too long. But it seems that no matter where I go, my problems continue to follow me.

Los Angeles, it turns out, is big enough to have two vigilantes, even bigger to make sure they never meet. It's quite amazing the entire time I've been roaming the streets, I've yet to meet the other. I can't tell if it's because they are good at hiding or if I've gotten bad at seeking.

The truth remains: I'm not the only vigilante in this city. I've walked the streets these past couple of weeks, trying to figure out who they might be, but there's no way to tell.

Every crime fighter has their own signature style, though it's only apparent when they make a move. Nightshield is a ghost, blending in seamlessly.

The vigilante being male is the only lead I have so far. Based on eyewitness testimonies, estimated height is at least six foot four inches. But for all I know, they could just be a haunted WNBA player. I'm willing to entertain any idea that gets me closer to solving either of the mysteries plaguing me.

Walking past the produce, I head straight for the cereal. I could buy actual groceries, except I never cook, and there's no point pretending that, at the end of the day, I won't order takeout.

The cereal section always feels like a dreamscape with its endless choices. I go toward the new stocks and try to pick the box that calls out to me.

"Winter?"

I raise a brow and lean closer to the shelf; who knew if I paid close attention, the boxes would actually speak to me? I didn't.

"Winter?" The voice doesn't come from the box this time; it comes from beside me. When I turn my head, I'm face to face with the last man I expected to be looking at on this fine day.

I nearly jump out of my skin, almost tripping over myself, but Xavier catches me. My entire being heats up, and I try to pry myself from his grip. He lets go immediately, and my cheeks flame with embarrassment.

"Xavier," I say, desperately trying to regain my composure. His presence overwhelms me, making simple tasks like standing upright a challenge.

I give myself a much-needed pep talk. *Come on, Washington, get it together; he's just a guy and I've fought literal villains.*

To his credit, Xavier doesn't look amused or awkward.

"Fancy seeing you here," he says. "It seems like fate is trying to make us reconnect by any means necessary."

His attempt at a joke falls flat, and I scramble to think of an excuse, looking everywhere but in his direction. "Listen, I know the coffee shop was awkward, but I really hope we can be friends again," Xavier continues, drawing my attention back to him.

"It wasn't that bad; I just really needed to leave," I say, trying not to imagine myself practically sprinting from there.

Xavier nods, pretending to believe me. "How about I make it up to you by cooking you a meal?"

I raise an eyebrow. Since the last time I saw him, he's cut his hair short, barely revealing the curls I associate with him. He's wearing a white t-shirt highlighting his biceps, and I discreetly swallow the lump in my throat.

"You can cook?" I ask.

He nods. "I can hold my own in a kitchen."

"Your place?"

Xavier grins so wide I feel my heart start to hammer in warning. What if I'm making a mistake? Maybe it's the pessimist in me, but I don't see—whatever this is—having a happy ending. A part of me wants to change my mind and walk away, yet something is forcing me to stay.

As Xavier and I maneuver through the grocery store aisles, I casually suggest, "Why don't we just keep it simple? Maybe sandwiches?"

He shakes his head, tossing a box of pasta into the cart. "No way. You're in for a treat tonight. We're having carbonara."

I raise an eyebrow again, amused by his confidence. "Isn't that a little ambitious?"

Xavier chuckles, grabbing a wedge of Parmesan from the

dairy section. "Not when you've got a chef like me in the kitchen. Trust me, a sandwich won't cut it."

I playfully roll my eyes. "Alright, Chef Xavier, show me what you've got. But don't say I didn't warn you when we end up burning the kitchen down."

He laughs. "Oh, ye of little faith. And you won't be anywhere near the stove. We both know you're not the best cook."

At self-checkout, Xavier and I struggle with the temperamental machine. For the fifth time, it blares a warning: "Please remove item from the bagging area."

"Again?" Xavier mutters, rolling his eyes. He reaches over, pulling a bag of apples from the highlighted area.

I stifle a laugh. "I swear these machines have a vendetta against you."

"Either that or they just really like to mess with people," he says, scanning the fruit again. The machine finally beeps approvingly.

"Think you can finish without it throwing another fit?"

Xavier smiles. "Let's not get ahead of ourselves."

With the last item scanned and bagged, Xavier declares, "Victory," and swipes his card to pay. He grabs the bags and leads the way out of the store. To my surprise, he lives as close to the supermarket as I do, just in the opposite direction. I ignore the thought that he might have been right about fate.

His apartment isn't what I imagined. It's not a penthouse, but it could easily be mistaken for one. The building is similar to mine, noticeably newer, as if it was set up just a few days ago.

"Water?" Xavier asks, pulling my attention away from his pristine space.

I nod and follow him into the kitchen, just a few steps from the living room. The entire setup is minimalistic. Unlike me, Xavier knows how to keep his place tidy—or maybe he always expects company. That would explain the lack of clothes thrown around, no dirty dishes in the sink, and no leftover pizza in sight. The place is immaculate, with no sign that he eats pizza at all.

Xavier hands me a glass of water, and I take a sip before downing the whole thing, realizing just how thirsty I am. "You can look around while I cook."

Although tempted, I know better than to take him up on that. "It's okay," I say. "I want to help you."

Xavier laughs, and I feel the corners of my mouth tug upward.

"You're my guest," he says with his back turned as he takes more ingredients out of his shopping bag. "I'm the one who offered to cook. And I told you, you aren't coming anywhere near these burners."

"Yeah, but I can chop—"

"Let me do this for you, Winter. I'll let you know when it's done."

"If you insist," is all I offer as I make my way back to the living room.

The white walls are adorned with eclectic art pieces, and forest-green curtains frame the windows. Xavier has a fascination with plants, and despite the limited sunlight, they seem to thrive. I wander from one plant to another, trying to guess their names before inevitably giving up.

He has a bookshelf filled with obscure titles—the kind I'd have if I didn't prefer eBooks. I pick up a physics book and flip through it, unsure of what I'm looking for, before placing it back.

There's a coziness to his apartment that makes me realize how unwelcoming mine is. I never found the time to decorate, and now, with Jessica gone, I don't think I ever will. Her unclosed case fills me with dread, and I force myself not to dwell on it.

A door to the left must lead to his bedroom. I glance over at Xavier, whisking something in the kitchen. I won't invade his privacy, but I can't help stare at the man in front of me. I do so unabashedly. He's grown into himself, his jaw more defined, a clear indication he spends a lot of time in the gym. Perhaps as much as I do.

I shake off the rising thought of us working out together. It's been a while since I've been in someone else's space without immediately undressing.

"It's ready," Xavier calls, and I move away from the wall and toward him with a smile on my face.

"You have a nice place," I say as I sit at the table.

Xavier looks around his house like he doesn't quite get what I mean. "If you say so," is all he says and goes back to plating the meal. He sets the dishes down and takes the seat across from me.

"Thanks for dinner," I say after noting the time on the wall. It's nearly five p.m.

Xavier waves me off. "It's nothing."

I take a bite of the food, and my taste buds come alive. When he said he would make dinner, I didn't expect him to blow me away.

"Dude, what the fuck!" I say and slap the table in excitement. "Why didn't you say you were a seasoned chef?"

He blushes deeply and bows his head a little. To taste the goodness for himself, he takes a bite. His face doesn't bear the excitement I'm feeling, and I scrunch up my nose a little at his reaction. "It's alright?"

"What do you mean by 'it's alright'? This is really amazing. The best meal I've had in maybe a month."

Xavier's eyes widen at this. "You should eat better," he

says, his voice losing the light-hearted tone it held a few moments ago.

"You should really look into opening a restaurant," I say to him. Xavier snorts at that, like it's the most ridiculous thing he has ever heard. For someone who spends a lot of her time in restaurants and ordering more food than the next person, I know what I'm talking about. "So are you at USC too?"

"Well, if you hadn't booked it from the coffee shop, you'd know."

I choke on my pasta, almost forgetting how sassy Xavier could be. "Yeah, well, you know, I had…" I stumble out, "I'm so sorry about that. I completely forgot I had to dog-sit. Mr. Fluffles hadn't gotten his food for the day yet."

With a coy smile, he says, "I completely understand. We couldn't have let Mr. Fluffles go hungry. I'm actually at UCLA; I'm finishing up my doctorate."

How does a UCLA student get an invite to a prestigious USC gala?

"I had to give a speech on the research I'm working on with USC," he adds, as if reading my thoughts.

"Oh, so you must be a big-shot doctor now?"

He leans into a laugh. "Something like that."

KOREATOWN – *Xavier's*
February 26, 21:07 PST

"I SHOULD GO," I say, standing up.

Xavier rises with me and looks at the clock. We've been talking for over four hours. This is the longest I've spoken to anyone since Jessica was killed. I shake my head a little.

"Are you okay?" Xavier asks, and I nod my head and make my way toward the door.

"I have to be up real early tomorrow," I say even though the truth is I need to get back to the case. Spending time with him was a nice change of pace; we caught up like we were supposed to at the café. Here, I didn't feel judged; I didn't feel like there was a part of his mind that was perceiving me in some way. The conversation was easy. But now it's getting late, and I have other matters to attend to.

"I got so caught up I forgot to ask how you really are," Xavier says, following me to the door. He talks quickly, trying to make me understand.

"How am I?" It's such a loaded question. Where would I even begin? I could mention my dead roommate, or perhaps I start strong and talk about my dead ex.

"Yes, the last time we saw each other."

"At the café? I really had somewhere to go."

Looking away, Xavier scratches his scalp. "Not the café or the gala."

It takes me a few seconds to register what he's asking. "Oh."

"I'm sorry," he lets out, and I shake my head quickly. I wonder what part he thinks is his fault. "I don't mean to make you uncomfortable, but after I pushed him off and restrained him, I turned around and you were just gone. I didn't know how to contact you to see if you were fine, a—"

"I'm fine," I say, turning away from the door to face him. "I really am fine; it happened. It was a long time ago. You keep thinking of me as that same girl, and I'm not. Far from it." I meant to keep the last bit to myself, but the confession was needed.

"Winter, I just wanted to address the elep—" He doesn't get the chance to finish. I close the gap between us in an instant, my hands gripping the collar of his shirt as I pull his lips to mine.

Xavier's hands wrap around my waist to catch me. He opens his mouth to let me in. His lips are warm and slightly chapped, but they move against mine with a softness that sends a shiver down my spine. He tastes just like pancetta and the rocky road ice cream we decided to eat for dessert, an oddly intoxicating combination. I press my body to his as closely as I can. His hands come up to cup my face, and this kiss—it's different but also familiar. His palms still cradle my face the same way he once did as a high school junior. The only difference is now he knows how to work his tongue. He licks the roof of my mouth, his teeth biting my lower lip.

There's no rushing. We're not ripping each other's clothes apart. It's been a while since I've been kissed just for the heck of it. I've missed it. The realization only makes me more desperate to have his hands all over me, but I have a feeling that Xavier isn't one to rush anything, not even a kiss.

I pull away, our foreheads resting against each other. My chest rises and falls as I stare into his eyes. Xavier leans in and kisses my lips lightly, and my throat chokes up.

"I should go," I say again, trying to control my voice. "I have an early day."

CHAPTER 22

HOME – *Lair*
   March 02, 21:19 PST

"K.A.R.M.A., run the algorithm again with my newest changes."

"Running decryption algorithm," she responds.

I lean back, rubbing my temples. I've never faced something this challenging before. The encryption doesn't follow any standard scheme, so naturally none of my usual decryption methods are working.

"K.A.R.M.A., any luck?" I ask, my patience wearing thin.

"Negative. The encryption remains intact. I'm afraid I have more bad news. Would you like to hear it?"

I let out a frustrated sigh. "Well, don't leave me to my imagination. Spit it out."

"It seems that after this failed attempt to decrypt the drive, I discovered the drive would wipe itself clean after ten incorrect password entries. We have seven total guesses remaining."

Lovely. I get up from my chair and start pacing the room. "No more guesses on the drive directly, K.A.R.M.A. From now on, only matches with a percentage greater than seventy should be attempted based on the hash. We need to be extra cautious." I pick up my nun-chucks and start doing figure eights. "What's the latest on Chris?"

"Chris Turner has been observed engaging in routine activities," K.A.R.M.A. reports.

"I don't see a clear motive for him yet. And it sounds like he isn't the only potential suspect in her life either," I mutter, thinking aloud. "What about the LAPD investigation, K.A.R.M.A.?"

"No updates since the substance from her toxicology report was identified as heroin. Her cause of death is still labeled as a heroin overdose."

Surveillance footage of random criminals plays across my monitors. I've been digging into all the drug activity in L.A., starting with the Omega Outlaws. For weeks, I've followed random members, slowly narrowing down the higher-ranked individuals.

"K.A.R.M.A., compile the latest intel I've gathered on the Outlaws," I instruct as I strip off my civilian clothes, preparing to go out for the night.

"Compiling data." Moments later, the screen fills with profiles of various gang members, each one more dangerous than the last. Any one of these people could've killed Jessica. Their rap sheets show none of them are shy to murder. I've also discovered the existence of at least seven distinct gangs in Los Angeles during my nightly outings. It's not logical to only keep watch on the Outlaws.

I sit down on the bench and grab my boots. I push my foot inside, but something feels... wrong. They're tight, way too tight. I shimmy my foot deeper, only making the pressure worse. I grit my teeth, trying to ignore the dull ache. Lately, my feet have been killing me. Going to the shop and getting fitted again seems like a nightmare. A pang of irritation ripples through me—a broken-in pair of boots shouldn't be this uncomfortable.

"Alright, K.A.R.M.A.," I say, taking a deep breath. Expanding my focus feels overwhelming but I force myself back to the here and now. "Let's re-prioritize our targets and cast a wider net. I need you to perform introductory research into the other gangs. Get me starting points for key members."

"Understood, I will begin assembling information."

Tightening the last strap of my boots, I ignore how they pinch. My feet throb, but I shove it down, pushing myself off the bench. There's no time to dwell on it. I've got work to do.

CHAPTER 23

HOME – *Bedroom*
   March 04, 11:28 PST

WHAT DOES one wear to a food bank?

Xavier called to tell me about his volunteer work and asked if I'd like to come along. Since the kiss, we've managed to stay out of each other's way. I needed to clear my head, and realign myself. His kisses are distracting, stirring up feelings I thought I'd buried. I believed I'd never encounter another person who could make my mind spin again. Though it's true, there's no one new, just the same old Xavier.

It was inevitable that he would bring up that night, but what I didn't expect was my own impulsive kiss. I wanted to show him I wasn't as fragile as he thought. Now, I'm stuck with the memory of his lips, the warmth of his hands.

Agreeing to join Xavier's volunteer work seemed like a good distraction—something to keep me occupied that didn't involve alley fistfights. He promised it would be fun, yet part of me still considers blocking his number, maybe even moving to a different city again.

Now, I'm standing in front of my closet, wrestling with the simple decision of what to wear. If Jessica were here, she'd have the perfect outfit picked out in seconds. She always had a knack for that, making sure I looked my best for any occasion.

I settled for denim pants and a black Tupac graphic tee. My hair takes a long time to tame, and I'm nearly covered in sweat by the time I've bound it into an updo with two coiled strands falling at the corner of my face. I'm almost out the door, putting on my lip gloss as my phone rings.

Grabbing my small bag, I hurry out of the building. Xavier leans on the hood of a shiny black car when I step out.

"Hey," he greets and stands straight. I wonder what the right way of greeting the man you've ravished in a kiss is, but I'm not given a chance to think too much about it when he envelops me in a small hug.

"You have a car," I say when he releases me.

"Of course I have a car, Miss Big Shot. You aren't in New York anymore. It's L.A., baby," Xavier says with jazzy hands before opening the door for me. I get into the car and watch him turn around, and my heart hammers a little at the familiarity of it all. It takes noticeable effort to force my mind away from the tragedy even though I'm hyper-aware and listening for sounds. I breathe easy when Xavier steps into the car. Safe and sound.

I manage to put on my seatbelt, grateful my hands aren't shaking. I don't think I'd be able to handle it if they shook. Until now, I thought I had dealt with Jayden's death. Or at least I thought I could get into a car with another person without freaking out. With Xavier returning, it shows me just how wrong I was.

"Are you ready?" I nod, and he starts the car, merging onto the road.

"What's the organization about?" I ask, trying to spark a conversation.

"We try to provide food for those who can't afford it," Xavier explains. "We also pay for school fees sometimes and healthcare if we have enough sponsors. I joined not too long ago, and it's been the most fulfilling thing I've done in a while. Today, the people we're visiting are going through a really tough time. I mean really rough. Most of the adults are heavily dependent on drugs, and more than half of the youth either sell drugs or resort to prostitution.

"We can't change the situation overnight, but we want to make a difference. The plan is to start with food, then hopefully build a school and provide permanent access to healthcare.

"It might not work, but we can try. Maybe when basic necessities are provided, they'll stop making harmful choices."

I've heard people talk about the beauty of watching someone discuss their passion, and for the first time, I truly get it. Xavier, even with his solemn expression, speaks with conviction. I can tell this community is at its worst; if there's one thing I understand, it's being at your lowest.

I think about it now; if my mother had some of these things available, would her addiction have gotten to the state it did? Would mine have? There's no way of telling, and it doesn't make sense to play shoulda, woulda, coulda now.

"I think it's amazing that you're doing this. I know it can't be easy."

Xavier spares me a look and smiles at me. "I'm glad you're coming with me. We aren't going to just serve food. There'll be a lot of fun games." He looks proud of this announcement, and I find myself laughing at the look on his face, but Xavier doesn't seem to care. "You look very pretty when you smile."

His eyes on me don't feel burdensome. He doesn't look at me with lust. I've seen it in enough men's eyes to know.

"Shut up and drive." I shove him lightly to hide my blush.

He shrugs me off. "Hey, I will pull this car over. Keep your hands to yourself."

There are people already setting things up when we arrive. I notice that his dark navy-blue shirt is actually a uniform and not an outfit choice. I see the logo of what looks like an embroidered dove on the left sleeve of every shirt in white.

Xavier leads the way, weaving between tables stacked high with produce and non-perishables. He gestures toward a group of volunteers, smiling warmly.

"Everyone! This is Winter, my childhood friend," he says, his voice full of pride.

I step forward, offering a handshake to each person. "Hi, it's nice to meet you all," I say, trying to match Xavier's enthusiasm. But even I am not that good of an actress. "I hear you're doing amazing work here."

They smile back, nodding in acknowledgment. "Thanks, Winter. We're glad to have you with us," says one of the volunteers, her face bright with sincerity.

As we continue our introductions, I catch myself wondering how I would introduce Xavier if the roles were reversed. Childhood friend? It's strange that I've never defined it in my mind, but he's right.

"Alright, folks, we've got a lot to get through today," the coordinator calls out. "Let's keep things moving smoothly. Winter, Xavier, you two handle the veggies. Make sure everything is bagged properly."

We nod in unison and turn to the pile of boxes at our feet. Xavier reaches for the nearest one, pulling out an eggplant that makes him pause, a smirk forming on his lips.

"Is it just me, or does this look a bit... suggestive?" he asks, holding up an abnormally large eggplant.

I shake my head. "Do boys ever get over pointing out things that look like penises?"

Xavier chuckles, placing the vegetable into a bag. "Not really, I'm afraid."

As we work, our hands brush occasionally, a comfortable rhythm developing between us. The pile of vegetables slowly dwindles, replaced by neatly packed bags ready for distribution.

"Hey, Winter," Xavier says, his tone turning more serious as he places a yellow squash into a bag. "I'm really glad we're doing this. It feels good to help out, give back, you know?"

I look up at him, our eyes meeting. "Yeah, it does," I agree softly. "It really puts things in perspective…"

The women with children show up first, and it reminds me of a time when things got so hard for us, we could barely afford anything; we were beneficiaries of such kindness. For my mother and I, the local kitchen a couple of blocks from where we lived came to our rescue. Sometimes, the kitchens gave out perishable groceries they didn't get to use that day, and sometimes, it was the food they didn't sell. On other days, it was both. It got us through some difficult times.

Xavier interacts with the community, wearing a smile so bright it warms my walled-up heart. He turns to look at me with another smile, different from the one he showed the locals. Xavier extends his arm toward me, and I make my way toward him.

With a puzzled expression, I grasp his hand. Xavier has a

serious look on his face when he demands, "Cornhole, you and me against Omari and Destiny."

I blink at him, momentarily thrown off by the sudden challenge, but three beanbags are shoved into my hands before I can even gather a response. "Wait, what—?"

"Come on, Winter!" Xavier is already jogging toward the makeshift field, where I assume Omari and Destiny are eagerly staking out their positions near the two wooden goal boards. They're bouncing on the balls of their feet, clearly pumped for this impromptu game.

Xavier motions toward me to follow, and I do as instructed at a more leisurely pace. "Didn't realize we were getting this serious," I mutter, but there's a lightness in my tone, something fun tugging at the corners of my mind. I don't remember the last time I just... played.

Omari, with his oversized jersey hanging off his small frame, holds up a hand. "You're going down, Xavier!"

Destiny, who can't be more than seven, giggles and adds, "Yeah! We're the champions!"

Xavier clutches his chest. "Oh, it's like that? Alright, you two are about to learn today!"

I'm standing beside Xavier now, watching the kids settle into their spots, and I can't stop the smile that spreads across my face. "You sure we're not gonna crush their little spirits?" I say, elbowing Xavier.

He leans down toward me, his voice low. "Nah, we'll go easy on them. Mostly." I can't help but roll my eyes.

"Are you two boyfriend and girlfriend?" Destiny asks as I get ready to throw the first shot, halting mid-swing. From the corner of my eye, I see Xavier's face flash red.

"Um, no, we're not dating," he says, his voice almost an octave higher than usual as he tries to keep his composure. "Winter's just a... friend."

"But why not?" the little boy chimes in, his curiosity unfiltered in that way kids have of getting straight to the point.

Xavier shifts his weight from one foot to the other, and I see him searching for a response as if looking for a safe place to land. "Well... Winter and I are just hanging out. We haven't seen each other in years, and she might have something else going on. She could be taken already."

"Ooooooo, Winter has a boyfriend," Destiny teases.

The beanbag slips a little in my hand as the words tumble out before I can restrain myself. "I'm not taken. I don't have a boyfriend."

He turns toward me, surprise flooding his face. Xavier studies me like he's trying to figure out what's really behind my words. "Wait, really? I thought you were with someone back in high school."

My fingers fumble over the rough fabric of the sack, nails scraping at the seams. "It... didn't work out," I say, trying to keep my voice steady. "But enough of this talk. We have a game to win, don't we?"

Xavier seems to catch on, offering me a small, understanding smile prior to moving aside to give me a clear sight of the board. "Right. Ladies first."

I get into position and take a deep breath before tossing the first one. It lands on the tip of the board. Not terrible, but not great. I catch Xavier's smirk out of the corner of my eye.

"Not bad, but let me show you how it's done," he says, stepping up with exaggerated confidence. He throws his beanbag, and it arcs perfectly through the air before landing squarely in the hole. Of course, he'd be annoyingly good at this.

Omari groans. "No fair! You're too good!"

Xavier winks at me. "Told you, kids. This is how winners play."

I shake my head, unable to hide how easily I'm slipping into this. The wholesome banter, the light competition.

Omari, ever the trickster, tries to get in my head. "Hey, Winter! Watch this!" he shouts, breaking into the most absurd dance I've seen all day. His limbs flail wildly, moving with absolutely no rhythm, but with all the delusion in the world. It's almost impressive.

I fight a smile, watching him from the corner of my vision. "That's your secret weapon?" I ask, lining up my shot.

Omari grins, clearly thinking he's got me distracted. "Yep! You can't resist it!"

Xavier's watching the whole scene with a smile of his own. "He's really going for it," he says, shaking his head.

I aim carefully. Despite Omari's best efforts to throw me off, the bag lands perfectly on the board and slides into the hole.

"Seriously?!" He stops mid-dance. "No way! I was doing my best moves!"

"Your moves were solid, Omari. But not enough to stop me."

"You weren't supposed to make that!" he complains, stomping his feet. He crosses his arms, glaring at the board like it's the real culprit.

Xavier steps over, giving Omari a pat on the back. "Better luck next time, kid. Winter's great at everything she puts her hands on."

Omari whines dramatically, "I don't want to play anymore. You two don't play fair."

I raise an eyebrow, holding back a laugh. "Maybe you need a new strategy."

The boy throws his hands up in surrender, walking away with inflated defeat. "Whatever, you cheated. I'm telling Destiny."

I meet Xavier's eyes, and he mockingly rolls them at me, a playful glint in his expression. "Kids these days."

When Destiny tosses her beanbag, it skids across the board before falling off the edge. "This game is rigged!" She pouts.

"Rigged?" I say, walking over to her and crouching down to her level. "Nah, you just need a secret technique." I lean in, whispering like I'm about to share the world's biggest secret. "When you throw, picture it already going in the hole. Like magic."

Destiny's eyes light up. "Magic?"

"Yep. It's all in the mind. You have to believe it first."

She giggles and tries again, her tiny hands gripping the sack tightly. This time, it lands on the board. Not in the hole, but close enough that she jumps up and down with glee. Her celebration is cut short when Xavier zooms past, chasing Omari with a beanbag after he catapulted one in his face.

He's so great with kids. I swallow the thought quickly, not wanting to dwell on it. But it lingers in the back of my mind as the game winds down. There's a rare sense of ease in the air, and I find myself enjoying the simplicity, the laughter, and the shared moments. Xavier's arm touching mine when he hands me a beanbag, Destiny's squeals of excitement, Omari's noteworthy protests when he misses a shot. Xavier throws the final bag and wins the game (to no one's surprise), causing Omari and Destiny to pitch a fit. They quickly get over it, running off to find something else to do.

As the kids jet away, Xavier and I stand side by side. He's grinning like a complete idiot, his eyes soft as they follow Omari and Destiny. My hand drifts down to my stomach, and I wonder what it could be like to have a normal life. A life not as a vigilante.

CHAPTER 24

HOME – *Living Room*
   March 09, 18:46 PDT

I SURVEY THE AREA, making sure everything is in order. I've paced the entire apartment from the living room to the kitchen, then to my bedroom, hoping to find some distraction before Xavier arrives. The place is spotless, the cleanest it's been in a while. I wonder what will catch his eye first when he steps inside. Whatever it is, I hope it makes our interaction interesting rather than awkward.

With midterms approaching, inviting him over for a study session made sense. He didn't hesitate to accept the idea. I have a stack of books on the dining table, my back-pack slung over one of the chairs. Snacks are neatly arranged —fruits, chips, nuts, juice, and water. My coffee brewer is ready, and Xavier promised to bring lattes and baked goodies.

It almost feels like we're meeting up to eat rather than study. The thought makes me chuckle despite the nervousness in my stomach. I tell myself not to worry too much; I've been to his place, so it's natural for him to visit mine.

I catch myself wondering if I'll kiss him again today. It's been hard to keep my hands to myself, and although I've assured him I'm no longer shaken about what happened, Xavier has been cautious, never going further than staring at my lips. If more kissing is to happen, or anything else, I need to initiate it.

A white crop top clings to my body. Skipping the bra was tempting, but I decided against it. It would've been too much for what I'm trying to achieve here. My boobs are the fullest they've ever been. They'll be hard to miss. The top I've chosen showcases my abs, or at least what's left of them. I look slightly bloated, and I'm hoping it goes unnoticed.

The doorbell rings, making my heart race. I take a final glance around the living room, trying to look casual as I walk to the door and open it. *Xavier looks like sin.* I swallow hard before smiling.

"Hey," Xavier says, and I don't pretend to not notice the way his eyes sweep over my body.

"Hey," I say, my voice a bit breathless. Xavier, ever the gentleman, pretends not to notice. I step aside to let him in and shut the door. He's holding a coffee holder with two cups and a brown paper bag. "Here, let me take that." I grab the items from him.

"Dope TV."

"Thanks. Tech is my only splurge category besides food." I offer a nervous laugh.

He looks around, noticing the bare walls. "You haven't lived here long?"

"Is nine months long?" I hand him his cup.

"Not a huge fan of decor then?"

I shrug my shoulders. When you move a lot, decorations

just become another box that you have to pack up and drag around.

"Well," Xavier says, "It looks lovely." I don't share the sentiments, but smile like I appreciate the compliment. "Hey, are you going somewhere?" He points to my gym duffel bag in the corner near the door. He stumbles. "Sorry, it's none of my business. I was just wondering with spring break coming up."

"It's all good, Xavier. That's just my gym bag. Honestly, I was just going to stay in L.A. for the break. I have a lot of things to catch up on outside of school."

"Well," he starts, "I'll also be in town too. Although, I think ours is a week after yours, but we should hang out. Assuming you get some free time on your hands."

"Let's do it." I clasp my hands. "So, I've set everything up on the table; is there anything you want to focus on?" I say and begin walking.

"Just some research, confirming lab results. You?" Xavier follows me to the dining table.

"Software Development Process. I need to build an app or whatever." I sit across from him. "Study for an hour, then take twenty-minute breaks?"

"How do you usually study?"

"I just get in a zone until I need a break. I usually never remember to take one."

"Same applies to me. We'll just work until whenever," Xavier says, and I nod.

"I almost forgot the snacks," I say, hurrying to the kitchen to grab everything I've set out.

Xavier's eyes widen and his jaw drops. "Wow, did you leave any food at the store for anyone else?"

"I wasn't sure what you liked."

"Thanks. This is great."

I smile shyly and take my seat. "We shall begin."

Xavier laughs but opens his notebook. "Yes, ma'am."

The only problem is, I can't begin. I try to get into my work, but my eyes keep flitting to Xavier, who seems to have no trouble concentrating. He's focused, erasing and rewriting notes with a precision that mesmerizes me. His black sleeves cling to his biceps, contrasting perfectly with his sandy brown skin. His glasses, perched on his nose, catch the light as he occasionally adjusts them with a tap of his pencil or a push of his finger. He runs a hand through his mousse-styled locks, and I suppress a groan, throwing my head back in frustration.

I don't want to distract him, but it's his fault I can't focus. All I want is to sit on his lap and have him devour me. I reach for the snacks, grab a slice of apple, and toss it into my mouth, chewing half-heartedly. Xavier reaches into the bowl and grabs a strawberry, and I know for a fact I won't be able to survive it. As he takes a bite, his lips encompassing the berry, I squeeze my legs together, feeling a tightness in my stomach I didn't know could be caused by someone simply eating fruit.

He takes another bite. "Xavier," I breathe, and he looks up at me, and I feel my heart-rate speed up. His lashes are the longest and prettiest things I've seen.

"Something you don't understand?"

There's a lot I don't understand, yet none of it has to do with school. I nod, and Xavier slips out of his seat, coming over to me. He glances at the notes I have in front of me and then at the empty text editor, which should contain the code I'm supposed to be writing.

"You haven't written anything," he says, as if I'm unaware.

"I don't know what to write in this situation."

Xavier frowns, his brows pulling together in a way that

makes me grip the underside of the table. He's driving me insane and doesn't even realize he's doing it.

"What part is difficult for you? Maybe you can bounce some ideas off of me. I'll do what I can, but I'm no computer nerd like you." He smiles at his own joke.

I hear his words but don't register them. When I don't reply, he looks down at me, and I lose control. Rising from my seat, I grab his face with both hands and press my lips to his. The pencil he's holding drops to the ground as one of his hands finds my waist and the other cradles my face. He keeps the kiss chaste, which only frustrates me more. I press closer, trying to deepen the kiss, but he doesn't open his mouth.

"Do you not want this?" I ask, not bothering to hide the frustration in my tone.

"I really want to," Xavier says, tugging at a strand of my hair. "But do you want to? That's what I really need to know."

"Are you kidding me? I'm not the one stopping anything. I told you, you need to stop treating me like I'm still a high schooler. I'm a grown-ass woman, Xavier."

He opens his mouth to respond, but I don't let any words fall out. I'm not interested in them, not even remotely. I take the chance of his mouth being open and slip my tongue in. He lets out a groan that I expertly swallow. His arms tighten around my waist, and then he lifts me and drops me onto the dining table. When I bought it, this is the last thing I imagined happening there. Xavier settles himself in between my legs, and I find it impressive he doesn't break the kiss the entire time.

I feel his erection against me, and I grind into him. The contact makes me whimper and drags a grunt from him. Suddenly, I feel like there's too much space between us. Xavier comes up for air to nibble on my neck. I tilt my head to give him more access, which is more than I've ever allowed anyone. He's kissing slowly, his tongue licking along as he goes. I notice finally that his hands are still resting on my thighs, squeezing lightly, but never going further than that.

"You can touch me, Xavier. I want you to touch me." I bring his hand above my waist, where my bare skin is visible, and press it there.

It's all the confirmation he needs. His hand slips underneath my top, and I lift my hands up as he tugs the shirt off me. My bra follows next. Xavier kisses me again, deep and short before dropping his mouth to my nipple. The heat has me arching my back up to meet him. His other hand kneads the breast that doesn't have his lips, and I'm overwhelmed by his thoroughness. I want him everywhere.

For the longest time, everything before this had been almost transactional. We were just looking for someone to fulfill our lust and get it over with. But Xavier is different. He's attentive.

The button of my shorts falls open, and Xavier grips my thigh even tighter as he switches nipples. My moans are climbing higher, and I question for the first time if the walls are soundproof. They don't seem like they are, and I wonder how my neighbors would react to my exclamations filling the air. I don't intend to be quiet, and if I'm being honest, I don't think I'd be able to.

I pull Xavier's shirt off and shove his pants down. He steps away from me to remove his boxers. And his dick is something to write home about. It stands nearly erect, and the tip of it glistens. I sink to my knees and crawl over to him. He looks down at me, his expression dark. I maintain eye contact as I kiss up his thighs.

He twitches when I wrap my lips around him. "Fuck,

baby." The term of endearment warms me, and I'm deter-mined to impress. I suck him expertly.

My head tilts back as his grip tightens and he thrusts into my mouth. The action seems like it was unintentional because he freezes. His entire length is buried down my throat. I gag around him and look up into his eyes.

"You look so sexy," he praises me and gathers my hair into his hands. "Squeeze my thighs if it gets too much for you."

Xavier pulls out slowly, and I cough. I nod in understand-ing, giving him permission to take my mouth. I hold onto his waist as his grip on my hair tightens with each oscillation.

He eventually retreats from my mouth, and I whine at the loss. Bringing me to my feet, he kisses me, sucking on my tongue.

"That was the hottest thing that has ever happened to me. Now, it's my turn." Xavier says while he picks me up and drops me back on the table. "You have no idea how long I've thought about this," he falls to his knees in front of me. "Touching you, kissing you, fucking you. I want to make you feel good."

He shoves my legs apart and trails kisses up my thighs. When he gets to my mound, he growls before burying his face into it. My hips buck as I press further toward him.

Xavier runs his tongue along my lips and sucks on my clit. A sob falls from my mouth, and my hand finds his hair, and I tangle it. He sucks and laps at me like a crazed man, and I'm no saner than he is. I squirm, wanting so much and getting too much all at the same time.

"Xavier," I plead and try to pull him off. The feeling is good, but I don't want his tongue, what I need is him. I just want him to bend me. Every which way.

Finally, Xavier is pliant and comes up easily. When I kiss

him, I reach down, positioning him in front of my entrance. I place my forehead on his and, for a while, we do nothing but share breaths. I can feel a sob coming, and I try hard to push it back.

It's just sex. But it doesn't feel like it is anymore. This doesn't feel like we're trying to quell an itch.

"Are you okay?" Xavier asks. "We can stop."

I shake my head quickly. I want this; I just didn't factor in how intimate the act would be. I expected it to be like every other time, but its not and I can't wrap my head around it. I'm aware of everything, like his tip hovering over my opening. If I pull him any closer, he'll slide in with ease because I know I'm wet enough for that. So, I do.

Xavier groans and drops his head onto my shoulder, and I feel him everywhere. I bury my face into his chest. I want him so much, it amazes me.

"Xavier," I say. I'm not entirely sure what it is I'm asking for, but I'm certain that if he doesn't move, I'm going to lose what's left of my sanity, and it won't be in a pretty way.

"What do you need, baby?" he says, defaulting to an affectionate nickname. I don't mind. All it does is make me squirm, and when I do, I feel his fullness.

"Fuck me, please," I breathe out.

CHAPTER 25

HOME – *Lair*
  March 18, 20:03 PDT

I DECIDED to take a different approach to Jessica's drive. Standard methods aren't cutting it, so I start thinking outside the box. I rule out the possibility that Jessica was a better cryptographer than the brightest minds in the field. Then I get to thinking, she was a music theory major. Maybe the key is a song? I had K.A.R.M.A. run an algorithm on every album from each artist displayed on her bedroom walls. No hits.

Pulling the last trick up my sleeve, I say, "K.A.R.M.A., expand the search to include Allen Glory's record label."

K.A.R.M.A. displays an album cover on my desktop showing a preteen Jessica hugging her dad. "One potential match detected with a confidence level of seventy-one percent. "Lost Child," an unsuccessful Allen Glory single released eight years ago featuring Jessica as the composer. It only sold 5,000 copies worldwide."

"Try it and see if it works, K.A.R.M.A."

"I must caution you, ma'am. Only two tries remain before the drive is completely wiped."

"I know, K.A.R.M.A., but we're running out of options. Do as you're told." I release a sigh of relief as ACCESS GRANTED is displayed across my screen.

"What am I looking at, K.A.R.M.A.?"

"I am able to decipher names, addresses, photographs, and shipping routes for what appears to be in relation to multiple drug cartels. I want to highlight the presence of a surprisingly detailed spreadsheet that seems to be of all the drug transactions she's had." A spreadsheet jumps across my monitor.

I notice something interesting about the data. The last few rows in the payment column are empty. If I know something about drug dealers, they don't care who you are; they only care that when they give you the product, you're slipping them their money.

My eyes zero in on the sheet. If I understand the file correctly, and I do, Jessica isn't the middleman for just one supplier. There are three drug gangs listed, and I can't imagine any of them are nice. The only ones I recognize are the Omega Outlaws. What the hell was she thinking? Dealing with three of them was already enough to put a mark on your neck, but missing payment for not just one, but all three of them was, dare I say, suicidal?

I'll never understand why she sold drugs when she was already well-off. With a father who's a Grammy-winning music legend and a mother who's won Emmys, Jessica grew up in a world where privilege was handed to her on a silver platter. She wasn't quite a child actor, but lived a lifestyle close to one—hobnobbing with L.A.'s elite, guest appearances at exclusive events, paparazzi flashes outside upscale restaurants. She had access to every luxury most people could only dream of. And maybe that was the problem. Because the more I think about it, the less it makes sense.

She had a bit of a wild streak before college: her name sprinkled throughout the tabloids for little stunts such as getting caught sneaking into VIP areas, underage drinking, and one particularly famous story of her "borrowing" a Ferrari just to "see what it felt like to drive one." It was the kind of trouble that comes with having too much too young and not knowing what to do with it.

Maybe she was chasing a high, trying to escape her routined and privileged life. Or maybe Jessica just wanted to do something that wasn't defined by who her parents were. To be something other than the daughter of Allen and Charlotte Glory. But it doesn't change the fact that she's dead. And one of these gangs most likely had something to do with it.

Let's bust a cartel. If things go right, I'll be a step closer to solving her murder.

"K.A.R.M.A., which of the three gangs has the lowest profit margin?"

"The Serpents, ma'am."

COMPTON – *Serpent Warehouse*
   March 24, 22:36 PDT

THE SERPENTS OPERATE out of the edge of South L.A., making them prime suspects in Jessica's murder. Their profits have been dwindling, especially if Jessica was missing payments for the drugs she was dealing. After some digging, I tracked their base of operations to a rundown warehouse near the harbor.

The warehouse is hidden in plain sight, nestled in a busy

area. I've scouted the location, hoping to find a way in. Locals swarm the area, and unless you know what you're looking for, you'd overlook the nondescript pharmacy on the corner. It looks auspicious, almost run down. The type of place you wouldn't give a second thought to.

For five days, I've watched the pharmacy. Only four people have entered or exited, and the only way in or out of the warehouse seems to be through that store. It should be easy enough to slip in there and get the drugs I need, testing them against the heroin found in Jessica's bloodstream. As of yesterday, her death was officially declared a murder investigation. Detective Gillian appealed to have a case opened after the medical examiners in Sacramento found enough marks on her body to prove foul play. It's about time the LAPD caught up to what I've known for months.

The man running the pharmacy is small, bald, and bespectacled. He sits in a suit, reading a newspaper, barely acknowledging the men who come and go. Someone else replaces him whenever he needs a break or does things men do. The entrance is not left unattended for long.

Finally, my patience pays off. The new guy covering for the old man is inattentive. He steps out almost immediately after taking over. Seizing my chance, I rush to the store and slip in, heading toward the back like I've seen the others do. A long, dingy corridor with ripped leather curtains greets me. They hang around like ghosts. I push them to the side, ignoring the moldy smell that clings to the air. It's nauseating.

The fluorescent lights keep blinking in and out. I don't pay mind to them; I focus on the hall in front of me. If I want to go far, I need to find a way to make sure I don't get caught as soon as I make it to the other end of the hall.

Will they have someone posted there? I start to feel uneasy. I see the other side and realize just how exposed it is.

I press myself to the walls, and hope that by the time I approach that point, the light will blink out. I just need a second to be able to get in without attention.

When I get close enough. I wait for the light to blink out. It does, and I don't waste another second. I make a break for it, careful not to put my weight on my feet.

Mounds of pallets fill the edges of the room. I run up to the closest one for cover and inch forward. Toward the center of the warehouse, from the corner of my eyes, I see the women responsible for packaging the drugs. They're wearing only their underwear. I'm positive the outfit choice has more to do with preventing stolen merchandise than the view.

I do an initial scan of the room to check that the coast is clear before I make my way over to where the drugs are lined up, jumping from pallet to pallet. I don't intend to start anything. This should be a quick job, in and out.

"Hey!" someone yells behind me. I freeze for a second, cursing under my breath. I was never the best when it came to stealth. I turn around to find a slender man walking over to me with his gun pulled out.

"Who are you?" he asks, and I roll my eyes even though he can't see me. My mask only allows him to see my lips, which are frowning now.

Instead of replying to the question, I charge toward him and slide down. He pulls the trigger and I don't think he had a target in mind because I manage to dodge every shot he dispenses at me. I blow him in the throat, and he drops the gun to clutch his neck. I grab the weapon and pistol-whip him.

I hear distant footsteps and yelling, and I groan. This was supposed to be a simple mission. I didn't want any problems, but here we are. With the gun in front of me, I step as carefully as I can forward. The shadows of the men who have come to find out what's happening grow larger. I go in the opposite direction of their silhouettes, pistol first, around each corner.

Suddenly, a strike to my hand knocks the gun to the ground, and I'm roughly pulled out into the open. Something hits my stomach, and a stab of pain rushes throughout my body.

The baby. When the next strike comes, I move out of the way, my instincts kicking in. I focus on the man in front of me, but more men join him, and they're all holding bats in their hands. I feel horribly outnumbered. There are way more than I anticipated, almost a whopping ten more. There's no way I can take them all on. I didn't prepare for a fight. I don't have the right gear. *I need to get the hell out of here.*

I just wish it didn't take a situation like the one I'm facing now to consider that I might actually want to be a mother.

The man directly in front of me is tall with a scar on his left cheek. He smiles with a twist to his lips, and I know I'm properly screwed. He charges toward me, and I move to the side when he brings his bat down and punch him square in the nose. He stumbles back, but I fail to dodge the strike on my back. I collapse to the floor, managing to roll away in the nick of time before an offender brings his bat down on me. I fall back only to regain my balance and receive a blow to my face.

"You should pay close attention to your surroundings," my *sensei says and delivers a punch to my jaw.*

The punch is reflected in the hit I take from the man in front of me. A few chuckles are let out around me as I struggle to my feet, the same way I did back when I trained. I try to pay attention to my surroundings like I was instructed, but all I'm met with is unsteady vision.

Another punch and my sensei huffs. "Your opponent will never wait for you to recover. You need to find a way to get to them. One window of opportunity is all you need."

A window of opportunity seems unattainable now, so I let the men hit me, and I stagger back until another hit forces me onto the table where the drugs are kept. In the midst of scrambling to my feet, I sneak two packs into my jacket because I refuse to let this fight be in vain.

My head aches, and I try not to think about it too much. I'm vaguely aware of the blood dripping from the side of my face. This is starting to feel like an unfair fight.

My stomach turns, and I heave out a breath. Fear starts to mix in with the pain. *What if something happened to the baby?* I shake the thought out of my head. I can't worry about a baby if I'm dead. I need to leave this warehouse alive.

I get hit in the gut again, causing me to wobble around disoriented as another bat swing to my back sends me forward. I feel like I'm crumbling. I need to think of a way out of here.

"You keep thinking of what to do. As a vigilante, you should be anticipating and reacting while you fight," my sensei says, *punching my gut. "You're still thinking. Get out of your head, and you might find a way out. You say you don't want to feel power-less? You need to get out of your head. You need to get up."*

Feet are raining down on me, they're taunting me. It's all fun and games to them.

"Enough!" silences the room and turns the heads of all my attackers.

Now's my chance. I reach into my belt and deploy a smoke bomb I've been developing, patent pending.

With everything in me, I rise to my feet and push past the two standing in front of me. My whole body aches, but I don't stop.

I pass by the old man in the store and run down the street,

taking a corner and disappearing into the darkness of the alley. My heart thuds, and I struggle not to pay attention to the stabbing pain in my abdomen. I need to get off the streets as quickly as possible. I do my best to prevent being tailed, but tonight, I don't have it in me for my usual thoroughness.

Stumbling into my apartment, I head for the bathroom, barely able to keep myself up. I turn on the shower and begin removing my suit in front of the mirror and let out a wail from the pain. A cry breaks out of my mouth as I shrug my jacket off and throw it to the side. My entire rib cage is on fire and heavily bruised. I'm sure I have at least three to four broken ribs.

I get into the shower and drop to my knees. The pain in my stomach is shearing, but there's nothing I can do. It's too late. My blood washes away, down the drain. I'm so tired that all I can do is watch it flow and push.

CHAPTER 26

March 26, 15:11 PDT

LIMPING into the dimly lit space, I feel colder than usual. I drop the assortment of drugs onto my workstation and with a sigh; I open the first package. A brick of cocaine, the white powder pristine and ominous. Carefully, I extract a small sample using a sterile tool and place it into the testing machine. The device hums as the screens around me spring to life.

Next, I turn to the heroin, its dark, compact form a strong contrast from the cocaine. I cut a sample, my hands unsteady, and add it to the second machine. The lab instruments whir as they begin their analysis, filling in the hollow silence.

"K.A.R.M.A., start running the initial tests on these."

"Ma'am, based on your vitals from the other night, you should be taking it easy. Your body needs time to heal."

"I don't have time to take it easy, K.A.R.M.A.," I snap, immediately regretting my harshness. I programmed her to care after all. "Sorry. Just... let's get this done. Begin testing both samples."

"Understood. Initiating tests," K.A.R.M.A. replies. I sit back and watch the process. The machines work methodically, breaking down the compounds and analyzing the chemical structures. I watch the white powder circulate through the device.

"K.A.R.M.A., can you confirm if the heroin is a match for the one in Jessica's system?" I ask, needing the distraction. I can't let myself think about it. Not now.

"Unfortunately, I cannot confirm with complete certainty. The preliminary results are inconclusive without further analysis. I can confirm the cocaine is pure and unlaced. And the heroin is of high quality," K.A.R.M.A. responds, her tone almost apologetic.

I wince, running a hand through my hair. "Looks like we need outside help. K.A.R.M.A., call Thorne." Every favor I ask of him causes me to slip further into a world I'm supposed to stop. Thorne's not someone I reach out to lightly, but desperate times and all that. What's yin without a little yang?

The phone rings twice before he picks up. "Snow." Thorne's voice is smooth, almost too smooth. "Twice in a quarter. It must be my lucky day. What can I do for you?"

"I need a favor," I say, cutting to the chase. "I've got some drugs here that I need analyzed. Can you get me in touch with someone who can confirm if they match the ones found in an autopsy?"

"I might know a guy. But you'll owe me for this."

"Fine," I say, too tired to argue. He's my best chance at keeping the investigation from slipping through my fingers. "Add it to my tab. Just get me the contact."

"I thought you would protest more to the favor, but

consider it done," he replies, a hint of satisfaction in his voice. "I'll send over a courier shortly to pick up the samples."

I hang up and lean heavily against the table, closing my eyes for a moment. The machines continue their work, the rhythmic sounds almost soothing.

K.A.R.M.A.'s voice pierces the quiet. "Ma'am, please take care of yourself. You're no good to anyone if you're not at your best."

"I know," I whisper, opening my eyes, exhaustion tugging at me. "But right now, I need to be doing something."

CHAPTER 27

THE DOOR CREAKS OPEN, and I step inside. As I cross the threshold, I see an envelope, stark cream against the dark floor. I bend down and pick it up, recognizing Thorne's flamboyant handwriting immediately.

I tear open the envelope and unfold the letter, my eyes scanning the text. It's the results of the heroin test. *Not a match.*

Frustration bubbles up inside me, a knot developing in my chest. I crumple the paper in my fist, the edges digging into my palm. Another dead end. My eyes instinctively land on my workstation, where the test samples lie.

IT TAKES LESS than a minute for the door to fly open, and I don't give him time to say anything. I throw myself on him and slot our lips together. A squeak of surprise escapes him, but he wraps an arm around my waist and pulls me closer. The movement makes me let out a sharp exhale. I guess my ribs aren't fully healed yet. Thankfully, I don't think he's noticed. I've been dodging his calls for weeks, and deep down, I know I can't stay brooding alone in my basement forever.

The door slams shut. Xavier's mouth is still on mine, shoving his tongue down my throat. He squeezes my waist, and it's a bruise that's still healing. I don't mean to, but I jump a little. Xavier pulls away from the kiss, and I try to bring him back. He doesn't budge.

I know what my face looks like. The bruises on my lips are fading, but the purple is still visible. I have a cut on my left brow and a few other bruises that are trying their hardest to heal.

Xavier frowns, and I can sense anger in his eyes. "Did someone hurt you? What happened to you? Who did this to you?"

"Whoa, sir, calm down. It was nothing serious. Just a workout hazard."

"Workout hazard?" He asks, and I nod quickly and try to kiss him again, but instead shuffles away from my reach, and I huff in frustration.

"Someone hit you this badly during a workout?"

"Yes, I was sparring at the gym. You're going to get hit when you box," I say with enough conviction and a frown on my face.

Xavier comes to stand before me. He tugs at the hem of my shirt, and I bite my lower lip but lift my hands up for him. The shirt comes off quickly. I scoff, still letting him do whatever he wants. I've stared at my stomach more times than he could dare to cover today. The first time after that night was the hardest. I had all sorts of marks. The bat marks, the boot marks, I looked a sight. Now, some of the physical welts have faded away.

Flames in his eyes, Xavier's fingers trail over the inflamed areas, pressing in lightly on more than one and gauging my reaction. If I wanted to get examined, I'd have gone to the hospital.

"Xavier," I say again and force his face up to look at me. "I am fine."

"Have you seen a doctor?"

I nod. "I have, and they say there's nothing to worry about."

Other than the fact that I lost my child.

The confession hovers in the back of my mind, but I push it back. And the more I try not to think about it, the more adamant the thought becomes, forever etched into my memory.

"Are you sure?" he asks, his hand cupping my face.

"I am. Now, will you stop worrying so much about nothing and kiss me." I'm not about to burden him with that information. He never knew I was pregnant, so it doesn't make sense to mention it now.

Xavier chuckles lightly and brushes our lips together. When I whine, he kisses me hungrily. His tongue darts into my open mouth as one of his arms hoist me up. I wrap my legs around him, and between kisses he continues, "You've been MIA for the past few weeks."

I ignore him, holding onto his neck as he carries me away. This has become a routine of some sort, and I know where he's going before he even starts to make his way out of the living room. I know he's going to deposit me on his bed and take his shirt off in an artsy way that'll leave me stunned every time.

With finals approaching, it's only natural we find the same comfort we provided each other during midterm season. After our first "study date," we decided to keep things casual. It works out fine. I'm over at his place some days, and he's over at my place some days. But we know what we are, friends with benefits. I don't have the time or energy to be falling in love right now. I think he felt the same way because he didn't protest the idea.

We haven't discussed the exclusivity of the agreement, but I don't show up at bars hoping to get railed in whatever secluded space I can find. There's something about Xavier I don't think I can get anywhere else. It's his softness that I try to refuse, and still, I'm surrounded by it. The way he pays attention to small details I don't think about. I don't remember anyone seeing me like that before.

Xavier hovers over me, and a giggle escapes me. "Hi."

He looks amused. "Hi."

And then we don't talk anymore. His mouth comes down on mine, and I forget everything.

HOME – *Living Room*
April 27, 13:23 PDT

THE COCAINE from the bust sits on my coffee table, and I'm trying to give myself a lot of reasons why it would be stupid if I was to snort any of it. I just stare at the package for a while.

I thought about seeing a therapist, but going to talk to someone about losing the baby in some way implied I cared about the existence of said child. The truth was I simply tried as hard as I could to not think about it. In a way, I believed if I ignored the pregnancy long enough, it would eventually work itself out. *I guess my wish came true.*

Xavier's kisses and touch were usually enough the past couple of weeks, but if he touches me in the state I'm in now, there's no telling what I'll do. I might not even jump his bones. I do suspect I'll cry my eyes out, and I don't want to cry anymore.

For over ten years I've been clean, but I can't help how I'm feeling now. For the life of me, I can't seem to crack Jessica's case, and Xavier and I are getting stupidly close for a friends-with-benefits situation. He's pieced together that something is up. I just keep claiming I'm fine. The truth is I am fine; I'm doing as okay as I can be in this situation. I still have all my vital organs, and it doesn't hurt every time I inhale or move, and the bruises on my face are healing nicely. So I guess I'm as right as rain.

I stand up sharply from the couch, pacing around the living room. I can take some, I rationalize; I simply need to take it in moderation. It's only cocaine, and the initial screenings K.A.R.M.A. ran show it's unaltered. I know how much is too much now. The idea makes sense, not the best one I've had, but it's still an idea. I don't need to take that much; I just need enough to calm me down. Just enough so I can focus on something else for a second. Anything else.

With enough conviction in my blood and shaky hands, I pull the encased package closer. My forehead sweats as I dump out a small quantity of the powder onto the table.

There's an anticipation in my veins that worries me. With a deep breath, I separate the substance into three different lines using an index card from my Information Security study set. I spend more time than necessary trying to make sure the lines are straight, and also to see if I'm going to snap out of it. But the itch to sniff overwhelms every other feeling, so I listen.

I bring my nose down to the first line and inhale it in one swift motion. The blood rushes to my head, and I feel everything all at once. The emptiness isn't gone, but it's dulled. And that'll just have to be enough.

My brain isn't running a million miles a minute. I no longer feel like I've lost something dear to me, and I no longer wonder about what would've happened if I didn't let my ego get the best of me and go inside that warehouse. It doesn't matter that I should've just let the police handle Jessica's case. Or that I have no business playing dress-up every night. All of that seems irrelevant.

CHAPTER 28

"WHAT'S the progress on Jessica's third gang, K.A.R.M.A.?"

"No updates, ma'am. I'm still following Black Syndicate transactions. But I do believe I'm close to narrowing down a few of their fronts in L.A." Data flows in front of me, revealing the various transactions. They seem to have a heavier footprint on the east side of town. Perhaps interrogating a Syndicate thug will clear up a few questions.

"Ma'am, you have an inbound call from Gina Washington. Would you like to answer?"

"Yes. Hey, Gina," I say, attempting to sound cheerful.

"Winter, sweetie! You were always a night owl. I figured I'd take the chance of calling."

"Is everything alright?" I absently brush a thin line of white together. My movements are deliberate, almost routine.

"Well," she continues, a hint of mischief in her tone, "I've been thinking that the family hasn't seen you in forever! Why don't you come visit us for the Fourth of July? It'll be good for you to get out of L.A. for a bit."

I hesitate, my eyes drifting to my cluttered workstation and murder board spread across the different screens. "I don't know. I've got a lot going on here right now."

She doesn't miss a beat. "Winter, you've been cooped up in that city for too long. A change of scenery might do you some good. And besides, we miss you. Come on, it'll be fun. Fireworks, barbecue, family... you need this."

I bite my lip. Maybe she's right. Maybe I do need to get out of L.A. to clear my head and gain a fresh perspective.

"Alright," I finally say as I lean forward, toward the table. "I'll visit for the Fourth."

"Oh, wonderful! I can't wait to see you, baby. It's been far too long," she says, her voice bright with excitement.

"Yeah, it has," I agree, taking a deep, swift inhale, leaving a sharp sting in the back of my throat. "I'll see you soon, Gina."

"Take care, sweetie. Safe travels," she replies before hanging up. I crouch toward my desk again.

"Ma'am, if you aren't busy, I've accessed the statement Chris Turner made to the police. Would you like to see the transcript of his interview?" K.A.R.M.A. announces.

"Why not?" I study the screen and wipe my nose, absorbing every detail. "It's about time I've done my due diligence and paid Chris an official visit," I say, standing up and grabbing my gear.

It's the dead of night when I arrive at the frat house. The quiet is almost oppressive. I slip inside, my movements silent and precise, making my way to Beta Alpha Psi's president's room. He's asleep, blissfully unaware of the storm about to hit.

"Christopher, wakey wakey." I yank him out of bed, my grip firm on his arm. "Rise and shine."

He startles awake, eyes wide with fear. He flails for a second, disoriented, while I drag him to the floor. "What—who are you?" he stammers.

"Immaterial," I say, dragging him onto the balcony. "And you know why I'm here." I push him against the railing, my eyes boring into his. "Jessica's dead, Chris. I need to know who her supplier was, or any information you forgot to mention to the police. Start talking."

"I don't know!" he pleads, his voice trembling. "I don't know anything about her supplier! I told the police everything I knew!"

"Sure you did." I roll my eyes, my patience thinning. "Let's start with an easy one then. How long had Jessica been selling drugs?"

His breath comes out in panicked bursts, and he sticks his hands up defensively, his eyes darting around like a trapped animal. "At least a year? Maybe more? I'm not sure. She was doing it when we started dating."

I shake my head, inching closer until there's barely a gap between us. "Tell me about that run-in she had a couple weeks before her death," I demand. "The one that had her terrified. Who was she afraid of?"

Chris's face pales, and he starts shaking. "She mentioned some guy... I don't know his name. She wouldn't tell me. She just said he was bad news and was following her."

"Where can I find him?" I loosen my grip, and if I release any more he will fall off the building.

"I don't know! I swear!" he cries, tears streaming down his face. "She mentioned a district... somewhere in East L.A. That's where she would go to do some of her drops. That's all I know, I swear!"

His fear is evident when the acrid smell of urine fills the air as he loses control, sobbing.

"Clean yourself up," I say coldly, taking a step back, releasing him on solid ground.

CHAPTER 29

XAVIER'S – *Front Door*
  June 22, 01:42 PDT

I STUMBLE AROUND, my body reeling from your non-traditional cocktail of coke and tequila. My thoughts are spiraling, and every movement feels like it's too fast and too slow all at once. The knock on his door sounds like thunder in my ears.

Xavier's eyes go wide as soon as he sees me. The shock is clear, but he masks it quickly. It's not that I don't come around; I do. It's just... I'm never like this. "Winter?" He says my name, the disbelief hanging there. "It's a bit late. Everything alright?"

"Perfect," I slur, forcing a smile that doesn't feel quite right on my face. "Can I come in, or are you just gonna leave me out here all night?"

He hesitates for a second but then steps aside, letting me through. "You look like you've had a night."

"Or a life," I mutter, heading straight for his couch and

flopping down, stretching out like I belong here. The cushion feels cool against my overheated skin, and I kick off my shoes, flinging them off to the side. My heart is racing, and I can't tell if it's the stimulant or the depressant. Maybe it's just being near Xavier which always does something weird to my pulse.

Xavier's standing there, unsure whether to sit or scold me, like he's trying to decide if he's supposed to play the concerned friend or just... let me be. He moves closer, sniffing the air, and I realize he can probably smell the bottle clinging to me. "You've been drinking," he says.

I shrug, avoiding his eyes. "It's been a difficult spring. Needed to take the edge off."

"Uh huh," he says, trying to keep his tone light, but I can hear the worry underneath. "How much have you had to drink tonight?"

"Enough." I toss my head back against the pillows, staring at the ceiling. The room tilts as I respond, "I don't want to talk about it. I came here to forget, not get a lecture."

Xavier lets out a slow breath, and I feel the couch sink as he sits down next to me. "Winter, what's going on? You're acting weirder than normal. This isn't like you."

I inch toward him, leaning in so close I can see the subtle flecks of brown in his eyes, the worry lines forming on his forehead. "I fear this is me," I say, my voice dropping faintly. "And you know why I'm here." I reach out to tug him by the shirt. "Let's... just have some fun. Forget everything else for a while."

He catches my hand. "No, Winter." The seriousness in his voice is enough to cut through some of the haze clouding my mind. "Not like this. You're wasted, and... whatever else you're on, it's not you."

"Why does it matter?" I snap. "You keep trying to 'save' me. But I don't want to be saved."

Xavier shakes his head, his grip on my wrist steady. "You're not thinking straight," he says softly. "And you're not going to feel better by doing... this. I'm not taking advantage of you when you're like this."

"Taking advantage?" I laugh, "I'm offering. You think I don't know what I want?"

"No, I think you don't know what you need right now. You can crash here tonight, but we're not sleeping together." His voice is gentle, but it feels like a slap. And he just sits there, solid as a rock while I'm spinning out of control. "Something must be wrong. Tell me what happened instead."

I yank my hand back from his, while he searches my face for something—an explanation maybe, a clue—but I... can't. Not with him staring at me like that. "Just... mommy issues. It's nothing," I mumble, shrugging like it's no big deal, like it isn't ripping me apart from the inside.

Xavier doesn't let it go. "Mommy issues?" he asks, raising an eyebrow. "What does that even mean?"

Evading his eyes, I focus instead on the fabric of the blanket draped beneath me, how it grazes my fingers. "My mother and I have a strained relationship, and I don't see it getting any better." I say, knowing that's the closest I'll get to being honest with him about this. It's the truth, but just half of it.

"Why can't it get better?" His voice is soft, and I hate that it's so understanding, like he can just pull the pain out of me.

"Can we just forget it?" I run my fingers through my hair, tugging at the knots as if the pain might distract me. "I'm not here to talk about her. I'm here because..." My voice fades, and I don't finish the thought. Because what? Because I wanted to forget? Because I wanted to bury myself in him and pretend, even if it was just for a second. That my real issue at the moment isn't with my mother? It's the fact that I'm not sure I'll ever be cut out to be one. *And I'm no better than her.*

Xavier watches me for a long moment, and I can feel his eyes trying to pull more out of me. But he doesn't press. He lets out a sigh, rubbing the back of his neck. "Okay," he says finally. "Get some sleep. I'll make breakfast in the morning."

I nod, grateful that he's letting it go but also hating how exposed I feel. I pull the blanket around my shoulders, hoping it can shield me from everything I'm wrestling with.

The sounds of Xavier moving around the room—the click of a light switch, the subtle shuffle of his footsteps—somehow make everything better. And as he disappears down the hall, I bury myself in the blanket, trying to quiet my mind. I find myself wishing I could just let someone in, let him in, and how impossible that feels.

CHAPTER 30

CALEDONIA, *Mississippi*
    July 04, 13:09 CDT

MY HOMETOWN IS a place that holds a lot of memories for me. The place where I was the happiest, and my life looked like it had so many possibilities. It's also the place that hurt me more than I thought I could endure.

I take a bus back home, leaning my head against the window, and watch the city and people roll by. Since moving away, I only went back home twice, but for my mother it never happened again. Apparently, it was too much for her to bear. The place made her too sad, and all she could think about was how Dad was never coming back. The loss, my mother said, was easier to bear when it wasn't staring you down at every corner. I believed we left because she didn't know how to live in a town with so much of my father and the absence of him.

It wasn't until later I learned the real reason—we left because she couldn't stand the pity. The endless advice on how to raise me, how to live, how to survive—it suffocated her. Affection, no matter how well-intended, can become a burden when overdone. At least, that's the explanation I try to feed myself whenever I think about everything I lost after moving away.

My mother wouldn't come with me, so she sends me off on my own because she doesn't want my aunts to keep accusing her of stealing me away from them. It's just for summer break, and I don't have anything else to do, so my mother lets me go with the promise that I'm going to come back.

I don't have any reason why I wouldn't, so I agree. Things were looking up for us. Mom had a new fancy job. I'm attending the same school in the fall. I just finished an amazing season as a freshman on the varsity basketball team. I'm finally starting to feel like I'm settled in for once.

I'm nervous about going back home, where I left without so much as a goodbye to all the people I care about. My thoughts drift to Jayden; is he okay? What if he's too angry at the way I left? Would he believe me if I said I had no idea we were leaving? That I came back to see we were already packed and ready to go? It didn't seem believable in the least, but it was the truth, my truth.

Aunt Gina is waiting for me at the bus station when I show up. I can see her even before we roll to a stop, and I watch her observe the bus to see if it's the one I'm in. She breaks into a smile the second I get off and run to her. Until I saw her reaction, I thought she didn't want me to come at all. Her arms open, and when I fly into them, my cheeks hurt from smiling too much. I realize I can't remember the last time my mother hugged me.

The thought comes as a shock to me, bringing with it tears that I didn't even know I needed to let out. Gina holds me through the cries, and I bury my face into her chest.

My mother is struggling, and it's killing me to see her suffer this much because I know that the reason she's being like this is because she wants to provide for me. I tell myself she's doing the best she can.

"I missed you so much," is all I can manage to say.

My aunt squeezes me even tighter. "I missed you the most, my love."

When I step out of the bus, Gina isn't there to welcome me this time, and I try to shake off the disappointment. I'm the one who refused her offer to pick me up because I wanted to take a look around while I walked to her house. She lives close enough to the bus station.

The town has changed since the last time I was here. The roads look better, and there seem to be more stores that offer more variety. The best thing about the town was the mall that went up when I was in fourth grade. It quickly became the hangout spot for most of the older kids. What were you even doing if you weren't going to the mall? Parks became outdated. If you wanted to see your friends or hangout with them, you better be making plans to meet them at the mall, which also came with an arcade. It was where I hung out with Jayden, his friends, and mine.

The mall is gone, I realize when I get there. It isn't gone gone—I mean, there's a shopping center there, but it isn't the one I know. I stand for a few minutes trying to put the new structure in my head, and I compare all the ways it's different. This one is bigger for sure, and it looks more appealing. There are a lot of people going in and out, but my eyes zero in on a group. They're messing around amongst themselves, and one of them is walking backward, telling a joke that's making everyone lose their minds. Two kids from the pack remind me of Jayden and I. They're stealing glances at each other whenever they laugh, and then eyes are being diverted.

"Winter," someone calls out to me, and I raise my head to

find a friend of Gina's, Mrs. Christie, waving her hand at me. I smile and return the act. "Did you just get back?"

I nod my head. "Yes, I'm actually coming straight from the bus stop."

"Welcome home," she says. "I'll see you later. I'm in a hurry."

I nod again and wave her goodbye. That's the thing with growing up in a town where everyone knows everyone, you'll get recognized almost instantaneously. No one needs to tell me that by now, Gina already knows I'm in town. Someone must have called her to let her know the exclusive, as she used to say. Now that I'm the subject, it doesn't feel like anything about the information is exclusive.

The houses here all look the same. It's almost as if they were built by a single person. Every property starts out green with black roofs and a little lawn. Gina is one of the last few to keep the green and mows the grass religiously. I ignore all the stares I'm receiving from the neighbors. They'll know who I am in a few minutes, but for now, I want to see my aunt.

Before I get the chance to knock, the door flies open, and Gina pulls me in for a hug. I let myself get hugged. It feels nice. I'm taller than my aunt, but hugging her feels comfortable. I bury my face in her shoulder and breathe in her scent. She smells of lemon and garlic.

"Winter," she says, pulling away from the hug, "Let me see you."

I step back a bit to give her a good view of the woman I've become. She isn't judging me; she's just taking me in. I know it's been a while since she's seen me, so I look at her smile instead. I wonder what she sees when she looks at me.

Gina is older than my father. She's easygoing and without a doubt the nicest of his sisters, which isn't to say they aren't all nice. But the thing with Gina is she doesn't go off getting angry without hearing both sides of the story.

Her hair is short; she's never been one to worry about vanity. She's the person who cuts her hair on impulse. It drives her sisters mad because it doesn't matter what style she has because she's a natural beauty.

"You look amazing, baby. I just know you spend too much time in the gym!" she says, pulling me in for another hug.

I hug her back, and the uneasiness slips away. Being back might actually be good for me. Gina pulls me into the house, and she's not alone.

"Look who's here!" Gina announces. A few of my cousins, uncles, and aunts sit up in the living room. I'm not familiar with a couple of them, but I allow myself to be spun around and commented on.

"Winter! It's been so long!" one cousin exclaims, pulling me close.

"How have you been?" an aunt asks. "What's new? Did Angela come?"

I answer as best as I can. "I'm in grad school now. My mother's doing well, just busy, so she couldn't come. She sends her regards."

As I speak, I can't help but think about my mother's reaction when she finds out I'm back home. She and Gina have reconnected, but the rest of the family is a different story. She says she's changed and wants to be part of my life again. A part of me wants to believe her, and that scares me the most.

"Winter, how is New York treating you? I've been thinking of moving there," my oldest cousin asks, pulling me out of my thoughts.

"I'm actually in L.A. now. And forgive me, Caroline, but aren't you married to a cow farmer?"

"You're right, it's a pipe dream. I know. But I can't take the boonies anymore, Winter! I'm so bored. I'm going insane." She sighs dramatically. "You were lucky, you got to get out early."

"That's me. Lucky..." I say with a polite mask and look around. "I'm going to go check on Gina and see if she needs any help."

I head into the kitchen. "Hey, Gina. Need any extra hands? Feel free to put me to work."

"No, shoo," my aunt says as she waves a wooden spoon at me, ushering me back to the French double doors that separate the kitchen and the living room. "Go. Mingle. Reconnect with your family, Winter."

I cross my arms. "Fine. I'll go back out there and answer the same questions for two hours. But you're making your cobbler and lamb chops again before I go back to L.A."

"Done. Whatever it takes for you to get back in there."

With a resigned sigh, I turn and make my way back into the great room, blending in with the crowd of similar yet distant faces. There's conversation and laughter, but I find myself gravitating toward the deck, drawn by the sight of the sunset fading in over the fields outside.

As I step out into the fresh air, the scent of the grill wafts over me. The neighbor I haven't seen in nearly a decade is expertly flipping burgers. His face is weathered, illuminating the passage of time, but his smile is just as big as I remember.

The sight of him takes me back to countless evenings spent in this very spot, summer fun paired with the sizzle of meat on the grill. I can't help but smile as I approach him, memories flooding back with each step.

"Mr. Johnson," I call out.

He looks up, squinting slightly against the bright sun. For a moment, there's a flicker of recognition in his eyes, followed by a wide grin that spreads across his face. "Well,

I'll be damned! If it isn't little Winter Washington, all grown up."

"It's been a long time, hasn't it? How have you been?"

"Too long," he agrees, setting down his spatula to pull me into a hug. His embrace is strong, comforting, a reminder of the stability this place holds. "I've been good, just holding down the fort around here. And you? How's my favorite city slicker doing? I hear you've been off chasing big dreams."

"That's one way to put it," I say as I pull back, matching his smile. "It's good to see you. It feels like everything's changed, but this place… it's like time mostly stood still."

He nods, glancing around. "This old town has a way of doing that. But you've changed, Winter. You're not the little girl who used to race around the yard anymore."

"Life has a funny way of making us grow up," I reply, brushing aside thoughts. "But some things never change. Like your legendary burgers. Mind if I steal one before they're all gone?"

He chuckles, handing me a freshly grilled patty. "Help yourself, kid. It's on the house."

I accept the burger with a grateful smile and take a bite. The flavors are as good as I remember. "I don't know what you do to these, but they're amazing." He gets a laugh out of that.

A voice interrupts our conversation. "You must be the prodigal cousin everyone is talking about," a woman sitting on the porch steps says, extending her hand. "I'm Claire. We haven't met before."

Intrigued, I shake her hand, still chewing the burger. "I didn't realize I had a reputation." I swallow quickly. "But it's nice to meet you, Claire." I gesture toward the clan of Washingtons in the house. "Which one is yours?"

She grins and points across the room to a tall man with

glasses animatedly talking to a group of relatives. "That's my husband."

I nod, recalling Derek's wedding invite from five years ago. "Ah, cousin Derek. He's great. I haven't seen him in forever. Does he still randomly break out in song?"

Claire chuckles. "Yes, he does. It's so annoying. I brought him to a work party two months ago, and he just started singing '9 to 5' to my line manager. I was so embarrassed." Claire doubles over, snorting as she laughs. Her laugh is so contagious, I find myself joining in.

"Classic Derek," I sigh. "That doesn't top the time the classroom hamster died in fifth grade and he held a funeral for it. He put on a whole production. He placed the hamster in a red toy RC car and sang 'It's So Hard to Say Goodbye to Yesterday' as he steered the car across the school auditorium stage."

She leans into me, wiping her eyes, laughing uncontrollably. "Nobody has told me this story. Oh, the shit he's going to get when we get home."

"There's plenty more where that came—"

"We have something we would like to share," a cousin announces as she walks to the center of the living room. Claire and I enter the house to hear better.

"We're pregnant!" she says as her husband, a wealthy man from a tech company, squeezes her hand proudly.

My eyes focus on her stomach, still flat, and I feel like I've been sucker punched all over again.

The room fills with congratulations, and I force myself to join in. "Congrats," I say, my voice steady despite everything. *At least she knows the father of her child.*

"Amazing news, Hayleigh!" Gina rubs her belly. "I can't wait to meet the new addition to the family! Food's ready, everyone, let's eat."

Soon enough, dinner comes to an end, and people start to leave. I stand dutifully by Aunt Gina to say goodbye to everyone.

"I was so sorry to hear about Jayden," my newest cousin-in-law says as she hugs me. I stiffen up on instinct and force myself to at least nod. They have nothing to talk about besides me at a dinner party. This town is too damn small for its own good.

When the final person leaves, I help Gina clean up the house and do the dishes. She doesn't say anything, but I can tell she knows my mood has been soured.

"Is everything alright?" She asks me, and I nod my head immediately, but I do it too quickly, so it doesn't feel convincing. I take a deep breath to calm myself, but it feels like a wasted effort, so I stop.

The tears are already coming, and I have no way of stopping them. One of the reasons why no one insisted I come back to visit was because of Jayden. Everyone knew about us, and they understood that coming back to the town where our love story began might be too much for me. Even after all these years, the truth hasn't changed. I still miss him.

I take a deep breath to steady myself; the last thing I want to do is worry my aunt. "I'm fine."

"Oh, baby," Gina says and walks over to me. She wraps her arms around me. "You don't have to pretend to be fine. Not with me."

And the tears I've held back flow out of me with a sob that racks my chest. Gina holds me, patting my back encouragingly. She doesn't ask me to stop crying; she just surrounds me. I press my face into her chest and let everything out.

When the tears stop after what feels like forever, Gina leads me to the living room and settles me on the couch. "I'll make some tea, and then you can tell me all about what's really bothering you. If you want. I know all those tears weren't just about Jayden."

I don't nod or respond, but it doesn't seem like she wants a response right now. I know if I don't talk about this with someone I'm certain holds no judgments about who I am, I'll never be able to talk about it with anyone.

"Now," Gina starts, settling down in the seat opposite mine. She places a cup of tea in front of me, but I don't know the flavor. She's an avid tea drinker, and her shelf bears testament to what I can say is an obsession. "Do you want to talk about what's upsetting you?"

I try to think of a reason why I shouldn't, but I come up empty, so I say what I've been trying to push out of my mind since the warehouse. "I lost a baby."

Gina says nothing for what feels like forever, and then she suddenly drops the teacup she's cradling in her hand and hurries over to me. "Oh, honey."

The tears are fresh again and falling from my face. Until now, I didn't understand just how greatly the loss of the baby was affecting me. I knew I wasn't doing fine; I mean, I relapsed after a decade of staying clean.

"I just don't know what to do, and it doesn't make sense that I'm feeling this way because I didn't even know I wanted the baby. It just happened, and I just wanted to see where it was going to go, and then..." I don't say anything more because I choke up and Gina pulls me further into her.

It's true, I wasn't enthused to be a mother, but the idea was gradually growing on me. Or at least the option to make another family happy and give the child away to people better equipped to raise them. I thought I still had time to hold off making a real decision. I kept telling myself it wasn't a bridge I needed to cross until diapers were needed.

"Losing a child isn't an easy thing," she says, her arms still around me. "Whether you planned on having the child or not, that emptiness is something you can't escape. And you went through all of this on your own. No one with you. You have no idea how proud I am of you."

"I'm not a good person. You shouldn't be proud of me." There's nothing for her to be proud of. The way I got pregnant, the way I lost the baby, the person I became—I have nothing for her to be proud of.

"Oh, honey, you have no idea how proud I am of you. You've gone through things that would break a simple person. The fact that you're still here means you've persevered and you'll continue persevering. It isn't easy to lose your father, move town and leave your friends and family. You had to survive with your mother, and then have the man you love die in your arms. You've done so well for yourself; hell, you're even getting your master's degree. You're doing amazing, sweetie. Even if it doesn't feel that way right now, I want to assure you that your father would be proud of the woman you've become. I'm proud of the woman you've become."

I cry again.

$$-\mathord{\wedge}\mathord{\wedge}-$$

I CAN'T SLEEP, so I step out of the house, making sure not to wake Gina. I don't know where I'm going yet, but I start walking around the neighborhood. With no destination in mind, it meant that I was free to go anywhere. The streets are dark and almost empty, except for the few people who are still gathered around making jokes and smoking joints. They don't bother me, but I wish they would so I can kick their ass just for the heck of it. Anything they did would have been a trigger for me, even something as simple as hollering at me. The men here are quite different from the ones in New York and California; they seem to want to mind their business.

Passing the library, I turn the corner and before I realize it, I'm on Jayden's street. From where I'm standing, I can see his house in the distance. My feet remain planted, watching the structure that has no lights turned on in it. *I wonder if they moved.*

I look around to see if someone is watching me, someone who might influence my next decision. I find no one. Left to my own devices, I make my way over to the house as slowly as I can. I have no idea what I'm hoping to find, but I can't refuse the pull the residence has on me.

On the off chance that Jayden's family still lives here, the last thing I want to do is encounter them. I quietly hop over the fence, my knees absorbing the impact. Now, it seems like the easiest task in the world. Unlike when I was a child who struggled to get her weight over the gate.

At the back of the house, the grass is overgrown compared to the front lawn. Maybe there really is no one living here. Even if there isn't, I don't want to draw the neighbor's attention to me. The Oxfords can be a nosy bunch.

I move quietly to the tree house Jayden's father built for him. In the treehouse where we spent most of our time together. I take my time going up the ladder, and it feels the same. I peek inside when I finally make it up there.

"Winter?"

I stand sheepishly on the top step, toying with my hands and keeping my eyes fixed on the ground. I don't want to look at Jayden and see he isn't pleased with my presence.

"Winter," he says again, but his voice comes out as a whisper, and I'm forced to raise my head to look at him. He looks even more

handsome than the last time I saw him, over a year ago. I don't even know what I was hoping would happen when I decided to show up and surprise him.

The truth is, I hoped that he'd be happy to see me, but he looks shocked, and I feel exposed. I don't get a lot of chances to second guess my answers because Jayden jumps to his feet and hurries over to me, his arms pulling me to his chest.

I do nothing but wrap my arms around him and squeeze him back. The tears come rushing before I get the chance to stop them.

"I'm so sorry I left without saying goodbye," I tell him in-between sobs. "I had no idea we were going to leave like that. I came home one minute, and the next we were leaving."

"You didn't say goodbye," Jayden says and hugs me tighter. "I thought I did something wrong, and you were avoiding me."

"I'm sorry," I say again even though I know there's no apology I can offer for this type of heartache. I made his heart ache.

He pulls away from me and shakes his head. I'm surprised to see the tears in his eyes. I didn't think he'd cry about my return. I wanted something other than his coldness when I came to see him, but this is even more than I imagined.

"You're back, that's all that matters," Jayden says, and I don't have the heart to tell him it's just for the summer. He moves me further into the tree house and settles on the bed before lying back down and pulling me into him.

"I missed you so much," I say to him, and he places a light peck on my neck.

"I missed you more," Jayden says and places another kiss on my collarbone. "Your aunts weren't sure you'd come back, but I never lost hope. I told everyone you'd be back; I kept telling them you wouldn't abandon me like that."

A sob appears in my throat, and I turn in his arms until I'm facing him. I don't think about our bodies touching and the fact that

I'm lying right next to him. I just focus on the fact that I'm with him again. And he missed me.

SUMMER IS ENDING *in a couple of weeks, and I still haven't told Jayden I'm leaving again. I tell myself that I'm going to do it tonight. I don't want a repeat of what I did before. It wasn't fair to him.*

I'm waiting in his treehouse because he'll be coming back from football practice any minute now. Stretched across the bed, I'm close to dozing off when I hear him climbing the tree.

I sit upright and ask, "Can you sit with me for a second?" His face, which had a grin before, turns into worry. I guess my tone is a bit serious, but he needs to know.

"I need to tell you something." I pause but continue before I lose my nerve. "I'm only staying for the summer. I have to leave soon."

"It's okay. I figured as much. Any time I talk about picking our sophomore classes for the fall, you always change the subject."

"I'm sorry. I'd stay if I could. But my mom needs me."

Brushing my hair away from my face, he places a light kiss on my lips. Jayden pulls my face back up and whispers, "I know. But this won't be the end of us."

He drops his lips to mine again. This time, his two hands cradle my face. This kiss is different, it's more than I hoped would happen tonight. I lean further into him, letting him take whatever he wants because I know in the long run, I want the same thing he does.

Jayden deepens the kiss, and I rut against him, causing him to groan. He pulls away and rests his forehead on mine. "Winter," he says, his eyes not opening to meet mine. "Are you sure you're ready to do this?"

It's sweet and all except I don't want to stop now. I want him more than ever. This isn't something I've done before, and it surprises me how much I know what to do. But there's something that I need, and he's the only one who can fulfill it for me.

"I want this," I breathlessly say to him. I continue moving my hips while I place light kisses on his face, his jaw, and then his neck. I nibble, but not hard enough to leave a mark. "I want you."

I must've said the magic words because Jayden jumps up quickly and my legs spread apart. He kisses me, and this time it's heavier. He gropes my hips tightly, so much so that it hurts a little, but the pain quickly translates into desire in my head.

"Jayden," I whine into his mouth, and he looks down at me.

"Are you sure?"

I nod my head; I want him to be the first person to have me like this, and I'm certain it'll be the best decision I ever make.

A loud noise startles me. I turn to the sound and watch the sky fill with colors. And it's beautiful. My gaze is glued to the window, watching the fireworks encapsulate the air.

The crackles and pops die down a bit, and I run my hand across my face, my eyes landing on the spot where I lost my virginity. The blanket is gone, as well as the little camping bed Jayden convinced his father to bring up for him. The tree-house looks nearly the same in that the fairy lights are still connected to the wall, alongside a few pictures still tacked to the planks. I can't help but give a sad smile at the poorly etched *J.W.* initials surrounded by a terrible excuse for a heart.

My hands run through every item in an attempt to hold on to something from the past, but all I get in return is dust. I lie down on the floor and inhale deeply. I don't remember what Jayden smells like, and that in itself makes me even sadder. Maybe he misses me, wherever he is, and it sucks I can't be with him right now.

I wonder how Xavier is celebrating the holiday. I catch myself and shake my head. There's no reason for my thoughts to be wandering over to him. The relationship we have doesn't require us to think about each other like that. It's purely physical. And I shouldn't even be thinking about him in Jay's treehouse of all places. It feels wrong.

Before I spiral out of control, I quickly get to my feet. For a while after coming down the ladder, I stare at the house and wonder if anyone would exit. The possibility of Jayden coming out is nonexistent, but I will for it to happen. Maybe all of this has just been some elaborate nightmare, and I'm going to wake up any second now. I think about Xavier again, how being with him these days doesn't feel like a dream anymore. But I'm not sure I want to face reality yet.

CHAPTER 31

MONTEBELLO – *Sketchy Laundromat*
 July 15, 23:11 PDT

LIGHT FLICKERS above me as the smell of detergent mingles with the harsh tang of fear. I circle the man tied to the chair, my boots echoing softly against the linoleum floor. He looks up at me, eyes wide, struggling against the ropes that bind him.

"Comfortable?" I ask, my voice a villainous whisper.

He glares at me, but I never forget a face. He's the same man who was following Jessica and I around during our hangout day. Part of the Black Syndicate, one of their many foot soldiers. *Security my ass.*

"Who the fuck are you?" he spits, eyes darting all over the poorly lit room, searching for an escape. His voice wavers, a mix of defiance and fear.

After tracing Syndicate money to this front, I ran into my now-bound friend here. I continue to circle him. "Just a pissed off and frustrated individual," I say, my tone icy and measured.

He sneers, "You think you can scare me?"

I stop pacing, leaning in close enough to smell the sweat beading on his forehead. "I don't think," A familiar cold smile tugs at the corners of my mouth. "I know."

Without another word, I produce a small knife from my belt, the blade catching the light of the lone bulb overhead. His eyes widen once more, and he tenses in the chair, instinctively pulling against his restraints.

"You're going to tell me everything you know about the Black Syndicate." I run the flat edge across his cheek. "Starting with why you were following Jessica Glory."

He laughs. "You think I'll talk?"

I press the knife against his skin, just enough to draw a thin line of blood. "Yes, I do." I whisper. "In fact, I think you'll spill your guts."

The bravado remains in his eyes. "Do your worst, bitch. I'm no snitch." He then proceeds to spit on my boot.

I shake my head, disappointed. "You don't get it, do you?" I press the knife harder, twisting it slightly, watching the blood drip down his cheek. He grits his teeth, trying to hold back a cry of pain.

"Fuck you," he says, his body radiating with fury.

Stepping back, I sigh and survey the array of tools on the nearby washer. "You know," I say, my voice dripping with mock disappointment, "I was really hoping you'd cooperate." My fingers hover over the instruments before selecting a pair of pliers, feeling their weight and testing their grip. "But I have been itching to break in my new toolkit."

He watches me, fear starting to creep into his eyes. "You won't kill me. Aren't you supposed to be some type of hero?"

"I don't know where people keep getting that idea from. I

might've saved a few lives, but I never claimed to be a hero," I correct, stepping toward him. "I need what's in your head. And I have all night to get it."

I grab his jaw, forcing his mouth open. He struggles, but the ropes hold him tight. "Last chance. Tell me why you were following Jessica Glory."

He shakes his head. "Go to hell."

I clamp the pliers around one of his molars and start to pull, feeling the tooth begin to give. Honestly, I'm doing this guy a favor. His wisdom teeth are extremely impacted. "Stop! Stop, please!" he begs, tears streaming down his face.

Giving him a moment to catch his breath, I release the pressure slightly. "Ready to talk?"

He nods frantically. "Okay, okay. I was following her because we needed to send a message."

"What was the message?" I ask, my eyes narrowing.

"That you can't stiff the Syndicate on payments and then go to the country club."

"I'm only going to ask this once," I say as I peruse my torture collection. I pick up a syringe. "Did you or anyone in the Syndicate kill Jessica Glory?"

"Of course not," he says quickly. "We just wanted to scare her a little. We'd never kill her. The Syndicate doesn't want the problems that come with killing the reigning 'King of Pop's' daughter."

I study him for a moment, weighing his words. The Black Syndicate is ruthless, but even they know better than to draw too much attention to themselves. Still, I need more.

"What else?" I ponder. "I want to know about the Syndicate's operations."

He hesitates, and I see the struggle in his eyes. Loyalty to his gang versus the fear of what I might do to him. *Will do to him*. Finally, when I begin extracting the contents from a vial into the syringe, he breaks.

"They're using this laundromat to launder money," he says quickly. "Cash from their drug operations, mostly. They funnel it through here, make it look clean."

"Tell me something I don't know! Where's the money going? Who's running the show?" I yell, approaching his arm with my thumb ready to push the plunger.

"There's a safe in the back," he confesses, his voice trembling. "The code is 2874. The big boss comes by once a week to collect. That's all I know, I swear."

"Can I count on you to fill me in whenever you discover more information?"

Enthusiastically, my captive nods. "Yes, yes, I'll do anything. Just… please…"

I straighten up and pack up my belongings. "Thank you," I say, my tone almost polite. "You've been very helpful."

He looks up at me, relief flooding his face. "So, you'll let me go now?"

"No." I shake my head slowly. "But I'll make sure you're found. And remember, I'll be watching. Oh, and since you asked so nicely earlier, the name's Cyber Huntress." I walk away, leaving him tied to the chair, cursing my name. I have what I came for.

As I approach the exit, I pause, a thought crossing my mind. *Hell, why not? I'm already here.*

2-8-7-4. The lock releases with a satisfying clunk. Opening the safe door, I'm greeted by a mountain of untraced dollar bills stacked neatly inside. A slow smile spreads across my face.

Looks like I'm having surf and turf tonight.

CHAPTER 32

XAVIER'S – *Bedroom*
July 24, 19:14 PDT

SOFT SILK SHEETS tangle around my legs, a thread count of perfection as I pull myself to the edge of the bed, reaching for my underwear. I can feel his eyes on me, the lazy, satisfied grin that's practically radiating from him.

Xavier hasn't brought up our last awkward encounter, which I'm thankful for. I don't really know why I showed up at his place in that state last month, but if I'm being honest with myself, I just didn't want to be alone.

"Stay a little longer." The bed creaks as he shifts, looping an arm around my waist and tugging me back slightly. "We could order food, hang out, do absolutely nothing. Doesn't that sound perfect?"

I smile at the thought, but it's brief. I'm already pulling my jeans up as the reality settles in. "I can't," I say bluntly, brushing his hand off my hip gently.

"You can," he insists, his voice dipping lower as he leans

into my neck, planting a tender kiss just beneath my ear. "What's the rush? It's summer. It's your birthday. Relax." His lips move against my skin, his attempt at drawing me back to the warmth of the bed, to him.

I pause, my fingers gripping the clasp of my bra tighter than they need to. *Relax.* He has no idea. I finish tying my shoelaces as Xavier sighs behind me. I'm impressed he remembered after all these years, but I've never been one to celebrate my birthday.

"Really?" The sheets fall away as he sits up, watching me with confusion blatant on his face. His voice shifts, almost serious now. "You're still leaving? I'll order whatever you want—hell, I'll cook. And I won't even sing the song. We can start that show you wanted to watch. Just stay."

I know he's joking, trying to make me have fun with his nonchalant charm, but ain't shit funny. The message from K.A.R.M.A. flashes in my mind, reminding me that time isn't a luxury I can afford. There's a lead waiting for me. The Black Syndicate boss had the kid I coerced for information killed, and he had the gall to threaten the Cyber Huntress next. K.A.R.M.A. just spotted him entering a raunchy place of business that I need to get to before he slips from my grasp. There seems to be some misunderstanding that I was hired by a rival gang that I need to take care of. The Cyber Huntress doesn't have partners.

Sliding my phone into my back pocket, I stand, waiting for my ride three minutes away. The life I've chosen doesn't come with free afternoons or birthdays in bed. I can't stay and pretend I'm not the Winter that's out there in the streets, hunting down killers and drug lords.

"You're not taking summer classes. No deadlines. You've got time. What do you need to leave for now?" Xavier asks, his eyes searching mine, the playfulness gone. "Where are you always running off to?"

My hands halt mid-motion, and the room suddenly feels smaller, tighter. I am always running. From him and from the mess I've gotten myself into. From the life I live at night. A truth I can never share with him.

I meet his gaze, the look in his eyes cutting through my armor, just for a split second. He's catching feelings, real ones, and I can't let it go any farther. Not with this double life pulling me in two directions. "I have somewhere to be."

His jaw tightens, and I see the hurt in his expression for a moment, though he quickly hides it. "You know..." He pauses, running a hand through his hair before he meets my gaze again, "I'm open to this being more than... whatever this is between us."

I knew this would happen. Eventually, this thing we shared —this easy, light thing—was bound to get messy.

There's a smidge of guilt twisting in my gut. I shouldn't have let it get this far. I step toward the door, tugging my shirt over my head, and forcing myself to say the words that need to be said. "Maybe we should just stick to what we agreed on. Friends with benefits."

The words taste bitter on my tongue, but they're necessary. I need to nip this in the bud.

Xavier blinks, his face frozen, but he doesn't argue. He just nods, revealing a terse smile. "Right. Friends with benefits."

I hate the way it sounds coming from his mouth, but another thing I can't afford is to let this blossom. Not when I have to walk out that door and meet a man wanting nothing more than to kill me.

"So, I'll see you soon?" I ask, though the question hangs awkwardly between us.

"Yeah... soon," he says and rolls over in the bed, facing away from me.

LONG BEACH – *The Midnight Oasis*
  July 24, 20:29 PDT

SHOUTS from the crowd are muffled by the deafening bass from the speakers. The air is covered in smoke, stale cologne, and desperation. Lights flash across the walls, showcasing half-naked strippers moving in rhythm to the beat. But I'm not here for the show.

Heads turn and faces are filled with shock, but no one dares to stop me. They know who I am. My reputation alone clears the path.

At the back of the club, Frankie "The Butcher" Garza holds court, lounging like a king on his throne in the VIP section. His bodyguards, all muscle and intimidation, stand watch, but I barely glance at them. They mean nothing to me.

Frankie's eyes catch mine from across the room. His smirk falters, just for a second, before he tries to recover, leaning back in his chair like he's still in control of this situation. He isn't.

I approach his table with purpose, my boots thudding against the sticky floor as I stop directly in front of him. His two bodyguards stiffen, hands twitching toward their guns.

"Touch those, and you won't make it out of here alive," I say, steady and ice-cold. They freeze, uncertainty spreading across their faces. Their boss waves them off, but he's not smiling anymore.

"Well, well, well," Frankie starts, trying to sound casual,

but his voice drops slightly. "Cyber Huntress graces my humble establishment. To what do I owe this pleasure?"

I don't respond. Instead, I pull out my phone, unlock it, and show him the image—his man, the dead one. A bullet through the head. The note beside his lifeless body: *You're next, Cyber Huntress. And your employer too.* He was even kind enough to scrawl his name at the bottom.

"Your guy... he didn't snitch," I say quietly, my voice relaxed but deadly. "But you killed him anyway."

Frankie shrugs, taking a long drag from his cigar. "What can I say? I don't like loose ends."

I lean forward slightly, my eyes locked on his. "That was a mistake. You killed him because you're paranoid. And now, you've made another mistake, thinking I'm going to let you get away with threatening me."

"You know how this works, sweetheart," Frankie says, his grin spreading wider as if this is some kind of joke. "You, you took my money. You crossed the line, Huntress. Now you get to deal with the consequences. You should have stayed in New York."

I take a deep breath, the table crackling with tension. Being soft doesn't work, and neither does trying to use reason. It only got the guy killed. Men like Frankie... they don't respond to words. They respond to fear. To pain. Violence.

My hand rests on the gun at my side as I get to my feet. He watches me, still smiling, but it's slipping. He can tell something's shifted.

"I'm not here to talk, Franklin. I'm here to make sure you understand that the next mistake you make is your last." I don't give him time to acknowledge my words. The combustion of the bullet overpowers the music as I shoot him in the kneecap.

The blast echoes through the room. His scream follows, high-pitched and guttural as he folds in the chair, clutching his leg. Blood pours onto the floor, staining the already red carpet. The bodyguards jump up, guns half-drawn, but I raise both of mine first, calm as ever.

"Sit the fuck down, or you're next."

They hesitate, glancing at each other, then at their boss writhing on the floor. They sit, chucking their arms across the room.

I crouch down beside him, watching his face contort, his hand gripping the wound as if it'll somehow stop the agony. His bloodshot eyes are active and undilated. *Good, he's alert.*

"You listen to me, and you listen well. I simply don't care about your gang or the territory you think you own. If you start a war over this, I will make it my personal mission to burn everything you've built to the ground. Front by front. Until there's nothing left of the Black Syndicate but whispers in the dark."

There's an ominous silence before I continue. "I didn't want it to come to this, but you left me no choice. You threaten me? Leave notes for me?" I shake my head slowly. "You're not the only one with power here, Frankie. Remember that."

He glares at me, his voice now rasp. "You can't kill me. That'll start the war. Everyone knows you work for the Serpents."

"I don't work for anyone. Especially not no damn Serpents. I work alone." I stand up, holstering one of my guns. "And I don't have to kill you. I just have to keep making your life a living hell until you wish I had. Now, while I have your attention, I just need you to confirm one little thing for me. Did the Syndicates have Jessica Glory killed?"

"Who?" Frankie belts in pain. "Who the hell is that?"

"Jessica Glory. Daughter of Allen and Charlotte Glory. Did you have her killed?"

"Why would I have her killed? I don't even know her." I study his expression and body language. Nothing tells me he's lying. It does line up with what the dearly departed goon told me. It's not far off to believe that he wouldn't be involved in the day-to-day operations, like which sorority girl is selling on a certain campus.

I turn to walk away, allowing the moment of brashness to pass. I linger at the edge of the table, my back to him. "If you stay out of my way and keep my name out of your mouth, we won't have any problems. You can have me as a neutral bystander or an all-out enemy. The choice is yours. One more step out of line, Frankie… and next time, I won't aim for your knee."

CHAPTER 33

BALMY AIR BRUSHES past me as I jog through the streets. Crack of dawn runs never seem to fail me when I'm stuck on a problem. The things I want to achieve keep running away from me. So, I figure I'll chase after them.

The Syndicates have been quiet. No more death threats. It seems they know their place, at least for now. I've managed to get my hands on the heroin found in Jessica's system, which means I'm currently looking for the person who supplies it. The dealers that sold it to me weren't of any use. Each of them said a different rival gang supplied them. How can that be true if they all match? This supplier seems to be the most evasive individual I've ever had the displeasure of not meeting yet.

"Pick it up," someone yells in the distance, and I look over to see UCLA ROTC cadets doing their PT training. There's a girl on the track running toward the trainer tracking her speed.

She stops, and the man checks the stopwatch in his hand.

"One would think you're here to measure just how slow you can be," Colonel Walters yells and looks down at the black timer.

I'm panting really hard, trying to get my breathing under control. Until I heard his voice, I was convinced this was my best time yet. In fact, I thought the ground behind me lit flames at my feet to show just how fast I was going.

"You're six seconds slower than your previous record."

Six seconds, I repeat to myself and shut my eyes. The last lap I ran, I was four seconds slower than the record I'm supposed to beat. I can't tell what's causing my speed to plummet, but it's really killing my mood.

I whine in defeat. "I don't understand how doing all this running is going to make me a better fighter." I wanted to win a boxing match, not become a damn track star. That's the whole point of taking time out of school to train me.

Walters takes off his cap. "I promised I would teach you how to protect yourself. Sometimes running is the best thing you can do. Now, again."

And just like that, I take off once more. If he truly believes this is the best way, then I'll have to trust him. I run as hard as I possibly can. As I'm gasping for air and collapsing to the ground, he throws a water bottle my way. I've trained with him enough to know, this was his way of expressing he's proud.

He checks his wristwatch and says, "That's enough for today. It's time to go. It's getting late."

I slam the door shut on Walters' truck, and he drives away from the school. It's been eight months since Walters saw me getting beat up in the school parking lot. I was running my mouth as usual, but I never learned how to back it up. The very next day was eleventh grade picture day, and I just knew I didn't need a yearbook.

The first thing he ever asked me was, "Did you want to get your ass beat or did you have a plan I seemed to miss?"

I would have laughed if it didn't hurt to breathe. And yet he was right; I was just picking fights at this point. I'm not even sure what my thought process was either. But I figured I can either be invisible at this new school or be a menace, so I guess I chose the latter.

He helped me up. "If you ever decide to direct your anger in a better way, come find me in the JROTC portable."

I wasn't sure what he meant at the time, but after a long night in the hospital three months later, I felt like I needed a change and some structure in my life. The next day I walked into his office and asked to join the JROTC. I've been a cadet ever since.

We still have a few minutes until we reach the apartment my mom and I share. I say share because we are more roommates than mother and daughter. Hell, I pay the rent more than she does.

"Why are you doing this? Going out of your way, spending your spare time training me?"

What does he get out of it?

He glances my way and wears a somber expression. "You remind me of my daughter. All the good and all the bad." He lets out a dry chuckle. "She was a troublemaker just like you."

I somehow know the answer to my question before I even ask, "Where's your daughter now?"

With his eyes glued to the road, he says, "She died, years ago." He pauses and continues, "But I wanted to help you the only way I knew how."

He drops me off at the front of my complex and drives into the night.

The contact in my phone stares back at me for what seems like forever. I was almost certain he wouldn't answer, but the line eventually connects.

"Washington?" he repeats, "Washington? Is everything alright?"

"I know it's stupid, but I ran into some UCLA cadets today and it made me think of you."

"Well, it's good to hear from you. We haven't had time to catch up since you upped and moved to Hollywood. How's the weather out there?"

"Warm and sunny. You know, typical L.A. weather."

"Must be nice. There's another tornado watch out here." He adds, "Now I know you didn't call just to talk about the sky, Washington. Tell me what's on your mind."

There's silence for a while before I say, "You know I had every intention of walking away. Setting the mask down for good. And then someone I knew died. Go figure, right? But I decided to come back to this life, and now I'm stuck on this case, and I don't know how to proceed."

"Well, it all comes down to w —"

"What you know and what you don't know," I say, finishing his sentence. "Yeah, yeah, yeah. But what if I don't know what I don't know, Colonel?"

"Then you simply don't know enough. Start fresh. Look at the case from another angle. Things are never random. They just lack context. It's your job to find the context."

K.A.R.M.A. interjects over the intercom. "Ma'am, I have made a discovery."

"Hey Walters, I have to go. But thanks."

"Anytime, Washington."

I end the call. "K.A.R.M.A., what do we got?"

HOME – *Lair*
August 07, 10:48 PDT

I CLOSELY MONITOR dark web forums, particularly those connected to the case. In several threads, I flagged users as potential gang members from Jessica's drive and noticed repeated references to a "Jeep." Initially, I overlooked it, assuming they were talking about a vehicle. But as I dug deeper, it became clear that "Jeep" was being mentioned more like a person.

The posts are cryptic, but the more I read, the more a pattern starts to emerge.

User *cr0ssfade* mentions: *"A jeep came through, made the drop, and just like that, the streets were flooded."*

Another user, *Spect3r*, adds: *"Whenever a jeep's involved, things run smoother."*

User *cryp7ic* chimes in: *"With a jeep, the job gets done."*

It's clear now that "Jeep" isn't just a vehicle—it's a key player. The way these users talk about Jeep; it's like they're describing someone who knows the game inside and out. The comments are always vague enough to keep things under the radar, but there's a pattern in how they talk about deals and operations going off without a hitch when Jeep's in the mix.

Fract1on posts: *"Whenever a jeep's around, Omega's numbers shoot up. Coincidence?"*

After looking into him more, Jeep, it turns out, is every drug dealer's dream guy. He doesn't just know who to sell drugs to, he knows how to get away from the cops, which people to blackmail, etcetera. Going through his files, I conclude he's more than a drug dealer, he's a businessman and broker. Not only that, he's the one who decides which cartel gets ahead and who stays behind.

Any gang he aligns with, their sales increase by almost fifteen percent, which is a lot considering the competition only raises by two percent per year, if that. In the long run, Jeep is something akin to a money doubler.

The only problem is there's no photograph of this Jeep anywhere. None. And I've looked everywhere, the FBI's database, DEA, ATF, every law enforcement agency that seems like they would know a thing or two about drug dealers and their associates.

I've even hacked some overseas accounts trying to find this man. There's absolutely nothing on him. That tells me I'm dealing with someone who is well connected and knows exactly what they're doing. But now that I know he's aligned with the Outlaws, I might be able to work with this.

CHAPTER 34

LAKEWOOD – *The Iron Spoke*
   August 15, 22:20 PDT

DURING MY INITIAL research into the Outlaws, I found a promising lead, Kane, real name Archie Lennon. Archibald is the closest you'd get to the top brass of the Outlaws on the West Coast. Kane's back in town after a long holiday traveling in Baja, California. One week—that's the length of time I've followed Kane and the entire time, he shows up at this one bar.

Two bouncers stand outside the building looking like they wouldn't hold back from breaking an intruder into two with their fists. The entire time I sit on the roof of the building across from them, they don't crack a smile once. They're all business and nothing else.

My eyes are locked on Kane, who stands near the entrance, shifting his weight impatiently. He checks his watch, glancing around before finally relaxing as a man approaches. The newcomer is tall, dressed in a casual jacket that doesn't quite fit the seedy atmosphere of the bar. They greet each other with a nod, then lean in, talking quietly.

"K.A.R.M.A., identify the new player." I zoom in with my binoculars to get a clear view of the man's face.

"Running facial recognition... Match found. The individual is Officer Daniel Mitchell, LAPD," K.A.R.M.A. reports.

My heart skips a beat. An LAPD cop meeting with Kane? I watch closely, noting their body language, the ease with which they converse. They're too familiar, too comfortable. This isn't a chance encounter or a casual meeting. I adjust my position, and Kane and Mitchell laugh about something, the sound faintly carrying in the wind. Mitchell claps Kane on the shoulder; there's a camaraderie there.

A dirty cop? It makes sense—the Outlaws exist in multiple states, so it would follow they have connections everywhere, and having someone inside the local police department would be invaluable. It would also explain the extreme lack of care they've shown in a case that should have the most eyes on it.

I watch as Kane hands Mitchell a small envelope, the cop pocketing it with a casual glance around. They part ways, Kane heading into the bar while Mitchell strolls back toward the street, blending into the crowd.

"K.A.R.M.A., log this interaction. We need to keep a close eye on Officer Mitchell. There's no telling how deep this level of corruption could be in the LAPD."

"Interaction logged. Surveillance on Officer Mitchell initiated," K.A.R.M.A. confirms.

A young girl stumbles out of the bar and bumps into one of the guards. Instead of steadying her, he shoves her away from him with a disgusted expression gracing his face. I frown at the interaction, but the girl doesn't seem phased by this; she hustles to her feet and rushes away from them.

There's something about her that feels familiar. It's the way she has her hands in the pocket of her hoodie like she's clutching something precious. Even when she fell, she didn't pull her hands out of that pocket.

I follow after her, keeping to the roof. It's dark out, and even if it wasn't, I'm sure she wouldn't even notice me, seeing how focused she is on getting away. She turns into an alley, and I settle on an adjacent roof. She pulls the hoodie off, and a gasp escapes me. She's so young, too young. There's no way she's even old enough to drink yet. She looks like she hasn't eaten in a while, and her hair looks scattered. With shaky hands, she shoves them into her pant pocket and pulls out a thin rope. I want to run over to her and stop her, but I feel frozen. Meticulously, she ties her arm as tightly as she can before taking the needle out of her pocket.

That's too much. Before I let myself think, I hurry down the side of the building. The girl is already convulsing when I get to her. She's shaking really hard, and if I waste any more time, then without a doubt, she's going to die. I grab her and throw her onto my back.

The only place I can go to is the hospital, and I curse the fact that in all the time I've been in L.A., I haven't let the thought of buying a car cross my mind. Now that I'm hauling another body across town with their life dangling by a thread, I see how stupid the decision was. I find the closest car I think I can hot-wire. She isn't going to make it unless I get this car started up. The hospital is over five miles away. After ignition, I take off like a scalded dog.

The hospital comes into view, and someone steps out of their car in the parking lot. A tall man wears a white coat and holds a briefcase. Without a doubt, I know he's a doctor.

I lower the girl to the ground while he stares at me.

"She overdosed on fentanyl," I say in a loud voice. His

eyes widen a fraction, and I step away from the girl. "Please, save her."

As he hurries over, abandoning his bag on the ground, I step away from them and blend in with the shadows. He takes her pulse and starts pumping her chest. He looks behind him toward the hospital. Then back at the girl. He picks her up bridal style and rushes inside the building. His briefcase sits in the middle of the parking lot.

I'm grounded in my spot, and from the corner of my eye, I see movement and follow it. The person I've been looking for without knowing if we'd ever run into each other stands in the corner, watching me.

Nightshield isn't as imagined. Looking at the body build, and how the outfit clings to them confirms my suspicion that the other vigilante is male. I tilt my head to the side to get a better look at him, but he shifts even further back into the darkness, and I don't need anyone to tell me he's gone.

"He said his bag is somewhere here, didn't he?" someone asks, pulling me out of my thoughts. Two women dressed in scrubs peer around the parking lot.

"Near his car, right?" the other one asks. "Where's his car?"

"That's it," the other replies, pointing toward the car the man stepped out from. "The black Honda."

"Of course, you'd know his car."

"He's a very good doctor," the first girl defends.

"Yes, I'm sure that's all there is to it."

I don't linger to catch more of their conversation, even though I would love to know if the first nurse and the doctor were having some scandalous affair. But watching that girl's body convulse drags me back to the night my mother was rushed to the hospital. It was the first time I'd ever ridden in the back of an ambulance. I knew she was addicted to drugs, but I had no idea how bad it had gotten until that night.

Her eyes were lifeless, and no matter how many times I shook her, she wouldn't wake up. In my panic, I didn't call Aunt Gina. There was only one person I knew who could keep me calm.

Jayden picks up on the fourth ring.

"Mom's going to die," I blurt out immediately, my voice coming out hysterical.

There's rustling, an indication I had just woken him up. "Winter, calm down. What's going on?"

"I came home from school, and she was just there on the floor. She took something," I reply, crying some more.

"Where are you?" Jayden asks.

He can't come, I realize immediately. I'm not within his reach. He can't hug me and tell me everything's alright. And somehow that makes me cry even harder.

"Deep breaths, Winter," Jayden says. "You're going to be fine. Have you called for an ambulance yet?"

I nod before remembering he can't see me. "We're in the hospital now."

He breathes out in relief. "That's good, Winter. You're doing really well. Now, I need you to take deep breaths to calm yourself for when the doctor comes to talk to you. There's nothing else you can do now. She's in the hospital; the doctors will take it from here. She'll be fine."

I don't believe him about my mother being fine. He doesn't know how many people I've seen overdose. Every day, there's a story about someone who's found in their living rooms, bathtubs, in some ditch, and hardly any of them survive.

"Jayden. I'm scared."

"Hey, she's going to be fine, you'll see."

"Yeah, but I'm not sure I'll be."

He pauses. "You know you can talk to me about anything, right, Winter?"

"I could've been admitted tonight too." I finally offer. I'm tired of secrets and being alone. I need to let someone in. "I was minutes away from taking the same laced drugs my mother took. If she wasn't on the ground when I got back, I'm not sure where I'd be right now."

I can tell I left him speechless, so I continue because I'm on a roll. "You were right. I haven't been myself. I didn't know how to tell you that I was raped last year. And I've been doing everything to try and get over it and forget. But it constantly replays in my mind. If I'm being completely honest, it's been a shitty few years overall, and getting high was the only way I felt any peace. But after tonight, I know I can't keep this up. I'm going to stop. I have to stop. I promise."

At this point, I'm full-on ugly crying, snot and all.

"Winter, I can't even pretend to imagine what you're going through. But I do know you don't have to do it alone. I'm here, and I'm not going anywhere. We're going to figure this out together."

Even though we broke up not too long ago, in the most dramatic fashion, he's still the one I turned to in my moment of pain. I thought I was still mad at him for ambushing me with a group intervention call on New Year's last month. I remember answering the phone and thinking maybe Jayden was willing to talk things out and we could move past what happened outside the dance. But it wasn't just him on the screen. There were three other tiles, yet my eyes zeroed in first on Jayden, who looked guilty and flat-out uncomfortable.

I had no idea why we were having a group call. I felt unsettled by it. There was something about it I didn't like.

The brothers, Michael and Jeremiah, look like they always do, happy and pleased. Since I've known them, I haven't once seen them lose their cool. And then there's Rebecca, the most put-together girl

I've ever known. Their intentions are pure, they're worried about me, but I don't appreciate the concern. They're the ones who've hardly picked up their phones for me for years. What do they mean by they care? Respectfully, they can shove this sudden need for consideration up their asses.

"Jayden and I are fine. We just had a fight."

"You broke up two weeks ago," Rebecca points out, and Jayden throws his face to the side as if the information hurts him to hear.

I roll my eyes. They have no right to come up on me like this. "It was his fault." Our relationship is none of their business anyways.

"I wanted you to tell me what was going on," Jayden yells, and Michael whistles loudly. "You never talk to me anymore."

"And you seem distracted too," Jeremiah adds. "You keep twitching, and you always look uncomfortable."

"Yeah, Winter, you've been acting different lately," Rebecca chimes in.

"I am fine," I say again. "There's nothing to worry about."

"Is it your mother again?" Rebecca asks, and I find myself sitting up to level her a look.

In a low voice I say, "Leave my mother out of this," causing Michael to whistle again.

"We're not accusing her of anything, Winter," Jeremiah says, and I can see Rebecca nodding again. Of the five of us, Rebecca and Jeremiah have always been the ones who can handle conflict. Michael would rather grovel than have a difficult conversation.

"I'M FINE," I repeat for a final time and slam my laptop closed.

I hear Jayden's voice in my head again. *You're going to be fine.* I take the longer way home and all of the shortcuts I know in case I'm being followed by Nightshield.

When I get home, I grab the stash of cocaine I have. Just because he isn't here anymore doesn't mean I didn't make a promise. Before I lose my nerve, I dump everything down the toilet and flush it away for good.

CHAPTER 35

THE IRON SPOKE – *Outlaws Hangout*
   August 18, 21:18 PDT

VENTURING INTO ONE OF L.A.'S most feared bars, I wear the shortest top I have, and I've taken the time to oil my skin so it glows when the light hits it just right. My skirt leaves nothing to the imagination. The catcalls start the second I step out of the taxi.

The musk of the establishment hits me when I open the door. I brave a smile and step in, ignoring the whistles as I make my way to the bar. The Outlaws' logo is splattered across the arms of half the men in here. I order a dirty martini because it has never failed me on nights like this, and I'm certain it's not about to start now.

I can't hear anything; the men are talking all at once, and none of them are listening to each other. They laugh even louder. There's a pool table in the middle of the room, and a group of them surround it. With each hit, whether a score or a miss, I'm unable to tell because their reaction to both is exactly the same, loud shouts.

A hand wraps around my waist and squeezes tightly. I don't look at the owner of it as I take time to school my expression. They're a gang, and one wrong move is going to take me from being desired to being prey. Although a prey is desired, they have a higher chance of being left for dead.

I turn my head to face the man beside me. I don't smile at him even though his grin is fit for a toothpaste commercial.

"How are you, milady?"

My vision alternates between his hand curled around my waist and then back at his face. I raise a brow, but he doesn't take the arm away. We engage in a staring contest, and I don't budge a bit. He gets the message after a while, but doesn't let go without a squeeze.

"I said—" he begins. However, I've decided I'm done entertaining him and turn my attention back to my drink. I can tell he doesn't have the information I want. He's a nobody. I wait for him to do something stupid like strike me or call me a slur. It'll be entertaining for the other men if I beat him up. It'll get me attention but perhaps not the attention I want to attract in a bar full of criminals. Fortunately for both of us, the man just walks away.

More screams erupt from the pool table. I turn my head slightly to see if I can tell the cause of the commotion this time, but the effort yields the same result. I sigh loudly and shake my head. Men, I suppose, will always be men.

"They've been at it for a while now," the bartender is kind enough to inform me. "For some reason, I thought they'd just drink and keep it moving."

"You make a mean martini," I say to him, ignoring his revelation about the people in his bar.

The bartender is lanky-looking, nothing like the rest of the men in the club. His skin is void of any piercings or tattoos. "Thank you," he says and offers me a smile. "I don't think I've seen you around here before."

Another shout. "I don't come here, never have, but someone told me I could find the best drinks here, and they didn't lie." I raise my glass to him. "Do you own the place?"

He shakes his head and leans in close so I can hear his words. "I just work for the man who owns the place."

"What do you do when you're not here?"

"I just hang around with them mostly. I don't have much to concentrate on right—hey, don't touch that. You're going to ruin it."

The offender is a shorter man, a little person if I must say. He's standing on a table and attempting to remove the deer head hanging on the wall. The people around him egg him on, and the bartender looks like he intends to march over there and drag the man down himself.

He doesn't get to see it through because the door opens and another man comes in. He looks pissed when he sees the small man on the table, and one look sends him scrambling down to the ground.

"And that would be the owner of the club," he informs me with a light laugh. The owner of the club is a large man in his own right, black with his head shaved clean. He has a mean look in his eyes as he scans the room. The noise has died down as everyone regards him.

"Come now, Abel," someone calls out to him, "You don't have to be so serious all the goddamn time."

A light laugh rings through the room and ends with a question, like they aren't sure if this is a situation to laugh in. Abel approaches the man who called him over. They talk for a few minutes, but the conversation is cut short when Abel yells out. "I said, keep it down."

Which is an odd thing to say given it was his first time announcing the need for silence. The men around the pool table pay no mind to him. They keep laughing and shoving each other roughly. I don't understand how hitting a ball with a stick is the funniest thing in the world.

"Uh oh," the bartender says. "Here he comes."

He hurries out of the space, and Abel walks in and grabs a bucket. He fills it with water and throws it toward the men at the pool table. I manage to move out of the way just in the nick of time.

Everyone's attention is turned toward the bar, and shouts fill the air. The bartender pulls me away.

"Do you want to go somewhere?" he asks into my ear, his hand grabbing my butt. If there's anyone who knows something, it'll be the one person who's here everyday.

Somewhere turns out to be the bathroom. Not very creative, but it gets the job done. He sits on the toilet while I straddle him. Our lips meet each other in a frenzy as the yelling picks up outside. I grind my hips down on his waist, relishing the grunts that fall from his lips.

"Do you have any drugs on you?" I ask and let out another moan. Someone outside whistles, and in response, the bartender squeezes my ass even harder.

"I have ecstasy," he says and licks a strip up my neck. I giggle at the contact, my hips grinding down again. To prove his point, he dips his hand into his pocket and fishes out a little baggie. "I swiped it off one of them."

"Aren't you going to get in trouble?" I ask in a whisper.

"They know better," he says as his lips meet mine again.

I can do ecstasy. It's not a hard drug, and if I don't take the pill he just popped, there's no way I can ask him my follow-up question.

With a wink, I place the tablet in my mouth and lean

down to kiss him. I force the pill down his throat and disguise it as a steamy kiss. I nibble on his bottom lip. *I guess I do mind taking ecstasy.*

"You don't have anything stronger? Like some H?" I ask.

He shakes his head desperately. It's ego-boosting when you have a man turn to putty in your hands. "There's regulation on it these days."

I pout at that, and he surges forward to kiss it off of me. Without a doubt, I have him deeper than I need him.

"Regulation? Why?" I breathe out and throw my head back when he latches his tongue to my breast. This is escalating a bit more than I intended it to.

"Some rich white girl was killed," he says, and I award him with a crotch massage. "There was an argument or something, no one talks about it much, but a lot of drugs have been off the street for a while. The cops are all over the case."

I moan out my response because he might as well have directly said the Outlaws were involved in Jessica's murder. For his honesty, I believe he deserves a little reward. This information just made my job a whole lot easier. I give him a final kiss as I inject him with ten CCs of my Night Night drug.

Sweet dreams.

CHAPTER 36

WESTWOOD – *Westwood Park*
   August 22, 16:12 PDT

THE SHIRT I'm wearing clings to my skin with sweat, and I take a deep breath. I'm losing, and I hate losing. Sure, it's been a while since I've played basketball, I just didn't expect to suck this badly at it.

Xavier throws the ball into the hoop, and I groan loudly. I'm no longer keeping score. That's how much I've lost. He laughs as he chases after the ball.

"You've gotten slow," he calls out to me, and I scoff loudly and roll my eyes. What does he know about being slow?

"I'm just letting you win because you clearly need it," I say with all the nonchalance I can muster. It isn't a lot. In fact, it sounds like I care so much about losing, and I'm sore about it. And being a loser isn't a problem, but being a sore one is just straight-up embarrassing.

"At what point are you going to pick it up?" he asks. "When I score one hundred points?"

I scoff and catch the ball when he throws it at me. "You wish you could get to one hundred points."

He tilts his head to the side, looking painfully amused. I want to reach over and smack it. "I'm at thirty points."

I mirror his head position. "What about it?"

"You've scored only four points."

My head straightens quickly, and I look at him with wide eyes. "That can't be true."

Xavier laughs loudly and claps his hands together, a clear indication he's having too much fun mocking me. There's no way he's at thirty points while I just have four. But the image of the two goals I scored comes back to haunt me because it was the first two shots of the match and I made such a big deal out of it.

"You've lost your mojo," Xavier says. "You've shot so many bricks we could build a whole neighborhood." Then to make matters worse, he *tsks* and wags his finger at me. "You've let yourself go."

I would have preferred to be pulled by my ears and called an idiot. It felt like a slap to my face, and I know he's just teasing, but I won't stand for it.

"I'll show you letting myself go," I mumble and move back a bit. I bounce the ball on the ground and look at him through slitted eyes. He doesn't know it yet, but it's time for war.

Louder this time, Xavier laughs again, but gets into position nevertheless. I already know my play. He must have forgotten how good I am at this game because he seems to relax. I charge forward, and Xavier stretches his hand to break my move. I fake left, but as I'm about to turn right, Xavier hits the ball out of my hands. Instead of going after the ball, he wraps an arm around my waist and pulls me to him.

"Hi," he says and places a kiss on my lips. "You look mad."

I struggle not to let the kiss distract me. Even more than that, I force myself not to think about how this doesn't feel like we're friends with benefits anymore. It feels like we're dating, and I can't imagine that Xavier doesn't feel this way too.

"I'm not mad," I say with a voice I hope is stern, but even to my ears, it sounds really weak. "I have a game to win."

"It's getting late," he says, and I look up at the sky.

The sun is still up, and cool air blows around us, rustling the leaves of the surrounding trees. I can see a few birds above, and from the corner of my eye, a squirrel dashes into the nearby shrub.

"What are you talking about?" I mutter. Xavier is still looking at me, and the look in his eyes makes me squirm in his arms, and the next words that leave my mouth are a whisper. "The day is beautiful."

There are children in the park running around, laughing, and a couple of dogs playing fetch with their owners. I don't even know what I'm doing now, let alone what my line of thought was when I agreed to come to the park with him. This isn't how I saw the day going. I'm aware of his arms around my waist. It's barely a hold; if I step away, his hands will fall free, but I don't move an inch.

Beads of sweat cling to his skin, and it's satisfying to know he spent as much energy as I did during the game. "Xavier," I whine, and he chuckles.

He places a trail of kisses on my neck. "What is it?"

"You need to let go. I have a game to win."

"We can say you already won."

I let out a huff. "Last game. And then we'll leave."

"Really?" He perks up at that.

"Yes," I say, and he lets me go. I run to the other end of the court while Xavier flexes his muscles, watching me dribble the ball. He's got that damn smile.

I look up to the net with a frown and sigh. It's the qualifying game for the Illinois Girls' Basketball State Championship. My opponent in front of me hops from one leg to another, with a firm look of concentration.

My task is simple; I'm required to score a point. Hers is simple as well. She's required to make sure I don't score. But all of that would have to wait because the buzzer signaling the start of half-time breaks my focus.

Exiting the gym and entering the hallway, I head for the concession stand. Starters get free food and drinks, one of the many perks of being a ninth-grader on the varsity team. Rachel's mom, the mother of our starting point guard and the head of the PTA is running the booth today.

I run up to the front of the line. "Can I get a blue Crocade?" Suddenly feeling parched, I grab a quick drink before the second half of the game begins.

"Sure thing." She turns to the boy running the booth with her. "Honey, can you get Winter one out of the cooler?"

As he reaches into the blue ice bucket, I can't help but notice the curls that cover his face when he bends down. He places the drink in my palm and says, "Here you go."

"Thanks." I squint and read his name tag. "Xavier."

"You play with my sister, right? Rachel?"

"Yep! Speaking of which, there's a huddle in the locker room I have to run to."

He grabs a protein bar and stops me as I turn around. "Well, take this and good luck. But I don't think you need it. Your jump shot is lethal."

When our hands touch again, I lose my breath for a second.

"Winter! Coach wants to see you before the third quarter!" I

turn around and see Rachel hanging out of the locker room. I nod my thanks to Xavier and skedaddle away.

It's only twenty seconds left in the game, and Rachel just passed me the ball because it's crunch time. I dribble the ball and make my way forward. One bounce after another, I try to come up with a game plan. Faking left and going right is an overrated trick. All the times I've tried it, the ball is always taken away from my grip.

This time, I'm determined to do something different and wipe the smirk off player 8's face. I tune out everyone watching from the bleachers. I don't need to hear them talk about the low chance I have of getting past her. She's a very good defender, best in the state in fact, but what this girl doesn't know is that I'm the best forward in the state.

I pick up my pace, and when I show up in front of her, I go left and pretend that I'm going right. As she goes right, I maintain on the left. I jump and shoot the ball through the hoop with nothing but net.

Three points. And just like that, we're going to state. At the edge of the court, Xavier's applauding me with a huge smile on his face.

"In yo face," I scream over at Xavier, who's still standing there looking at the ball bounce away. "And that's how you play a game." I receive a few claps, and take bows before turning my attention to Xavier to taunt him more. He's already looking at me when I turn, and the next words die in my mouth.

Oops rings in my ears when Xavier rushes toward me. I run away and ignore the idea of being a hypocrite, catching feelings after I explicitly drew the line. It doesn't matter, at least not right now, because the sun is shining, the guy I like is chasing me through the park with a grin on his face, and I might actually be happy.

CHAPTER 37

SOUTH LOS ANGELES – *Abandoned Parking Lot*
  August 27, 20:47 PDT

MY EYES ARE FIXED on the empty car spaces. Word on the street is there's going to be a money transfer tonight for the Outlaws. I watch Kane, who I've been tracking for weeks, step out of a beat-up sedan.

"K.A.R.M.A., run facial recognition on our new guest," I whisper, my voice barely audible through the earpiece. Below, Kane meets with someone new.

"Processing."

I zoom in with my binoculars, watching Kane hand over a large duffel bag full of cash. The other man, tall and imposing, takes it, exchanging a few words.

"Subject identified as Holden, higher-ranking member of the Omega Outlaws," K.A.R.M.A. reports.

"Elaborate more on Holden, K.A.R.M.A."

"Holden, real name Tim Collins, is one of the members with the most jail time and press presence. He is constantly on the move, traveling between the various Outlaw hubs in the states. He is one of the Outlaws' top men. He is considered to be a loose cannon, but still one of their most indispensable. According to police records, he has escaped prison for some of the most mundane reasons, from wanting a cup of coffee to seeing the sky out of the prison yard. Holden has recently been released from a short stint in prison for minor tax embezzlement."

So this might be the link I've been looking for. Holden, a wildcard higher-up in the Outlaws, is right in front of me. I watch as he flips the duffel over his shoulder, a satisfied smirk on his face.

Holden leaves just as I shift my attention to the heavily guarded Outlaw armored truck idling nearby. They're making a transfer tonight, and I'm going to intercept it.

"K.A.R.M.A., get ready to disable the truck's engine on my mark," I instruct, moving swiftly down the fire escape.

"Understood. Awaiting your signal."

I hit the ground running as the truck begins to move, and I match its pace. As it pulls out of the lot, I launch forward, latching onto the side. I pull myself onto the roof, the wind whipping around me as the truck picks up speed.

The truck barrels down the street, the roar of the engine and the rumble of the road beneath me. I maneuver carefully, positioning myself above the passenger window. With a quick motion, I smash the glass and reach inside, yanking the door open. The guard inside barely has time to react before I'm on him, delivering a swift punch to his jaw that knocks him out cold.

"K.A.R.M.A., now!" I shout and slide into the cab, my eyes locking onto the driver. He glances at me, startled, and fumbles for his gun.

"Disabling engine," K.A.R.M.A. responds.

I grab the driver's arm, twisting it painfully and slamming his head into the dashboard. He slumps forward, unconscious. The truck engine shudders, but it's still moving.

"Well, that didn't work," I mutter as I shove him aside and grip the wheel tightly, my heart pounding as I wrestle control of the massive vehicle. The guards in the back start shouting, realizing something's wrong.

The truck careens down a narrow alley, sides scraping against the walls. I spot a dead end up ahead and slam on the brakes. The truck skids to a halt, the guards in the back thrown off balance. I climb out the window and jump behind the van from the roof, my staff in hand, ready for a fight.

The first one stumbles out, gun raised. I duck under his arm, delivering a sharp blow to his ribs and another to his head, taking him out. The second guard is more prepared, firing a shot that whizzes past my ear. I roll to the side, coming up behind him and disarming him with a quick twist of my wrist. A knee to the gut and an elbow to the back of his head, and he's out like a light.

Breathing hard, I open the truck doors. The briefcases are still secure, untouched amidst the chaos. I open one, the sight of neatly stacked bills confirming my success.

"Let's see how these Outlaws function without any funds."

CHAPTER 38

USC CAMPUS – *Computer Architecture Lecture*
   September 02, 13:57 PDT

MY PROFESSOR HAS ALWAYS BEEN a man of many words, and until today, I never believed I would be one of those who found the habit irritating. He's saying a lot of valuable things, but all I can think about is how I'll give anything not to be in class anymore.

This is the last lecture I have before the start of Labor Day weekend. Xavier and I made plans to spend it together. Not only that, we're going to make a trip of it.

Xavier decided it'd be better if he was in charge of the planning. I had no reservations about the request, so I let him. I've tried to get him to tell me any information about where we're going, but he's as elusive as he's handsome.

A smile appears on my face, and I'm quick to wipe it off. I've caught myself doing it every time I think of Xavier recently. I pat my cheeks with both hands and shake my head, telling myself to snap out of it. I definitely won't fall for Xavier. I can't. I've read enough comic books to know that having a relationship while being a vigilante always ends terribly. But every time I think of him, I feel a way I haven't felt in years, and it almost feels like a betrayal to Jayden. I'm scared I could be happy without him, which hurts more than I'd like to admit.

In my apartment building, I head for the elevator instead of going to the basement like I usually do. I don't want to think about the case or my lack of progress. I keep picking up one loose end after another. The more I try to track down someone, the quicker the trails disappear.

Any minute now, Xavier will be here, and I'd rather not have to explain why I have a basement full of high-tech equipment. Falling in love with Xavier will mean hiding this part of myself from him. It's at times like this that I have to remind myself that it's best that we're not together that way.

My phone buzzes; it's Xavier. "I'm downstairs. If you're not ready, I can come up and wait."

I roll my eyes, zipping my bag closed. "How very generous of you. But I'm heading down already." I hang up the phone and walk to the door.

"Ma'am. Before you leave, I have a new potential status alert."

I groan. *No progress all week, but the second I want to go somewhere.* "What is it, K.A.R.M.A.?"

"The LAPD scheduled a last-minute sting operation for the Hazard Gang this afternoon. Would you like more information?"

Hazard Gang? From what I know, they're famous for human trafficking. Could they be involved in Jessica's murder? I hover over the doorknob. Should I stay and follow this potential lead? There might not even be a connection; Jessica was only affiliated with the Omega Outlaws, the Serpents, and the Black Syndicate. No mention of Hazards.

I take a deep breath. "K.A.R.M.A., stay close to it. Monitor all the communication channels for this op. Find and save any relevant paperwork from police servers. I have to go, but I'll be back Monday evening for an update."

"Certainly, ma'am."

Xavier is leaning against the *No parking* sign in front of my building, staring with conviction at a tablet. On seeing me, he stands straight and quickly pockets the device.

I walk to him, and he pulls me into a hug. I wonder briefly if no-strings-attached partners hug each other in public like this, but the thought doesn't sit long with me because Xavier pulls away and kisses me softly on the lips.

"Will you tell me what the plan is now?" I ask.

Xavier chuckles and throws open the passenger-side door. "I'm sure you'd like to know."

"Well, I don't think I know you well enough to assume you're not leading me to my death," I reply and get into the car. Xavier laughs and shuts my door. I don't clench up as much as I used to when he gets to the other side. *That's progress if I've ever seen it.*

His laugh follows him as he gets into the car, leaving a smile on my face. "Trust me, that's the last thing on my mind."

I say nothing but roll my eyes and buckle my seatbelt, connecting my phone to the car's speakers. Xavier's only request besides packing a weekend bag was for me to create a playlist for the ride. The first song that plays is one the basketball teams used to blast whenever we got together. Xavier's grin widens as he cranks up the volume.

Hours pass in comfortable silence, the road stretching out

before us. My phone vibrates, a message from K.A.R.M.A. lighting up the screen.

> Status Update: I know you are on a trip, ma'am, but I found more information on the case. A blood sample from Jessica was 'lost' in the chain of custody from the Sacramento lab. I believe Officer Mitchell played a role in this mishap to prevent conclusive results from being found. Will investigate further.

"Figures," I mumble, rubbing my temples. The suspicion of Mitchell being dirty is no longer just a hunch—it seems he's played an active role in sabotaging the case. I can't help but wonder if the supposed backlog in Sacramento was just another of his fabrications. There's no telling what else Mitchell has done to aid the Outlaws.

Xavier glances over, catching my frown. "Everything alright?"

"Yeah," I automatically reply, forcing a casual tone. "Just annoyed. A group member suddenly wants to meet this weekend for an assignment."

"Oh... Well, if you want, I can turn back."

"No, please continue driving to this mystery location. They'll just have to wait."

A small smile plays on his lips as he exhales in relief. "Good, because I didn't want to go back. I've planned something special, and turning around wasn't part of the deal."

I raise an eyebrow, intrigued. "Special, huh? You're really not going to give me any hints?"

He chuckles, eyes still on the road. "Nope. You'll just have to wait and see. Patience is a virtue, grasshopper."

"Since when did you become so mysterious?"

"Since I realized surprises make things more interesting," he quips back, glancing at me with a playful energy.

As he continues driving, the conversation drifts back into silence, the landscape gradually shifting. Finally, orange arches come into view, and it's clear where we are.

"San Francisco?" I ask, a hint of excitement in my voice. "You know I haven't been here before."

"Exactly," he says, pulling up to a hotel that's all glass and modern luxury—definitely not a place for a struggling graduate student.

When he opens my door, I keep looking at him, and this time, he does well to look back at me. I'd like him to explain, but he doesn't say anything. Placing the keys in the valet's hand, he simply smiles widely, and I swear he has the prettiest smile in the world.

"What's going on?" I ask as he helps me out of the car.

"We're staying here," Xavier says and gestures to the hotel behind him. I've stayed at hotels in my life, but never of this caliber.

"Are you serious?"

Xavier nods, putting his arm around my shoulder. "I promised you something special, didn't I?" He leads us over to the receptionist's table. I'm being pulled along because I'm taking in everything. The large chandelier hanging in the center of the room resembles an oversized golden ornament. The floors are covered in black-and-white marble tiles.

"Thank you," Xavier says, guiding me before I can bring myself well into the present situation and award the receptionist with a smile. He takes me to the elevator, and I follow diligently.

"It looks expensive," I note. I know his family has money,

but he has this need to be independent of it. A sentiment I don't understand but share in a totally different way.

"Don't think about it too much. We're here to relax for the weekend. And then we'll have to return and deal with all the stress that comes with our degrees."

The reminder makes me groan and place my head on his shoulder. "That's something I don't want to think about for a while."

I feel him nod his head in agreement when the elevator comes to a stop. He leads us down a large corridor with royal blue carpets while I try to control the rapid beating of my heart. I pay attention to the sound of our shoes when they hit the floor, which is a soft thumping sound.

The door opens, and Xavier pulls me in along with him. The room is larger than I thought. A gigantic bed with rose petals takes up most of the space in the middle of the room. The hotel has taken it upon itself to have a fruit bowl ready for us with a bottle of champagne, and I know it's only possible if Xavier made a special request.

I look over at him, and he's putting his bag away. I'm overwhelmed by how thoughtful the entire act is. I don't register dropping my duffle on the floor and moving to him until he turns around and watches me with raised brows.

When I get to him, I cradle his face in my hand and kiss him deeply. The kiss feels like every kiss we've shared, but I hope he'll know how grateful I am. I'm not sure what I expected him to do, but the six-hour drive and the hotel seem like a lot.

There's a pang in my heart, and I know what it means. I'm just refusing to dwell on it. I don't want to think about how the man who now has his hands on my waist is making me feel all kinds of things. Things I forgot I've felt before.

A shiver runs through me when he lifts my shirt to make

contact with my skin. Over and over, it rings in my head I'm falling for him, but I don't harp on how scary the thought is. I keep kissing him, and he keeps responding. When we pull apart for air, Xavier caresses my cheeks, pecking me lightly on my lips.

"Are you okay?" he asks. I don't open my eyes because I don't want to look into his. I can feel his fast breaths matching mine when I pull him in for a hug. Laying my face on his chest, I'm distracted by how firm it is.

Xavier holds me tighter, and I bury my face in his shoulders, and I try not to think about what changed. I don't even want to know when it changed. But it only sounds right when I think about it.

"Do you not like the room?" Xavier asks, "I can get another one if you like."

"I like the room. It's a lovely room." I pull my face away from his chest. "The bed looks amazing."

He coughs out a laugh, and I know that's the last thing he was expecting me to say.

"We should eat dinner," Xavier says, but he doesn't stop holding me, and I embrace him back. I feel safe right now in his arms. The last thing I'm thinking about is food, and I know he feels the same way if the bulge pressing into me is anything to go by.

"We can eat later; I'm sure the hotel will be glad to deliver room service," I say and palm his erection.

Xavier twitches and hugs me even tighter, his breath hitching a bit. "Winter," his voice comes with a warning, and I hum. "We need to eat," he says, and I've heard him try to be stern before to know he's doing a very bad job at it.

I hum again and release him long enough to unbuckle his belt and dip my hand through the band of his jeans. Xavier shivers, but he doesn't let me go, and I use my free hand to tether him to me.

He inhales a shaky breath by my ear when my hand wraps around him, and I feel goosebumps cover my skin. "You like that?" I ask, even though his body language is a good tell. Xavier says nothing, his breath strained.

I pull him into a kiss, and it's the hottest one we've shared today. Another tug on his dick has him gasping into my mouth, my tongue dipping inside to explore him. The effect I have on him sends a thrill through me. Breaking away, I push Xavier onto the bed and help him out of his pants. When his underwear comes off, he springs free, standing at attention, and I grin widely at him.

"You're enjoying this more than you should be," he says, a smirk playing on his lips. I reach down and squeeze it again. Xavier drops his head on a pillow with a groan, and I don't wait for him to recover before putting him in my mouth.

If I thought the first groan was the loudest he could be, I'm proven wrong when he grunts even louder. I laugh around him because it's the funniest sound I've ever heard him make. Xavier, abandoning all caution, grips my hair tightly. He thrusts his hips upward, causing me to gag. With my hands, I pin his waist down and continue. There's a plan I'm working with, and none of it includes having him do whatever he wants. I want him at my mercy. It's about giving him pleasure without him having to take it. I'm catering to him tonight.

"Winter, come on," Xavier whines. "I'm not going to last long if you keep sucking me like that."

I pull away, and he looks at me with dilated pupils. "Who says that's not the goal?"

"Fuck," he pleads, dropping his head back on the bed. "You're killing me here."

"I hope it's a happy death."

I put him back in my mouth before he can say anything and get back to business. Only this time, I'm stopping every single movement, restraining his hips. Xavier twitches and squirms, but I don't let up. He pulls my hair a little tighter, and I moan around his dick.

"Winter," he cries out my name, and I know for a fact he's on the edge, and all I need is to push him a little. And I do just that, squeezing him lightly and dragging my fingernails up his shaft until he finishes. I swallow while maintaining eye contact with him. His eyes never leave my mouth, and I move over to him and slot our lips together. I kiss him hungrily, hoping he can still get the taste of himself from my tongue.

"It's really amazing what your mouth can do," Xavier breathes out against my lips.

I throw my leg across his body and grind down on him. He becomes quite vocal, and I know it's because he's starting to feel overstimulated, but I don't relent in my movements. I can feel him growing again; this time, I allow his rutting.

Every time I brush against him, his rising erection presses into me and sends me into a frenzy, making me whimper.

"Xavier," I moan out, and he grabs my hips and guides them down to his cock, and I shudder above him.

"Tell me what you want?"

I know if I ask him to do me like I'm itching to, he'll flip us over and have me screaming his name, but I don't do anything like that.

"I want you to stay put." I slide off him and start to strip while his eyes follow me with rapt attention.

"I think room service closes soon," Xavier says, his voice coming out hoarse. He clears his throat and tries again. "It's pretty late."

"Well, I'm not sure what you had in mind to eat. But I can

think of something that might satisfy you in the meantime," I say as I remove my panties.

Xavier swallows as he takes in my naked body. "We can eat later."

I smile at him and settle into his lap. His hands immediately grip my bare ass, and he squeezes hard. The routine of the act makes me shiver a little.

"Hi," I say to him before placing a light kiss on his lips.

"Hi." Xavier leans in to kiss me again, but I move my head out of the way. If he thinks the blowjob is the highlight of this day, then he's painfully mistaken.

"I'm going to ride you now," I say and push him down slowly, laughing at the groan that leaves his mouth.

"You just might be the death of me this weekend."

I sink down his length, swallowing a little to give myself time to adjust. When I start to move, the sensation is familiar yet foreign. Xavier's hands hold onto my waist as I rise and fall. I throw my head back and do nothing to quiet my moans. I don't care about the reports the neighbors will give the front desk. I only care about satisfying the man beneath me. Our orgasms hit at the same time, and it feels unreal. I crumble on top of him, and he pulls me close and holds me as our breaths mix with each other.

"Damn, girl, that was amazing," Xavier exclaims, and a sad smile escapes me. The last time I heard that phrase, I was in another hotel room, only this time, it was my grad trip to Hawaii, and it was Jayden lying next to me.

I force the thought out of my head; I'm in bed with another man for crying out loud, and all I can think about is Jayden. I don't want to think about him anymore; I'm tired of living in the past.

Xavier's arms tighten around me, and I snuggle deeper into him. "We should really shower and order room service. I have a full day planned for tomorrow." I groan loudly even though I know he's right.

"But before we do that," Xavier begins, "I would like the snack I was promised."

He loosens his grip on me, leaving a trail of kisses down my stomach and thigh. He pushes my legs apart, his stubble tickling me, and claims his meal voucher.

CHAPTER 39

THE ROOM IS QUIET, and he waits for me to speak. His eyes are on me, but I'm trying to figure out what to say. I have a lot to say, in fact, and still there's no way to let it out of my mouth without giving myself away. More than I already have. Xavier believes I'll be affected by the decision he makes, and I don't want him to think that at all.

"That's good news." I force the words out and make it look like I mean all the syllables falling from my lips. "Congratulations."

I don't have to be a lab scientist like him to know the chance he's being offered is what some would call a once-in-a-lifetime opportunity.

Xavier nods, but he does it very meticulously, his eyes following me, and I start to feel a little uneasy from his scrutiny.

"When do you leave?" I ask.

"I have until Christmas to decide."

The way he says it, and the way he keeps looking at me makes me uncomfortable. At this point, if I was okay with the news, I would've stood up and offered to treat him to dinner to celebrate. I tell myself to do it, yet my mouth remains closed.

Now, Christmas looks like it's a good while away, but it'll creep up on us soon enough. I can't tell him to stay, and I can't be with him if he leaves. I still have a job to do here. I've done long distance enough to know I can't handle doing it again. This wouldn't even be a conversation if I stuck to my plan and avoided falling for him.

I grab my things because even if I can pretend to be alright, I can't do it for long. I need to get out of here before the ache in my chest becomes something I can't rein in. Leaving Xavier's apartment is an art in and of itself. I can never leave too quickly, or he'll know something is off with me, and I can't leave too slowly for the same reason.

"Winter," Xavier says when I get to the door. I'm hyper-aware of how I act, and I need to do it right. For someone who's a vigilante, I suck at subtlety. I have zero control over my feelings right now. How is it I always pick the worst time to be in touch with my emotions?

"Yes," I say and turn to face him with a smile on my face. I can't let him know how I feel. That'll just make things more complicated. How could I be so dumb?

I WAS NOT supposed to fall in love.

Xavier doesn't say anything, and my heart is hammering loudly. There's no mistaking the look in his eyes. He knows I'm struggling with the news. It's the same look of pity from our time at the coffee shop. I feel dreadful.

"I'm really happy for you. Really. Harvard's a big achieve-ment," I offer, which is an upgrade from running from him. I am running, but I'm doing it with a bit of grace this time. I don't wait for Xavier to say anything. I open the door and step out into the hall. I take a few moments to catch my breath. *This is the last thing I expected to happen.*

It isn't in my best interest to stand in front of his door and pretend I'm not breaking down, so I pull myself together before he decides to come after me. I head for the elevator, and despite moving forward, I feel like I'm back in high school all over again. I want him to take the opportunity. I think I want us to be together too, but I know I can't share him with anybody else. He's the reason I don't do long-distance relationships anymore.

The happiness sitting in the pit of my stomach causes me to twirl around the room Aunt Gina provided me this summer. I'm thrilled, and there's no other way to explain it.

Jayden and I talked. We both knew I'd be leaving in a few days. Summer break will be over soon, and who knows the next time we'd have to talk like that again.

I didn't want to be without him, and Jayden said being without me was impossible. What was even harder for him was the chance that if he let me go, another guy would swoop in and steal me away from him.

There's no denying the butterflies that swept through my stom-ach. It meant a million things all at once. He not only thought I was beautiful enough to catch the fancy of other guys, but he was scared I'd fall for their charms. If I'm being honest, I haven't met anyone who has managed to catch my attention the way Jayden has, but I find it cute he thinks about such things.

"We can keep this up after you leave," Jayden said, placing a light kiss on my lips.

"Keep this up?"

"Yes," Jayden looked at me with the brightest, saddest eyes. Until then, I never knew a person's eyes could hold two conflicting emotions. It made me want to hug him.

Falling into my bed, I hug my pillow tighter before bringing it to my mouth to help me muffle my screams. I repeat it to myself, recalling how he held my hands tightly, "Let's keep dating after you leave. If anybody can make long-distance work, it's us."

I kick my legs in excitement and roll over in my bed. This is nothing like the way I expected my summer to go. I thought we'd hang out, and I'd go back to my mom and start the tenth grade.

But this is even better.

IT'S LATE OCTOBER, and I've been away for too long, or at least it feels like it. In the span of three months, the friend group no longer included just the five of us. I know Jayden has always been popular, but the way his popularity has grown overnight since joining the football team is ridiculous.

We aren't spending each passing moment together on the phone like we used to. There are new friends, new girls who don't care who I am and don't want to learn. Girls that steal his attention, and he allows them while I find myself fading into the background until he remembers to call me.

However, Jayden wasn't the only one whose attention was diverted. After meeting Xavier at the entry game last year, we seem to naturally gravitate toward each other. Our paths crossed frequently; before long, we were saying hello in the halls and eating lunch together. Athletes had the same lunch block, so it made sense.

We sit across from each other in the cafeteria, the noise of chattering students filling the air. Xavier leans in and says, "Did you hear about that fight in the locker room yesterday?"

I roll my eyes, taking a bite of my sandwich. "Yeah, it's all anyone's talking about. What happened, exactly?"

"Apparently, Jake and Tom got into it over something stupid after practice—like who used up all the hot water in the showers. Tom accused Jake of hogging it every day, and things escalated from there." He chuckles, shaking his head. "Coach was not impressed."

I laugh, imagining the scene. "Typical high school drama. You'd think they'd have more important things to worry about."

Xavier smiles. "You know how it is. Any excuse for guys to throw punches, they'll take it. It's like we're living in a bad teen movie."

It was a relief to have someone like Xavier around. Our friendship came easily. I wasn't socializing much, and if I'm being honest, I didn't see the need for it. I couldn't afford to have a lot of friends. I had Jayden, and that was enough.

"Hey, speaking of practice," Xavier says, shifting the conversation, "I'll pick you and Rachel up later today. Sound good?"

"Yeah, that'd be great. Thanks." The bell rings, signaling the end of lunch. We gather our things and head to our respective classes.

It's the end of the day, and the three of us leave the gym after practice. We get to the door as I throw my shorts into my bag. "Hey, I don't see my homework. Go on without me; I'll just be a sec."

"Rachel, take the keys," Xavier says, handing them over. "I'll help Winter look for her homework."

We head back down the hallways, which are now quiet and deserted. I fumble with the combination once we stop at my assigned spot, frustrated with myself for being so forgetful. As I reach into my locker, Xavier steps closer, and the next thing I know, he has my back pressed against the wall.

"Winter," is all he lets out before pressing his lips to mine.

Something takes over me, and I drop the book I came back for, linking my arms around his neck to kiss him back properly. Our lips slot together, and it's a struggle on each of our parts not to let our hands wander.

It takes everything in me to snap out of it and pick up my text-book. "We should head back. Don't want to keep Rachel waiting."

CHAPTER 40

SUNSET BOULEVARD – *Behind The Gilded Tavern*
   October 07, 22:17 PDT

HALF of the letters are burned out in the sign above me, practically pleading to be repaired. A bouncer stands by a dumpster, arms crossed, eyes cold. The kind of guy you don't make small talk with. I approach him, keeping my posture casual but confident.

"Blackjack's Whisper," I say. His eyes run over me, assessing, before he steps aside and lets me through.

The underground gambling den is covered in an aggressive plume of cigarette smoke. Dim, buzzing bulbs hang from the ceiling, highlighting the chipped tables. The space reeks of bad decisions and adrenaline—things that keep places like this alive, and me within them.

Tugging the collar of my leather jacket higher, I blend in while every instinct in me stays sharp. I scan the room, taking note of the exits, the type of clientele lounging at the bar, and the dealers working the tables. I can't see Mitchell yet, but he'll show. The dirt always surfaces in places like this.

I sidle up to a table, easing into the empty chair. My eyes meet the dealer's briefly before studying the faces around the table. Hardened expressions. Shifty eyes. A couple of regulars. They don't spare me more than a glance.

"Buy-in's fifty," the dealer announces. I toss the chips onto the felt surface, keeping my movements deliberate, smooth.

As the cards slide across the table, the man to my left watches me curiously. He leans back in his chair, sizing me up in the low light, his greasy hair falling over one eye.

"You got a name, or you just like playing the silent type?" he asks, his voice rough like he's been chain-smoking for decades.

I barely glance at him, letting my fingers trace the edge of my cards. "Raven," I reply, keeping my tone flat. Raven Steele, a reliable alias I like to keep in my back pocket for occasions like this. I orchestrated her whole past, making sure to add a criminal record here and there. Some are real, some fake. Ms. Steele has gotten me out of a couple of binds in New York.

He pauses, his lips twisting into a smirk. "Raven, huh? Heard about someone using that name recently. Are any of the rumors true?"

I feel his eyes on me, but I don't give him more than a flicker of recognition. He's fishing, and I'm not about to give him any bait.

"People talk. Never know what's true these days."

He chuckles darkly, leaning in a little closer. "Well, if half of what I heard is true, I'm sitting next to one hell of a player tonight."

I raise an eyebrow, finally meeting his gaze. "Then maybe you should pay attention to your cards instead of mine."

The man shifts uncomfortably in his chair, but I've already turned back to the game, focused on the real target. I catch his reflection in the dusty mirror above the bar as he strides in, his presence pulling eyes across the room.

Mitchell's energy is loud, cocky, and just slimy enough to make your skin crawl. A couple of Outlaws greet him.

"Good to see you, my boy," one of them says, clapping Mitchell on the back. "Where's Sal tonight? Ain't seen him in a minute."

"Sal's lying low for a bit. Some heat came down on him recently. Happens." Mitchell says, waving them off with a lazy grin.

They laugh it off like it's no big deal, but I make a mental note. Sal. That's someone worth looking into later. *An accomplice, I'm sure.*

Mitchell moves to the high-stakes table, and I gather my chips and follow, sliding into a seat across from him. The dealer starts shuffling as I observe the criminal in disguise. He's too relaxed, too sure of himself. At home almost.

"Name's Raven," I say, catching his attention as the first hand is dealt.

He raises an eyebrow. "Raven Steele? Heard the name these past few weeks. Never thought I'd actually see you in person. You usually operate off a different coast, no?"

I suppress a smile. Nice to see my pseudonym still has some clout. If he were a real cop, I'd be worried. "I got tired of the snow. And sometimes you've got to get your hands dirty."

Mitchell chuckles, leaning back in his chair, his eyes never leaving mine. "Ain't that the truth."

The cards are a distraction from the real game we're playing. Each bet I place is calculated, but my focus is on him. On the way, his jaw tightens slightly when he's bluffing. On the flicker of his gaze toward the exit when someone new walks in. He's hiding something—more than a cop being on the take.

"You don't seem like the type to get too comfortable in a place like this," I say after a few rounds, keeping my tone casual. "What brings you here?"

Mitchell shrugs, taking a sip of his whiskey. "Same as anyone else. Money, connections. Fun."

I tilt my head, watching him closely. "Connections, eh? What kind of a connection do you get out of a place like this?"

His eyes narrow just slightly, but his smile doesn't budge. "You're asking too many questions, Raven. Not sure I like that."

I hold his gaze, unflinching. "I'm just curious. I've been in L.A. long enough to know that not everyone is a friend I want to have."

He leans forward, lowering his voice. "And what about you? Playing in places like this, dealing with people like me? What brings you here, Ms. Steele?"

I smile and say, "Raise, twenty-five." Pushing a large stack of black chips to the center of the table and add, "I'm smart enough not to get caught in someone else's mess."

His eyes alternate between the dealer and me. He knows I'm pushing. Knows I'm not here just to play cards.

"Call." He matches my bet and places the same amount of chips into the pot.

"As someone new to the West Coast..." I start as the dealer flips the third card and I watch Mitchell become less calm. "Anything to do up north? Bay Area, maybe?"

"Depends. You can get into a lot of trouble around the Oakland area. Stockton too if you want to branch out. Funny enough, I was up north not too long ago. Food isn't half bad in the capital either."

"Small world." I say, raising another ten thousand dollars. Mitchell huffs and folds, throwing his two cards to the center of the table. I collect my winnings and rise from my chair.

He looks at me with questioning eyes. "You don't want to go another round?"

"I like to quit when I'm ahead."

HOME – *Lair*
October 08, 03:09 PDT

"K.A.R.M.A., go through the LAPD database and find every cop with the name Sal. And pull up Detective Gillian's profile."

Each screen fills with bits of information—names, faces, people of authority. A small chime cuts through the silence, and K.A.R.M.A.'s voice follows.

"Processing complete. One potential match found. Officer Solomon Parks."

Parks? The screen shifts, and a photo of a young cop fills the display—a fresh-faced kid in blues, the same rookie that took my statement. *The first cop on the scene.*

"Parks graduated from the LAPD police academy one point five years ago. Officer Mitchell is listed as his training officer. He just completed his rookie training."

My eyes narrow in on the screen. Mitchell's been busy. He's got this kid wrapped up in his dirty dealings too. Seems like Parks wasn't given a choice but to follow his mentor's path. One that leads straight into a life of corruption. A newbie who didn't have a clue what he was getting into when he signed up. *Or maybe he did.*

Another chime. "And the profile as requested."

Detective Jonathan Gillian's information slides across the screen. His photo shows the same man I met in the police station, mid-forties, clean-cut, jaw set like stone, and a pair of sharp, no-nonsense eyes that speak to a career built on busting criminals. Married, of course. No kids, though, or at least none that the file mentions. A decorated officer, won the California Investigator of the Year Award. Twice. His track record is spotless.

Gillian has led Jessica's investigation from the beginning. If it wasn't for him, the case wouldn't be open. She would've been another statistic in the war on drugs, the same story of a celebrity lost to the needle. From what I have observed of Gillian, I know enough to know he's thorough and relentless. The type of cop who doesn't stop until he gets the answers he needs.

He has no idea that he's being intentionally sabotaged in his case by a fellow badge holder. I don't think he's dirty. But after tonight's Casino Royale with Mitchell, who ever really is clean?

I sit back in my chair, replaying the poker game in my mind. That Texas Hold 'Em chat revealed more than I expected. He was definitely in Northern California when Jessica's evidence was tampered with in Sacramento. That much is clear. The problem is, there's no record of him buying any plane or bus tickets. I combed through his financials—nothing. His city-issued car, the only vehicle he owns, never left L.A. County. So how did he get up there?

My phone vibrates on the table, interrupting my thoughts. The message is from Xavier, and I consider ignoring it for a second. But curiosity wins out.

Haven't heard from you... Are
we good?

Instead of replying, I toss the phone aside, exhaling hard. There's so much going on right now, I don't have the headspace to deal with Xavier's upcoming relocation. The case comes first. It always has.

"K.A.R.M.A., does Mitchell have any family or close connections not listed on his profile? I need to know who else might be involved," I ask, rubbing the bridge of my nose. The lack of sleep is catching up to me, but I can't stop now. He's not married and doesn't have any siblings. So who else is there? There has to be someone else.

"No other immediate family but I found a sealed court case from San Diego."

My eyebrows raise. "Sealed? Open it."

A string of legal documents fill the screen. It's a custody case, buried deep in the records. Mitchell's name is listed as the defendant in a paternity suit. And right there in black and white, I see it. He has a child. A child with a woman named Carla Vasquez. I lean closer, scrolling through the details. Carla, his baby mama, lives in Richmond, California. My gut twists. "K.A.R.M.A., cross-reference any flight or travel bookings from Carla Vasquez's accounts in the past year."

K.A.R.M.A. processes for a moment, then pulls up a flight itinerary from LAX to SFO, purchased ten months ago. The date aligns perfectly with the evidence-tampering timeline.

"Carla bought the ticket," I mutter, realization settling in. "Mitchell didn't have to leave a trace. She did it for him." He thought he was slick by having her book the trip. Smart. But not smart enough.

I stand up, my mind racing. This complicates things. Mitchell's more careful than I thought, using Carla as his shield. It makes sense now—no digital trail to follow, nothing that could link him directly. But he was in Sacramento, evidence was mishandled, and it was under the radar.

CHAPTER 41

CRENSHAW – *Steel & Chrome Auto Works*
   October 30, 22:37 PDT

MY HEAD RESTS against a gutted car in the salvage yard. The moonlight highlights the maze of abandoned vehicles and scrap metal, creating the perfect cover. My senses are on high alert, every creak and rustle amplified in the stillness of the night. I inch closer to the dilapidated car repair shop, searching for movement. The place reeks of rust, a fitting scent for an Outlaw operation.

K.A.R.M.A. and I have been occupied these past few weeks. We shut down a drug den on 5th Street, dismantled a gambling ring on Maple Avenue, and took out a weapons cache near the docks. Each hit has been pushing the Outlaws closer to extinction. I want to systematically dismantle every operation they have. They need to be desperate and careless. The more pressure we apply, the more mistakes they'll make. The fewer places they have to hide, the easier they'll be to take down.

I pause at the edge of the yard, staying low as the smell of oil wafts in the air. "K.A.R.M.A., is this the right location?"

Just as I'm about to move, a bullet whizzes past my ear, embedding itself in a nearby car door with a thud. *That answers that question.* I roll to the side, finding cover behind a heap of demolished cars. Gunfire echoes through the yard, and I take a moment to assess. Five shooters.

"Affirmative. Multiple sources indicate this is the main chop shop for the Outlaws."

I pull out my earpiece in frustration and peek around the corner. The nearest gunman progresses closer, maintaining a bounce in his stride. I take a deep breath, aim, and fire. The bullet hits his shoulder, and he drops his weapon with a cry of pain.

Four to go.

I move swiftly, keeping low. Another gunman rounds the corner, and I fire twice, hitting him in the leg. He goes down, screaming. A third shooter engages, bullets ricocheting off the metal around me. I dive behind a pile of tires, return fire, and hit him in the chest. He slumps to the ground.

Two more shots ring out, narrowly missing me as I duck behind a stripped-down car. I scooch to the side, aim, and execute, hitting the fourth gunman in the arm. He drops his weapon and falls to his knees.

The last man, a heavy-set brute, charges at me with a roar. I sidestep, using his momentum to throw him into a stack of car parts. He groans, trying to get up, but I place my gun to his head.

"Don't move," I hiss, quickly restraining his hands and feet before securing the other wounded men. All five thugs neutralized.

"K.A.R.M.A., alert the cops."

"Understood."

I move to the back of the repair shop, where the office is. This is where the brains of the operation will be, and where I'll be able to get my answers. I kick the door open and find someone reaching for a gun on the desk, but I beat him to it, aiming my pistol at his head.

"Ah, ah, ah," I almost sing, "Drop it."

He freezes, his hand hovering over the gun before slowly raising them in surrender. "Alright, alright. No need to get hasty."

My gaze locking onto his, I demand, "Who killed Jessica Glory?"

"You're in over your head, girl. You think you can just waltz in here and—"

I shut him up with a punch to the gut and a knee to the face, making him double over in pain. "I'm not here to negotiate. Who. Killed. Jessica. Glory?"

He spits blood. "Look, I don't know who exactly did it. All I know is the Outlaws haven't been selling dope for a while because of it. And I've been up my ass in trying to keep up with all the stolen vehicles they're trying to move instead." He stops and hesitates. I cock the gun and insert it under his chin. "I've heard rumors. Something about an expansion gone wrong. If it was something that big, that means the higher-ups were involved."

"Give me names."

"Kane, maybe? Could be higher? I'd just be guessing. They don't tell me shit. I just work on cars, okay."

"Where can I find him?" Kane has dropped off the face of the Earth since the money transfer over two months ago.

"Hell if I know. Look around, crazy goggle lady. I don't run a criminal organization. I get paid a little extra to turn the other way when VIN numbers don't add up."

I step back, nodding. He's right, a scrapyard mechanic

doesn't have all the answers I need. I knock him out and exit the shop, the sound of sirens growing louder. *They're right on time.* The authorities will take care of the cleanup.

CHAPTER 42

THE IRON SPOKE – *Adjacent Rooftop*
   November 13, 01:28 PST

"YOU HAVE an incoming call from Xavier Harris, ma'am. Would you like to answer it?"

"Yes, answer it," I whisper, keeping my voice low.

"Winter? It's late. What are you doing up?" His surprise is evident, even through the phone.

"Oh, I don't know. Maybe it's the same reason you're still up," I reply, my eyes still trained on the figure below. My attempt at a joke is met with silence. "But what's up?"

"I was going to leave a voicemail, but I just wanted to let you know I can't make our usual time for lunch later today. Something came up," he says, sounding a bit frustrated.

"That's okay. We'll reschedule."

"I hate to cancel on you. We were starting to make this a routine." I can hear the sincerity in his voice, but I can't help the twinge of disappointment.

Lunch breaks with Xavier have become a welcome escape

from the constant grind of work. More often than not, they end with us tangled in sheets, momentarily forgetting how Christmas is rapidly approaching.

"No worries," I say, forcing a smile he can't see. "We'll meet up some other time."

"How's everything else going?" he asks.

I delay my response, looking at the night sky. "It's... complicated. I've gathered a lot of information for this project I'm working on, but I'm not sure how to piece it together yet."

"You'll figure it out," he says. "You always do. Hey, I wish I could talk more, but I've got to go," he says softly before hanging up, returning my mind to the task at hand. The target stops at a corner, glancing around nervously.

I've been tracing a new possible suspect for the last few days, a guy named Dragon. I suspect the name comes from the dragon tattoo on his left arm. He's the only person I've seen interact with Holden besides Kane since I started following him; based on how their discussion went outside the bar, I suspect he knows a thing or two about Holden, or at least, he might be doing a task for him.

Dragon is everywhere on the police database. He's been arrested for everything from breaking and entering to tax evasion to stealing cars. But there's nothing on him for murder or drugs.

The thing with Dragon is, he isn't an Outlaw. He's a Hazard. So what does he want with Holden then?

I stay hidden, following behind him. Dragon is a large man who looks like he spends more time in the gym than in the real world. Given his line of work, I suppose it helps him feel intimidating. Yet, he lacks any sort of situational awareness someone in his profession should have. He seems not to have a care in the world. He's smoking a cigarette, and this is the third one he's on. He left the bar a while ago and has been walking around this section of town. He doesn't live in the area, so he must be waiting for someone.

The screech of tires pulls my attention from the man below me. I look to my right to see two headlights barreling down the road; I spare Dragon a look and see he's traded the cigarette in his hand for a handgun. I tilt my head to the side and step away from the edge of the building, but not so far that I don't get a view of what's about to happen. Dragon takes aim, and I expect him to pull the trigger. Instead, he hesitates long enough for the car to roll by and open fire on him.

I watch his body shake as each round fires into him. I stand frozen for the longest time, even after Dragon's body hits the ground, even after the people on the street rush over to check if he's still breathing, even after the car is nowhere in sight.

My heart hammers at the sight of his blood pooling around him. I step further away from the edge of the building. I fall to the ground and will myself to get it together.

There goes my fucking lead.

CHAPTER 43

HUNCHED OVER MY WORKBENCH, tools and parts litter the table. The glow of the work lamp illuminates the circuit board in front of me as I carefully solder delicate connections for my latest project—a compact device meant to scramble communication signals. Every wire, every connection needs to be perfect.

Xavier's name lights up my phone screen, taking me out of my technical trance. "Hey. How's it going? Are you busy?"

"Not too busy," I answer, leaning back in my chair. "Just doing some homework."

Before I can say more, a sudden spark erupts from the circuit board, followed by a string of smoke. Soon enough, the board engulfs into flashes.

"Son of a..." I cough as I swat the smoke away with one hand. *I left the damn iron on the board.*

"What happened? Are you okay?" His concern is immediate.

"Yeah, just one sec," I say, trying to downplay the incident, rushing to get the fire extinguisher out of the cabinet. I pull the pin and approach the flames cautiously, spraying the contents of the canister. I peer at the now-charred and damp circuitry. The room fills with the smell of burnt plastic, and I kick the chair over in frustration. I've done this a hundred times before. But I've never been so careless.

"And what homework are you working on exactly?" Xavier asks sarcastically. "But seriously, are you alright?"

"All good," I insist. "So, what's up?"

There's a brief pause, then he speaks. "I was wondering if I could come over. I could use the company."

I feel a smile tug at the corners of my mouth. "Sure. I've been staring at screens for far too long. Come over whenever."

"Great. I'll be there in about an hour."

"See you soon," I say, hanging up. I set my phone down and tidy up my workstation, throwing my melted idea in the trash. I leave the basement, a place the property manager thankfully hasn't requested a survey of.

I clean up the clothes I have lying around the apartment because I don't want to seem like a slob to Xavier, not that I think he's going to care so much. As long as the bed is made, I'm sure the clothes I have everywhere won't matter.

The doorbell rings a few minutes later, and I open it to find Xavier standing there with a smile and a pizza box.

"I brought pizza," he announces as he enters, placing a kiss on my lips. It seems almost domestic. The type of thing someone would do to their wife, not the girl they're hooking up with, but I don't comment on it. I have limited time to be with him. I'm not going to question it, nor am I going to allow myself to enjoy it because it will be taken away from me before I even knew what was going on.

He places the box on the dining table before heading into the kitchen to grab plates. I stand by the door, watching how comfortable he feels in my apartment. I know for a fact when I show up at his place, I'm the same way. Why did I never notice it before?

"What are you studying for?" Xavier asks, coming into the living room area with two plates, looking at the large Database Design textbook I'm currently skimming through.

"Just making sure I haven't forgotten everything I've been taught so far." Which isn't a lie, but it isn't exactly the truth, either.

"During Thanksgiving break?"

I shrug my shoulders. I'm hoping to find a trick that'll allow me to break into a database I found that may contain information on Jeep. "My thesis class is next semester, and I still don't know what I'm going to write about."

Xavier nods, opening the pizza box. I settle down next to him, accepting the slice he offers.

"So, what's your dissertation topic?" I ask, trying to keep the conversation light.

He shrugs, taking a bite. "Something about genomes and sequencing. How they can be altered to fight off cancerous cells. Honestly, it's still a bit up in the air. I don't want to specialize but all my advisors are telling me it's the only way to get published. And getting published is the only way to get a permanent lab position."

I nod, pretending to understand. The inner workings of university research will always remain a mystery to me. "Sounds complex."

"It is," he admits with a chuckle. "I haven't fully decided

what angle to take yet. Might be moot though, since I might not be finishing it at UCLA anymore."

The unspoken reality of his imminent departure lingers between us. I don't dare to ask more, afraid of the answer. Alternatively, I focus on his face, how his eyes light up when he talks about his research, and how his lips move.

Talking to him feels strangely underwhelming. I crave his touch, his warmth. Knowing he won't be around for much longer makes every moment feel precious. When he leaves, I'll be back to picking up random men at the bar, men who will never be Xavier. It feels like a waste not to seize every second we have left.

I finish my slice but don't take another. Instead, I watch him eat, waiting for him to finish. When he finally does, I scoot closer, feeling the heat of his body next to mine. Without a word, I press my lips to his, pouring everything unspoken into the kiss.

The pizza crust falls from his hand, and he wraps an arm around my waist and pulls me onto him so I'm straddling his lap. I press myself into him, and he squeezes my thighs.

"Winter," Xavier says in between kisses, and I don't let him speak. I can't let him talk because if he does, I know he'll say something I'm in no mood to hear. "We need to talk."

I shake my head slightly and bring his lips back to mine. "We can talk after," I say. As far as I'm concerned, we don't have anything to discuss.

The only issue is Xavier isn't interested in talking after. He wants to talk before we go any further, which frustrates me even more. I sigh and take a deep breath, but when I go to dismount him, he holds me in place.

"What do you want to talk about?" I ask, crossing my arms.

Xavier tugs at one of my curls and twists the hair around his finger before letting go. "Boston."

I suppress a groan and rest my forehead on his. "I thought we already talked about it."

"Did we?"

I nod frantically and try to kiss him, but he expertly avoids my lips. I audibly groan this time and throw my head back.

"Of course, we did," I say. "At your apartment, you told me, and I wished you all the best."

Xavier bites his bottom lip, and I focus my attention there. I don't dare to look him in the eyes. Otherwise, all my thoughts will fall off from my lips, which won't do any of us any good.

"Winter," Xavier says and pulls on another lock of my hair, "Why won't you look at me?"

"I don't know why you think this conversation is necessary. You're going to take the job at Harvard, and that's all there is to it. It's an amazing opportunity, and it makes sense for your PhD and career. Why do you think it's something we need to discuss?"

The anger is building up, and I try to slide off his lap, but he won't let me leave. I don't appreciate being held down like that. My heart is thumping too fast, and I feel cornered.

"I want you to tell me how you feel."

I force myself out of his grip and walk to the other end of the room. "I thought we were just having some fun. What do you want to hear from me, Xavier?"

"Damn it, Win! The truth," Xavier yells, pushing his seat back. The frustration I feel is starting to be evident in his voice too. At least, that makes the both of us.

"What truth? We're fuck buddies. There's no need for us to act like we have a special relationship. If you leave, I'm sure you can find someone to replace me as easily as I can find someone to replace you."

His face goes void of all emotion, but I can't turn my back on what I feel. There's no need to try to get him to stay. I don't want him to choose to stay. *He's better off without me.*

"How long are you going to deny your feelings for me?"

I laugh to be cruel. "Feelings for you? I feel something for you, and it starts and ends with sex. The company is good, and we relieve some stress for each other. Except now, I'm not feeling very thrilled by this conversation. You should be helping with my stress, but you're at the center of it."

"That's bullshit, and you know it."

"Think what you must," I say and look around my apartment. Has it always been this small?

Xavier takes a step toward me, and I take one back. I need distance between us. So much has happened that he doesn't know about. I'm so much that he doesn't know about. He slowly approaches until my back hits the wall, and he stands in front of me. I still don't look at him. I look past him. I won't let him do this to me.

"Aren't you tired of this game?" Xavier places a light kiss on my shoulder, and a shiver runs through me. "Why do you keep insisting this is nothing?"

I open my mouth and close it. I don't want to respond to that.

"We're so much more," he says, his lips kissing up and down my neck. I tilt my head to the side to give him more access, and he takes it. He sucks on every inch as though he's trying to mark me up.

"I can't do this," I say finally, unable to stop myself. I don't know *how* to do this.

Xavier steps away and nods his head. *Hold it together. I can't fall apart right now.*

"I'm going to go," he says, and I don't move to stop him.

HOME – *Living Room*
  November 27, 14:23 PST

THE TEXTBOOK in front of me makes less sense the more I read it. I've been staring at the Incident Response section for more than an hour now, but I haven't flipped a single page yet. My thoughts keep finding their way back to Xavier. Whatever he thinks we have between us will just have to be ignored because it doesn't matter at all. Why did we have to reconnect if I was going to fall this hard and get left behind?

A knock on my door pulls me out of my thoughts, and I hurry to it, hoping to find Xavier with another box of pizza. I knew he wouldn't let me spend Thanksgiving all by myself.

The smile on my face falls. My mother smiles at me and gives a little wave.

"Surprise," she says and looks inside my place. "I thought I'd wish you a Happy Thanksgiving."

I slam the door shut. In the hallway she yells, "I brought Chinese food!"

Opening the door again, I notice the takeout bag in her hands. I snatch the food and close the door for a final time.

"Come on. Winter, don't be like this," she says through the door. "I'm trying here. Let me in. Now."

I step back and stare at the door between us. *Let her in?* Who is she to give me demands? A long time ago, I made a promise with myself that I wouldn't let her disturb my peace again. And this door is the only thing keeping it intact. I don't intend on breaking the streak anytime soon.

"Winter, I just want us to talk," she says in the hallway, almost pleading, but there's something rehearsed about it.

"Talk? About what? About how you sold me out when I needed you most? Or is this about how you want to feel better about yourself now that you've got your life together and realize you're getting older with nothing to show for it?"

It's going to take a lot more than crab rangoons to bridge the abyss she left between us. After being her payment for a couple of bottles of Xanax when I was fifteen, how could I believe anything has changed since? There's a long list of things I can forgive, but I can't forget.

"Winter, I've changed," she insists. "I'm trying to make amends. I want to make things right."

"Yeah, right." I let out a bitter laugh. "You're trying to make yourself feel better. Let's not pretend this is about me."

"Winter, I know I hav—" My mother begins, but I cut her off. "It's always about what you want, what you need. *Me. Me. Me.* And what about what I want? That's never mattered to you. Not then, and not now." My words ooze with years of built-up resentment. "If I was unclear the first time, let me spell it out for you. Get out of L.A. and leave me alone!"

CHAPTER 44

"WINTER, do you think this section on market analysis is comprehensive enough?" Sara asks, her eyes glued to the document in front of her.

I glance at the highlighted text, my mind half-focused on the words. "Yeah, it looks good. Just make sure to include the latest stats I found last night. That and the proceeding relating to our topic."

As Sara nods and makes a note, my eyes drift to my phone lying on the table. The screen lights up, but it isn't Xavier. I haven't heard from him in weeks. He isn't picking up my calls, and I refuse to believe he'd ignore me like this. If he wants nothing to do with me, I want him to say it to my face.

"Winter?" Nathan's voice pulls me back. "What did you think about this class?"

"Yes," I say, forcing myself to focus. "I thought it was very theoretical. I'm more of a hands-on, in-the-code person. But it definitely gave me a new perspective."

"Agree. I didn't think Cybersecurity at USC of all places would be so focused on theory," Sara states.

"Yeah," I muster, struggling to stay present. My thoughts keep returning to Xavier. Each attempt to reach him has been met with his voicemail. Even though I was kind of a bitch the last time we spoke, I don't think he would leave without attempting to say goodbye. Xavier isn't the type to up and disappear.

"Once I finish the formatting, I'll send the email to the professor. The extension did come in handy, but I'm so ready to be done with this final project." Nathan sighs.

"Perfect." I gather my things. "I hope everyone has a great Christmas," I say, imitating a smile.

"Thanks, Winter," Sara says, giving me a concerned look. "You okay?"

"Yeah, just tired. Let me know if there's anything left I can help with." I step out of the library into the crisp evening air. The campus is growing quieter now, the day and the semester winding down.

Standing in front of Xavier's building, I pull out my phone one last time. I dial his number, the familiar sequence almost automatic. The call rings once, twice, then goes straight to voicemail. My heart sinks.

"Xavier, it's Winter. Call me back."

Determined, I push open the door to his building and ride the elevator up to his apartment. I reach his door and knock, no reply. I knock until a neighbor takes pity on my knuckles and comes out. "I don't think he's around," he says with a frown on his face, but I don't pay much attention to it.

"Has he been gone for long?"

The man tries to think about it. "I haven't seen him for at

least a couple of weeks now. Maybe he traveled. You should call him." I don't tell him I've already tried that. Instead, I thank him as he retreats into his apartment.

The next option would be to leave, but I can't. Something feels off, and it isn't a feeling I can shake.

I stare at the door for the longest time. Sighing, I reach into my bun and grab a hair clip. Xavier's deadbolt is harder to pick than I thought it'd be, but I get the final tumbler and I step inside, shutting the door behind me.

As always, the house looks immaculate. There are a few books on his table, and his laptop is there too. Everything in his apartment looks the same and in tip-top shape. When I peek into his bedroom, I don't find anything out of place. His bag is here, and none of his clothes seem to be missing. I wonder if I know any of his friends, but I come up short.

I look back at the laptop and wonder if taking it with me is a good idea. I have a bad feeling, but how am I going to explain taking his computer while he's away? I could tell him I took it to ensure he speaks to me no matter what. It seems like a good enough reason to me, so I grab the device and walk out of his apartment building.

HOME – *Lair*
December 22, 18:14 PST

UNLIKE HIS DOOR, his laptop is fairly easy to get into. I don't know why, I just expected him to take his digital security more seriously. He clearly has no clue how easy it is for someone to hack into his accounts. I thought he was listening to all my rants during our pillow-talk sessions.

As I look through his laptop, I see why his password was

so pitiful. There are no folders. No photos. No documents. No videos. It's empty. Nothing about the drive reveals that it was wiped recently either.

Why would someone have an empty laptop? Why does *Xavier* have an empty laptop? I navigate to his browser and see no prior browser history, but there's one bookmark labeled Cloud. I click on the link and it directs me to a login screen. There's a username and password required, and when I guess, I'm made aware I have just two chances remaining.

"K.A.R.M.A., find all instances of Xavier's social media presence. Use those usernames to find a hash of his password on the cloud's server. Then use my offline brute-force script to crack his password. Start with keywords like close friends, family, or pets."

Voila, two and a half hours later, I'm in. Given the level of entropy for his password, I'm certain he was listening to me the entire time. I suppress a smile.

I'm presented with seven folders labeled *Year 1-7*. I double-click on *Year 1* and a voice recording auto-plays. I hear Xavier's voice describing his first day patrolling his neighborhood. He talks about a string of robberies and wanting to stop the person responsible before he went back to college in the fall. I exit out of *Year 1* and go to *Year 5*. This folder holds more than just voice recordings. There's suit design sketches, addresses, and blueprints. I recognize the logo belonging to the other L.A. vigilante.

There has to be a misunderstanding. *It can't be.*

My hands shake as I stare at the screen. Xavier is Nightshield, the vigilante I saw at the hospital. I've spent this entire time sleeping with the other vigilante. I don't know if I should laugh or cry. How is it that the person I've been trying to find has been right under my nose for the longest time?

Rising from my chair, I pace from one server tower to another, shaking my head at the absurdity of it.

I try to recall something that could've hinted at Xavier being a vigilante, but nothing comes to mind. Well, actually, Xavier is absolutely ripped. There's no explanation for why a biochemical engineering PhD student needs to be that swole. I do know we were both constantly in and out, yet we always seemed to have similar availability. Maybe that should've been the reddest flag. Now that I think about it, we rarely had nightly link ups. I suppose both of us were patrolling the streets then.

A laugh leaves my mouth. *Xavier is a vigilante.* It's as outrageous as it is true. Perhaps he was right about fate because this is simply unbelievable.

There are so many entries to go through, and instead of getting to them, I decide to make myself a cup of tea to help me calm down, taking a page out of Gina's book. I can't over-think the situation. A steaming mug of tea now positioned next to my keyboard, I return to my chair ready to delve deeper into Xavier.

I start the recordings from the very beginning. A part of me wonders what his excuse will be when he gets back. Should I pretend I don't know what he does with his nights? The ones he doesn't spend with me. Or should I come clean too and tell him about myself? The next diary entry I find causes me to stop short. It has my name in it, and it's Xavier wondering if I'm doing alright after what happened to me.

Holy shit. I'm the reason he decided to become a vigilante. He says he felt so powerless when he found me, and he didn't want that to happen again. All I can think about is Xavier dedicating his life, vowing what happened to me won't happen to anyone else under his watch. It squeezes my heart and makes me desperate to see him.

Flipping from one folder to the next, I find the very last entry. Xavier is waiting for a guy named Macey. I wonder why I never thought of doing reports. They seem fun and informative. If I was the one who went MIA and Xavier was trying to find me, I'm certain he wouldn't find anything.

"I'm going to tell Winter I love her," Xavier in the tape says, and my heart rate picks up. "I just want her to be honest with me. I'll give up Harvard for her. For us."

After everything, he still wants to be with me. My vision becomes blurry slightly.

A *bang* forces my teary eyes to the screen. "Boss, we have him."

I stare at the black void long after the audio ends. I look at the metadata from the MP3 file and the date is from two and a half weeks ago. My heart rate picks up again. While I was busy going from one final to the next, hoping Xavier would call me, he was in the hands of whomever this is.

"K.A.R.M.A., search every known database for a Macey." I say, biting my fingernail and bouncing my leg as I await her response.

"One match found. Macey, real name unknown, is an alias for a member of the Hazard Gang."

Hazard Gang. "K.A.R.M.A., pull up the police op intel you gathered from Labor Day weekend," I say, putting on a pot of coffee. *Tonight's going to be a long night.* "What provoked the sting on the Hazards?"

"Accessing data," K.A.R.M.A. responds. "The Hazards have been using containers at the Port of Los Angeles for a portion of their operations. Container numbers B47, C53, and D12 were flagged for suspicious activity by customs."

A creak escapes the chair when my weight sinks further into it, trying to think clearly. "Do we have any footage or recent activity on those containers?"

After a few seconds, the screen fills with grainy images of the port. "These are the most recent feeds available from a month ago."

The thought gnaws at me that if I hadn't been out gallivanting in San Francisco with Xavier, I could've helped the cops capture these criminals. Then maybe Xavier wouldn't be in this predicament.

I watch the footage, searching for any sign of the Hazards. *Is he even alive?* After almost three weeks of being held captive, the chances seem slim.

Slim is good enough for me. I jump up from my seat; the docks are a solid lead to act on. I can't afford to be slow with this case. His life is on the line. I get dressed in black, wearing my recon suit. I load up with my sniper rifle, my two handguns, my belt, and a buttload of ammo.

As I secure my gear, I whisper a simple prayer: "Please let me find him alive."

CHAPTER 45

"UNDER MY DIRECTION, the homeless population has decreased by over four percent. A vote for Governor Nelson is a vote for a housed California. W—" I turn off the car radio. I'm not in the mood for political ads.

I decided to procure a vehicle for this mission because I thought a getaway car might be necessary. I have no idea what I'm walking into. As I drive to the pier, every home I pass by is covered in festive lights. If by some Christmas miracle I get Xavier back, this will be our first Christmas together.

"Xavier is a vigilante," I whisper to myself, still unable to believe it.

With the aid of my binoculars, I'm able to get a clear visual of the front of the shipping yard. I climbed to the top of a crane to get a bird's-eye view. There are at least ten guards at the entrance, and they aren't just staying put. They're moving from one place to another. I don't have time to figure out how their movements work.

Neither the range on my sniper scope nor my binoculars is far enough for me to see how many hostiles are inside. The last time I tried to infiltrate somewhere blind, I got my ass handed to me. But none of that matters because the most important thing is getting in there and getting Xavier back. Alive.

Descending the crane, I start my advancement toward the containers. Overhead lights come on and move in all directions. I almost get struck by one of them. *Great, now I have to deal with the guards and the lights.*

As I get closer to the perimeter of the fence, I realize how much of a fool I am for this. There's no guarantee he's even in this yard. There are hundreds of containers, maybe even thousands, and I doubt any of them are labeled *Xavier is here.* And there are at least a baker's dozen worth of people I need to avoid.

Despite that, I inch toward the back side where the ocean stares back at me. No one hears me when I cut through the wires of the fence. I cut just enough so I can squeeze through, and if needed, Xavier can too. When the light passes my way again, I hide behind a dark orange container. Casing the yard, I stick close to the sides of the cargo crates.

I scan every crate I pass by using the x-ray feature on my goggles and groan. *Jesus,* this is going to take forever to check each container. Then there are sounds of movement, and I reach for one of my dual pistols. This time I came prepared with a silencer. I turn off the safety and make my way quietly toward the noise. I'm a few boxes away from what I assume are Hazard goons.

"Pick up the speed! We don't have all day." I tap my goggles and see a line of women and a male figure pushing a young girl into one of the open boxes. I count four men who aren't restrained.

After they lock the container, I pop out and head-shot everyone but one. As the remaining one grabs his gun, I shoot his hand and run toward him. I throw him against the crate as he clutches his wrist. "Where is he?"

"Where is who? Who are you?"

"Don't act stupid. Where is Nightshield? I know your gang was the last to encounter him."

"I don't know!"

I press my gun into his crotch and whisper, "You have three seconds to respond or your 23andMe ends with me."

"I swear I don't know. Juan would have known." He proceeds to point to one of the three bodies I just dropped.

Goddamnit. I really need to ask more questions before I shoot to kill. That's my bad. I take a deep breath. "Cool and collected" Winter has a better chance of getting out of here with Xavier versus "vengeance shall be mine" Winter, blinded with rage.

"Well, Juan can't help you anymore, but I can. If you don't want to end up like him and your lil friends, you're going to tell me everything you know," I say, adjusting my grip on him.

"Okay. Okay! All I know is that we are holding somebody and he might be in one of our shipment yards. Either here or Long Beach. We have a few men guarding him." I cock the gun, and he trembles. "Look, that's all I know. Please don't kill me."

I slam his head against the container and knock him out. I'll let him live because he was kind of useful.

Before I go, I reach into the snitch's pocket, pull out the restraint keys, open the container, and throw them in. Before closing the door, I tell the girls, "Be smart."

This isn't my battle tonight.

I leave to do another survey of the shipyard, listening closely for movement. About twenty rows down, I hear a crate clink open. As covertly as I can, I make my way there, climbing atop of a container.

There's a figure tied up in the distance when I inch toward the corner. It's Xavier. There are four guards on each side of the shipping container with another two inside taunting him. Xavier seems to be a little out of it. His face looks swollen and purple. His chest is exposed, showcasing a bunch of newly added bruises and cuts.

"Hey Shield," someone calls out to Xavier, and I immediately duck out of the way. "Should we wake him up?"

"I think he's had enough. We don't want to actually damage him before the big boss gets here," another one replies.

Who is this boss, and why did he take Xavier? And after weeks of holding him, why hasn't he seen him yet? Maybe a better question is why haven't they killed him by now?

"I can't believe we actually got him," the first one says, and the others nod in agreement.

"I'm going to go take a leak," another one says. He doesn't wait for a response; he just makes his way out of there. The other men start to joke amongst themselves, while I analyze the situation. If I decide to start a shootout, I won't be able to get Xavier out or myself.

"Hey someone else is here," someone yells to the guards in front of his crate. I peek out of my hiding spot to find the rest of the men making their way to the mess I made several rows down. *It's go time.* I scale down the shipping container.

"Xavier," I whisper and pull out my knife to cut the ropes that bind his hands. Seeing him like that, struggling to open his eyes, breaks my heart. I repeat, "Xavier," and wipe the sweat on his face. He coughs loudly, and I take the chance to take off my hood, mask, and goggles.

"Winter?" I don't respond because I'm busy cutting his feet free.

"You're here," he says, and I can tell how hard it is for him to speak. I feel a different type of anger taking over me. It'd be stupid to go against all the people outside. There are too many of them for only me to comfortably handle. I'm riled up enough, but it wouldn't be a smart use of my time. And I don't think Xavier is up for an all-out fight right now.

Xavier shakes his head as if I'm a hallucination he's trying to fight. When he opens his eyes again, I'm still kneeling in front of him. In a desperate attempt to confirm my own presence, I press my lips to his. The kiss is slow, and I'm as careful as possible about the bruise on his bottom lip.

"You're here," Xavier whispers again against my lips, and as if he came to his senses, his eyes fly open. "How are you here?"

"Long story," is the reply I go with. Whatever we have to discuss, we can do it when we're well away from this place.

"How did you know to come here?" Before I can respond, he states, "You're the Cyber Huntress," as I look around for the best exit strategy out of here, putting my gear back on.

"And you're Nightshield," I reply, fighting the urge to add, *Keep up.*

"Winter, wait," Xavier says and pulls me back to him. "What's going on?"

I blurt out, "You tell me. I'm only here to get you out because you disappeared, and I thought you were avoiding me. Then I go over to your place, and your neighbor says he hasn't seen you in weeks. I thought you'd left for Boston already, but I didn't want to believe the last time we saw each other ended like that.

"So I break into your apartment—your lock is really hard to pick, by the way—and I find your laptop. Okay, now I'm thinking you can't leave for Harvard without your laptop, so I take it back to my apartment and I find all these files. I find out that you're Nightshield.

"Then I hear you get knocked out in a recording. That's when I realized I'm in love with you, and I was scared to lose you. So, I came here to get you." I flail my arms around to indicate what I mean by here.

I wipe the tears falling from my cheeks, I tell myself not to cry, but there isn't much I can do because Xavier is staring at me with his eyes widened and his mouth parted slightly. He's in shock. I want him to say something, and at the same time, I don't want him to say anything.

"You love me?"

A part of me wants to turn away and avoid the conversation, but I have skirted this for long enough. There are plenty of valid reasons why we shouldn't be having this talk at this very moment, and those reasons are exactly why it's now or never.

"Yes, I love you, and I know my actions don't make any sense. So much has happened, and I wasn't sure how to use my heart anymore. If I'm being honest with myself, I'm still not completely sure. I don't know where we go from here, but I'm open to being vulnerable again, for you."

Xavier steps forward and presses his lips to mine. I kiss him back with everything I have.

"Where is he?" booms through the shipyard, forcing Xavier and I apart.

"We need to go," Xavier whispers, and I, drunk on the kiss, nod my head and point behind me. "How do we get out of here?" he asks as the light finds us and stays on us while we try to outrun the minions on our tails.

I lead Xavier toward the cut-out I made in the fence. We just need to go through it and make our way to the car I parked near the pier. The path we're supposed to take already has men suddenly swarming it. I have no idea where they all came from. Did they have a shipping container full of henchmen?

With my head, I gesture upward toward Xavier, hoping he'll get the hint to climb. I grab hold of the closest container to me and ascend to the top. I spot Xavier doing the same thing a couple of crates away. Jumping from crate to crate, Xavier and I stop at the end of the yard near our escape route.

Below us, waves crash into the sides of the ship to our right. We have nowhere to go. I hear the men closing in on us. I don't know the distance between the edge of this container and the Pacific Ocean beneath us. Jumping without knowing doesn't feel like fun.

There's rustling behind us, and when I turn, I find a man training a gun at Xavier. Without a second thought, I shove him out of the way. My chest is on fire as I find myself falling. Xavier's voice follows me all the way down.

CHAPTER 46

"YOU CAN DO IT, WINTER," Xavier cheers from behind me, and I bow my head to stop Dr. Anderson from seeing me blush.

Given how long he has accompanied me to physical therapy, one would think I'd be used to all his antics, but it's like Xavier finds a new thing to do every single time. Thankfully, this is my last mandatory session, meaning I won't be subjected to this feeling every time it's decided I'm doing a good job rolling my shoulder around.

It's almost been two months since Xavier's kidnapping, since I got shot. When I woke up, he was ecstatic, and I could tell from the bags under his eyes that the week and a half hadn't been easy on him. He looked like he didn't get an ounce of sleep. A beard was also coming in. It looked good on him.

"Hey, sleepyhead."

In a voice I didn't recognize, I asked, "How long was I out?"

"Ten days."

The timeline registered in my head. "You can't be here," I said to him. "What happened to Harvard? You should be in Boston."

"Nothing happened to Harvard. I couldn't leave you. Don't be ridiculous."

"Ridiculous?" I tried to yell and sit up, but the pain in my left shoulder was debilitating.

"Lay back and relax, Winter. There will be other opportunities, but I'm not going to give up on us because of some beakers and pipettes. If you don't already know by now, I love you too."

And that was New Year's Day.

Dr. Anderson concludes today's session with a final stretch. "Remember, Winter," he says, his voice gentle but firm. "Take it easy for the next couple of months. Give yourself time to heal. Do those stretches every day for a speedy recovery."

I nod. "Thanks, Doc. I'll try."

"Appreciate your help, Doctor." Xavier shakes Dr. Anderson's hand.

"Of course, Xavier. Take care of her," he replies, glancing back at me with a stern look.

Xavier is holding a bouquet of flowers, something that wasn't present when he drove me here today. I try and fail to keep the smile off my face as I approach him.

"Look who just finished her therapy," he says, grinning. He hands me the roses, and I can't help but smile up at him.

"You're too much."

Xavier shakes his head, a playful glint in his eyes. "On the contrary, I think I'm just enough. Happy Valentine's Day, babe." He leans in, pressing a gentle kiss to my lips before helping me up into the car. I try not to think about it being Valentine's Day.

Xavier squeezes my hand as if sensing my thoughts. "You okay?" he asks softly.

I nod, forcing a smile. "Yeah, I'm fine. Just... in my head."

"Well, get out of there." He kisses my forehead. "I'm thinking we can stay home and order in. Maybe watch a movie. All up to you tonight."

As we drive, I find myself antsy to get back to the house. Since getting shot, we haven't gone beyond kissing. It's the commercial day of love, after all, and I want more.

"You seem excited," Xavier comments as he parks the car. I watch him as he makes the turn, his eyes are on mine, smiling.

He leads me out of the car and into the building. The ride up to my apartment is full of me restraining myself from pushing him up against the wall. I don't want him to be careful with me anymore. He's always cautious of where he places his hands whenever he kisses me.

"When you get better," he said one evening, "We can do whatever you want."

And the universe knows there's a long list of things I desire right now. Xavier opens the door, and I follow him inside. The second it closes, I push him up against the door. It feels good not to have a sling across my arm anymore.

"Hi," Xavier says with humor in his voice.

I look down at his mouth before looking back at him. Xavier bites his lower lip, and he must know what that does to me. I'm forced to stare at it again. It's a nice lip, but I require something else entirely. I want to be ravished the way I deserve after being denied for so long.

"Hi," I say after I press my body closer to his. "You made a promise."

"Did I?"

I nod my head quickly. "You said as soon as I get better."

Xavier can't control his laughter then. "Are you trying to seduce me right now?"

I nibble along his neck. "Is it working?"

"Yes, it is. But your injury."

"It's completely fine, and I feel neglected," I say, making sure to add a pout to my voice.

"Well," Xavier says and picks me up, eliciting a giggle from me, "We can't have that."

He takes me into the bedroom and lowers me onto the bed as opposed to throwing me on it. No matter how much I tell him I'm healed, I know he's never going to believe me. The best I can do is get with the program and enjoy it as much as I can. Xavier crawls up to me, kissing my lips. I place my arms around his neck and pull him closer. I want all of him. I want him so bad that it aches physically.

"Xavier," I whine, but he doesn't budge. Instead, he presses another kiss on my collarbone, and I shudder.

"Patience, princess," he says, another thing I've grown accustomed to with Xavier. He drops pet names whenever he can. And for the first time in a long while, I feel like I might be ready to face another Valentine's Day.

CHAPTER 47

HOME – *Bedroom*
March 03, 08:23 PST

I STIR, the warmth of the bed cocooning me as I blink against the morning light. Turning my head, I find Xavier beside me, his face relaxed in sleep. For a moment, I simply watch him, the even rise and fall of his chest soothing. The lines of worry and tension that usually crease his brow are smoothed away, leaving him looking almost boyish. I reach out, my fingers brushing lightly against his stubbled cheek. His eyes flutter open, a sleepy smile curving his lips.

"Morning," he murmurs, his voice rough with sleep.

"Morning," I reply, my hand lingering on his cheek before I pull it back. Propping myself up on one elbow, I shift, causing the sheet to rustle softly. "Were you serious about what you said the other night? About helping me with my case?"

He reaches out, taking my hand in his, his grip warm and reassuring. "Of course. I meant every word."

Searching his eyes for any hint of doubt, I study him. But I find nothing unwavering in his gaze.

"Come with me. I want to show you something." I lead Xavier down to the lobby toward my lair entrance. I unlock the door, and purposeful lighting illuminates the space.

"Wow, the Cyber Vault," Xavier exclaims. His eyes widen as he takes in the columns of computer servers running along three of the walls. The fourth wall is made up of weapons glistening in the low light. On one side, a compact training area is filled with various pieces of gym equipment.

"The Cyber what now?"

"The Cyber Vault," he repeats, stepping further inside. "So you, AKA The Cyber Huntress, have a whole fan page online. All of your fans have deemed your hideout the Cyber Vault." His hand trails over my work area scattered with gadgets I've been developing. He picks up a seemingly normal tennis ball.

"Hey, put that down," I warn as the motion timer in the ball initializes. A hiss escapes the device within it, releasing a cloud of knockout gas. Xavier's eyes roll back, and he collapses to the floor.

"This is why I don't let anybody in here," I mutter to myself and grab a vial of smelling salts from a nearby drawer. Waving it under his nose, I watch as he jerks awake, blinking rapidly.

"Just don't touch anything from now on," I say with a wry smile.

He groans, sitting up and rubbing his head. "Probably the safest option."

"Here." I chuckle, helping him to his feet. "K.A.R.M.A., you there?"

"Good morning, ma'am. I see we have a guest," she announces from the speakers.

"Xavier, meet K.A.R.M.A., my AI assistant."

He raises an eyebrow, glancing around. "K.A.R.M.A.?"

"Knowledgeable Analytic Reconnaissance Mitigation Assistant," K.A.R.M.A. explains. "I assist Winter with her vigilante activities."

Xavier looks impressed. "Nice to meet you, K.A.R.M.A."

"The pleasure is mine, Xavier Elliot Harris," she responds. "Ma'am, shall we brief Xavier on the outstanding case?"

"Let's," I say, leading him to a cluster of screens displaying various pieces of the puzzle. "I've been investigating the murder of my old roommate, Jessica Glory."

"Hold on, you were Jessica Glory's roommate? Since when?" Xavier's expression turns serious. "You know what, nevermind. What do we know so far?"

I gesture to the screens. "Her killers tried to disguise her death as a heroin overdose. After stalking her boyfriend Chris, I learned Jessica was a drug dealer. I ruled the boyfriend out as a prime suspect a long time ago; there was no motive, and the only thing he can kill is a keg stand. Then, I found an encrypted USB drive hidden in Jessica's mattress that revealed she dealt for The Black Syndicates, The Omega Outlaws, and The Serpents. She missed quite a few payments toward the end for each gang.

"I started with The Serpents. They relied heavily on Jessica's cash flow," I say, my voice tight as I stand up and begin to pace, unable to stay still. "So, naturally, I thought they were the ones who killed her when the money dried up. But they're too disorganized and not advanced enough to pull this off; also, their heroin didn't match what was found in Jessica's system." My steps quicken, and I wring my hands as if trying to shake off the frustration. "K.A.R.M.A., take over."

K.A.R.M.A. chimes in, projecting images onto the larger screen. "Before Jessica's death, a Syndicate member was tailing Winter and Jessica around for a day. After some persuasion, Winter received confirmation that they weren't behind Jessica's death. Their goal was just to scare her."

Xavier's eyes narrow as he watches me pace. Finally, he interrupts, holding up his hands. "Time out." His voice is gentle but firm. "Winter, would you stop bouncing around? You're making me nervous. Are you alright?"

I pause, caught off guard by his question. My hands, now clenched into fists, loosen slightly. "Yeah, I'm fine. Just thinking," I say, but even I can hear the strain in my voice.

"Really, Winter? Just thinking? You just glitched out talking about the Serpents and the timeline is right when you came over to my place covered in bruises. That can't be a coincidence."

"Okay, fine, yes. The mission didn't exactly go as planned, but can we just stay on track and finish the rundown?" I was able to let him in, but I'm still having trouble letting parts of me out. Some secrets are still only mine to bear. At least for now.

Xavier just sighs and says, "Alright, continue."

"Finally, that brings us to the Outlaws. So the Outlaws are in a few major cities across the US, and it's the gang out of the three with the most prolific killers. K.A.R.M.A., put Kane and Holden up on the screen."

"Kane is an Outlaw lieutenant for the West Coast. Winter learned his movements and managed to get intel that The Outlaws were definitely involved in Jessica's murder by going undercover at one of their bars. Winter also discovered that the Outlaws have at least two moles within the LAPD. Kane eventually led Winter to Holden, someone higher up in the Outlaw food chain. Winter has created a noticeable dent, taking down the Outlaws' businesses in L.A. But the question still remains, which one of them actually did it?"

Xavier nods, absorbing the information. "And what about leads?"

"So we got Dragon," I say, pulling him up on the screen. "I saw him interact with Holden right before he was killed."

"Yes, I'm familiar. Dragon was a Hazard Gang member. Surprisingly, pretty high up," Xavier chimes in.

"I haven't found out much about why Dragon was killed. But, I'm thinking if we answer the question of why a Hazard met with an Outlaw, we might be closer to solving this case."

"Maybe I can help with that. I've been in the Hazard world for quite a while. I'm looking for the man who runs the Hazard Gang. I mean top upper echelon. And I'm close. If I had to guess, that's why the Hazards held me for so long. For the past few years I've been working on trying to stop child trafficking, at least in this region."

He rubs his neck and adds, "Back to Dragon, I can't say for certain why he was gunned-down. But I do know he killed a rival gang member by accident. It could've been retaliatory. However, I have a strong inkling it had to have been done by someone who knows his moves, somebody close enough to him."

Xavier studies the screen, his brow furrowed. "Hey, how does this guy connect in your case?" Xavier points to a photograph of Jeep, which I barely managed to find in an off-site CIA server.

"He seems to be some gang intermediary and broker? Honestly, it's unclear, but he's come up a lot during my research into the Outlaws."

"Well, that's funny, because it's the same for me but the Hazards."

"K.A.R.M.A., go through Xavier's files from his cloud storage account again and find all references to Jeep."

"Remind me to change my password," Xavier snips.

I smile. "All that's going to do is just slow me down. I'll still get in."

"Processing complete." She shows me various photographs of a shipping port. Macey and Jeep are conversing with another guy, muscular with a rugged look, covered in tattoos.

"I took those at a shipment yard in Long Beach over two and a half years ago. I had no idea who Macey was meeting with at the time. But he looks just like your Jeep guy. I never managed to figure out who the third one was."

"K.A.R.M.A., run facial recognition."

"That appears to be Rico 'The Wolf' Santana. He's an Outlaw from Atlanta."

"These meetings only make sense if…" I start and in unison we say, "They were working together." Our eyes lock and we continue, "The Hazards must supply the drugs and mules for The Outlaws."

Xavier leans against a very expensive server in deep thought. "So these girls are given drugs to swallow before being transported through the border. The drugs are then handed to the Outlaws, who might buy the kids off the Hazard's hands."

"Damn it!" I yell, punching one of my monitors, causing the screen to go rainbow. "I should have known this." *How did I not see this?* The Hazards were involved from the start.

"Whoa, Winter. At the expense of making a terrible dad joke, you need to chill out." Xavier reaches out and starts massaging my shoulders. "You couldn't have known this. You weren't even here two years ago."

As a half-hearted attempt to calm down, I take a deep breath. This revelation does confirm some things. From the abundance of files on her drive, Jessica managed to stumble upon information that wasn't hers to find. I was able to piece together that there was a large shipment of girls, young girls. As of now, my best bet is that The Hazards sourced them. I don't think Jessica knew the extent to which children were forced to transport drugs. She witnessed a girl no older than thirteen, Jessica's memo said, being made to cough up the drugs she had swallowed. When the product was out, a gang member had smiled before saying, "Shipment."

Whatever she found must have haunted her for days, pushing her to gather everything she could on that drive. It likely tore Jessica apart—trying to do the right thing while realizing just how far things had spiraled out of control. She must have known she couldn't handle this alone. I can only assume whoever killed her did it because she missed her payments. If they believed she had incriminating evidence on that drive and plans to expose them, they would've broken in to take it. They already knew where she lived—and where I live.

After a while, I break the silence. "So it's settled. We're basically working on the same case. Let's team up. I think after a few more strategic nights out, we can finish this together. Let's follow anything Hazard or Outlaw related."

"We? Nope. You're staying here doing all the hacking while I go out and do all the fighting."

"If you think I'm not seeing this through, I should've left your ass passed out on the floor."

"Winter, think about it," he says, and I roll my eyes. There's absolutely nothing to think about.

"Xavier, I can handle myself."

"I know you can, but you were just shot a few months ago. Can you honestly say you're back to a hundred percent?"

I hate that he's right. My arm feels so much better than the week when I first woke up; still I can't draw my gun as quickly as I'd like to. But that's never stopped me before.

"I won't be here worrying about if you're okay," I say with enough force in my voice.

"You won't be worrying about me," he says, rolling his eyes as if I'm being unnecessarily stubborn. "We'll be talking to each other the entire time."

He taps his ears to demonstrate an earpiece. It's tempting, except there isn't any earpiece on the market that can cover the distance. To do what he's suggesting, I'd have to build an office into one of those vans, and those aren't easy to build and drive around.

"That's not a good idea. And you know why."

"If we go out together," Xavier starts, and I know he's about to take a whole new approach, "We'll spend too much time looking out for each other to even make progress."

"Maybe we should just spread out, cover more ground."

"Baby, please don't be difficult. We can build a minivan, and I'm not saying this because I don't trust your skills. In fact, I trust you completely, and I would love it if you directed me."

After an intense staring contest, I comply, "Fine, but if you need backup, I'm stepping in." If we investigate together, I can prevent him from being grabbed off the street like last time.

Xavier beams at that, and I fight the urge to smack him over the head. He stretches out his hand. "Partners?"

I begrudgingly shake it. "Partners."

CHAPTER 48

DOWNTOWN LOS ANGELES – *Grand Park*
March 15, 13:48 PDT

"IT'S a great day for a stroll. Isn't it?" Thorne all but demanded to meet here. I don't think I'll ever understand him. He flashes me a smile. "Not sure what you need with a high-tech van, but here you go."

He places a set of keys in my hand and continues, "Before you leave, indulge an old man and walk with me, Snow." We progress a few yards before he asks, "Do you think you know the meaning of life?"

"Is this a rhetorical question? Or..."

He fixates on the palm tree directly in front of us. "That is the question, isn't it? There is no universal answer, is there? Does that imply there is no answer? If everything matters equally, does nothing matter at all?"

"Jesus, Thorne. What has gotten into you?"

"Oh Snow, it's more like what I haven't gotten into. You see, I'm having lady troubles..."

"Please don't finish that thought," I beg. I'm not interested in hearing any of Thorne's sexual escapades. Or lack thereof.

He laughs and turns to look at me. His gaze is always investigative. He arches a brow in my direction and motions at me. "Something is different here."

"What are you going on about? What's different?"

"I can't put my finger on it but you're smiling, like genuinely. I caught you a couple of times. I just haven't seen you like this before."

His words surprise me; I never imagined Thorne paid that much attention to me. Noticing the subtle shifts in my mood, reading me like I'm an open book. It makes sense how he's managed to stay invisible yet wield so much power. He understands people—knows them better than they know themselves.

At this point, we'd already walked a few blocks from the park. We stop in front of a white van with *Pacific Power* written across its side.

"Oh well, here's the new whip. Let me know how it drives." And with that, Thorne walks away.

CHAPTER 49

WATTS – *Adjacent Alleyway*
April 17, 21:21 PDT

WE'RE PARKED, concealed by the darkness but with a clear line of sight to the Outlaw traphouse. The van monitors give my face a blue tint as I go over the plan with Xavier one last time.

"Okay, listen closely," I say, turning to him. "You need to act desperate. Get in close, like you really need more dope. The bug isn't invisible, but it's tiny, so it has to go somewhere they won't notice."

He nods, his jaw set. "Got it. Where exactly should I place it?"

I pull out the small device and hand it to him. "On his jacket, near the back collar or maybe go for the belt. Somewhere he's not likely to check."

Xavier takes the bug, studying it for a moment before slipping it into his pocket. He looks up at me, his eyes serious. "Are you ready?"

"As ready as I'll ever be," he says, exhaling deeply. "Let's do this."

"Wait one second." I step closer, ruffling his hair and ripping his shirt a bit. The fabric tears easily, exposing his chest. I can't help but glance at his pecs, momentarily distracted.

"My eyes are up here," he puffs out, a hint of amusement in his voice.

Ignoring his comment and stepping back, my eyes linger. "Now you fit the part."

He exits the van, his shoulders hunched and his steps uncertain, mimicking the movements of someone in desperate need of a fix. He approaches the traphouse, the muffled thump of music and conversation growing louder.

From the van, I listen through the surveillance equipment. Xavier knocks on the door, and it creaks open, revealing a burly gang member.

"What do you want?" the gang member growls, his tone laced with irritation.

Xavier falls forward, tugging at the man's sleeve. "Please, man, I just need a little. I'll do anything."

The gang member glares at him, clearly annoyed. "Back up," he snaps, shoving Xavier. But as Xavier stumbles, he manages to place the bug on the guy's jacket.

"Come on, just one more hit," Xavier pleads with feigned desperation.

"Get outta here, junkie," the gang member yells, slamming the door shut.

Xavier makes his way back to the van, his steps quicker. He climbs in, closing the door behind him, breathing hard.

"Did it work?" he asks, breathless.

I check the feed, adjusting the volume. Voices crackle to

life through the speakers. "We're live," I confirm, handing him a headset. "Good job."

Gang Member 1: I'm just glad they're letting us sell more now. That break was brutal.

Gang Member 2: Yeah, can you believe we were losing customers to the Serpents of all people?

Gang Member 3: I knew messing with that sorority chick was bad news. But Holden wanted to break into the student market and no one seems to be able to tell him no.

Gang Member 2: Turns out she was that Glory guy's kid.

Gang Member 1: Well that explains why we've been so cautious. I just wish Biggie looked into who she was before he killed her.

Gang Member 3: That would require him to have a brain that didn't follow Holden's orders like a dog.

Gang Member 2: Wait, Biggie did it? How come nobody ever tells me anything?

Gang Member 1: Relax, I didn't know until last week. Kane and I did a job and it came up. We found out together.

I take the headphones off and wheel myself to another screen in the van. "K.A.R.M.A., find me everything you can on an Outlaw named Biggie."

"Unfortunately, ma'am, I am unable to find any useful information on Biggie, real name unknown. However, I believe I found a potential description based on FBI records."

Three photos are displayed with multiple men. It seems Biggie is a bit of a misleading name. The only constant in these images is a smallish-looking man with a disturbing mustache. He's not a big poppa at all.

"Winter," Xavier chimes in with his headphones still on, "One of the thugs just said they're going to a big drug exchange sometime tomorrow. It's all hands on deck. Apparently, Holden is back in town and will be present. Presumably Biggie too."

"Looks like tomorrow's the big day."

CHAPTER 50

FASHION DISTRICT – *Abandoned Rooftop*
   April 18, 17:48 PDT

A GLITTERING maze of lights expands before me. On the edge of the rooftop, the late afternoon air brushes against my skin. I delay dialing Gillian's number, but eventually activate my voice modulator.

"Detective," I say, my voice unrecognizable. "This is the Cyber Huntress."

"Cyber Huntress," he says, stewing over his response. "This is unexpected. What's going on?"

"I need to cut a deal," I begin, glancing out over the city. "I've got some information I think you might find useful. You will be able to put a lot of people away. And solve a high-profile murder case."

Gillian is silent for a moment, digesting my words. "What makes you think you can trust me?" he asks finally, his voice guarded.

"I don't," I admit. "But this isn't information I can turn

over to just anyone. I need someone who will take it seriously, who isn't dirty. You seem to have a hint of integrity."

He sighs, the sound crackling through the phone. "Alright, tell me what you have."

"Two deadly criminal empires are operating in the city together. The Hazards and The Outlaws have an arrangement. I'll do my best to deliver Holden and Macey. Bigger arrests than Nightshield and I. We would like to do this the right way. Are you willing to back off the hunt for us if we give them up?"

There's a silence that stretches between us, filled with muted fears and hopes. Finally, Gillian speaks. "Why are you coming to me now?"

"Because if we don't stop them, more people will die. And because I need to believe there are still good people left in the system."

He takes a deep breath, his voice softening. "Alright, Cyber Huntress. I'll entertain this tip. But just know, not every cop is as gracious as I am. What exactly do you need from me?"

"Gather a group of cops you trust. I'll be in touch later tonight. Just do your part, and I'll do mine."

The call ends, and I look up to the sky, wondering what Jayden thinks when he looks down at me. About what I've become? I thought about it a lot, and for a while after hunting the people that murdered him, I was obsessed with knowing whether or not it gave him any peace.[1] Because it didn't give me any. Not like I thought it would anyways.

The roof door opens, and Xavier walks toward me. "What do you think?"

Between the both of us, he takes a longer time to get into

---

1. A story for another time.

his suit. Xavier has so many complicated parts to his outfit, which he claims are all equally important, but if I'm being honest, I don't think they are. His pants are a snug fit. He wears a fitted jacket with a giant shield across his chest. Within it is a crescent moon in the night sky alongside a star. He has a belt with an X as the buckle and a single gun holster. It isn't the outfit I usually see him in.

"What happened to the old one?"

"I thought it was time for an upgrade." Xavier says, pulling me closer to him before hugging me tight. "Are you okay?"

Having someone who wants to check up on you feels really nice. I don't want to lie, so I tell him the truth. "I just don't know what to expect. I want Jessica to rest in peace."

He rubs my back and says, "I have a feeling everything's going to work out tonight."

CHINATOWN – *Random Alleyway*
   April 18, 19:33 PDT

THERE MUST BE a festival because the streets are unusually loud and lively. The vibrant color, the lights, the food and culture of Chinatown never really changes regardless of what city you're in. It takes everything in me not to gawk at it all. It's too soon to tell if the busy streets will be useful or a detriment tonight.

Our leather fabrics collide when my glove connects with his own, swatting Xavier's hand away. "Would you stop fidgeting? I need to install this camera correctly."

"Sorry, you're just so close." He clears his throat and

continues in a deeper voice, "So I've been meaning to ask, who's this Thorne guy?"

"Just some criminal from the East Coast." I say as I secure the lens over the star on his chest.

"Some criminal from the East Coast that's always in L.A.?" I assume he has a raised eyebrow behind his mask.

A smile breaks across my face. "Is that jealousy I detect?" I grab his hand and open it. "Here. Put this in. I built an app that lets us talk to each other for long periods of time without needing a phone call." It uses some mics I found on the dark web and an undetectable custom radio frequency. This very well could be the future of vigilantism.

"Well, have you guys ever..." He trails off.

"Not the time nor the place, Xavier!" I yell into my earpiece. "Mic check. 1-2-3."

He reaches for his ear. "Ow! What the hell, Winter!"

"Nightshield, I need you to focus. You are about to walk into a warehouse full of hardened criminals. Get your head in the game."

"You're right. You're right." He agrees and reaches for the handle on the van door. "Tonight, let's focus on making the arrests we need and getting these girls off the street."

Without thinking much about it, I reach for him and pull him back. "Good. Now, stay safe." I give him a quick peck on the cheek. He nods and exits the van.

"Are the visuals coming through?"

I look at my screen and see what Xavier is seeing. "Yep. All good."

Xavier makes his way through Chinatown to save the girls he's looking out for, and to make the arrest of the man who killed my roommate. I thought he would stick out like a sore thumb in his suit. Luckily for us, the people don't seem to pay much mind to him when he navigates through the crowd.

"How do we get in?" Xavier asks as he walks past the warehouse being guarded for the second time.

I bring up a 3D map of Chinatown and say, "There's a side entrance, but it's all the way at the back, and we know it's guarded."

"By four people."

"If you take them out, we're going to draw attention to ourselves."

"I don't think it matters much if I'm being honest. We either get this right, or we're going to be chasing ghosts again. Everyone you've pinned on your wall is probably going to be in there. This is our last chance to get them."

"Fine." This has been a whole year of my life, and I need to close this chapter.

Xavier makes his way to the back where the people are at the corner, talking amongst themselves and sharing a cigarette.

"I need a diversion, or I'm going in swinging."

Quickly thinking on my feet, I pull up all the traffic lights in the area. I update their timing mechanisms so it'll cause a traffic jam in front of the warehouse. All the commotion causes the men in the back to see what's happening. Xavier slips into the building undetected.

I can hear the voices before we see who they belong to. Instead of going through the front like the henchmen do, Xavier walks up a small ladder. It leads to a small room that has a balcony overlooking the scene. He lies on the floor and crawls toward the edge.

Holden leans on a black car, smoking his cigarette, and has an amused smile on his face. Next to him is Biggie, who looks like he's having the time of his life. They're facing someone who has their back to us, but I figure it's someone from the Hazards.

"We had a deal," Macey says, and Holden laughs.

"I know that. It just seems like the terms are no longer favorable to us."

The other man runs his hand through his hair, pacing back and forth. "The drugs are yours," he says, and Holden nods. "You came out of prison to oversee this transaction."

"I'm overseeing the transaction?"

"You're trying to screw us over. We have a container full of women with drugs in them. Hazards don't deal drugs."

Holden smiles. "Of course. Your convoluted moral code. You'd rather sell a person than a product."

"Listen here, you piece of shit," the man says and rushes forward, but Biggie steps in front of Holden. I feel my blood boil. This is the man who killed my friend. Seeing how he is for his boss, I have no doubt it was Holden who gave the order to kill Jessica.

Holden drops the cigarette on the ground and steps on it. He ignores the Hazard goon and looks at Macey. "I'm just messing with you, Macey. Of course, we'll take the drugs off you. We'll take the drugs and the girls."

Macey shakes his head. I can understand his frustration. It's almost as if Holden is pretending not to hear anything they've been saying. I'm sure Macey just wants the drugs out of the girls so he can get right to trafficking them.

"And the girls? Are you out of your damn mind? These girls need to be moved. The feds are watching both of us now thanks to you." Macey sounds reasonably pissed even when Biggie steps closer to him. He doesn't back down. He just maintains eye contact with Holden, who's still looking pleased with himself. "You killed Dragon; we're not even getting mad at that."

"Oh please. Stop with the woe is me act, Macey. Hazards are just as guilty as me. I was the only one with the balls big enough to do something about the girl. An example needed to be made. Besides, I keep a few friends in strategic places so there's no blowback. And Dragon was killed because he couldn't follow instructions. Idiots can't be trusted."

"He was one of our best men."

"You shouldn't be proud to say that out loud," Holden says, and I find myself nodding in agreement. Having Dragon as one of their best men is not something to tell the whole world.

"We need to let the cops know where we are," Xavier whispers to me.

"K.A.R.M.A., send the signal over to Gillian." I say before returning my attention back to the screen.

"Does Jeep know what you're doing?"

The smile on Holden's face shifts. Biggie steps to the side, and Holden gets in Macey's face. Macey squares up to face Holden, and I almost applaud his bravery. Macey's goon stands by his side looking trigger-happy.

The thing with Macey, the reports said, is he's very timid until he doesn't have to be. He's to the Hazards what Holden is to the Outlaws. What differentiates the two is Macey doesn't make a habit of getting arrested. He could be found at a crime scene, but he'll always walk away because the last person you'll find drugs on is Macey. And he makes sure none of the girls ever see his face. If Jeep was present, he would've been the buffer to allow Macey and Holden to have a conversation without all this posturing.

"Biggie," Holden says, still looking at Macey, "get the briefcase." Biggie hurries off to do as he's told. "We'll take the drugs only." Holden hands the briefcase to Macey.

Macey accepts the briefcase, pops it open, sifting through

the contents as if he's trying to find a counterfeit. With the way Holden's jaw tightens, he must be doing that to provoke the man. Satisfied with his inspection, Macey dips his hand into his pocket and pulls out a key. "The girls are at the port. E46. Happy harvesting."

Biggie takes the key from his hand. My panic starts to rise. The cops aren't here yet; we can't just let them leave.

Xavier pulls out his gun and aims for Biggie before I can interfere. The bullet hits the henchman behind him. All the other men pull out their guns and train them at each other.

"What the hell was that for?"

Bullets zoom past, and Xavier responds, "We need to stall for time. If they walk out of here, we've lost them."

"Oh, so you were just going to kill Biggie to stall?"

"Of course not. The goal was to have them shoot at each other until the cops came. And even though I'm against it, don't you want him dead anyways?"

"That's not the point. He's not yours to kill! If someone's going to do it, it's me."

The sound of sirens cut our squabble short. Gillian took me seriously. I peek back at the screen, wondering why they aren't coming up to see who fired the bullet.

"They're leaving," I yell out. I slam the van door and run toward the warehouse, toward Xavier. I know he thinks he has it under control, but I can't sit in that damn van for much longer. "I'm on my way."

"No, wait in the—"

And just like that, our connection is severed. I pull my phone out of my pocket. "K.A.R.M.A., give me a map of the surrounding streets. Overlay the city archives and schematics of the warehouse."

The map has three color-coded layers. "There are a series of tunnels from the prohibition era connecting Chinatown to downtown L.A. They appear to triangulate on City Hall."

Tunnels. How did I manage to miss something as big as this?

"Although not crucial, I would like to add that City Hall is a bookable venue space, and tonight, it has been reserved for Hamilton High's Senior Prom. To find out more information on how to book this location please visit lacityparks.org."

"K.A.R.M.A., remind me to review your training model on followup information. Now, I need you to call Detective Gillian and activate my voice changer." I have to assume Xavier followed them into the tunnels. This wasn't supposed to be how this went. Who's to say they won't be waiting for him to catch up to them? Macey knows Xavier, and his henchmen do too.

"You've got Gillian."

"Detective, don't bother coming to the address I sent in Chinatown. Head to City Hall. They're taking a tunnel leading that way." I don't wait for confirmation, I hang up and approach the back entrance of the warehouse. The men previously standing guard are gone. No time to think, I rush inside.

The building is decrepit, its walls lined with rusted metal shelves and broken crates. The atmosphere is damp. Shafts of moonlight filter through cracked windows high above, creating eerie patterns on the ground. The floor is littered with debris—discarded tools, torn tarps, and the occasional rat skittering away at my approach.

Navigating through the maze of forgotten machinery and toppled shelving units, my footsteps echo in the empty space. Ahead, a heavy steel door stands ajar, leading to the basement. The faint sound of water dripping escapes from below.

I push the door open, the hinges groaning in protest, and descend the spiraling staircase. Grime surrounds me as the temperature grows colder with each step. At the bottom, I find a narrow passage, barely wide enough for two people to walk side by side.

The tunnels are a labyrinth. The distant and distinct sound of combat is my guiding beacon as I move silently, each step measured and deliberate. I quicken my pace, causing my heart to pound in my chest. Ahead, the path splits three ways.

I pause, uncertain. "K.A.R.M.A., which path should I take?"

"Calculating, one moment please." I duck under a wild swing, the whoosh of the blade slicing the frizzy ends of my wig. Firing off two quick shots, I take him down. But another goon tackles me, his weight slamming me into the tunnel wall. Pain jolts through my barely healed arm as I'm thrown, the impact knocking the breath out of me. My gun skitters across the floor, out of reach.

So much for taking it easy.

"By all means. Take your time, K.A.R.M.A." I struggle out of my attacker's hold.

"Second path on the left," she replies, but I'm already in motion, rolling away from a knife strike aimed at my head.

On the ground, I spot a loose boulder and grab it, swinging it with all my might. The rock connects with the side of the goon's knee. He howls in pain, collapsing. The third one charges, his fist catching me in the ribs. I grunt, but twist out of his grip, elbowing him in the jaw. He staggers back, dazed.

I lunge for my gun, fingers closing around the grip just as the fourth goon raises his weapon. I fire first, the bullet hitting his shoulder. His gun and body drop with a cry of agony. Breathing heavily, I walk over to him and knock him out with the butt of my pistol.

"Second on the left," I scoff as I charge down the middle tunnel.

CHAPTER 51

DOWNTOWN LOS ANGELES – *Underground*
   April 18, 20:59 PDT

TURNING A CORNER, I see him. Xavier is fighting off six henchmen. They're overpowering him. Their sheer numbers and brute force wearing him down. He parries a blow from one attacker, only to be struck from behind by another.

Firing my gun, the shot takes out one sneaking up behind him. "Still think I should have waited in the van?" I say, delivering a swift kick to another attacker.

"About time," he grunts, evading an attack. "I knew you couldn't resist ignoring my clear instructions."

"And let you have all the fun?" I call out, taking out another one.

Xavier blocks a punch aimed at his head and glances at me, a quick flash of gratitude in his eyes. "Not a chance."

He lands a powerful kick to one goon's chest, sending him sprawling. I punch another henchman, causing him to double over, and I finish him with a quick jab to the jaw.

"Behind you!" Xavier shouts, and I spin, narrowly avoiding a knife thrust. I twist the assailant's arm, disarming him and inserting a bullet in his shoulder. I deliver a knee to his gut, making him crumple to the ground.

Another shot rings out, and I duck, the bullet embedding itself in the wall behind me. Xavier and I exchange a glance, and I toss him a smoke pellet. He catches it, throwing it into the midst of the remaining goons. The tunnel fills with an encompassing smoke, and we move through it, striking down the remaining disoriented attackers.

We catch our breaths, and I gesture toward the tunnel that leads deeper into the darkness. "Ready for round two?"

Xavier pounds his chest, leading the way. "Let's do this!"

A fresh wave of goons wearing ski-masks emerge from the shadows. I count twenty. Half of them bearing the Hazard symbol and the other half the Outlaws insignia.

"You take left, I take right?" Xavier responds with a simple nod.

They rush us, but we're ready. Xavier launches a barrage of smoke bombs, the thick fog overtaking our attackers. I use my night-vision goggles, picking them off one by one.

Click. *I'm out.* "Back to basics," I sigh, reaching for my belt. I duck under an aggressive punch, using my momentum to strike another goon in the ribs with my staff, providing me with a satisfying crunch.

Gunshots echo, closer this time. I squat, feeling the heat of a bullet whiz past my head. Grabbing the nearest goon, I yank him in front of me just as a spray of rounds erupts from the darkness. The thug jerks as the bullets enter him, and I use the moment to push forward, shoving the lifeless body into another aggressor.

I toss a flashbang, and the explosion of light and sound

surprises our attackers. Xavier and I move in unison. We press forward, taking down goon after goon.

Xavier sweeps the legs out from under another attacker, then faces me with a smirk. "Does this count as foreplay?"

"Focus," I shout, blocking a punch and retaliating with a sharp uppercut. He drops, clutching his throat. I turn just in time to deflect a blow meant for Xavier.

"Sorry," he grunts, spinning to deliver a kick to another assailant.

We're surrounded, but Xavier and I are synchronized. He disarms a goon, tossing the gun aside as I deliver a swift elbow to another's temple. One lunges at me with a knife. I evade a slice, grabbing his wrist and twisting until he yelps in pain and drops the blade. I follow up with a knee to his crotch, and he goes down hard.

Xavier's by my side again, our backs to each other. "Please tell me you have more tricks in that Santa bag of a belt you have," he says, deflecting a blow aimed at his head.

"Well, I would've if I had packed for combat," I say, ducking under a swinging bat and delivering a kick to the attacker's knee. He collapses with a moan. "But I remember a certain someone saying I got it all under control, babe. You won't even need to leave the van."

"Okay, I was a bit cocky earlier," Xavier admits.

I ignore him as we continue fighting, the numbers dwindling but the intensity never waning. At last, the final goon drops. I take a moment to catch my breath, looking around at the bodies littering the ground. Xavier stands beside me equally winded, but alive.

"We did it," he says, a note of disbelief in his voice.

"For now," I reply, scanning the area. "But this isn't over."

The tunnel widens into a cavernous chamber, and the

entrance to City Hall lies ahead. Biggie fumbles with the hatch while Macey and Holden stand watch.

"Think you can take them?" Xavier asks, his tone light but his eyes deadly serious.

Biggie's eyes narrow as he assesses us. "Who the hell are they?"

Macey perks up, recognition dawning on his face. "The tall one is Nightshield," he sneers, pointing at Xavier. Then, turning to me, he adds, "And that bitch is—"

"The Cyber Huntress," Holden interjects, his gaze locking onto mine. "She's been giving the Outlaws a hard time."

Holden charges at me like a freight train, all muscle and fury. I evade just in time, my staff whistling through the air as it connects with his ribs. The impact reverberates through my arms as Macey lunges from my left, his gun catching the dim light. I move quickly, twisting his wrist until he yells and the weapon clatters to the floor.

Behind me, Xavier and Biggie collide. The room vibrates as each punch begets a thunderous sound in the confined space.

Holden isn't down for long. He swings at me again, a wild haymaker aimed at my head. I crouch low, my staff sweeping his back. He crumples with a groan, but he's tenacious. Before I can kick his weapon out of reach, he grabs my ankle, yanking me down hard. The ground rushes up to meet me, but mid-fall, I manage to wrench my leg free. My elbow collides with his face, resulting in a sharp crack. Blood sprays from his nose, and he's still reaching for me, stubborn as ever.

I scramble to my feet as his eyes burn with fierce determination, and even as blood pools around his nose, he lunges at me again, refusing to go down without a fight. I sidestep his attack, my staff crashing into his ribs, but he barely flinches. His hand shoots out, grabbing my wrist with a crushing grip, and he yanks me toward him. I twist, breaking free with a jab to his gut. Macey tries to intervene, lunging at me. I bend his arm sharply, forcing him to the ground. Holden takes advantage of my distraction and connects his fist with my healing shoulder. The impact nearly knocks me off balance. I recover quickly, retaliating with a hard strike to his left knee. He staggers, but his grip on my arm tightens, dragging me down with him. I struggle to break free, delivering a kick to his face. His bloodied hand claws at my leg, pulling me closer.

In the corner of my eye, I catch Macey aiming at Xavier. My heart pounds as I free myself from Holden's grasp, charging at Macey before he can pull the trigger. I tackle him to the ground, wrestling him into submission and restraining him with zip ties.

The sound of fists connecting with flesh pulls my attention back to Xavier. He's locked in an exchange with Biggie, the smaller man fighting like a cornered animal. But with one last powerful strike, Biggie sinks to the ground.

Breathing hard, I turn back to Holden, who's still trying to pull himself up, his face a bloody mess. His stubbornness is almost admirable, but I'm not letting him get the upper hand again. I swiftly bind his hands with zip ties, forcing him to stay down.

I glance at Biggie, lying motionless on the tunnel floor, an unconscious small man, yet he looms large in my mind. *He killed Jessica.* The anger, the grief I've buried deep, all of it surges up like a tidal wave. My fists clench tightly when I step toward him, every fiber of my being screaming for revenge. I could end it here—make him pay for what he did.

Biggie stirs, groaning. I stand over him, the weight of the past year pressing down on me. "You killed her," I say, my voice trembling with controlled fury. "You killed Jessica Glory."

He looks up and states, "It was orders."

"Shut up!" I explode, my voice echoing through the chamber as I reach for my utility knife. My breath comes in ragged gasps. "No one told you to open your mouth."

"Cyber Huntress." Xavier steps closer and rests his hand on my shoulder, his voice a grounding force. "We said we were going to do this right. You're better than them."

Xavier says the last bit with confidence, as if he's merely stating facts, yet I'm not sure that I am. Despite his presence, the anger surges and my grip around the knife becomes tighter. The blade hovers an inch from Biggie's throat. He cowers, eyes riddled with terror. For a long, agonizing moment, I'm on the edge, the choice teetering in my mind.

He deserves it. Man, does he deserve it.

My body fights an internal war, and with a shuddering breath, I lower the knife. Killing Biggie isn't going to change a damn thing. I've been down this road before. Justice, not vengeance. For Jessica. *For me.*

I let Xavier restrain Biggie's hands. The law will deal with him and Holden. They'll face the consequences of their actions.

My biceps flex and my muscles struggle in an attempt to pry the hatch open. "Hey, could you help me with this?"

Xavier rushes over. "Here you get the top and I'll get the bottom." Together we manage to get it unlatched.

"LAPD, come out with your hands up!" Gillian's voice announces from the other side of the metal dome.

"Detective. Holden, Macey, and Biggie have been subdued. I'm going to open the door now. Don't shoot."

"Stand down!"

Xavier's hand brushes mine as we push the door fully ajar. Gillian stands waiting, his team placed in strategic corners of the old wine cellar.

"Hello, Detective," I say, making my way to shake his hand. Xavier stays back handing off our zip-tied friends to the officers.

"How did you know about them? We've been trying to track them for a while."

That answer isn't something I'm interested in revealing. Instead of responding, I hand him a flash drive containing evidence of their crimes. The drugs, the trafficking, and Jessica's murder.

I begin walking toward Xavier as I say, "That should help you make sure the charges stick."

"Miss Huntress," Gillian calls out. I turn back and meet his eyes. "You're off the hook for tonight, but tomorrow you and your boyfriend are back to being fugitives. L.A. criminals aren't yours to play with."

"Well, I'm looking forward to the chase then, Bradley." His eyes widen at the use of his middle name not on any public database. "Oh, and I'd keep a close eye on Officer Mitchell and company if I were you."

The beat from upstairs is still blaring, and it's amazing to know that through all this pandemonium, there are people who kept living their lives. "What's that music from?"

"Prom."

Xavier pulls me along. "Let's go peek. I never took you to prom." I refrain from mentioning he'd have some competition back then.

"Oh my God," someone yells, "It's Cyber Huntress and The Shield."

Xavier mumbles, "It's actually *Night*shield." But he still seems pleased at the recognition. He extends his arm, bows his head and asks, "A dance, my queen?"

I grab his hand as everyone cheers. Xavier leads me to the middle of the room and wraps his arms around my waist. I place my arms around his neck, and we sway to the music. A small smile plays on my lips as I keep my eyes on him.

"We don't work well together, you know," I say, and he laughs loudly, throwing his head back. "I'm serious. You just went in. No warning. No nothing."

"Hey, it worked out, didn't it?" I roll my eyes behind my mask. "And if I'm being honest, I didn't think too much about it. I knew you would come in after me."

"And if it didn't?"

"We'll learn," Xavier says after a while. "To work together, I mean; it's going to take some time, but we'll make it work. Now would you shut up and kiss me already?"

I pull him closer and press my lips to his.

CHAPTER 52

THE BLACK DRESS clings to my body, billowing slightly as I walk through the graveyard. Although it's my first visit, I know exactly where Jessica is buried. The man who killed her has been apprehended, and it's all over the news. I feel a grim satisfaction knowing I've granted her justice the only way I know how.

Clutching a bouquet of lilies—chosen simply because they're pretty—I navigate the plots, crypts, and crosses. When I reach Jessica's grave, I find it already adorned with flowers, their petals wilting. Gently, I push them aside and place my fresh lilies in their place. I stand in silence, staring at her headstone.

JESSICA GLORY
singer, writer, daughter
Our Muse, gone too soon

"Jessica," I finally whisper, "I caught him for you. I'm sorry I couldn't protect you. Everyone knows you lost your life trying to be a hero in the end."

I pause, struggling to steady my breath. "Graduation is tomorrow, and I know you would've loved it. It won't be the same without you…"

"I reconnected with someone. You would've liked him…"

The tears well up despite my efforts to hold them back. "I can never fully express how grateful I am that you were my friend. You know, you were the only one who replied to my housing post. When I moved to Los Angeles, you didn't hesitate to help me, showing me around and suggesting places to visit."

"I've been looking absolutely horrendous lately because you're not here to evaluate my fashion taste. But I know you'd love the dress I picked for tomorrow."

I wipe my eyes, chuckling through the sadness. "You accepted me for who I was, without judgment. I'm sorry I wasn't there for you when you needed me most. I have a feeling if we got to know each other a little more, none of this would've ever happened."

"Jessica, you are and forever will be missed," I say, my voice breaking as a sob escapes me. The pain of losing someone never gets easier, no matter how many times it happens to me. Or how briefly they were in my life.

"I'm sure she misses you too," a voice says faintly. I look up to see Jessica's parents standing there, their faces soft with understanding. Charlie hands me a tissue, and I take it with trembling hands.

"I'm sorry. I didn't mean to intrude."

"Intrude? We're just glad someone other than us is visiting our little girl," Allen says.

Charlie smiles warmly. "We're extremely grateful the man

responsible was caught. We can't thank those vigilantes enough." I nod, but Charlie's gaze lingers on me, as if she knows more than she lets on.

"It goes without saying, if you need anything, just let us know," Allen adds with a kind smile.

I say my thanks and turn to leave. Charlie calls out, "And happy graduation. Jessica would be so proud of you."

USC CAMPUS – *L.A. Memorial Coliseum*
May 15, 14:56 PDT

ON THE SPRAWLING GREEN FIELD, I sit among my fellow graduates. The sun beats down on us, a sea of black caps and gowns with orange hoods. If someone had told me by the time I completed this degree, I'd reconnect with an old friend who'd make me want to feel again and uncover the truth behind Jessica Glory's murder, I would have laughed them off. Yet here I am, looking at Gina and Xavier sitting next to each other in the crowd as the announcer reaches my name.

"Winter Octavia Washington. Receiving a master's of science in Cybersecurity from the School of Engineering."

I collect my diploma and shake the necessary hands. I don't waste a second more before I run straight into Xavier's arms. "You know, I never did thank you."

"Thank me? For what?"

"Everything really, but mostly for being patient with me."

"For you, Octavia, always." I playfully shove him. He knows I don't like being called by my middle name.

"We should do something after all this, just the two of us. I'm thinking... Europe."

Xavier nods in agreement and says, "It's like you read my mind. That sounds perfect."

OFFICIAL PLAYLIST

Enhance your reading experience with the official soundtrack of *Decoding the Heart*!

Visit **https://cyberhuntresschronicles.com/playlist/** or scan the QR code below to listen to the carefully curated music pairing.

BONUS CONTENT
CAN'T GET ENOUGH OF WINTER AND XAVIER?

The hardcover edition of *Decoding the Heart* includes **exclusive** bonus chapters told from Xavier's point of view — moments you didn't get to see the first time around. If you've only read the ebook or paperback, you're missing parts of the story.

Visit **https://cyberhuntresschronicles.com/** to get your copy. Signed copies available while supplies last.

CONTENT NOTICE (CONT'D)

This novel includes sexually explicit scenes, strong language, and themes of sexual assault, substance abuse, violence, child abuse, and grief.